An Elegant Encounter

Buttoning her silk blazer against the cool evening breeze, the woman followed the driver out of the Air France terminal to the silver Rolls-Royce at the curb. Paris lay beyond, glittering on the horizon.

As she approached the car, the rear door swung open. The creamy-beige interior of the Rolls was covered with rose petals of the palest pink hue and redolent of the most expensive Right Bank *parfumerie*. Glimpsing a familiar silhouette in the back of the car, the woman smiled, then slid effortlessly onto the bench seat, carefully skirting a large crystal champagne bucket.

A handsome gray-haired man eased out of the shadow and kissed the woman passionately. "Take off your clothes," he whispered as his lips caressed her neck.

"But what about . . . ?" the woman murmured, responding to his touch.

"Don't worry," he replied.

There was a soft whir as an opaque pane of glass rose from the front seat, separating the driver from his charges.

"Is that better?" he asked.

"Much," she answered with a devilish grin, as the silk blazer slipped from her shoulders onto the carpet of porcelana roses. . . .

WHITE SATIN NIGHTS

MARIANNE KANTER

ST. MARTIN'S PRESS/NEW YORK

WHITE SATIN NIGHTS

Copyright © 1990 by Marianne Kanter and Richard M. Lieberman.

Pillows of California represented by: Park B. Smith Inc.,
295 Fifth Avenue, New York, New York 10016.
Natori Lingerie, New York, New York.
Fur coat by Goldin-Feldman, New York, New York.
Fur hat by Lenore-Marshall, New York, New York.

ISBN: 0-312-92002-4   Can. ISBN: 0-312-92003-2

Printed in the United States of America

First St. Martin's Press mass market edition/January 1990

10 9 8 7 6 5 4 3 2 1

To the ladies of my round table—
Frances, Judy, and Bonnie

When she saw the liveried driver outside the customs gate, the young woman was more concerned than angry. She had expected him to be waiting there for her. It was, after all, his habit, and he had promised. Buttoning her silk blazer against a cool evening breeze, the woman followed the driver out of the Air France terminal to the silver Rolls-Royce waiting at the curb. There was a hint of rain in the air, and Paris, glittering on the horizon, looked ill-prepared for it.

As she approached the car, the rear door swung open. She inhaled a sweet scent that overpowered the oily kerosene smell that normally hung over the airport. The creamy-beige interior of the Rolls was covered with rose petals of the palest pink hue and redolent of the most expensive Right Bank parfumerie. Glimpsing a familiar silhouette in the back of the car, the woman smiled, then slid effortlessly onto the bench seat, carefully skirting a large crystal champagne bucket.

A handsome, gray-haired man eased out of the shadow and kissed the woman passionately. "Take off your clothes," the man whispered as his lips caressed her neck.

"But what about . . . ?" the woman murmured, responding to his touch.

"Don't worry," he replied.

There was a soft whir as an opaque pane of glass rose from the front seat, separating the driver from his charges.

"Is that better?" he asked.

"Much," she answered with a devilish grin, falling to her knees as the silk blazer slipped from her shoulders onto the carpet of porcelana roses.

PART 1

Chapter 1

Room 523 was brighter than any of the other court-rooms on the floor, and certainly cheerier than any of the courtrooms in the Criminal Courts Building down the street. The blond woodwork gave off a pleasant glow, enhanced by the fluorescent lights tucked into cells in the pebbled ceiling. A vinyl floor, institutional beige and badly scuffed, validated this time-honored decor. The only highlight in the windowless room was the single dark panel behind the judge with the words IN GOD WE TRUST fixed to it. Over time the W and E had somehow come loose, leaving just their outlines and a curious admonition on the wall.

Jessica Wheeler shifted uncomfortably in her chair while she waited for the judge's verdict. A numbness had gradually crept up her leg and was working its way into her left buttock. The young woman tried vainly to restore sensation by tapping her foot on the floor, but only succeeded in distracting her client, Mrs. Rios, from her rosary beads, and drawing a strange look from the opposing counsel at the other end of the long table. Unable to bear the discomfort any longer, Jessica got up, casually brushing her short blond hair away from her face, and walked unsteadily to the empty jury box.

As circulation returned and her leg slowly warmed, she raised her head and glanced out into the half-empty courtroom. In the last row she noticed a dark-haired man in his mid-forties staring back at her. He had a legal pad on his lap and seemed to be making notes. She didn't recognize him, but from his bearing, as well as his expensive suit and colorful silk pocket square, she assumed he was a lawyer.

Suddenly self-conscious, Jessica picked a tiny piece of lint off her blue skirt and returned to her seat. Fair-skinned, with soft blue eyes and high, wide cheekbones, her face had an almost classical perfection, which was interrupted by a small scar under her slightly uneven chin. The result of horseplay with her younger sister when they were children, the scar flared when she was angry, collected tears when she cried, and gave her youthful beauty character.

The judge finally reentered the courtroom around two o'clock and was immediately besieged by petitioners awaiting his signature on various documents. Mrs. Rios, by now used to the constant intrusions, continued with her rosary. She was a sturdy, middle-aged woman with spunk and determination, who, with the help of Jessica Wheeler and the others at the People's West Side Advocacy, had decided to take on her absentee landlord, a powerful New York real estate developer—or, to be more specific, the president of one of his subsidiaries.

Feeling a penetrating gaze on the back of her neck, Jessica looked over her shoulder at the man in the back of the courtroom. This time the man nodded and smiled politely. Since he was neat and clean and seemed to pose no immediate threat, Jessica nodded in return, then directed her attention to the bench.

Shuffling through the papers to his right, the judge motioned to one of the court officers. There was a brief exchange, then the judge peered down soberly at the litigants and lawyers sitting at the table in front of him.

"As regards the matter of docket number 270, Rios versus East 118th Street Realty," he intoned in a dispassionate monotone, "I find that the defendant has consistently failed to make the repairs cited in the building inspectors' reports, has deliberately withheld services endangering the health and well-being of the tenants, and has engaged in activities that could only be construed as criminal, to force the tenants to vacate the building. Therefore, I find for the plaintiff, Mrs. Carmen Rios, and order that the repairs at 545 East 118th Street begin immediately and that the building be placed in receivership. I will also ask that the findings in this proceeding be forwarded to the District Attorney's Office for possible criminal prosecution."

With tears of joy streaming down her cheeks, Mrs. Rios threw her arms around the blond attorney, drawing Jessica down to her. The young woman held her. "I told you we'd win," she whispered triumphantly. "And don't worry about the repairs, Mrs. Rios, I'll have Jerry from our office get someone to the building first thing tomorrow morning."

From the other end of the table Jessica could hear legal pads being thrown into briefcases and latches snapping shut defiantly. As she led Mrs. Rios from the courtroom, her opposite number, Chick Beresford, brushed by with his client. Beresford, an impeccably tailored, coiffed, and well-connected young attorney, had recently been elevated to partner at Wheatley, Paget and Greene, one of New York's tonier law firms. He also was a poor loser and more than a bit of a snob when it came to landlord/tenant cases involving minorities.

"See you on appeal, counselor," he said confidently.

"Chick, I would think you'd want to cut your losses now," Jessica replied, "especially with a possible criminal indictment hanging over your client's head."

"And, pray tell, how would I do that?" he asked sarcastically.

"Well, you could admit your client's bad faith, offer to completely restore the building, and then turn the title over to the tenants," she said.

"Dream on, counselor," Beresford replied with a sneer, continuing down the aisle.

"Well, it is something to keep in mind," said the young woman dryly as she trailed after him. "Who knows, when the time comes, your client might welcome it in lieu of ninety days on Rikers Island."

Whipping open the door, Beresford, with his bulldog-faced defendant in tow, quickstepped down the crowded corridor, his hundred-dollar haircut bobbing imperiously above the rabble.

As she and Mrs. Rios were about to leave the courtroom, Jessica felt a hand at her elbow.

"Ms. Wheeler."

Jessica turned, coming face to face with the enigmatic note taker, who seemed to tower over her.

"My name is Winston Avery," the man said with an easy smile. "I'm an attorney with Turner, Welles and Lambert."

Jessica hadn't recognized the lawyer's face, but she knew his name and the law firm. Turner, Welles and Lambert was an even more aristocratic partnership than Wheatley, Paget. It was the firm of choice for at least twenty Fortune 500 companies and had fattened and protected the pocketbooks of some of New York's wealthiest individuals. It was prestigious, discreet, and above all, very expensive. Billing began at over two hundred dollars an hour. Jessica knew that Winston Avery was one of their top men in real estate, having recently concluded the terms for the development of the controversial Phoenix Insurance Center.

"How can I help you, Mr. Avery?" said Jessica warily as they moved out into the hall.

"I was wondering if I might have a few minutes of your time," Avery replied.

"Certainly. But first I want to get my client a taxi," answered the young woman. "Then we can go to my office."

They managed to flag down a cab on Centre Street. Jessica bundled Mrs. Rios into the backseat while Winston Avery gave the driver the address and an extra ten dollars to take the woman uptown.

"You didn't have to do that, you know," said Jessica as they walked back across Centre Street and entered the small park in front of the Civil and Municipal Court Building.

"I didn't mean to offend anyone," replied Avery. "It just seemed like the right thing to do."

"It was. And thank you," she answered apologetically. "I'm sorry if I seem defensive. After a couple of go-rounds with rich, fat-cat lawyers like—" Fortunately, she caught the thought before it left her mouth.

"Like me," said Avery, completing her sentence.

"I was going to say like Chick Beresford," she replied, trying unsuccessfully to contain an embarrassed smile. "Anyway, after a while you begin to distrust English tailoring."

Long shadows had begun to inch across lower Manhattan and into the park as the sun dipped behind the World Trade Center. A cool breeze crept out of the shade and chased away what remained of the warm April day. Winston Avery stopped for a moment and slipped on the tan cashmere topcoat he had been carrying over his arm, then the pair continued on. When they reached a bench in the last circle of sunlight near the southwest corner of the building, Jessica sat down.

"I thought we were going to your office," said Avery inquisitively.

"This is my office," replied Jessica as she set her briefcase on the green wooden slats next to her. "Actually, this is the downtown branch. The uptown office is in a storefront on Broadway and 161st Street."

With his cashmere coat clearly in jeopardy, Avery carefully sought out a soot-free section of the bench, then, deftly balancing his posterior on the fewest number of slats, occupied only one third of it.

"Ms. Wheeler, I'll be brief," he began.

"I think you'll have to," replied Jessica, looking west at the approaching shadows. "We're running out of sun."

"Are you always this glib?" asked Avery.

"Only when I'm tired and someone is trying to sell me something. You are trying to sell me something, aren't you, Mr. Avery?" Jessica said.

"Definitely not, Ms. Wheeler," answered Avery. "In fact, we're in the market to buy."

"We?" she asked suspiciously.

"Turner, Welles and Lambert," he replied, with an inspiring, patrician reverence. "You see, we're looking for someone for our real estate department with litigation experience. Someone with a sharp mind, a commanding presence—"

"And a glib tongue?"

"If necessary," he answered calmly. "Look, Ms. Wheeler, let me stop beating around the bush. We've heard some impressive things about you from some of the people that fund the People's West Side Advocacy and from colleagues you've faced in court."

"I like the work."

"I could see that in court," said Avery. "You got a kick out of cutting Wheatley, Paget's rising star off at the knees, didn't you?"

"I got a kick out of getting Mrs. Rios some justice and maybe scaring a little compassion into one of Sidney Fein's henchmen," Jessica replied, perhaps a little too self-righteously. It was just that she regarded Fein, one of New York's biggest real estate moguls, as the real villain in the trial. For an instant her gaze drifted out over the park, then settled back on Avery. "All right," she admitted, shrugging her shoulders, "it felt good to take Beresford down a peg."

"Winning is no sin."

"It could be winning for you."

"Don't sell us short, Ms. Wheeler," Avery said. "We do our share of pro bono work. We will even consider leaves of absence if we believe the work poses a conflict of interest. We're not all hired guns in British woolens."

"I'm just wondering how many people like Mrs. Rios you represent," she said.

"To be honest, very few," he told her. "But we do represent organizations that advise and support groups like the Advocacy, which represent thousands of Mrs. Rioses. . . . You know, it's worth thinking about. With access to the top, you might be able to make more of a difference than one-on-one at the bottom."

"Are you guaranteeing me that kind of access?"

"No, but in time it will come. To earn the $75,000 we're offering, we intend to keep you very busy."

"Seventy-five thousand," she repeated, after taking a deep breath to keep her voice evenly modulated.

As the sky darkened and the lights along the two paths crisscrossing the park began to glow, Avery looked down at his watch.

"Listen, Ms. Wheeler, I know this is short notice, but Jonathan Lambert, our senior partner, is anxious to meet you," he added hurriedly. "He's having a cocktail party at his apartment this evening. It's a small fund-raiser for the governor. Anyway, he said if our conversation got this far, I should invite you to the party. . . .

It's seven o'clock at the Dakota. Do you think you can make it?"

"I think so," Jessica answered softly, still overwhelmed by the $75,000 offer.

"Wonderful. Then, I'll see you later," Avery said. He rose from the bench with an awkward twisting motion as he tried to catch a glimpse of the back of his cashmere coat.

"It's okay, you got away unsullied," Jessica assured him. She only wished she had been so lucky. In their half hour together, Avery had thrown money, power, and influence at her, and though she had tried to parry his advances, he had hit his mark at least twice. Now, as Avery crossed the park toward Broadway, Jessica suddenly felt co-opted by her good fortune. Unable to turn away from the opportunities before her, she just hoped she wouldn't have to sacrifice the dedication of the past two years. She cared, and she wanted to continue to care.

Chapter 2

Even with the carpeting, the stairs in the old Chelsea brownstone creaked and groaned. Unfortunately, they didn't creak and groan above the third floor, which left the two apartments on the fourth floor defenseless. The building, constructed for a wealthy ships' chandler in the late 1850s, had, over the years, settled gently into its moorings on West Twenty-second Street and, like an indulgent grandparent, tolerantly overlooked the furtive comings and goings of its roster of tenants and the wounds time had inflicted upon it.

As she put her key in the lock, Jessica could hear voices in the living room and the sound of people scurrying about. Cautiously, she opened the door and stepped into the apartment. The room seemed in order, the television, stereo, and half-empty coffee cup all where she had left them in the morning. However, she soon noticed they had been mysteriously joined by a pair of men's black underwear which were hanging precariously from the back of the overstuffed love seat.

A slight rustling noise in the hall leading to the bedroom abruptly diverted her attention. She glanced quickly down the short, dimly lit corridor, briefly catching sight of a naked man as he disappeared behind the bedroom door. Now aware of what she had interrupted, she walked boldly to the bedroom door and knocked.

"Meredith," said Jessica insistently, "I have to talk to you."

"Why are you home so early?" a woman yelled from the other side of the door.

"It's an emergency."

"What kind of emergency?" the woman shouted back.

"I need to know what to wear to a fund-raiser at the Dakota."

"Wear a checkbook," scoffed a man's voice from behind the door.

"Shut up, Gary," Meredith shot back. "Great advice from a man who's never even owned a checkbook, let alone clean pants."

"I'm an artist," the man protested.

"And I'm Calvin Klein . . . Gary, you are what you call yourself on your tax return."

"So I'm a cab driver?" he replied.

"Right," answered Meredith. "And I'm an assistant marketing director with a lot of style."

"Do you two have to argue over everything?" Jessica interrupted impatiently.

"No."

"Yes," Meredith shouted back.

"Meredith, this is important! I have forty-five minutes to get dressed and get uptown," Jessica shouted through the door. "Are you going to help me or not?"

"Come on, Gary," Meredith said quietly, "get dressed."

Seconds later the bedroom door opened and a

barrel-chested redheaded man in his mid-twenties emerged, wearing a faded leather jacket and a sheepish grin.

"Jess, if you want, I can come back for you in a half hour and take you uptown," he said as he slipped by her.

"That would be great, Gary. Thank you," she said appreciatively.

Pulling a sweat-stained Mets baseball cap from his jacket pocket, Gary started out of the apartment. "Hey, Max, you'd better stay home," he shouted from the doorway. "'Cause I'm gonna call you later."

"Max?" Jessica said as she walked into the bedroom.

"He thinks I'm too tough and feisty to be a Meredith," replied her roommate. The petite young woman slipped a heavy terry-cloth robe over her black silk teddy and sat down on the edge of the rumpled bed, tucking her short, tanned legs underneath her.

Jessica wasn't sure that Meredith's cab driver/artist wasn't right. Meredith Werner was tough and feisty, but she was also warm, loving, and loyal to a fault. She had been Jessica's first roommate at Vassar and had given the wide-eyed Texas beauty a crash course in eastern social graces. Coming from a wealthy Long Island suburb, she knew how to break bread with the upper crust, how to keep her powder dry and her lips moist. And she passed these skills on to Jessica, protecting her flank while she honed them. In addition, she helped rid her friend of her heavy West Texas drawl and her blue eye shadow. Jessica would always be grateful; Meredith had given her something more than style—class.

After college they had gone their separate ways—Jessica to Yale Law School and Meredith to the fashion business on New York's Seventh Avenue. But they kept in touch through phone calls and occasional visits. In fact, it was one of those visits to New York that eventually led Jessica to the People's Advocacy program.

During her second year of law school, Meredith had taken Jessica to a Christmas party in a loft in lower Manhattan. There she had met a dedicated, thirty-five-year old lawyer named Eric Burgess. Although wheelchair bound as a result of a childhood accident, he was vibrant and energetic, bursting with ideas. A mesmerizing speaker with a magnetic personality, he held court in a corner of that Tribeca loft, trying futilely to make activists out of hedonists. He did make one convert, however, and they had lunch the next day.

Jessica found Eric Burgess inspiring not only for the way he dealt with his disability, but because of his concern for others. As the recently appointed director of legal outreach programs for the Alewhite Foundation, he was determined to improve legal services for the disenfranchised urban poor. Over a corned-beef sandwich and cream soda, he laid out his plans to the young law student.

Buffeted by his logic and reason, Jessica finally fell victim to his compassion and promised him she would consider public service upon graduation. There was no denying such persistence. But once back at Yale, it wasn't long before persistence came from another direction. Praise from professors and election to the *Law Review* soon brought offers of summer jobs from several important New York law firms. By April of that year, keeping her options open wasn't easy. And since social activism didn't help defer the costs of an Ivy League education, she opted to become a summer associate at a major New York firm.

Warfield, Weiss, Cleary and Burns had three floors of offices on Park Avenue just south of Fifty-fourth Street and at least a million dollars worth of art on the walls. They were a young, dynamic firm with a strong real estate department and a reputation for paying their summer associates very well.

During that unusually mild summer, Jessica found herself under the tutelage of Victor Cleary, a forty-three-year-old partner in the firm. After interviewing the six summer associates, Cleary, the head of litigation, had picked Jessica to do research for a major product-liability case he was preparing. They spent long hours together, many times working through dinner and, as the case progressed, into the weekends.

Jessica was astounded by the depth of Victor Cleary's intellect and his razor-sharp memory. He could retrieve obscure facts with computerlike efficiency, analyze them and formulate forceful arguments from them in a matter of seconds. He also had a low, soothing voice and deep brown eyes that seemed to engender trust and devotion in the people around him. His critics called him manipulative, Svengali-like, a cunning predator just waiting for the right moment to strike. Ascribing jealousy to his detractors, Jessica dismissed these accusations out of hand, preferring to see Victor Cleary as a skillful and accomplished attorney.

It was toward the end of July, while watching him take a deposition from a key figure in the lawsuit, that Jessica's feelings toward Victor passed beyond simple admiration. The man, an engineer, more accustomed to the finite security of stress tests and statistical evaluations, was clearly nervous about the interrogation and concerned about his future with his employer. With the man's reluctance to answer questions obvious, Cleary sought first to allay the poor man's fears, displaying assurances from his client, the engineer's employer. Then slowly, with tremendous sympathy and understanding, he peeled away the middle-aged man's defenses and got his answers. By the end of what became more of a catharsis than an interview, practically everyone in the room was near tears. It was as though

Cleary had managed to tap into the man's soul. Jessica had never seen anything so dramatic. It was such an overpowering display of emotional transference that Mr. Yepremian, the witness, even apologized for his zealousness, and as he left the office, actually embraced his interrogator.

Later that night, over dinner in a quaint beaux arts French bistro, Victor and Jessica went over the engineer's statement. Slim and graceful, with silver hair, an iconic face, and long, delicate fingers, Victor seemed almost saintlike in the flickering orange gaslight. The wine, the hour, and the fire in his eyes made Jessica more and more desirous of the man in front of her. To covet power was one thing, but to hunger for someone's humanity was quite another. And if only for a moment, she wanted to share that part of him.

As Victor looked across the table at her and gently touched her hand, Jessica understood what was happening. Arm in arm they walked the two and half blocks to his apartment on Park Avenue, gliding by the doorman and soaring silently up to his penthouse apartment.

Then and there, it didn't matter to Jessica that Victor was a summer bachelor, with a wife and two children tucked away in some sprawling beach house in Easthampton. Neither naive nor headstrong, she wasn't thinking beyond this night. Studying in New Haven, then working in New York, she felt alone and apart, cut off from her feelings. Tonight she was going to reconnect, to return to the wellspring of her emotions.

Victor led Jessica through the broad, colonnaded living room, then out onto a terrace that swept around half the apartment. As they stood by the weathered stone wall that ringed the terrace, Jessica could feel the cool night air invade the soft folds of her silk blouse and caress her skin. It felt clean and purifying.

Victor studied Jessica's face in the glow of the city

lights. They exchanged words of little meaning, small talk that filled pauses and heightened the sexual tension. After sweeping a strand of hair away from her face, he kissed her, tentatively at first, then passionately as she responded to the warm touch of his lips.

"This shouldn't be, but it seems so right," he whispered as he took her hand.

"I know, but it is," Jessica replied breathlessly.

Victor guided her back into the living room, then down a hallway to the other end of the apartment.

The master bedroom was enormous, all coral and gray, with hints of black and streaks of pale green. They undressed each other in front of the white marble fireplace, their naked bodies dimly reflected in the etched-glass doors. Victor gloried in her beauty, running his fingertips over the smooth planes of her body and pressing himself against her soft, supple curves.

Together they mounted the carpeted riser to the large bed and, tossing aside the silk moiré bedspread, slipped under the cool sheets. Immediately they fell into each other's arms, urgently trying to translate the ethereal into the corporeal, to merge their emotions and their senses. Their bodies became damp and shiny, their desires pushing them toward the precipice.

Jessica moaned loudly as she felt Victor tense. She threw her arms around his neck and pulled him down to her, her lips hungering desperately for his passion. With time seemingly suspended around them, they came together in one wrenching spasm, his heat piercing the essence of her being.

Afterward, he held her and they slept—satisfied, reassured, no closer to truth or God or righteousness or compassion, and no better or worse than the day before.

Their affair was sweet, exciting, and over by the time Jessica returned to Yale. There were no animosities or scenes at the end, no threats or reproaches. It was a relationship of a place and a time, not entirely guiltless, but still free enough to be thought of fondly in the months and years that followed. In time, it would remind Jessica of a flower pressed in a book, a pleasant memory, albeit slightly faded, whose perfume existed only in the thick vellum around it.

In the early spring, as graduation neared and job notices began to appear on the Law School bulletin board, Jessica got an unexpected call from Eric Burgess. Frustrated by the local jurisdictional disputes over his programs and the internal politics at the Alewhite Foundation, he had decided to return to a more hands-on method of providing legal services for the poor. He became director of the People's West Side Advocacy, a fledgling storefront operation in Washington Heights which he himself had begun funding while at Alewhite.

Over dinner in an inexpensive New Haven restaurant, Eric regaled Jessica with tales of glory, of heroes and villains, and of good and evil. Playing on her sympathies and her sense of justice, he showed her one or two briefs from ongoing cases, trying subtly to give her a feel for the work. Eric understood the enormity of his task. Recruiting Jessica for the People's Advocacy was like asking a college all-star from North Carolina State to play basketball in Israel for a year. It just wasn't going to happen, but he persevered.

"No, nothing but coffee for me, thank you," said Jessica politely as the pudgy, young waitress waited to take their dessert order.

"I'll have coffee too, and the rice pudding," Burgess answered.

The girl ambled off toward the kitchen, scribbling furiously on a small green pad. With her eyes narrowly glued to the pen point, she was almost sent sprawling across the dining room when one of the beige Formica doors leading to the kitchen flew open in front of her.

"I hope you understand that I drove all the way up here just to see you," said Burgess, turning back to Jessica after the commotion in the dining room had died down. "Which, I might add, was no easy task for a man in a wheelchair."

"Eric, don't try and test my sympathy," Jessica replied cynically. "I happen to know you drive a Mercedes."

"All right, so I have wealthy parents who love me," he answered. "Look, Jessica, I have to be frank. I can't offer you what the big firms are going to throw your way. I'll be lucky if I can offer half of what they'll pay. The hours are long, the clients sometimes impossible, and the office primitive. But I think this is something you should do . . . Why?" he said, before she could open her mouth.

She smiled and nodded.

"Because you'll learn to handle yourself in a court-room, and at the same time help some people who really need it," he said spiritedly, "maybe even balance out the scales once in a while." Eric paused, then plunged on. "Look, Jessica, I didn't come up here to preach to you. What I'm offering isn't for everybody, and it may not be for you. I just thought with a promising career ahead of you, you might want to put something in before you start taking out."

"Can I think about it, Eric?" she asked. "And I'm not saying that to put you off. I mean, take some time to think about it, seriously."

"Why not? I didn't think my good looks and—what did they call it?—a Mulligan burger, would win you over right away. Give it some thought and call me," he said, handing her his card.

"I will, Eric. I promise."

"Good," he replied as he spun his wheelchair away from the table.

A week later Jessica called Eric Burgess and accepted his offer, or more to the point, his challenge. Growing up in Midland, Texas, pampered and protected by a doting father, Jessica had never come face to face with herself and the harsh realities of life until her father died. Then her mother stepped in, managing what was left of her father's business and keeping the creditors at bay. Although a genteel, southern lady with antebellum manners, Nedra Wheeler had the maternal instincts of a grizzly bear, cautiously shepherding Jessica and her sister Kendall through adolescence with a crook and a loaded forty-five by her side.

Confident in her ability, Jessica felt the time had come to leave the safe and secure behind and break away, maybe even making that difference Eric Burgess had talked about. In June, Jessica picked up her degree, packed up her life, and moved to New York.

"A cocktail party, huh? What you need is a black Chanel suit," said Meredith as she watched Jessica flip through the clothes in her side of the long closet.

"I don't *have* a black Chanel suit," replied Jessica.

"That's not my fault," answered Meredith, preparing to point the finger of responsibility. "How long have we been roommates?"

"Nearly three years."

"And how long have I told you to get a Chanel suit?"

"They're too expensive," Jessica said, pulling an ivory silk blouse out of the closet and tossing it on the bed next to Meredith.

"Don't play stupid. You know what I mean," Meredith replied. "You can't wear this," she grumbled, snatching up the blouse. "It's stained. Every stylish woman should have a black Chanel suit."

"You don't."

"I'm too dark and too short. Those suits make me look like Minnie Mouse."

They found a black wool jersey dress in the back of the closet. While Jessica concentrated on her hair and makeup, Meredith went through her jewelry box and came up with pearl earrings and a gold pin. Good bone structure and fashion sense eventually prevailed. By ten to seven Jessica was standing in front of the mirror, dressed and ready to go.

"Not bad," remarked Meredith, admiring her handiwork. "From legal eagle to social butterfly in twenty-five minutes."

From the street they could hear the raspy howl of Gary's taxi horn.

"Well, good luck, Jess," said Meredith.

"How do I look?" Jessica asked nervously as she headed for the front door.

"Just great," replied her friend. "Oh, try to remember, no pledges, the rent's due next week."

Chapter 3

The Dakota was a massive antique. It had stood at the corner of Seventy-second Street and Central Park West for over a hundred years, peering down somberly at the urban life evolving in front of its shadowy gateway. Notwithstanding the intent of Henry Hardenbergh, the architect, the building, with its gables and dormers, had always seemed to evoke in passersby childhood fears of ghosts and demons, feelings undoubtedly more acute in the late 1800s, when the foreboding structure stood alone at the edge of Central Park.

As she stepped out of the elevator and into the small foyer on the fifth floor, Jessica could hear muffled voices from inside the apartment. She quickly checked herself in the mirror over a narrow antique Shaker table, then pressed the door bell.

Two plainclothes members of the state police checked her name against a list while an efficient, gray-haired woman in a black dress took her coat. Then one of the officers escorted her down a cavernous hallway, lined with rare Sargent drawings, into the living room.

The living room, a stately affair, seemed to run the width of the building. One long wall was punctuated with windows looking out over Central Park, and the other with paintings arranged to counterbalance an imposing sixteenth-century Flemish tapestry hung above a jewel-like Louis XIV escritoire. Two finely knotted oriental rugs divided the immense space, picking up the rich tones in the tapestry and the gilt furniture, upholstered in an exquisite silk brocade. Jessica held back a gulp as she thought of the Chelsea apartment, with its rickety Parsons tables and Goodwill chairs.

There were seventy or eighty people in the room, most of them at the far end where a bar had been set up. Beyond, in what appeared to be a formal dining room, Jessica could see others milling about another bar and a long buffet table.

Transfixed by the headlights twisting through the park, Jessica stopped at one of the windows to watch the last of the rush-hour traffic make its circuitous trek uptown.

"I'm glad you could make it," said Winston Avery as he joined her by the window. "After I told Jonathan about our discussion this afternoon, he's been anxious to meet you."

"And I him," replied Jessica, reaching out to shake Avery's hand.

"And so you shall," said Avery, taking Jessica's arm and leading her down to the end of the living room where a group of people were huddled off to one side of the bar.

In the center of the group was a short, trim man in his early seventies, with white hair, a pencil-thin moustache, and a black patch over his right eye. Avery walked up to the man, spoke to him briefly, then returned with him to Jessica.

"Ms. Wheeler," Avery began, "I'd like you to meet Jonathan Lambert."

"Mr. Lambert," replied Jessica, extending her hand.

"Ms. Wheeler, I'm so happy you could join us this evening," said Jonathan Lambert politely. "I've been quite anxious to meet you. In fact, why don't you and I have a chat in private before the governor arrives. But first, excuse me for one moment."

Lambert returned to his small circle of guests, singling out a beautiful Asian woman in a no-nonsense black-and-white-checked Armani suit. He whispered something to her. She nodded. Then he rejoined Jessica and Winston Avery, who immediately went off to greet some new arrivals.

"Good. Now that everything's taken care of, why don't we have that chat," he said amiably.

Jessica followed Lambert a short distance to a corner of the room. There, he opened an unframed door, which led to another door at the end of a short, low-ceilinged passageway. Passing through the second doorway, they entered a smaller room, which Jessica assumed was an office or study. While tastefully Georgian in character and aristocratic in spirit, the study nevertheless seemed less pretentious and more inviting than the Versailles-like living room on the other side of the double doors.

"Please, sit down, Ms. Wheeler," Jonathan Lambert said, motioning toward a tufted brown leather chair.

As Jessica slid onto the taut leather, Lambert glided around an elegant Regency desk, taking the chair across from her. As he sat down, he unconsciously ran his hand along the thin band of material that held his eyepatch in place and on through his snow-white hair. Rumor had it that he had lost the eye when he was nineteen in a barroom brawl over a woman, a rumor he steadfastly refused to either confirm or deny.

In addition to practicing law, Jonathan Lambert was a successful novelist, an avid art collector, a trilingual raconteur, and above all, a gentleman. He was one of those exceptional men who found integrity an asset rather than a liability, and he had parlayed this asset into a comfortable fortune. As the surviving member of the triumvirate that had founded Turner, Welles and Lambert, and with an awesome client list, Jonathan Lambert still took an active role in the running of the firm, with time out, of course, for his outside interests. A widower and one of the city's most sought-after dinner guests, he was seen in the company of some of New York's most interesting and exciting women.

Jessica studied Jonathan Lambert carefully. From the gold Phi Beta Kappa key dangling from his watch chain to his conservatively tailored navy-blue three-piece suit, white shirt, and boldly patterned Turnbull and Asser bow tie, he looked the sartorial, if not the professional, blueprint for every high-priced lawyer she had ever battled in court. Sitting across from him, she suddenly felt like a traitor, as though she were about to sell out her principles and her clients for 75,000 pieces of silver. On the other hand, she felt flattered by the invitation to join such an influential firm and the opportunity to rub elbows with the governor. She had never realized that this kind of attention could be so intoxicating.

"Tell me a little about yourself, Jessica," Lambert began, using her first name to break the tension.

"Well, I got my B.A. from Vassar in 1977 and my law degree from Yale," Jessica replied.

"No. I meant, where did you grow up, what do you do when you're not making life difficult for the Sidney Feins of the world?" interrupted Lambert tactfully.

"Oh, you know about that?" she said, surprised he was aware of the case.

"Winston's a very good scout," he answered. A gentle smile softened Lambert's rather raffish features. "So, where are you from, Jessica?"

"Midland, Texas."

"Nice town. Good people there."

"You've been to Midland?"

"Once. In 1938," he replied, working on a memory. "I came in on a boxcar and went out on the back of a fertilizer truck heading toward Albuquerque . . . What happened to your drawl?"

"You haven't gotten me up at three in the morning."

He laughed and his face flushed. "Is your family still there?"

"No. After my grandmother died, my mother moved my sister and me to Houston," answered Jessica. "That was just before I went off to college."

"And they're still in Houston?"

"Yes. My mother teaches elementary school. And my sister is married and works in a real estate office."

"Younger or older?"

"Three years younger."

"What about your father?" Lambert asked cautiously.

Jessica paused briefly, sifting through the faded images in her mind. "Well, he was a real anachronism, one of the last dyed-in-the-wool West Texas wildcatters. Long on talk when he was short on capital," she said, lapsing into her drawl, "and with more flash than a lightning bolt. . . . He died two days before my sixteenth birthday," she added, her voice reliving the sadness. "He was killed in an automobile accident."

"I'm sorry . . . He sounds like quite a character."

"Oh, he was," she replied quietly.

Recovering quickly from this awkward moment, Lambert segued to the topic at hand. "Jessica, I know Winston has presented our case, but I was wondering if you had any questions about us; perhaps something that came up after the two of you spoke."

"As a matter of fact, sir, I do," answered Jessica, straightening up in the high-backed chair as though bracing for a fight. "There's a whole city of qualified attorneys available to you, most of them with a lot more experience than I have, so why me and why now?"

"Because, Jessica, and I'll be frank," Lambert said firmly as he leaned forward to meet her challenge, "you're dedicated, you know your law and your way around a courtroom, you've got integrity . . . and you're a woman. Now, before you get ready to show me some of that integrity," he added quickly, anticipating the young woman's response, "let me explain. Lately I've been trying to recruit more women and minorities into the firm and have been running into the opposition of some of our, shall we say, more conservative partners. And now that we have an opening in our real estate department . . ."

"You want me to play Jackie Robinson to your Branch Rickey."

"Interesting analogy," replied Lambert. "Do you follow sports, Jessica?"

"Just enough to talk to cab drivers and make interesting analogies," she answered cagily.

"Then you understand, given the temperament of the time, how important it was for Rickey to hire the right man." Jonathan Lambert had made his point and eased back into his seat. "Now let me ask you a question. Do you think you're ready to leave the Advocacy?"

"You make it sound like some sort of graduation," she told him, "as though I'd be moving on to something better."

"We hope it would be."

"Even if it would be something better, the real question is, do I *want* to leave the Advocacy," said Jessica candidly, "and I don't know the answer to that."

Their conversation was interrupted by a knock at the door. The door opened slowly and the exotic, sloe-eyed woman in the Armani outfit entered.

"He's here, Jonathan," she said quietly.

"Thank you, Mei," Lambert replied. "I'll be right out."

The woman slipped noiselessly out of the room,

leaving behind the heady scent of jasmine and tube-rose.

"I must be getting back," said Lambert, rising from his chair. "The governor has arrived . . . But I do have one more question, Jessica," he added as he moved around the desk. "If you're so uncertain about all of this, why did you decide to come this evening?"

"Curiosity," she answered as she rose to meet him. "Mr. Avery offered me the chance to plug into the system, and I guess I came to see if you were really connected."

"And?" he asked, amused by the young lawyer's brashness. "Are we, as you say, connected?"

"That depends on whether or not I get to shake hands with the governor," Jessica added with a coy smile.

"I'm sure that could be arranged," said Jonathan, ushering her back to the living room, "even without a campaign contribution."

The governor was gracious and charming and ig-nored the shallow rumblings of Jessica's stomach. As she listened to the small talk and nodded approvingly, in the back of her mind she could hear her mother lecturing her on the consequences of skipping meals. With her confidence ebbing, she excused herself and retired to the security of the dining room.

Jessica began to move slowly down the buffet table, plate in hand, liberally sampling the array of canapés and cold salads spread out before her. In no time at all she had arrived at the caviar in the middle of the table. Poised over the mound of glistening black eggs, she reached for the small ivory spoon resting on the lip of the glass bowl. Suddenly, out of the corner of her eye, she spied a man at the end of the bar who bore a more than striking resemblance to Warren Beatty. Momen-tarily star-struck, she turned her head, her gaze follow-ing the man as he stepped away from the bar and strolled out of the room.

"Thank you, miss, but I think I'd prefer my caviar on a plate," intoned a disembodied voice.

Snapping out of her daydream, Jessica looked down and saw that, while in her trance, she had inadvertently smeared caviar on the hand and sleeve of the man standing next to her.

"Oh, my God," she gasped as she watched the oily black beads slide off the cuff of the man's light gray suit and onto the white linen tablecloth. "I'm so sorry," she said, blotting at the stain with her napkin. "I don't know what came over me."

"Please, these things happen," he replied sympathetically. It had been obvious what had caught the young woman's attention, but the man saw no need to embarrass her any further.

"You must let me pay to have that cleaned," said Jessica, fumbling in her bag. "Here's my card. I insist you send me the bill."

He took her card, and as he did, she got her first real glimpse of the man. He was tall and lean, with thick gray hair that matched the fine wool threads in his suit. His face, tanned and lined, was handsome in a way women his age found maddening. Time had taken away nothing. It had simply added character and wisdom to his youthful good looks. Although nearly fifty, his steely blue-gray eyes had lost none of their vitality and wonder. There was something about him, though, that immediately set him apart. Whether it was the cut of his suit, the way he carried himself, or simply the aura that surrounds the rich and powerful, Jessica knew that this man was different, special.

"Well, Jessica Wheeler," he replied as he tucked her card into his pocket, "my name's Mark Laidlaw. And I wouldn't worry about my dry cleaning."

Working in a profession dominated by men, Jessica, in an attempt to break through to her coworkers and dates, had taken to reading the New York sports pages. In the last two years, as the new owner of the New York

Knights basketball team, Mark Laidlaw's name had been mentioned regularly in the New York papers, often with considerable resentment. A wealthy man, he had come out of semiretirement to buy the Knights, the perennial last-place finishers in the Atlantic Division of the NBA, determined to turn them into a winning team. Some saw him as a fan on the ultimate ego trip, a rich kid let loose in a candy store. For others, mostly diehard fans, Mark Laidlaw was the great rich hope, the one who could possibly bring back the salad days of the early seventies to New York, when championship banners were unfurled from the rafters of the Arena, the team's home court.

"Tell me, Ms. Wheeler, what exactly does a lawyer for the People's West Side Advocacy do?" he asked.

"We provide legal services for the indigent on the upper West Side," Jessica answered as if by rote. "Mostly landlord/tenant disputes, divorces, wills."

"Wills?"

"Surprised?" she said. "In truth, the wills have nothing to do with money. They're more about dignity and a person's last chance to control his or her destiny. Some of them, the way they are dictated to me, are really quite moving."

"I had no idea."

"Most people who have anything to really leave don't," said Jessica offhandedly. "For them, it's mostly reducing the tax liability to their heirs or fashioning some financial memorial." She caught herself lecturing, then abruptly returned to her original train of thought, "Anyway, once in a while, for a little excitement, we take on a developer or a class-action suit. Helps us work out the kinks."

"So, I can take it you're not a wealthy lawyer here to make a contribution?" said Laidlaw with a disarming grin.

"I think that would be a safe assumption."

"Then what brought you to this gathering of the rich

and power hungry?" he asked, his curiosity piqued by the attractive young woman. "Were you dragged here by some wealthy lawyer sniffing around for a judge-ship?"

"Actually, Mr. Laidlaw, I'm here alone," replied Jessica. "And what about you?" she continued, playing his game. "Are you poor and alone?"

Laidlaw looked at her, his grin widening. "Neither, I'm afraid."

"Now how did I know that?"

"I don't know, I guess some men just look married."

"No," Jessica shot back, her blue eyes flashing devilishly, "I meant that you weren't poor."

"Ah, Mark," said Jonathan Lambert, joining the pair and interrupting their banter. "I see you've met Ms. Wheeler. As a long-time friend and client, I hope you can convince her to join us at Turner, Welles."

"I see, a new recruit," replied Laidlaw as the young woman became less of a mystery.

"Not quite yet," Jessica reminded them both, with a Cheshire-cat grin.

Lambert's eye fixed on a short, stocky man in his late fifties, with thinning chestnut hair and puffy red cheeks, elbowing his way toward them from across the dining room. In his beefy right hand he held a glass of champagne which he emptied halfway through his journey, and in his left a sheet of paper which he waved spasmodically as he shunted aside those in his path.

"Jonathan, your people have got to take this on," the man demanded as he reached the trio, still brandishing his paper standard. "This is the third one of these nickel-dime tenant suits that Wheatley, Paget has blown. This time that asshole judge wants to get my brother-in-law thrown in jail."

"Sidney, I've told you before, we'd like to take you on as a client, but we don't do that kind of work," replied Lambert diplomatically.

"Jonathan, I'm talking about bringing all our work

over from Wheatley, Paget," declared the short man as
he wiped away the thin line of perspiration that had
formed on his upper lip.

"Hello, Sidney," said Laidlaw calmly.

"Hello, Mark," replied the man, reluctantly acknowl-
edging Laidlaw's presence. "Great season you had," he
added derisively.

"At least the office has stopped getting those threatening letters," Laidlaw replied.

"Wait until you've owned the team as long I did.
They'll turn on you. Just wait," the man warned him.

"I don't expect to keep losing."

"Right . . . Look, Jonathan," said the agitated in-
truder, redirecting his attention to Lambert, "I need
your help. This butch lady lawyer from this damn
tenants' rights group uptown has decided to bust my
balls." At that moment he noticed Jessica standing next
to Mark Laidlaw. "Oh, excuse my language, miss," he
said politely.

"Oh, Sidney, I'd like you to meet Jessica Wheeler,"
Jonathan Lambert began artfully. "I've been trying to
persuade her to join the firm . . . Jessica, this is Sidney
Fein."

After they shook hands, Fein looked away quizzically.
"Wheeler, Wheeler," he repeated to himself. "The
name is familiar. Have you ever done any work for us,
Ms. Wheeler?"

"For you, no," answered Jessica tactfully. "On you,
definitely . . . You see, Mr. Fein, I'm the butch lady
lawyer who's been busting your balls," she revealed
boldly, underscoring her remark with a cool smile.

Sidney Fein blanched, then turned an alarming
shade of crimson. "Jonathan, is this some kind of a
joke?" he croaked. "I mean, what the hell is this woman
doing here?"

"Sidney, Ms. Wheeler is my guest," replied Lambert,
plainly unruffled by the shorter man's belligerent tone.
"And I hope, shortly, an employee of the firm."

"Christ, Jonathan, are you crazy?" Fein, his back to Jessica, growled in a terse stage whisper. "This woman hates everything we stand for."

"On the contrary, Sidney," Lambert answered. "If I understand Ms. Wheeler correctly, she despises everything *you* stand for."

Apoplectic with rage, Fein spun around and stalked off toward the living room, muttering to himself while his arms flailed at some invisible assailant.

Apparently unnerved by the scene, Jessica glanced first at Lambert then at Laidlaw, hoping for some support. However, both men had turned away and seemed as though they were about to explode.

"I'm so embarrassed," she said apologetically. "I really had no right to say what I did."

With Fein a safe distance away, Lambert and Laidlaw shattered their reserve and broke into laughter.

"I think I should really go now," she declared, convinced she had offended everyone within a thirty-mile radius of the dining room.

"Nonsense," said Lambert, regaining his composure. "You're not going anywhere. Moreover, I thought you handled yourself brilliantly. Didn't you, Mark?"

"Superbly," Laidlaw replied reassuringly.

Lambert moved closer to Jessica and took her arm. "Now, my dear, I'm going to introduce you to everyone here." He took two steps, then looked back at Laidlaw. "You never told me about any threatening letters," he said.

"Believe it or not, he sent me a file full of them the week before we closed the deal," answered Laidlaw. "I think in his own lunatic way, he was trying to warn me about what could happen."

"I tried to warn you too," Lambert reminded him, "but you bought the team anyway." Then he gently patted Jessica's hand. "Ah, there's the mayor. I wanted you to meet. Frankly, he's a lot more interesting than the governor."

As Jonathan led her from the buffet table, Jessica swung around to face Laidlaw. "And don't forget that bill," she said earnestly.

"Oh, I won't," he answered, tapping the pocket where he had put her card. Mark Laidlaw was suddenly envious of his old friend as Jonathan escorted the attractive young woman into the living room. She moved with a catlike grace, her long legs, sheathed in black nylon, imparting a steady rhythm to her hips. While he watched Jessica walk away, a delightfully erotic fantasy began to unfold in Laidlaw's brain. It vanished the moment he spotted some errant grains of caviar glued to the edge of his French cuff.

Chapter 4

The pressed-tin ceiling in the storefront office was at least twelve feet high, while the glass and steel partitions surrounding Eric Burgess's desk were only half that, affording little, if any, isolation or privacy. Outside the cramped cubicle, two rows of bent and bruised filing cabinets lined the whitewashed walls. Six gray metal desks and two-dozen pink and green molded plastic chairs, arranged in a geometric formation, made up the rest of the furnishings. By nine in the morning most of the chairs were usually occupied by prospective clients. The lawyers and paralegals, who did the interviewing, filtered in twenty minutes later.

In his shirt-sleeves, Eric Burgess sat with his arm slung over the back of his wheelchair. A pungent French cigarette dangled menacingly between his full lips. Squinting to avoid the unwinding curls of smoke, his whiskey-colored eyes seemed to bore into Jessica, making her uneasy.

"What can I say?" he concluded, plunking the cigarette into a half-empty coffee cup. "It's a terrific opportunity. It's a great firm, and you certainly can't complain about the money."

"God, I wish you wouldn't do that. It makes me sick," she said, gingerly picking up the paper cup and dropping it into the wastebasket.

"Then use it as an excuse to leave," Burgess replied facetiously. "It's as good as any."

"Fuck you, Eric."

"You want me to make this easy for you, don't you, Jess?"

"I want you to help me make a decision," she replied.

"I won't. I can't. Because I need you here," he said, making a show of his sincerity. "And because I'll miss you."

"God, you're so manipulative."

"You think that's manipulative?" he said. Pushing away from his desk, he wheeled himself to the doorway of his office. "Gloria," he shouted to a tiny, pear-shaped Hispanic woman on the other end of the room. "How far are we backed up this morning?"

After counting the heads in front of her and the files on her desk, she shouted back, "If Mosley gets back from court this afternoon, ten. If not, fifteen."

"You hear that," he said, whipping back into the cubicle. "Fifteen today. How many won't we be able to get to when you're gone?"

"Thank you, Eric. This isn't tough enough?"

"You see, that's what I could do if I were really manipulative."

"That's great," she said sarcastically. "But what about me, Eric? What about my life? . . . Look, weren't you the one who lectured me about putting something in before I started taking out?"

"Did I say that?" he replied with feigned innocence.

"Yes, you did. In New Haven, over the worst meal in my life, nearly three years ago to the day."

"All right, I said it," he conceded, "but I didn't mean it."

"Damn it, I know you meant it," Jessica said indignantly. She felt uncomfortable defending an argument she hadn't fully resolved in her own mind. "Eric, I'm sorry," she began, reaching out to him, much the same way he had in that restaurant three years earlier. "I'm just not the starry-eyed idealist anymore. I want things. I want to feel like I'm moving forward."

"That must have been some party."

"It wasn't the party," she answered ruefully. "It's where I can go and what I can do. It's also what I can't do here."

"You know, the air is rarefied up there."

"I know," she replied, remembering the line of limousines on the street as she'd left the Dakota, and the ride back to the apartment in Jonathan Lambert's Rolls-Royce.

"It sounds to me like you've already made up your mind," Eric said.

"That's the problem. I really haven't."

"Don't worry, Jess," he told her. "I'll be behind you one hundred percent, whatever you decide."

Jessica got up from her chair, bent over and hugged Eric. "Thank you, Eric," she whispered.

"Now get back to work. We just got three new complaints from another Fein building. . . . Oh, there is one more thing," he added as she was halfway out the door. "On your way to the top, or wherever you're going, try thinking of us as your favorite charity and get some of your fat-cat clients to throw some money our way."

"It's a promise," she said with a laugh. "You'll be my tax deduction of choice."

Back at her desk, Jessica hurriedly read through two files before she walked over to the reception desk for her next client.

"Jessica, there's a call for you on line two," said Gloria as Jessica neared her desk. "It's a Mark Laidlaw."

"You're kidding," said Jessica, at first surprised, then concerned, recalling the caviar incident.

"Honey, does this look like a face that kids?" The receptionist glowered, her mouth frozen in a threatening scowl.

"No, Gloria, it doesn't," said Jessica. After all this time, she was still unaccustomed to the woman's personal animosity toward lawyers. Everyone in the office just assumed that somehow she had been horribly wronged by a lawyer, either emotionally or financially, and had come to the Advocacy in search of revenge. Yet on the plus side, she was terribly supportive of the people who came into the Advocacy, and in addition, kept the office running smoothly, not to mention getting everyone to court on time. "Line two, Gloria?" Jessica asked, staring at the four flashing buttons on the telephone.

"Right, line two," the woman growled back.

Mark Laidlaw's voice was relaxed and slightly deeper than she had remembered it.

"I hope this isn't about your suit," Jessica said warily. "I'd feel just awful if they couldn't get the stain out . . . They did get the stain out, didn't they?"

"I'm afraid they couldn't," he replied, "but that's not why I'm calling."

"They couldn't?" Jessica said, sensing the end of a promising career before it had begun.

"No. Something about the oil and the color dying the fabric, but that's not important. What I—"

"Then you must let me replace the suit," interrupted Jessica before he could finish his thought. "Please, how much was it? I'll send you a check."

"Ms. Wheeler, that really isn't necessary."

"I insist. Just tell me how much the suit cost."

"Well, it wasn't a new suit."

"That's all right. Just tell me what it will cost to replace it," Jessica replied stubbornly.

"If you insist," he said.

"I do."

"Well then, the suit cost fifteen hundred dollars when I bought it in Rome a year ago."

Dumbfounded by his answer and compelled by the utter absurdity of all this, she blurted out mindlessly, "Was that with or without the air fare?"

There was a frightening pause, then Laidlaw began to laugh. "Are you this obsessive in a courtroom?" he asked finally.

"I prefer relentless," she replied as she felt the tension ease.

"Always?"

"When it suits my purpose," she answered cautiously. "No pun intended."

"Would it suit your purpose to have dinner with me tonight?" he asked pointedly.

In three days Jessica's life had picked up speed. Now it seemed ready to veer out of control. Mark Laidlaw was seductive, like maple-walnut Häagen-Dazs at three in the morning or a cashmere sweater marked down at Bloomingdale's. But she also sensed from a sadness in his eyes and his bittersweet smile that she could be risking a lot more than a pound or two on her hips or an overdraft on her checking account by accepting his invitation.

"I'm not sure," she answered. "Is there some reason for this dinner?"

"How about the failure of New York dry cleaning or the way you handled Sidney Fein?" he said. "Or maybe just the way you walk out of a room."

"Those are good reasons," she teased, "but not good enough to accept your invitation."

"Can I ask why?"

"Because I'd be very uncomfortable."

"Uncomfortable?"

"Yes. Because you're married, and I'm older and less interested in a pointless flirtation than I was the last time I got involved with someone who was married," she answered, falling victim to her better judgment.

"Who said this had to be pointless?" he asked.

"I would think that would make it worse."

"Maybe. Maybe not."

"I'm sorry, Mark. I can't take that chance. Not now," she said firmly. "I just can't go out with you. Maybe another time, when things are different."

"I understand," he said, unconvincingly. "I'm just sorry these things always seem ugly or sordid. That certainly wasn't my intent."

"What was your intent?"

"To have dinner with an interesting woman," Laidlaw replied.

"Now, if that doesn't sound like an invitation to scandal, I don't know what does," she said, feigning indignation. "Look, Mark, you're tempting, but your life is too public. Too many things could be misconstrued by too many people, by too many of the wrong people. And frankly, I'm much too insecure for that . . . I hope that's not confusing."

"Confusing, no. Disappointing, yes," he answered. "Perhaps another time, then."

"Perhaps," she said softly.

"Good-bye, Jessica."

Annoyed and frustrated with herself, Jessica hung up the phone. Since Friday she had started viewing everything in terms of extremes. The choices before her had suddenly become too important, the risks too great. She felt her life was being controlled and measured by some future happiness, some nebulous goal. Whatever that goal was, it put her more fanciful desires out of reach.

She reran their conversation in her head. Hearing Mark Laidlaw's words again, she became furious with his arrogance. How could he presume, no matter how attracted to him she might have appeared, that she'd jump at the chance to go out with him? Never mind that he was charming, wealthy, and terribly sexy. He was married. The nerve of the man, she thought. What kind of woman did he think she was? Well, whatever he thought, she wasn't that kind of woman and had no intention of becoming one.

Then it crossed her mind that she had misread him. Maybe it was just an innocent invitation. Worse yet, if he and Jonathan Lambert were so close, maybe he was going to make another pitch for Turner, Welles. For an instant she considered calling Laidlaw back, then reasoned she would be opening a whole can of worms by doing so. There was simply no graceful way to handle this now. Paralyzed by indecision, Jessica simply stared at the phone.

"Oh, Ms. Wheeler," Gloria called out, her voice dripping with irreverence. "Are you ready to see Mrs. Williams?"

"Yes, yes," Jessica snapped, impatient with her own uncertainty. As she stood up to greet the round black woman who was still trying to pry herself loose from the plastic chair, Jessica glanced down at the top of her desk, at the mound of files, the empty coffee cups and the telephone. She realized that nothing had changed on that desktop for the last three years. "No, Gloria. Please have Mrs. Williams wait," she told the receptionist just as the large woman managed to free herself from the chair.

"I don't think that would be a good idea," Gloria advised, glaring back at Jessica.

"Fine," she relented. "Send her down." Jessica sat down and began rummaging through her purse, looking for her wallet. Damn Gloria, she thought, and damn Eric and Mark Laidlaw. Everyone, it seemed, wanted a piece of her. She found the business card she had tucked away in her wallet just as Mrs. Williams's shadow obscured her desk.

"Please sit down, Mrs. Williams," said Jessica politely as she motioned to the plastic chair by her desk.

The black woman looked down at the small chair wordlessly and shook her head.

"And no reason why you should," replied Jessica as she jumped up from her seat and wheeled over a larger chair from behind one of the empty desks.

The large woman smiled at her appreciatively and sat down.

"Now, if you would excuse me for one minute, Mrs. Williams," said Jessica, reaching for the phone, "I have an important call to make." Jessica dialed the number on the business card and then waited. In the back of her mind she heard a voice, shouting at her. *Are you crazy?* the voice said. Immediately, there was another voice, this time her own, higher and thinner, shouting back, *Don't worry, I know what I'm doing.*

On the third ring a receptionist came on the line. Jessica paused for a second, then spoke slowly and deliberately, "Jonathan Lambert, please. Jessica Wheeler calling."

Chapter 5

"Jess, are you crazy?" Bobby Ray Masefield shouted, trying to make himself heard over the rushing wind.

"Don't worry," replied Jessica as she lifted herself on top of the front seat of the car. "I know what I'm doing."

The red Mustang convertible flew down the darkened highway. Slicing through the cool blackness, the headlights exposed the broken white lines dividing the lanes and blurred them into ivory ribbons that seemed to stretch all the way to Odessa. With no moon, and the flat Texas countryside comfortably cloaked in the inky night, the two teenagers felt as though they were rocketing through an endless tunnel, joining time and space rather than Midland and Odessa.

Bobby Ray Masefield was a dusty-haired boy with broad shoulders, deep creases in his cheeks, and a slightly crooked smile. A smile that had vanished the moment Jessica Wheeler started climbing up the front seat. This was his second date with the popular blond

cheerleader, and so far, considering their raging hor-
mones, they had both obeyed the rules. His reward to
date was one very wet kiss and an implied promise of
some future pleasures. But now she was acting crazy
and he was concerned. With his attention split between
the highway and the girl perched on the top of the seat
next to him, he began to slow the Mustang down.

"Don't slow down!" Jessica yelled. "It won't feel the
same if we're going slower."

Wanting more than anything to taste her warm skin
against his lips, Bobby Ray reluctantly kept the speed-
ometer at an even sixty miles an hour. Bewildered and
at the same time curious, he carefully adjusted his
rearview mirror so he could watch the girl and the road
at the same time.

Clad in his purple and gold varsity jacket, Jessica
appeared to him in the mirror as a mystical vision. Her
arms were spread out as though resting on the wind,
and her long blond hair danced around her face in a
golden fury. The jacket had billowed open, fed by the
constant rush of air, while her eyes remained tightly
shut. She seemed to hang there, contemplating some
distant time. Finally, a low moan passed her lips and she
slid back down into her seat.

"Jesus, Jess, you scared the hell out of me," said
Bobby Ray, looking over at her flushed face. "Just what
was that all about?"

"I don't know," she replied dreamily. "I thought it
would be fun."

"Fun?"

"Yes, fun. You know, like you playing football and
everyone around you cheering," she answered.

"And was it . . . fun?" he asked hesitantly.

"Better than fun. It was like a dream," she mused.
"It was sorta like riding into the future in a spinning
kaleidoscope."

"That's too weird," replied Bobby Ray. Then, noticing Jessica shake her head in the spontaneous and

unaffected way that began all his fantasies, he reconsidered his hasty opinion. "Well," he admitted, "maybe not that weird."

They could see three small fires on the rim of one of the sand dunes as they pulled off the highway. The Sandhills around Monahans, Texas, were a favorite hangout for any teenager in the Midland/Odessa area with a car, a six-pack of beer and romantic intentions; the natural bowls and hidden niches carved out of the shifting sand providing more than enough privacy when the time was right.

After climbing up to the ridge line, Jessica and Bobby Ray huddled around one of the fires with two other couples and shared some beer. The six gossiped and joked about school and friends until one by one the other couples drifted off into the darkness, leaving Jessica and Bobby Ray alone in front of the fire.

"Have you had many offers?" Jessica asked the boy while she stared into the flames.

"So far just A&M and TCU," he replied. "But I've got an appointment in Austin in two weeks to talk with Texas."

"Is that where you want to go?"

"I want to go where I'll get to play and be seen," answered the teenager. "I mean, that's the only way the pros are going to find you."

"Is it so important that they find you, Bobby?" she asked as she slipped under the young man's arm.

"Very," he replied intently. "Jess, you're not the only one with dreams. It's no secret I'm not as bright as you, and that's why football is my only chance to be somebody."

"You are somebody, Bobby," she said, turning from the fire to look into his earnest face.

"You know what I mean, Jess," he answered. "With all your grades and stuff, you must want to do something special, be somebody famous."

"Like on TV or in the magazines? . . . No, I don't think so." She thought for a second. "All right, maybe one cover story in *Time* or *Newsweek*," she admitted with a giggle.

"And what would you want them to say about you?"

She looked at him with an impish grin on her face. "That I was the only woman who could wear a short skirt and still be taken seriously."

"Really, Jess."

"You don't like my legs, Bobby Ray?" she teased, extending a long denim-covered leg.

The teenager felt the heat from the fire leap across the sand and inflame his groin. He loved her legs. He wanted to touch and caress them. He also wanted to play for the Dallas Cowboys someday, but he knew deep down that would never happen either. "They're great Jess," Bobby Ray answered as he concentrated on keeping his voice low and even. "And Lord knows, I do take you seriously."

Jessica liked Bobby Ray. With his soft brown eyes, and mop of unruly hair, he reminded her of a huggable puppy. Although a year older and, as quarterback of the high school football team, the object of adulation and adolescent infatuations, Bobby Ray had always been awkward and self-conscious around her. It wasn't until he finally asked her for a date that she learned how intimidated he was by her. On the surface they appeared to be the perfect couple—the cheerleader and the jock—but in reality it was an odd match, more like teacher and pupil. Yet they seemed to find a common ground in these simple, late-night talks.

"God, Bobby, I can hardly wait until I'm out of here," Jessica said, staring into the fire.

"The dunes?" he asked anxiously.

"No, I meant Midland," Jessica replied patiently. "There are just so many things I want to see and do."

"Like move mountains?"

"Maybe just a molehill or two," she answered modestly. "At least so someone'll know I've been here."

"Like your daddy did?" the boy asked perceptively, his tone reassuring.

"Yes, Bobby," she whispered. "Exactly like my daddy did."

He held her close, shielding her from the cold and from the sadness that threatened to invade their innocence. Below them in the still, murky shadows, interrupted by high beams and roaring engines, the interstate made its way back toward Odessa, a grim reminder of her father's frailty.

PART 2

Chapter 6

"She's been with you nearly two years now," Mark Laidlaw began, "but do you think she's ready for something this big?"

"She's very good," replied Jonathan Lambert, nodding at the waiter as he set an icy vodka martini in front of him. "Winston tells me she's got a tremendous feel for the real estate market. He says it's almost intuitive. In addition, her contract work is outstanding. I've also heard from some of the people she's been up against. And they say that in a negotiation there are few her age—or, for that matter, any age—who can get the better of her. What can I say, Mark? She's diligent, bright, and knows how to get right to the point."

"You're telling me," said Laidlaw, recalling a polite rejection and his wounded pride.

"Ah, I forgot. You and the young lady have already met," Jonathan replied coyly as he took his napkin and blotted a tiny drop of vodka at the edge of his moustache.

"That's another question I have," said Laidlaw. "If she wouldn't even have dinner with me, what makes you think she'll want to work for me?"

"Absolutely nothing."

"Wonderful," Laidlaw replied cynically.

"I wouldn't worry, Mark. The girl's a professional . . . Look, if you like," he added, "I can just assign her to you, make it a fait accompli, and you two can work out any differences you have over drinks on a neutral battlefield."

"Believe me, it never got that far."

"Then why worry?" said Lambert calmly. "She's exactly what you need."

"That's what I'm afraid of," Laidlaw replied.

"Now, why don't we forget Ms. Wheeler," advised Jonathan, beckoning the captain to the table, "and order some dinner."

The bar at 21 had begun to fill slowly. The cold rain that had plagued the city throughout February had continued over into March and had kept midtown traffic at a perpetual standstill, making everyone late for everything. New Yorkers, though, a generally plucky band, had adapted to the urban flooding and attendant gridlock by mentally rescheduling their appointments a half hour later.

Coming up from his office on Wall Street, Jonathan Lambert had stopped to pick up Mark at the Arena around six, then the two continued on to 21. Greeted warmly by the maître d', they were led into the bar, with its dark woods, banquettes, and toys slung chockablock from the low ceiling, to Jonathan's regular table in the horseshoe by the kitchen.

During dinner they exchanged stories and a wave or two with old friends at nearby tables. The bar at 21 was like a club, albeit a very select club, whose membership was limited to the wealthy and powerful, commoners being relegated—most courteously, of course—to banishment in the upstairs room.

After dinner, while the waiter removed their dishes, Jonathan lit a cigar. "How are you and Ruth doing?" Jonathan asked sympathetically.

Mark waited until the waiter had disappeared into the kitchen before he answered. He still considered his floundering marriage, long ago the focus of gossip and obscene innuendo, a very private matter. "Worse, if that's possible," he told Jonathan. "Since Patty went off to school in September, Ruth's drinking has, frankly, gotten out of hand."

"What happened with that expensive treatment program?"

"She dropped out after the second week," Mark admitted painfully. "Jonathan, I don't know what to do. I just can't seem to reach her. We can't even talk without her waving a glass of vodka in my face." Embarrassed about what he was going to reveal, Mark leaned over the table and lowered his voice. "You know, at first I thought it was the kids. With me wrapped up in the business, not being around, I figured Douglas and Patty had become too much for her. So we sent them off to boarding school, but nothing changed."

"But that's when the kids were younger. They must be some comfort to her now," said Jonathan.

"Patty was, but now she's off at college. And Doug," added Mark, "he's in Los Angeles, pretending to starve and write. So that just leaves Ruth and me in this horribly twisted relationship."

"You could leave her," Jonathan offered guardedly.

"Not the way she is. Anyway, why should I hurt her?"

"Mark, you don't have to hurt her," replied Lambert, "but you do have to save yourself."

"I'm trying," he answered.

"I don't mean the affairs."

"They're not affairs," Laidlaw insisted.

"What are they, then?" asked Jonathan stubbornly.

"Lapses, stolen moments . . ." Frustrated, he turned away, as though he could find a more understanding face elsewhere in the dining room. "Damn it, Jonathan," he said, turning back to his friend, "I get lonely. Every once in a while I need to feel close to someone."

"That's no crime, but I think deluding yourself is," said Lambert. "You think you can live like this for the rest of your life. What happens if you meet someone you really care about and who cares about you? Then what do you do?"

"Probably become more frustrated and guilty than I am now."

"That's ridiculous," replied Jonathan. "You have a right to happiness."

"And so does Ruth," Mark said flatly.

Disheartened, Lambert shook his head, conceding defeat. "Look, Mark, this conversation has come full circle," he declared, "and I'm tired of playing devil's advocate. You know you're the only one who can change things, and I know you'll only do it when you're finally pushed far enough."

"Jonathan, I appreciate your concern," said Mark, "but right now the only thing I'm going to push for, with the help of your Ms. Wheeler, is the completion of this deal. So, unless you want another go-round with this, let's change the subject and order some dessert."

"What do you mean, is it life threatening?" Jessica shouted into the phone. "It hasn't been this hot in March since 1955. The windows are sealed shut. And I'm wearing a wool suit in an office that feels like Houston in July . . . You're damn right, it's life threatening. Your life, if you don't send someone up here to fix the heat . . . Thank you, and I'll be sure to pass that bit of information on to the New York Department of Buildings," she said acidly, then slammed down the receiver.

"Everything all right?" Winston Avery asked, standing in the open doorway.

"Great, if you have plans to panel over this office and turn it into a sauna," Jessica replied sarcastically.

A wall of heat smacked Avery in the face as he entered Jessica's small office. "I take it that was maintenance on the phone."

"A Mr. Kelso, to be specific," she answered.

"Any luck?" asked Avery as he slipped into the chair by her desk.

"Not unless you're interested in Mr. Kelso's scatological description of the heating system in this building," said Jessica dryly.

"Wonderful. How's Rosenfeld coming along?"

"The property should clear escrow tomorrow."

"Good." Unusually restless, Avery got up and walked over to the window. He stared down pensively at Wall Street, watching the ant-sized figures darting in and out of the shadows. "Tell me, Jessica," he began casually, "you have anything else pending? Anything that requires your immediate attention?"

"Well, there's the closing on Joshua McMurty's co-op on Wednesday, and the Wesguard meeting next week," she answered, a little suspicious of his tone. "Why, Winston?"

"Listen, Jessica, if you wouldn't mind, I'd like to put Donald on the Wesguard meeting," he said, still looking out the window.

"But I do mind," Jessica shot back. "Come on, Winston, you know Wesguard is important to me. A private sector, middle-and-low-income housing project, and you want me to hand it over to Donald? Be fair, Winston," she said, spinning her chair around to confront him. "Isn't this the kind of thing you dangled in front of me to get me to come over here?"

"And seventy-five grand," he added testily as he turned away from the window. Clearly, he was uncomfortable with whatever he was about to say.

"Woo," replied Jessica. "Now it's getting a little cold in here."

"I'm sorry, Jessica. I'm just a little on edge today," Avery said apologetically. "Listen, after you finish with Joshua's closing, why don't you take the rest of the week off. I know you could use the rest. You haven't had a vacation since—"

"Christmas. Look, Winston, I don't want a vacation," Jessica countered. "What I want is the Wesguard assignment."

"I can't give it to you, Jess," he said regretfully.

"All right, Winston, what's going on?"

"You'll have to ask Jonathan," he answered, crossing the office to the door, their conversation obviously nearing an end.

"Jonathan?"

"Yes. He wants to see you in his office nine o'clock Monday morning."

"Do you know what about?" Jessica asked anxiously.

"Nine o'clock Monday morning," Avery repeated ominously. "Oh, and have a nice weekend." Then, grabbing hold of the doorknob, he added, "You want this open or closed?"

"Open," she said curtly while she dabbed at her forehead with a tissue.

Jessica was angry and confused. In the almost two years since she had joined the firm, this was the first time she had been reassigned. And to make matters worse, it had been done without any discussion or opportunity for appeal. Perhaps because it was so sudden, so arbitrary, she felt she had been deceived. There were promises that had been made, and she was determined to point those out to Jonathan on Monday. Unless, of course, he fired her the moment she walked in the door. After all, there had been rumors of cutbacks among the associates.

She played these senseless mind games for another fifteen minutes until the heat in her office became unbearable. Then, certain she would be reduced to a puddle of bodily fluids if she remained any longer, Jessica gathered up an armload of files, a handful of pens, and a legal pad and fled her office for the sanctuary of the law library one floor down.

Around five she grudgingly dropped off the Wesguard file on Donald Riegert's desk. Riegert, a brilliant but self-effacing young attorney, was exceptionally contrite. From behind a closed door he railed against the imperious nature of the reassignment and denied any complicity in it. Whether he was offering his regrets for this or some future injustice, Jessica was uncertain. It did seem strange, however, that at this particular time Donald suddenly felt compelled to apologize to Jessica for any slight or professional faux pas, real or imagined, anyone at the firm may have inadvertently committed since she first came to work at Turner, Welles.

Shaken, Jessica returned to her office. As she reached behind the door to get her coat, she noticed a man, clad in a beige jumpsuit, on his hands and knees behind her desk.

"Mr. Kelso?" she asked tentatively.

The man stuck his head up. He had jet-black hair and a wide, reddish, pockmarked face. "No, Rivera," he said, pointing to his name stitched in script across his breast pocket.

"Well, Mr. Rivera, what do you think?"

"You were right," he replied thoughtfully as he wiped the back of his neck with a crumpled blue bandanna. "It is hot in here."

"Thank yooou," Jessica wailed futilely. Then, with her coat over her arm and frustration oozing from every pore, she threw some notes into her wine-colored attaché case and headed out the door.

Maybe I *should* take a few days off, she thought as she hurried down the hall toward the elevator. Fly down to the Virgin Islands for a quiet weekend in the sun or just lock myself in the apartment with four large bags of popcorn, a box of tissues, and a *Breakfast at Tiffany's* tape.

She stepped into the elevator and, remembering her dinner plans, checked her watch. She had just enough time to get uptown to her apartment, change clothes, and meet the others at the restaurant. As the elevator rapidly descended the thirty floors to the lobby, Jessica began to have second thoughts about the dishing that took place around these monthly round tables, but on the other hand, these were her friends and they had an obligation to help her make some sense out of this screwed-up day.

Chapter 7

"Faith, you want to bring me Donatello's swatch book. Fabrizio's pink looks like Pepto-Bismol," Meredith Werner shouted to her assistant in the outer office. "I'm looking for something more floral than pharmaceutical."

"How about blush wine?" asked her assistant, standing in the doorway of the office, a small piece of pale pink silk in her right hand.

"Too tentative. I'm trying to make a statement."

"With pink?"

"It's a cruise-wear statement," Meredith replied caustically. "Have you got Donatello's book?"

"Right here." She handed Meredith a small portfolio, covered in a canary yellow silk moiré and bound at one end with an artfully braided silk cord.

Meredith flipped rapidly through the sheets of colored material, her red-framed glasses slipping closer to the end of her nose with each sweep of her hand. Her thick ash-brown hair was cut short, like a fifties rock and roller, and suspended by mousse and careful combing, hung over her forehead. Her body was wrapped in black wool jersey.

"Meredith, you don't want me to stay late, do you?" inquired her assistant.

"Jesus, is it five-thirty already?"

"No, it's a quarter to six."

"Damn it. No, that's all right, Faith, you can go." Meredith began to rummage through the clutter of sketches, photographs, and bits of cloth that littered the desktop. After a minute or two she found the television remote-control unit, switched on a small color set at the opposite end of the room and turned to one of the local news channels.

She continued to jot down fabric numbers until a cool, lean brunette in her late twenties began a report on young, successful, New York career women who want "it all." Whatever "it all" was. Meredith never ceased to marvel at the reporter's professional detachment and how she could affect that strange nasal speaking voice, a gooselike sound, that commonly afflicts women television reporters and cocaine addicts.

A series of inane questions from the anchorwoman followed the reporter's story. Christ, thought Meredith, what would the viewing public think if they knew both these women would give it all up for the love of a man who wasn't married or an axe murderer.

"Thanks, Liz," said the unctuous voice on the screen. "We'll have more of Liz Copley's report on New York's wonder women at eleven."

"That's it. This wonder woman is out of here," Meredith said to herself. She flipped off the television and began to pick notes and sketches off her desk and hurriedly stuff them into a black woven Bottega Veneta envelope. Then, with one eye still evaluating the desktop litter, she deftly scooped a silvery raccoon coat off a nearby chair and struggled into it. Finally, satisfied that she had taken everything of earthly value, she quickly glanced at her watch, snatched her handbag off a counter behind the desk, and rushed out the door, thankful she still had thirty minutes to get a cab and get up to Sixty-sixth Street.

Elizabeth Copley stood in front of the Council Broadcasting Studios waiting impatiently for a taxi, the cold wind whipping her long brown hair around her face. She was anxious to get to the restaurant early this time because she felt guilty about missing last month's dinner and because there was so much to talk about. She was also due back at the station at ten-thirty.

The monthly dinner circle had begun two years ago. Two friends had called two other friends to meet for dinner at an Italian restaurant on the upper East Side. Everyone enjoyed themselves, so they arranged to meet the next month. Soon the four became six, then eight; however, life being what it is in New York—the pressures of success, the humiliations of failure, the odd possessive boyfriend or new husband—the number gradually fixed at four. No one complained. There was solidarity and security in the number four. It also made for generous seating, and usually deterred predatory single men.

An on-duty cab stopped abruptly in front of Liz. Through a half-opened rear window a muffled voice drifted out from the darkened recesses of the backseat. "Whoa, lady, do you want it all or would you settle for a cab ride?"

Liz flung open the rear door. "It's freezing. I'll take the ride," she said as she got in. She looked over at the smiling face at the other end of the seat. "Meredith, what kept you?"

"Your riveting report and the traffic on Eighth Avenue."

"What did you think?" asked Liz hesitantly.

"We should have taken Tenth Avenue."

"What did you think about the story?"

"Honestly?"

"All right, I asked for it," Liz answered. "Honestly."

"It had no real depth, but that's not your fault. That's electronic journalism. But for what it was, it was good. The women you interviewed were a bit too messianic and made me want to throw up, but the pacing was great and I loved your outfit."

"Thanks for the compliment, I think," replied Liz stoically. "I take it you think women shouldn't want it all or at least try for it?"

"That isn't the point, Liz. If the opportunities are there, we should take advantage of them. It's just that trying to have it all has become a test of a successful woman's femininity. And God help you if you miss something on the list. But this whole thing is skirting the real issue."

"Which is?"

"Which is making the tough choices in life. We have to consider our options and decide what's important. No one tells a man he has to be the breadwinner, a physical specimen to rival the Greek gods, manager of two households, expert cook, or nurturer. He picks what he wants from life. Why shouldn't we have that right?"

"We do. Only we're women," replied Liz. "Perhaps we know we are capable of more. We're more complex. We're more nurturing. We're more adaptive. We live longer. We're—"

"At the restaurant," interrupted Meredith, reaching into her bag for the fare.

"Tell me, Meredith—not that I could ever use it against you—how do you always manage to get me on the defensive in these discussions?"

"Donald Greenleaf," Meredith said, fumbling with her wallet.

"Our philosophy professor at Vassar? What has he got to do with anything?"

"After I slept with him," replied Meredith, "I could

see you thought I walked away from his bed with the wisdom of the ages tucked smartly between my thighs. You bought recklessness for sophistication. Face it. I intimidated you then, and I still do," she added smugly.

"What!" Liz responded incredulously.

"Keep the change," Meredith told the cab driver. "In fact," she said, turning back to her friend, "the only thing I walked away with was an embarrassing social disease, but if I told you that nine years ago, consider all the wonderful arguments we would have missed. Now get out of the cab."

Gerardo and Giuseppe Bruno greeted Meredith and Liz effusively as they entered the restaurant. Charming, ebullient men with flashing eyes and mischievous smiles, they owned Sistina, along with their uncle and two brothers. While Giuseppe, the taller of the two, checked their coats, Gerardo led Meredith and Liz to their table in a corner of the soft-beige dining room. Lit by wide flaring sconces that bounced warm light off the blond woods accenting the walls, the room carefully avoided any airs of pretense or puffery.

Jessica and an attractive woman in her mid-twenties with honey-blond hair were deep in conversation at the table as Meredith and Liz joined them.

"Jessica Lee, honey, don't you look just tasteful," Meredith teased affectionately in an overblown southern accent, her head bobbing from side to side as she inspected Jessica's outfit. "Dear, isn't that an—" she began, her accent reverting to its Long Island roots.

"Anne Klein Two," Jessica announced with a wry smirk, dutifully playing along with her friend.

"Yes. It's functional, yet so nondescript," Meredith replied stingingly.

"And I got it right off the rack at Bloomingdale's," Jessica added proudly.

"Oh, my God," Meredith shrieked in mock horror, "and she paid retail, no less."

"You know, Meredith, you make the loveliest snob," said the other blond woman.

"Not really. I'm not tall enough. It helps if you can look down on people. Now, Julie would make a perfect snob," Meredith said, turning first to Liz, then to Jessica, and finally back to the blond woman. "God knows, you're tall enough. All we would have to change would be the nose, cheekbones, and hair. You look too inviting."

But it was that look that had made Julianna, née Julia Ann Vericki, one of the highest-paid fashion models in New York. Having arrived in the city five years earlier with driving ambition, an M.A. in anthropology from Stanford, and an impressive list of West Coast credits, the sensuous San Diego beauty quickly found herself a home at the Ford Agency. A year and a half later she became one of the chosen few, a member of that inner circle of unforgettable faces that are the bread and butter of any large agency. A college classmate of one of the original "ladies who dine," Julie Ann remained after her friend left the group and New York for a new life in Los Angeles. Julie Ann prized these monthly get-togethers. It was a chance to touch base with the real world, or at least that small part of it that Meredith, Liz, and Jessica represented.

"First, he tried to stick his tongue down my throat. Then he whispered to me, in no uncertain terms, how wonderful the rest of the evening was going to be."

"What did you do?"

"I told him not to bother getting out of the cab. My God," exclaimed Liz, stirring Sweet'N Low into her espresso, "the man used to be a priest."

"That should tell you why he isn't a priest anymore," replied Julie.

"Or a human being," chimed in Meredith.

"What is it with me? I have a healthy six-figure income, a body I've spent thousands on—not to mention, starved for—and I still can't find a nice man to share my life or even dinner," lamented Liz.

"And you never will," said Julie between mouthfuls of raspberries. "Not with that outlook on life."

"How do you eat so much and never gain an ounce?" asked Meredith. "I can't say the word chocolate without gaining weight."

"Good metabolism and a positive attitude."

"Positive attitude? Julie, this is New York," said Liz. "You mean you've never been depressed or felt yourself becoming cynical?"

"Well, only once. After a weekend in St. Croix with Michael Weinstock."

"Michael Weinstock, the investment banker?" asked Meredith.

"Well, it's more like Michael Weinstock, convicted felon," replied Julie. "He pleaded guilty to insider trading six months ago. You know, he writes me some very touching letters from prison."

"There's nothing like the threat of gang rape to bring out the sensitivity in a man," Meredith said sarcastically.

"Jess, you've been awfully quiet. Still trying to figure out how you're going to pay for that co-op of yours?" asked Liz.

"It's not that," Jessica answered haltingly. "Actually, it could come to that."

"What do you mean?" said Meredith, suddenly noticing the uncertainty written all over her friend's face.

"I had one of my cases reassigned to another lawyer today," she answered.

"Is that so unusual?" asked Julie.

"It happens. But it was the first time it happened to me," replied Jessica.

"Come on, Jess. What is it really?" said Liz. "It isn't like you to let your pride get in the way of your work."

"It was the way it happened, Liz," explained Jessica. "So offhandedly, without any real whys or wherefores. It was as though I was removed because I wasn't going to be around to follow it through."

"You think they're going to fire you, Jess?" asked Liz incredulously.

"It certainly looks that way," answered Jessica.

"Be serious, Jess," Meredith told her friend. "Didn't Avery once tell you you were the most productive associate they had?"

"That's not what he said this afternoon," said Jessica. "And that's not the half of it. Monday, I have to face Jonathan Lambert."

"Maybe it's a step up," Julie suggested optimistically. "Maybe they're assigning you to a heavyweight client."

"I appreciate the encouragement," responded Jessica. "But if that were true, why keep it secret?"

"Look, Jess, there's no use working yourself up when you don't even know what the old guy has got to say," Meredith advised, putting her arm around her friend's shoulder.

"I guess you're right," answered Jessica stoically.

"But if worse does come to worse, you can always sell the co-op and move back in with me," added Meredith.

"God, if it were me, I'd rather die first," scoffed Liz.

"If it were you," Meredith shot back, "that would be the only way I'd take you."

Jessica began to laugh. To be able to articulate her fears made her feel less afraid, less worried, less alone. Working so hard, she had often felt cut off from the world, from its laughter and zaniness, its warmth and compassion. She was thankful that these three women could bring all that back for her.

Chapter 8

Jonathan Lambert's office, two floors above Jessica's, was a baronial affair, reminiscent of a grand Tudor library. The walls were paneled in dark English walnut and hung with eighteenth-century English country landscapes and one or two small Holbein portraits. A massive antique desk, set in front of two large windows framed with heavy green silk draperies, dominated the room and, intentionally or not, focused a visitor's attention on the man seated behind it.

Jessica had first visited this office a week after she had phoned Jonathan Lambert to accept his offer. She remembered it clearly as she stood in the reception area Monday morning waiting to be announced. She remembered the anxiety she had felt over her future with what Eric had called "the opposition" and the quiet awe and reverence when she was finally admitted into Lambert's inner office. Now the fear was back— not over joining "the opposition," but of losing her position in it.

As Jessica entered the room, Jonathan was standing by a small tile fireplace, talking with a tall, gray-haired man. The man, an unfamiliar figure in a dark pinstriped suit, had his back to the door. His presence made Jessica more uneasy. Perhaps it was the idea of being fired in front of a total stranger.

"Good morning, Jessica, I'm so glad you could join us," said Jonathan courteously.

The tall man turned around and Jessica immediately recognized Mark Laidlaw. His piercing blue-gray eyes and disarming smile, not to mention the memory of beluga caviar dripping from his sleeve, had been difficult to forget.

During the weekend, while watching Audrey Hepburn and George Peppard fall in love in Tiffany's for the third or fourth time, she had spun lurid fantasies about how this meeting would turn out. There were screaming and shouting scenarios, tearful and distressing ones, but nothing with quite this refined level of humiliation.

"Since there are a few things we'd like to discuss with you," Lambert continued innocently, "why don't we make ourselves comfortable." He gestured toward a grouping of brown leather armchairs in front of the fire. "I think you already know Mr. Laidlaw," he added casually.

Jessica nodded nervously, then slipped into the chair closest to the fire. The leather was worn soft and supple. It reminded her of another chair in a small, sparsely furnished living room on the outskirts of Midland, Texas, where life had been simpler and she had felt safe. As she sank deeper into the dark leather, her confidence returned, restored in a rush of child-hood memories.

"Jessica," Jonathan began, "I've been quite impressed with some of the work you've done recently. According to Winston, you've handled yourself and your clients' interests with the utmost discretion and sensitivity."

"Thank you, Jonathan. But most of the credit should go to Winston. In many cases I was only support," replied Jessica modestly. If this is fawning, she thought, so be it. She was going to fight for this job in any way she could. Besides, pride would not help make the payments on the East Seventieth Street co-op.

"Jessica, we think, based on your performance," Jonathan continued, "that you're the perfect candidate for a very important assignment that Mark has asked us to handle. At the moment all I can tell you is you'll be working independently of the firm and closely with Mark. . . . Needless to say," he added with particular emphasis, "successful completion of such an undertaking would be looked upon most favorably by the senior members of the partnership."

Jessica shot a suspicious glance at Mark, who sat stone-faced throughout Jonathan's short monologue. Clearly, he had heard Jonathan Lambert try to sell this patrician hustle to other unsuspecting attorneys. But Jessica wasn't buying. She had already dodged one very enticing invitation from Mark Laidlaw, and didn't relish tempting fate a second time. She could see trouble written all over him—the kind of trouble, her father once told her, that made grown-ups do foolish things. In addition, she wanted that Wesguard project. After two years and a score of fat and happy clients, she reasoned, they owed her that.

Looking back at Lambert, Jessica decided to beard the lion in his den and state her case. "With all due respect, Jonathan—"

"Ms. Wheeler," interrupted Laidlaw, breaking his silence, "why don't you just save your 'with all due respect' speech and give this opportunity some serious thought."

"Opportunity?" Jessica said to Laidlaw coolly.

"Yes, opportunity," he answered contentiously. "Then, after you've thought about it, you can give me that speech of yours."

"Over dinner?" Jessica snapped back, angry at Laidlaw for cutting her short, then angry at herself for the cheap shot.

"Let's say tomorrow morning at nine in my office at the Arena?" he said calmly, ignoring her remark.

"I'll be there," she replied, giving in.

Five minutes later, as Jessica left Jonathan Lambert's office, she realized her father had been right about troublesome people, because she suddenly felt very foolish.

The taxi pulled in behind a long line of cabs in front of the Seventh Avenue entrance to the Arena. Jessica paid the driver, then crossed the broad promenade that led to the white marble building, eluding two surprisingly well-dressed panhandlers in the process.

For a time the Arena was more a state of mind than a place. Since the turn of the century, when the first hippodrome called the Arena was constructed eleven blocks southeast of its present location, the name had managed to evoke vivid images of blood, sweat, and thick gray cigar smoke. It was that corner of a man's soul where dreams were born and hopes died. It was where men took their sons and where those sons took their sons. It was where male bonding was toasted with cheap beer and loose women.

Yet, in its third incarnation, built in the early sixties over the bones of a grand beaux arts railroad station, the Arena had become a business. Gone were the architectural charms of the first building on Twenty-sixth Street and the Broadway hipsters of the second Arena on Eighth Avenue. Bland and sanitized, the newest Arena represented the era of the bottom line, and excitement suffered because of it. Championship boxing had fled to Atlantic City, and the once proud

New York Knights barely managed to share perennial mediocrity with the New York Blades, the resident hockey team. Sadly, the only link to the glory days were the annual visits of the circus and horse show in the spring and fall.

As she rode the elevator to Mark Laidlaw's office, Jessica honed the fine points of a first-rate rejection speech. It was to be a professional effort, a courtroomlike summation of the facts, with no allusion to or mention of that unsettling phone call. First, she would appeal to Laidlaw's vanity. A man as successful as Mark Laidlaw, she reasoned, had to be supporting a major ego. She would simply claim that his professional standing in the community demanded a senior member of the firm. If that failed, she had prepared a more pragmatic, albeit sexist, position: a female attorney would be more of a liability than an asset in the male-dominated world of pro sports. And finally, moving from self-deprecation to self-interest, she would plead for her career. Any prolonged independent assignment, she was ready to argue, would reduce her visibility at the office, and Jonathan's claim aside, any chances for an early partnership. Jessica was still debating whether, as a last resort, she should slander all professional sports or just basketball, when the elevator doors opened on the twenty-third floor.

Jessica stood alone in Mark Laidlaw's office, dazzled by the spectacular views of southern Manhattan and eastern New Jersey. The room itself was a study in understatement. A simply sculpted, burnished oak desk set on an immense oriental rug of the richest blue and creamiest beige wools, anchored the room. The two walls of the corner office were paneled in light woods and accented with small impressionist paintings and drawings. In front of the wide floor-to-ceiling window to Jessica's right, four black leather and stainless-steel Barcelona chairs silently stood guard over a large Mies van der Rohe glass coffee table. The room, like the man it mirrored, was not what she had expected.

"Not what you imagined, is it?" said Mark Laidlaw, emerging through a door to Jessica's left. He wore a charcoal-gray double-breasted Zegna suit, which had been carefully fitted over his muscular frame and was set off by a burgundy silk pocket square. "The trophies and team pictures are in a room we use for press conferences," he added. "I happen to prefer the Caillebottes and Bonnards to photographs of twelve tall men in their underwear. Won't you sit down, Ms. Wheeler? Or would you prefer to state your case standing up?"

They moved to the chairs by the window, where Jessica began her arguments. She made her case with the intensity and assurance of a seasoned trial lawyer, judiciously excluding the slur on pro sports, but she quickly realized from the expression on Mark Laidlaw's face that she was contesting the uncontestable.

"You really are very good, Ms. Wheeler," Mark replied, maintaining the formality to avoid any hint of impropriety or duplicity. "And I appreciate your candor. In fact, that's what attracted me to you in the first place."

Jessica crossed her arms over her chest, leaned back in her chair and eyed him skeptically.

"What I meant was," continued Laidlaw, trying to recapture lost ground, "your selection for this job was not some whimsical decision. You were picked—and this may or may not sound flattering—because you're an unknown commodity, because you're a woman, and because Jonathan says you're a damn good lawyer. And, if you screw up, you're expendable and I can throw you to the wolves."

With that checkered testimonial, any idea that this was to be more than a business relationship began to quickly fade. Dropping her arms, Jessica shifted forward in the chair. "And what if I don't fancy being thrown to the wolves, Mr. Laidlaw?" Jessica asked forcefully.

"Frankly, that's what I'm counting on for this enterprise to succeed. Jonathan seems to think that under those good looks and smooth southern manners, you're a real street fighter," he replied.

"Not much of one, if you've already got me between the proverbial rock and hard place."

"Look at it this way, Ms. Wheeler. I'm giving you the opportunity to make partner at Turner, Welles, in one giant step."

"Or end my career trying."

"Come on, lady. Take a chance," Laidlaw joked, hoping to crack the tension. "I'm really very easy to work for. And I promise no more errant dinner invitations," he added with a boyish grin.

"I really don't have a choice here, do I?" said Jessica, recognizing she had been outmaneuvered by both Jonathan and Mark.

"Not really," he answered.

"I don't even know what you need me for."

"Know anything about basketball?"

"Not that much, I'm afraid."

"Fine . . . Now, I hear you're a whiz at real estate. Is that true?"

Jessica smiled. It was easy to see he already knew the answer to his question. "I have a working knowledge," she answered.

"A working knowledge? Don't be coy. Avery says you're an ace."

"Okay, I'm an ace."

"Terrific," he replied. "When we're finished here, I want you to take your ace to the office we've set up for you on East Twenty-eighth Street. Dorothy, out front, will give you the address." Laidlaw got up from his chair and walked over to his desk. "I want you to begin work setting up two New York corporations and a Delaware holding company. You pick the names. Some-

thing you'll be comfortable with, but not too esoteric."
He pulled a sheet of paper off the desk, then returned
to his seat, handing the paper to Jessica. "These are the
officers."

The memo, addressed to Jessica, was stamped CONFI-
DENTIAL and bore yesterday's date. She quickly ran her
eyes down the page and saw her name listed as president of the primary New York corporation. It was
apparent Mark Laidlaw was not in the habit of taking
no for an answer.

"Do you have a real estate broker you can trust?" he
asked.

"Yes."

"Well, get hold of him, or her, and work out a deal
for his commissions and some hefty incentives for early
acquisition and low purchase prices."

"Whoa," Jessica interrupted. "You sound like you
want all of this done yesterday. When do I get a chance
to clear up my work at the office?"

"Tomorrow."

"Tomorrow?"

"Right," he said, then continued barking instructions. "Then, after you've finished up there, I'd like you
to meet me at Le Cirque for dinner . . . so I can fill you
in on the project," he added, anticipating her reaction.

"I'm not sure if I'll be free for dinner, Mr. Laidlaw,"
Jessica replied cautiously. "It's going to take quite some
time to wrap things up at my office."

"Try," he insisted. "And let's forget the formality.
After all, you've already tried rejecting me twice. I
think that entitles you to use my first name."

Jessica found herself reluctantly captivated by his
spirit and self-assurance, but at the same time made
uneasy by them. *Damn Jonathan Lambert,* she thought.
Why did he have to toss her out into the cold with only
her wits and this determined man for a safety net? It
would have been more humane to have simply fired
her. She had felt something between them the first

time they had met, something unspoken, unfathomable. She had tried walking away from it once, but was forced to face it now, drawn to him like a moth to a flame.

"All right, then, Mark," she replied dutifully. "What time should I meet you at Le Cirque?"

Chapter 9

The woman was held in and streamlined by blue and silver Spandex. On her feet were a pair of pristine Reeboks, and around her forehead, a navy-blue terry sweatband. The mandatory leg warmers sagged fashionably over the tops of the sneakers. In her late forties, Ruth Laidlaw was lean, with a tan just approaching leathery. Small purplish circles under her eyes were visible through her makeup, and tiny flaps of skin were evident on her neck, her first face lift two years ago already a memory. She struggled to raise her torso from the black foam floor mat, and grunted in a more or less regular cadence halfway through each sit-up.

Standing over her, chanting the fitness mantra, "No pain, no gain," and watching her sweat, was Teddy Breed. Teddy Breed was paid to make people sweat. Mostly, he made women sweat—beautiful women, ugly women, heavy women, lean women, but always wealthy women. A man of few words, most of them monosyllabic, Teddy was one of New York's many hyphenated careerists. In his case, it was personal trainer–actor, the obvious combination for someone with rank optimism and even ranker good looks. He enjoyed his work and its fringe benefits—the odd limousine ride, an extra theatre ticket here, some gratuitous sex there—but he was always careful to remember that he was only hired help, and that sound wisdom kept him from becoming more than a minor irritant to the husbands of his chic clientele.

Ruth Laidlaw finished her fiftieth sit-up and remained on the black mat, exhausted and out of breath. The morning sunlight danced through her frosted blond hair as it bounced around the room, first off the mirrored wall and then off the stainless-steel rods and tubing of the gleaming exercise equipment.

The gym had been Ruth's idea. When they first moved in, it had been an intimate little guest room, painstakingly decorated but rarely used. House guests seemed to prefer the gentility of the slightly larger bedroom across the hall. Eventually the guest room had become the warehouse for the sprawling fifteen-room Fifth Avenue apartment, until a year ago, when Ruth found Teddy.

"That's it for today," said Teddy, helping Ruth off the mat. "Let's cool down with some stretches."

Ruth moved to a barre along the mirrored wall and began a series of wide, graceful extensions.

"You do that very well," Teddy said, admiring Ruth's fluid movements.

"I studied dance when I was younger," she replied. Her breathing was deep and relaxed.

"So you were a dancer before all this?"

Ruth dropped her right leg to the floor, turned around and swung her left leg over the barre. "No," she answered, glaring at the young man as she stretched out over the top of her thigh. "And what makes you think I married into 'all this'?"

"I don't know. I can't think of you poor," he quickly

replied, trying to back away from an obviously sensitive issue.

"When my husband and I got married, twenty-three years ago, we lived in a tiny one-bedroom apartment over a bakery on West Thirteenth Street. It's taken most of those twenty-three years to build 'all this,' as you call it. It didn't come easy. So don't make it sound like this dropped into my lap."

During the embarrassing lull that followed, Ruth Laidlaw finished at the barre, threw a towel around her neck, and walked to a small steel cabinet at the far end of the room.

"I think it went much better than yesterday, don't you?" asked Teddy, attempting to restart the conversation.

"No, I don't. You should know by now Teddy, darling, that I find progress a bore," Ruth replied. She filled a tall glass with ice from a Lucite bucket on top of the cabinet, then poured three fingers of vodka into it from a bottle she produced from a yellow canvas sack. She took a long swallow of the icy liquid, stripped off the blue sweatband, and walked, glass in hand, into the gray-tiled bathroom to the right of the cabinet.

"You know, Ruth, I really don't know much about you," he yelled over the noise from the shower.

"Why should you? You're only my trainer, not my analyst," she shouted back, her voice reverberating off the smooth tiles.

Shaking his head in disbelief, Teddy grabbed a pair of chrome dumbbells off a long wooden rack and began doing curls in front of the huge mirror. "Jesus, Ruth, you piss me off. Why have you got such a goddamn chip on your shoulder? Oh, and tell me one more thing," he asked, as he admired his biceps rippling in the mirror. "If you're so bent on drinking yourself to death, why the hell have me come in five days a week and sweat the booze out of you?"

"Because, lover, if I'm killing myself, I want to look good while I'm doing it," she said, the bathroom echo gone.

Teddy pulled his eyes away from his reflection just long enough to notice Ruth standing nude in the entrance to the bathroom. Her body was glistening with droplets of water and streaked with lather. She held a white washcloth in her right hand, which she slowly rubbed across her tanned abdomen and between her thighs.

"Now, why don't you come in here and help me do my back," she ordered, tossing the wet washcloth at his feet.

Teddy put down the dumbbells and picked up the washcloth. He rubbed it against his face, inhaling her scent and the aroma of the perfumed soap. Then he pulled his T-shirt over his head and walked toward the bathroom.

He stopped in front of her, a shock of black hair spilling over his forehead. He could feel the desire radiating from her naked body. Ruth threw her arm around his neck and drew herself to him. She kissed him with a fierceness that he had known few times before; her hot tongue explored his mouth while her free hand worked furiously at the waistband of his shorts.

"Come with me," she whispered, her voice hoarse and gravelly as she led him into the bathroom.

Teddy dropped his shorts onto the blue tile floor and stepped into the shower with Ruth. She rubbed her soapy body up against him, making him slick and hard. The young man's head was swimming amid the steam, spray, and passion. He felt her nails clawing the back of his thighs. His reaction was swift and uncompromising. He spun her around, bent her over, and entered her.

"Oh yes, yes," Ruth cried, her head resting against the gray tile. "God, it feels so good."

At her urging, he drove himself into her, savagely,

unrestrained. As her moans grew deeper, she reached back and pulled him from her. Her soapy hands stroked him gently, then moved him up.

"Do it to me there," she groaned.

"We don't have to," he stammered, trying to muster some compassion for the lonely woman. "I don't want to hurt you."

"It has to hurt," she hissed as she forced him into her, "or it wouldn't be right."

They rocked back and forth together, the water falling in sheets from Ruth Laidlaw's back as the young man victimized her body and validated her pain.

Chapter 10

It was nearly noon by the time Jessica arrived at the nondescript office building on Twenty-eighth Street, just east of Park Avenue, where Laidlaw had rented a suite of offices for her. She took an elevator to the tenth floor, found the office, and apprehensively opened the oak door that separated Room 1014 from the dreary hallway.

Inside, Jessica was greeted by Stephanie Artis, a very professional and very exotic-looking young black woman in her early twenties. Sheathed in a vibrantly patterned Vittadini knit dress and wearing heavy gold-hoop earrings, she made more than a good impression. She set the level of sophistication for the entire enterprise.

"The only thing we're waiting on are business cards and stationery," the young woman told Jessica as they toured the suite. "Oh, and Mr. Laidlaw's office called to say if you didn't like the way they had the office done, it could be changed to suit you."

"This is just fine," replied Jessica.

It was clear that Mark Laidlaw—or more likely, one of his employees—had taken great pains in decorating the three small rooms that made up the suite. Coordinated in burgundy, gray, and black, and highlighted by a stainless-steel lathe ceiling, the office had a deliberate, efficient thrust, much like Laidlaw himself.

"If I could add a personal note," said Stephanie as they stood in Jessica's office, "I would understand if you would feel more comfortable hiring your own assistant. I was brought over from the Arena with the understanding that setting up the office might only be a temporary assignment."

"Thank you, Stephanie, but I think both you and the office seem perfect," said Jessica.

"Thank you, Ms. Wheeler," replied the young woman gratefully.

"I think I'd prefer Jessica," she responded, settling into the black leather chair behind her desk and checking the fit. "Considering it's just going to be the two of us."

When she was alone, Jessica pulled open drawers, cabinets, and closets, giving the office a thorough inspection. From the bar to the small marble bathroom, nothing had been overlooked. She had to hand it to Mark Laidlaw. He assumed, and things happened.

After she completed her inspection, she took a yellow legal pad from the well-stocked desk and began to list prospective company names, starting with acronyms, then quickly switching to the Greek alphabet for inspiration.

"Oh, I don't mean to take up any more of your time," said Stephanie from the doorway. "Only there are one or two things I have forgotten to mention."

"Please, come in," said Jessica, putting aside the yellow pad. "You've been so conscientious, I can't imagine what you've missed."

"One is the combination to the safe."

"The safe?"

"Don't worry. It's more like an armor-plated piggy bank." Stephanie smiled and walked over to the long black cabinet behind Jessica's desk. She pressed a button hidden in the molding and instantly a front panel sprang open, revealing a one-foot-by-one-foot pebbled steel plate with a black handle and dial. "Voilà. And here's the combination," she said, handing Jessica a slip of paper.

"Impressive. I mean the camouflage, not the safe," said Jessica. "Is there anything in there I should know about?" She had no intention of testing her manual dexterity in front of her assistant.

"There's three thousand dollars that was messengered over this morning from the Arena."

"What on earth for?" asked Jessica suspiciously.

"The note from Mr. Laidlaw's secretary called it a discretionary fund."

"Well, that's perfectly clear," said Jessica facetiously. "Now, what was the second thing?"

"Your American Express card," replied the young woman, reaching into the pocket of her gray knit dress. She handed the gold plastic to Jessica. "That's it for now. If you need anything at all . . ."

Jessica looked down at the names on the list. "Stephanie, how does Delta Associates sound to you?"

"Honestly? Like a front for the CIA."

"Funny, that's what I thought." Jessica circled three names on the pad. "Could you get me Robert Zerndorfer on the phone. He's at—"

"Cole and Zerndorfer," interrupted Stephanie. "I'll get him for you right away."

"I was right. You are perfect."

Moments later Jessica picked up the intercom.

"I have Mr. Zerndorfer on line one for you," Stephanie announced crisply.

"Thank you," replied Jessica. She touched the green

light on the phone. "Hello, Bobby. And no, I will not marry you," she said, preempting his customary opening remark. "Listen, Bobby, something important has come up. I need a real estate maven. Can you meet me for lunch on Wednesday?"

At the end of the day, Jessica took the subway down to Turner, Welles, to finish up some paperwork. But once she got down to Wall Street, she had second thoughts about returning to the office. From the subway station she called Eric Burgess and arranged to meet for dinner and information. The morning's events and the outward appeal of her new employer had raised a lot of questions in her mind. And she needed answers before tomorrow night's dinner with the enigmatic Mark Laidlaw.

"I don't get it," Eric said, setting down his coffee cup. "Your firm represents the guy. Why did you come to me?"

"Because I haven't seen you in four months and wanted to talk?" Jessica suggested unconvincingly. Lying was not one of her strong suits.

"Bullshit," growled Burgess.

"Okay. Because I trust you, Eric," Jessica said. "And because I know you'll accept that."

"Well, that certainly makes me a lousy friend if I ask any more questions, doesn't it?" He took a large envelope from a pocket alongside his wheelchair and slid it across the table. "This is for steering the Harrison grant to us."

Jessica took the envelope and set it on the banquette, under her handbag. "This is it?" she said facetiously. "No summary, no opinion?"

"You want analysis," Burgess teased, "that will cost you extra."

"Agreed."

After taking another sip of coffee, Eric began. "All right. Laidlaw's one of those legendary self-made men.

Only he didn't make it overnight, like today's whiz kids. He's a real plodder. Grew up right here in New York, in Hell's Kitchen."

"Really?" said Jessica incredulously. "He seems like he was born to money."

"If you know him," Eric started to ask, "why all the—"

"I've only met him twice," Jessica interrupted. "And the point is, Eric, I *don't* know him."

"Well, your street kid overcame the odds and won a scholarship to Columbia," Eric continued, "then a fellowship to the Harvard Business School. . . . If I can remember correctly, I think his first job out of the blocks was with some New York investment bank. Anyway, a few years after that, with some experience under his belt and the right contacts, he left the bank, got a small loan, and started a data-services company. Called it D.P. Services. The D.P. are his kids' initials. Really, not much of a story after that. Just twenty years of long hours and hard work. Then one day a few hundred million dollars later, he wakes up and decides he wants off the treadmill. I think that was about three—no five—years ago."

"Why?" she asked.

"Couldn't find an answer, only a lot of theories," replied Eric. "Some thought it was clever timing. Technology stocks were riding a crest at the time. Others thought it was male menopause or boredom, or maybe that he just wanted to have some fun. Anyway, six months later he sold D.P. Services to Allied Motors for around 350 million plus a six-year consultancy worth another three or four million.

"After two years of sailing around the world, trying to make peace with his kids, and doing all the other crap that men like him put off until they have a few years free, he sat down with our old friend Sidney Fein one afternoon in 21 and bought the New York Knights and the Arena. From what I've heard, there were no negotiations. He simply asked Fein for a price and agreed to it on the spot.

"Word has it that two hours later Fein was like a crazy man. He had unloaded a perennial last-place basketball team that had been nothing but red ink on his balance sheets, plus a twenty-year-old building badly in need of renovation, at a price that was inflated by at least ten million dollars, and he was miserable. You see, it was all too good to be true. He figured that Laidlaw had an angle or that he and his people had overlooked something. In fact, right up until the day the final papers were signed, Fein still had people on the street checking on Laidlaw.

"Fein just didn't understand. The guy was a fan. Laidlaw didn't buy a team. He bought a crusade, a new purpose. He was going to rebuild the Knights."

From the inquisitive look still on Jessica's face, Eric could tell that he had, consciously or not, omitted the truly relevant parts of Laidlaw's story. "Oh, let's see. He's fifty-two," he added parenthetically. "Married, to a woman he met at Columbia. Has two children—a daughter, nineteen, and a son, twenty-two. And lives in an apartment on Fifth Avenue in the Seventies. Aside from the Knights, for now, he has no other interests except maybe trying to keep his wife sober. Word has it she has a terrible drinking problem. Anything else you want to know?"

"Eric, where did you get all of this?" asked Jessica, somewhat surprised by the extent of his knowledge.

"Seriously, Jess," he said, "you should know better than to ask."

"Okay," she said, deciding not to press the issue of his source's credibility, "but if that's the summary, what about the analysis?"

"You really want my opinion on this guy?"

"Not really," Jessica answered sarcastically, "but since I'm picking up this dinner, I think I'm entitled to it."

"Okay, then. Here's my off-the-cuff appraisal," replied Eric casually. "Like I said before, he's a plodder. He's also single-minded, a fast study, and surprisingly, a bit of a dreamer."

"That's it?" Jessica declared impatiently.

"What do you want for a two-star meal? Whether or not I approve of his morals?"

Jessica stared across the table at Eric. "And do you?" she asked cautiously.

"Look, Jess, the man's wife is a drunk."

"You mean he's unfaithful," she replied.

"It's only rumor," he told her. "He's a very private person, and very discreet. Besides, I can't fault someone who's learned to live with his special kind of loneliness." There was a sympathetic tone in Eric's voice. Although saddled with a withered body, he had the same needs as any man and understood the emptiness when those needs went unfulfilled.

Jessica didn't know how to reply; instead, she fiddled nervously with her napkin. She certainly hadn't meant to pry so deeply.

"If that worries you," he said, tactfully picking up the conversation, "just keep your distance."

"I don't think that's going to be possible," Jessica replied mysteriously.

"Try," warned Eric. He was curiously tempted to violate their understanding and ask a question, but immediately thought better of the idea. "Anyhow, he's much too old for you."

"You think so?" Jessica asked dubiously.

"Seriously, Jess," he answered, "what have you got in common with a fifty-two-year-old man?"

"I'm not sure, Eric," she told him, "but I have a feeling I'm going to find out. And soon."

Chapter 11

Except for the frivolous eighteenth-century-style painted panels adorning the walls, the dining room of Le Cirque was much like any other elegant and expensive French restaurant in the city. What separated Le Cirque's taupe suede banquettes, white linens, and impressive floral arrangements from the other chic "Le's" and "La's" was the seductive aura thrown off by its powerful patrons. It tinted the pale walls utterly bewitching hues that tempted and teased the odd yuppie or ambitious provincial who came to rub shoulders with the high and the mighty.

Selecting those colors from his palette of personalities was Sirio Maccioni, a charming and urbane Italian, who ran Le Cirque with a delicate blend of grace and efficiency. He had just seated Mark Laidlaw at his usual table when Jessica entered the restaurant. She stood by a tall porcelain vase, overflowing with sprays of rubrum lilies and orange blossoms, and waited patiently for Sirio.

Jessica moved gracefully through the restaurant as Sirio led her to Mark's table, her light gray Anne Klein wool jersey skirt accentuating her long legs. At the same time, her darker gray cashmere V-neck sweater contrasted with her pale skin and titillated with a hint of cleavage. A simply tailored gray sequined jacket pulled the dramatic look together.

"Well, good evening," said Laidlaw, standing as she approached the table. He extended his hand, overwhelmed by her sheer physical beauty. The sequined jacket, exquisite diamond studs, and her honey-blond hair captured the diffused room light, concentrating it around her face. Sirio pulled the table away and Jessica slid onto the banquette, placing a silver scallop-shaped Judith Leiber minaudière on the table in front of her. He held the table away, waiting for Laidlaw to be seated.

"Sirio, if it's all right, I'd like to have a chair," said Laidlaw. "I think I'd like to sit across from the lady." The chair arrived in seconds and Laidlaw sat down. "Nothing against Sirio," he said to Jessica, "but you're far and away the most fascinating person in this room tonight."

As she listened to him talk, his eyes flashing, his engaging smile creasing his tanned cheeks, Jessica found it difficult to focus on business. But whose fault was that? she wondered. He had suggested Le Cirque. And she had said yes. She had spent two hours getting ready. And he looked divine. Perhaps, she reasoned, it was some cosmic conspiracy—the romantic setting, the soft lights, the heady scent of expensive colognes and perfumes, and Mark Laidlaw.

"Tell me a little about yourself," he urged. "Did you have a life before Turner, Welles, Yale Law School, and Vassar?"

"Well, I see you did some homework," Jessica answered, obviously flattered.

"You came highly recommended, but without much of a biography."

"And you'd like to know a little more?" she asked coyly.

"I am interested in the person in whom I'm going to place a lot of faith and trust, not to mention several hundred million dollars."

Her eyes, already fastened on his, widened.

"But we'll get to that later," he added casually, sidestepping her reaction.

"Well then, in the interest of faith and trust. I was born and raised in Midland, Texas," she began. Spinning out the story of her childhood, she included, intentionally or not, both the tremendous love and insecurity in the Wheeler household. "My father was our only excitement when my sister and I were growing up," she went on. "He must have been in and out of the oil business at least nine or ten times before he died."

"I'm intrigued," said Mark.

"We all were," replied Jessica. "My sister and I could never understand how we could be living in this big house on Scarborough Drive one day and have to move in with our grandparents on the other side of town the next. Up to that time, all our clothes had come from Grammer Murphy, and then suddenly we had nothing but my cousin Trudy's hand-me-downs. We must have moved in and out of that house four, maybe five times. The first time, I'm sure my mother had no idea what was going on."

Thinking back to the early days of his own marriage and the failure of that ambitious partnership, Laidlaw shook his head.

Misinterpreting his reaction, she responded defensively. "You have to understand, when she met my father at college, my mother was this sort of southern belle who majored in education, knew when to wear white gloves, and went to parties with handsome young men. And my father was a beautiful man . . . charming, like Cary Grant, Fred Astaire, and a country preacher all rolled into one. The way she's always told it, the instant they met, there was magic between them. Over the years, though, the magic was replaced by something stronger, and Mother began to understand Daddy all the more. I think that's when she finally explained all the packing and unpacking to us. I remember it was the Thanksgiving after the second move. That time Daddy simply needed the rent money from the house to cover his expenses while he tried to get a new stake together for his next well."

"Quite a wheeler-dealer," said Laidlaw. "When did he die?"

"Twelve years ago," she replied solemnly. "He had just closed a big deal in Odessa and was driving back home when he lost control of the car. They say he had been drinking."

"He meant a lot to you, didn't he?"

"He was my personal one-man cheering section," Jessica answered nostalgically. "His energy fueled my world, my dreams. I know he wasn't a perfect father, but at the time he certainly seemed that way. And it took me quite a while to get over his death."

"What was it like, growing up in Midland?" asked Laidlaw, trying to steer the conversation back to a happier memory.

"What was it like?" she echoed. "It was hot, flat, and twice in the spring and six times in the summer it rained mud. That's what it was like," Jessica said derisively, "and that's why we left."

"There must have been more to Midland."

"Right. I forgot. There were pickup trucks."

"Seriously, weren't—"

"Seriously," she interrupted. "Everyone owned one. Whether they needed one or not. Sort of like Jeeps in Connecticut. Every color, every style."

"Come on, counselor, you're being evasive," he protested. "You mean, aside from natural disasters, there were no adolescent adventures, no boyfriends, no moral transgressions? Nothing that shook up Midland?"

"Nothing that *I* did," answered Jessica with feigned innocence. "After all, Mother was an Episcopalian."

"What about adventures and boyfriends?"

"And moral transgressions?" she added facetiously.

"And moral transgressions."

"As far as adventures, as you call them, and boyfriends, there were a few, but no one or nothing really that wild," Jessica answered, recalling the occasional late-night trips across the railroad tracks to drink beer or the outings to Monahans with Bobby Ray. "And as for moral transgressions, don't you think you're being a little presumptuous?"

"Yes," he replied unashamedly.

Mark spent most of the dinner questioning, probing. Not in an offensive way—more, she thought, like a young boy on a playground at the beginning of the school term, auditioning new friends. By the entrée, feeling less defensive, Jessica had quit the verbal sparring; by dessert, the interrogation had evolved into a dialogue.

"I've been answering all the questions," said Jessica as she dug enthusiastically into the creamy center of a golden Grand Marnier soufflé. "I think I'm entitled to hear the secrets of Mark Laidlaw."

"You mean you didn't check me out?"

"No," she fibbed. "I thought I'd find out for myself."

"Well, there really are no secrets," he replied. "Since I bought the Knights, every move I've made, plus some I haven't, have become fodder for sports reporters in the second-guessing business, and gossip columnists in everybody's business."

"Assume I don't read."

"All right. Let's see, you want secrets," he muttered,

searching for a reference point in his life. "I'm fifty-two. I have two grown children. Whatever that means. Who think of me as Attila the Hun with money. A rocky marriage, a lot of gray suits. I'm partial to gray. Oh, yes, and I voted Democratic in the last presidential election. That's the best I can do."

"Maybe I asked at the wrong time," Jessica replied, embarrassed by his candor.

"Maybe I answered the wrong way," he said, responding to her embarrassment. Laidlaw looked down at his watch. "Do you think you'd like to see the end of a basketball game while we have coffee?"

"Is that like an invitation to see the view from your penthouse?" she asked warily.

"I don't think so," replied Laidlaw. "Actually, I'm not sure. I've never had a penthouse."

Even perched high above the Arena floor, the roar from the crowd below was almost deafening. There were just three minutes left in the final period, and the Knights trailed by three against league-leading Boston. Jessica stood at the window of the sky box. She squinted trying to read, through the bright lights and stale smoke, the championship pennants that hung just above the circle of two-tiered private boxes rimming the top of the Arena.

"I think it's more exciting to be down there in it," said Mark as he poured coffee into two white china cups on a small mahogany table.

Jessica turned back to face him.

"I mean in the crowd," he added. "Up here it's too objective, too remote. You can't see the sweat on the floor."

"Did you ever play?" she asked, walking over to the table where he was sitting.

"Never pro. Just the playgrounds, high school, and one year at Columbia. I injured my knee halfway through my first season and became a spectator."

"Do you ever wonder what it would have been like if you hadn't been injured?" She looked at him over the edge of the coffee cup.

"No," he answered. "Frankly, growing up the way I did, I've never had time for 'what ifs.' I'm more interested in what will be. Which brings me to you, Jessica, and what we're going to do together."

She had wanted to seize the opportunity and ask about his childhood, but found herself more anxious to hear what made her so important to him.

"I've had an offer from a German consortium for the Arena," he began. "They want to tear it down and build an office tower. It makes good sense and it's a terrific deal, but I didn't buy the Arena and the Knights because it was a good investment. Sidney Fein can tell you that. So, I found myself caught between good intentions and greed. Then it dawned on me how I could make the deal, build a fire under the team and the fans, and maybe even do something good for this city."

Jessica watched him closely, eager to participate in his growing enthusiasm.

"This is where you come in, counselor," Mark continued. "And everything's predicated on your success. We're going to build a new Arena." He paused for a second to let the weight of his words sink in. "And your two corporations—"

"Delta Associates and Artaud Enterprises."

"Right." His voice trailed off as he absorbed the names, then he shrugged off any comments he was about to make and continued. "Delta and Artaud will assemble the site for it. We've picked a two-block area south of Houston and West streets. I'll have a map in your office tomorrow morning. Then, once you've secured the land—"

"Just like that?" she interrupted.

"Quicker than that, if possible," he replied with a teasing grin. "Then, the P.R. phase will begin. We'll start to leak stories about falling attendance, about our dissatisfaction with the Arena, even about moving the franchise."

"Manipulative, but very clever."

"Not really. Everything is true. Attendance has been falling steadily and so has the building, around our ears. This glorious structure," he added disparagingly, "besides being an architectural monstrosity, is a maintenance nightmare."

"What about moving the franchise?" Jessica asked impertinently.

"I'll take a few trips to New Mexico or Florida, meet with people. If you live it, it isn't a lie."

"I love your integrity, Mr. Laidlaw."

"Thank you, Ms. Wheeler." Mark got up and walked over to a small bar at the rear of the tiny room. "Would you like a cognac?" he asked.

"Please."

The game had ended and the Arena quickly emptied. As the lights were shut off, Jessica moved to the large window and stared down into the deserted amphitheater.

"Now, where was I?" asked Mark, joining her at the window.

"New Mexico or Florida, meeting with people," she said, taking a brandy snifter from him.

"Eventually, these stories will attract the attention of the mayor. Losing a sports franchise in this city these days is a major political liability," he said. "It's tantamount to having someone blow up the Brooklyn Bridge. So the mayor and I will talk. Or more likely, a representative of the mayor, some big-time Manhattan lawyer who knows me or thinks he knows his way around a locker room. He'll say, 'We want the Knights in New York.' I'll say, 'We want to stay in New York, but the Arena, as it is, is costing us a fortune.' He'll say, 'What about remodeling?' I'll come back with, 'What about a new Arena?' He'll say, 'Where?' 'In the city,

naturally,' I'll say, with the greatest respect and reverence, 'but I'll want variances and abatements.' 'For
that,' he'll argue, 'the city will want public amenities,
road improvements, reconstruction of the nearest subway station.' We'll haggle some more. We'll each threat-
en. He'll ask for season tickets and then we'll agree."

"You're very sure of yourself, aren't you?" said
Jessica, her voice smoky from the warmth of the
cognac.

"Why shouldn't I be?" he replied. "Everyone wins.
The Germans get their office tower. We get a new
Arena and, perhaps, a few thankful fans. The city gets
two new tax bases and a revitalized neighborhood. And
you, Jessica Wheeler, return to Turner, Welles and
Lambert, more the wiser, a little the wealthier, and still
as beautiful. . . . By the way, are you seeing anyone
right now?" he asked offhandedly.

"I think you're being presumptuous again," Jessica
chided.

"Not really," answered Mark. "Since I plan on
monopolizing most of your time for the next several
months, I thought it would be only fair for you to give
anyone you're involved with ample warning."

"Several months?"

"At least two . . . Why? Is the prospect of spending
that much time with me so unappealing?" he joked.
"Or is it that your boyfriend won't approve?" Trapped
for an instant in a narrow beam of light, his eyes flashed
mischievously as he searched hers for an answer.

"Well, no," she replied haltingly.

"No what?" he continued, his smile exposing the
previously invisible lines around his eyes. "That he
won't approve or that I'm not that appealing?"

"Now you're toying with me," Jessica answered,
"and I don't know what to believe."

"You're perfectly right, and I apologize," Mark
responded. He looked at her intently, as though he
were trying to find in her face the emotion he desper-

ately needed to reclaim for his own life. "Actually, this *will* take several months," he quietly acknowledged. "And I *will* be taking up a lot of your time."

"That's not going to be a problem," replied Jessica, taking a sip of cognac, her eyes glittering at Mark over the snifter. "I have quite a bit of free time these days."

His real question answered, Mark, greatly relieved, brightened up. "Well, that's good to hear," he told her. "Very good to hear."

Chapter 12

Robert Zerndorfer was a born contrarian. He followed trends only to bet against them. And usually, by doing so, he found himself on the crest of the next new wave. It was an attitude he had greatly refined since graduating Dartmouth in 1968, a year in which most of his classmates either headed for Santa Fe to make belts or for Chicago to protest. Instead, he headed for New York to learn real estate.

First as an assistant to a broker, then as a broker himself, Zerndorfer quickly learned the intricacies and vagaries of New York real estate. In the early seventies he bought his first property, a small commercial building on Manhattan's West Side, along with Ashton Cole—another young, like-minded broker in his office —and a well-financed bank loan. Within a year they had sold the building to Sidney Fein, who needed it to complete a site for an office tower. And since the opportunity was there, they also sold Fein on the idea that their new firm, Cole and Zerndorfer, should

broker the space in the completed building. The deal
was a minor coup, which won them kudos from the
cognoscenti and a good table at 21.

"I really like your new digs, Jessica, but I thought we
would be going out," said Zerndorfer, stabbing at an
orange wedge on the Styrofoam plate in front of him.
"I thought I'd finally win you over with a dazzling
lunch at Le Bernadin."

They were seated at a smoked-glass table in the
conference room of Jessica's new office, plastic lids,
paper napkins, and Styrofoam cups spread before
them.

"I didn't think it would be a good idea for us to be
seen together just now," replied Jessica.

"It's because of the weight, isn't it?" he said playfully.
As he spoke, Zerndorfer, in shirt-sleeves and yellow
suspenders, carefully wedged his potbelly against the
edge of the table. "I'm working on that right now." He
triumphantly held up the orange wedge he had finally
run through with his fork.

"Be serious, Bobby."

"Then it's true," he responded in mock surprise,
"you're trying to hide us from him."

"Him who?"

"The king of cookies, your latest beau, of course,"
said Bobby. "That is what you call them in the south?"

"Not since William Faulkner died. And that relationship was over with months ago," replied Jessica, referring to her three-month roller coaster ride with Barry
Weiss, the owner of Mr. Chips, New York's largest
chain of chocolate-chip-cookie stores. It was an almost
comic mismatch, the half-baked entrepreneur and the
lady lawyer, but they had fun while it lasted and parted
friends. "But there is someone else," she added quickly.
She much preferred Bobby Zerndorfer as a friend
rather than an ardent suitor.

Jessica had met Bobby a year and a half ago at a
Christmas party at his partner's Sutton Place pent-

house. She had gone with Winston Avery to represent the firm. Winston made the initial introduction, then unceremoniously disappeared, leaving Jessica to her own devices and Bobby Zerndorfer, who spent the rest of the evening asking—and, when she refused, citing a nonexistent company policy, pleading—for a date. She found it difficult to deny his sad puppy-dog eyes and cherubic face, and went out with him several times. There was never any romance between them, although Bobby liked to pretend he was in love. She soon learned that was simply his way of flattering his female friends. With his ego, he just couldn't send roses.

"Bobby, I don't want us to be seen together because of this." Jessica cleared the table, then took a rolled-up sheet of paper from the chair next to her. She spread the sheet in front of Bobby. "Know the area?"

"Not exactly a garden spot. Mostly warehouses and lofts," answered Bobby, studying the map Laidlaw's office had sent over that morning. "There was a little speculation over there before they announced Westway, but when that got shot down, the play ended. Something interesting going to happen over there?"

"Maybe," said Jessica cautiously, "if you can assemble that site for me."

"For you?"

"For Delta Associates and Artaud Enterprises."

"Who are?"

"Delta Associates and Artaud Enterprises."

"Oh, I see. It's going to be one of those," said Bobby.

"Right now all I can tell you is you'll be definitely involved with both buildings."

"Both buildings?" replied Zerndorfer, musing over the opportunity. "Well, then, that's all I need to know, isn't it?"

"We'd like you to use one of your subsidiaries for this," Jessica added. "The more layers of anonymity we can add to this the better."

"No problem."

"How soon can you start?"

"I'll have my gnomes get on it as soon as I get back to the office."

"Thank you, Bobby."

"Clearly, it's going to be my pleasure. Now, let's discuss our dinner plans."

Jessica skillfully shrugged off the invitation. She wanted to be available if Mark should call. She also needed time to sort out her feelings for the man, feelings of trust and confidence she had associated with her father, and also feelings colored by passion and romance.

By two o'clock the next afternoon it was sixty-five degrees in Central Park. A weatherman called it a southeastern thermal, but Dorothy, Mark Laidlaw's secretary and closet mystic, saw it simply as a sign from the gods, or some such thing. And Laidlaw, for once, seemed ready to agree with her.

He had spent the last hour in the team's training room beneath the Arena, trying, as Dorothy joked, to turn back the clock. Returning unusually exuberant, he worked hard to clear his schedule of calls and appointments and leave the office early.

Mark was reading the last of the scouting reports when Dorothy buzzed him on the intercom.

"It's Mrs. Laidlaw on line two," she announced.

"Tell her I've already left," he said, trying to avoid another argument or drunken harangue.

"I think you can take this one," Dorothy advised confidently.

Mark shook his head in frustration. He found it hopeless to deal with a secretary who was a cross between a mother hen and a father confessor, but he had managed it for the last fifteen years and saw no reason to give up the most loyal and dedicated employee he ever had because of a minor character flaw—his, to be sure. Also, Dorothy had, over time, developed the ability to read his wife's state of mind over the phone, a talent worth twice the salary he was paying her.

He punched the red button on the phone. "Hello, Ruth," he said evenly. "I was just on my way out."

"Then I'm glad I caught you," replied his wife. Her voice was gravelly but still intelligible, which meant she had only had one or two drinks at lunch. "We can't seem to find your new tuxedo. The cleaner doesn't have it and it's not in your closet."

"I think I left it here," Mark answered. "Why the sudden concern over a tuxedo?"

"I wanted to have it cleaned for you," said Ruth. "Don't you remember? We have the party for the ballet Friday night, Ronald's birthday the following Wednesday, and the affair at the museum the week after. All black tie."

In the background, Mark could hear ice cubes colliding against the sides of a glass. He dreaded that sound as much as he dreaded the evenings out with Ruth. It was hell wondering how long before she tripped or spilled a drink on someone or alienated a friend. Perhaps, he unconsciously left his tuxedo in the office to avoid these ordeals.

"Of course I remember, Ruth," he lied. "Don't worry, I'll drop it off at the cleaner on my way home."

"And when will that be?" she asked meekly.

"Soon," he answered. "Soon." He hung up the phone, leaned back in the soft leather chair and closed his eyes. Soon faint images of Jessica began to form in his mind. There was a purity about them, a hopefulness that seemed to strip away his disappointment and offer the chance of escape from his tortured solitude.

There was no ugly postmortem after the museum gala two weeks later and no angry recriminations. Those things, for them, had ended years ago. They rode up in the elevator in silence, Ruth Laidlaw hanging on her husband's arm, the smell of alcohol and expensive perfume stinging his nostrils. Laidlaw tried to detach himself mentally from her by staring at the floor numbers blinking on and off above the elevator door and remembering the sheer escape of the past two weeks.

He met Jessica twice for lunch the first week and three times the second. They met at small, out-of-the-way restaurants, away from prying eyes and gossip mongers. This was allegedly to avoid jeopardizing the Houston Street project, but it also protected something they were both less certain about. At these lunches they spoke about business and about each other. They sensed their need for each other, but never put it into words, for fear of shattering what, for now, could only be a romantic illusion. He too wanted to analyze his feelings, break them down into their components, but he couldn't. She was just there, beautiful, sensitive, and understanding, and he wanted to be with her.

He loosened his black grosgrain bow tie, then started a fire in the white marble fireplace, poured himself a large brandy, and stretched out on the worn leather chesterfield. His gaze drifted from the flames to their outlines on the burled wood walls of the narrow study. As they leaped and flickered, the darkened room pulsated with orange and gold bands of light.

"God, how macho," said Ruth, standing in the doorway. She held a tall glass in her right hand and still had on the black strapless sheath she had worn to the party. "All you need is a golden retriever lying at your feet."

Mark sat up as she walked unsteadily toward the davenport.

"Have I ever told you how sexy I find men in tuxedos?" Her words were slurred, jumbled carelessly together in an alcoholic haze.

"Yes, you have, Ruth," Mark replied calmly. He tried not to sound patronizing.

"Don't worry, darling, I only violated your sanctum sanctorum because I needed you to unhook me," she said, making a slow shaky turn in front of Mark.

Mark reached up, found the tiny hooks in the folds of the delicate Fortuny pleats, and freed her. As the material parted, Laidlaw could see a tiny bead of perspiration slip down his wife's spine and disappear behind the black silk. For an instant he remembered how truly desirable she once was.

"Thank you, darling," Ruth said, wheeling around to face him. She emptied her glass, then stepped back and put it on the liquor cabinet. "And now, off to bed." With her arms behind her, she arched her back slightly and unzipped the gown. The bodice of the dress fell away, exposing her naked breasts. The soft white skin around the nipples washed orange and gold in the firelight. "Remember how good it was, Mark?" she whispered, her passion fueled by vodka and despair. She edged closer to the chesterfield. "This should help you remember." She tugged at the material hanging on her hips and let the dress slip to the floor. Then, steadying herself on the armrest, she stepped out of the circle of crumpled silk, revealing black stockings and a garter belt.

"Don't do this, Ruth," Mark pleaded.

She stood with her groin inches from his face, her fingers touching, probing.

"But I want you, Mark." She put her hands behind his head, pulling him toward her.

"No, Ruth," he said firmly, breaking her grip.

"Then I'll do you." She fell to her knees in front of him, tearing furiously at his pants.

"Come on, Ruth, get up. You know this isn't what either one of us wants." He struggled with her and somehow managed to push her away, then took his dinner jacket from the back of the sofa and drew it around her to cover her naked body.

"This is what *I* want!" she screamed at him.

Mark examined her face in the dim light, searching for the gentleness and understanding he had first known twenty-five years before; in its place he found a hideous mask, streaked with mascara and contorted with hatred and rage. "I can't," he said, shaking his head. "I have nothing left for you."

"You self-centered bastard, I wanted your cock, not your love."

He reached down and started to help her off the floor.

"Get your hands off me," she snapped. "I don't need anything from you, not anymore." He let go of her and she slowly climbed to her feet, glaring at him defiantly. She walked over to the liquor cabinet, grabbed a bottle of vodka, then paraded past him, a vicious smile pinned to her lips. As she came even with the fireplace, Ruth realized she was covered with Mark's jacket. With a faraway look in her eye, she rubbed her cheek against the silk lapel and lingeringly stroked the soft, rich wool, then, in one quick movement, pulled it from her shoulders and tossed it into the fire. "Not anything," she snarled, as she continued out of the room.

Laidlaw made no move to rescue the jacket. He simply watched it, in much the same way he had watched his marriage, smoke and smolder and finally burst into flames until there was nothing left to save.

Like an injudicious afterthought, the Seventy-ninth Street Boat Basin leapt out into the Hudson River, creating a meddlesome scene along the even shoreline. With the gray water slapping at their sides, an array of pleasure boats tugged at their mooring lines as the incoming tide tried to drag them upriver to sure destruction against the jagged boulders at the foot of the George Washington Bridge.

Nodding to the guard, Mark led Jessica through the security gate and toward a trim hundred-foot ketch tied up at the foot of one of the narrow piers. The large sailboat rocked sleepily in the water while the halyard whipping against the metal mast rang out a tinny lullaby in the wind.

Mark had met Jessica at her office under the pretext of lunch but then had swept her off to the upper West Side for what he said was an important appointment.

"Dives?" asked Jessica, eyeing the name painted on the stern of the boat.

"I think it's pronounced 'di-vez,'" answered Mark.

"Which means?"

"You're not going to believe it," Mark said with a broadening grin.

"Try me," she challenged him.

"Well, it means rich man . . . At least, that's what the broker told me."

"Then this isn't your boat?"

"Not yet," replied Mark.

"Not yet?"

"I've been thinking about buying it," he said as he helped Jessica up the short gangway. "I hope you don't get seasick," he shouted into the wind.

"I hope so too," she replied, groping for the railing in anticipation of the next roll of the deck. "By the way, who are you meeting?"

"You'll see."

They made their way below deck, where they were greeted by a uniformed steward who took their coats then steered them to a dining area off the main salon. The space, dominated by a formally appointed table large enough to seat eight but set for two, was surrounded by hand-rubbed mahogany and teak joinerwork that radiated classical elegance. Against one wall a long Regency sideboard, decorated with dazzling and intricate marquetry, groaned under the weight of a tantalizing assortment of foods. Above the sideboard, between a pair of brass sconces, the inhabitants of two delicate Rembrandt etchings sat in quiet repose, staring down hungrily at the heavily laden table.

"You can begin now, Brian," Mark told the young steward.

As the young man turned and left the cabin, Jessica smiled puckishly, then nipped a perfectly formed strawberry from a bowl on the sideboard and popped it into her mouth. "You lied to me," she said as she wiped a tiny drop of pink juice from the corner of her mouth with the tip of her finger.

"I know," replied Mark softly. "I thought we had just about run out of restaurants and that this would be a refreshing change."

"This is certainly a change," Jessica said, looking out a porthole at a sea gull gliding over the river.

The steward returned shortly with a bottle of champagne, then, joined by a second young man, served them lunch. After a brief review of her progress on the acquisition, and two glasses of champagne, Jessica began to regale Mark with mythical tales about her grandfather—a man twice as notorious and ten times as lascivious as her father—who reportedly succumbed at the age of seventy-five in the bed of a thirty-five-year-old married woman.

"I can't tell you how confident I feel now, knowing I have Benson Wheeler's granddaughter working for me," Mark teased. "Tell me, Jess, what should I worry about—kissing the Arena deal good-bye or being seduced and abandoned?"

"What do you think?" Jessica said, flirting.

"I think," replied Mark, reigning himself in, "Brian should pour the coffee."

They moved into the main salon for coffee, sitting across from each other on matching chintz love seats.

"Well," said Mark, setting his cup on the pink marble coffee table between them, "you think I should buy it?"

"Buy what?" asked Jessica.

"The *Dives.*"

"I don't know," answered Jessica, surprised that he would ask her such a question.

"Okay, then," he began, "do you think you could be comfortable here?"

"Mark, it's your decision," she replied, trying to deny the implication of his question. "Why are you asking me?"

"Because, Jess, what you think is important to me," he confessed. "In fact, everything you think and do is important to me."

During the silence that followed, Jessica could feel their tacit understanding eroding. She knew they could no longer keep their feelings at arms' length. They had become too strong. In the short time they had known each other, through looks, through words, through unspoken thoughts, it had become clear they needed to be together—not for convenience or dependence, but simply because they seemed to have always existed in each other's lives.

"Mark, I . . ." Jessica hesitated. She wanted to repeat his words, to tell him what he meant to her now and the first moment she saw him, but she couldn't. She was afraid. Afraid her admission would undermine their feelings and rip apart her fantasy. "I really have to go," she told him. "It's late and I have to meet some friends for dinner."

"Stay a little longer, Jess," he said. "I have so much more to say to you."

"Please, Mark, not now," Jessica replied anxiously. "I don't think I'm ready for this."

He lowered his eyes for a moment, then looked up at her. "I understand," he said, realizing what he was asking and what he was risking. Perhaps it was just too much, too soon. "I'll take you back," he said, getting up.

"I wish you wouldn't," she replied. "I think I need some time by myself."

The steward brought her coat, then Mark led her back through the paneled dining area and up to the deck. The sun, now a smoldering copper disk, was slipping behind the old Hoboken ferry slip as a blanket of cold air began to descend on the city. Jessica pulled her coat up around her face, then reached into her pocket for her gloves.

"I'll call you tomorrow," Mark said patiently.

She wanted desperately to kiss him and tell him they would be fine, but instead she smiled weakly and walked down the gangway, disappearing moments later into Riverside Park.

Chapter 13

"The guy never gives up. I swear, if it wouldn't mean my job, I'd sleep with him in a minute. Anyone want more wine?" asked Liz Copley, pouring the last of the white wine into her glass.

A busboy removed the ice bucket, then began clearing their dishes. It was almost ten-thirty, Sistina was beginning to empty, and the April "ladies night" dinner was winding down toward dessert.

"I take it, Liz, you don't have to do the eleven o'clock news tonight," said Meredith.

"Correct," Liz answered, raising her glass. "I'm also celebrating philandering husbands' month in memory of the dear departed Daniel Fleming."

"My God, Liz. Daniel died?" said Julie.

"Close," replied Liz. "He went back to his wife."

"Liz, these are not healthy relationships," said Meredith. "Maybe you should consider becoming a lesbian."

"I don't think it would work out," replied Liz. "You

three don't do anything for me, and you're the most exciting, attractive women I know."

"I'm not sure how we should take that," said Jessica.

"How about I love you all, but I don't want to sleep with you?" offered Liz. "For now, at least. Who knows? You might look better to me six months from now."

"That's fair," Julie Ann chimed in. "At least there's a chance."

"If we could leave the unfulfilled world of the Cosmo woman just long enough, maybe Jess could tell me who or what is Delta Associates. It sounds very cloak and daggerish," said Meredith. "Tell me, darling, Turner, Welles, didn't fire you and force you to become a missionary for the CIA?"

"You mean mercenary, don't you?" Liz corrected.

"Whatever," Meredith replied, ignoring the tipsy brunette. "Any position is a job."

"Goddamn Vassar graduate," muttered Liz.

Jessica couldn't help smiling at the rapid-fire exchanges that always took place between Liz and Meredith. They had become an expected part of the monthly dinners as much as Giuseppe's flirting and the chef's sinful *tirami su*. "I'm sorry to disappoint you Meredith, I'm not getting into bed with the CIA and I haven't been fired."

"God help us, then," Meredith said cynically. "We're going to hear another incredibly tedious tale of yuppies in action. Can we bear it?"

"Try," answered Jessica. "It'll save me telling you later when you serious up in the cab."

"I knew she had to do that sometime," grumbled Liz.

"What about the job?" asked Julie.

"Delta Associates is just a client," replied Jessica. "They have a lot of heavy contract work, so I've been loaned to them, like a temporary in-house counsel." One had to admire the versatility and simplicity of a well-constructed lie, Jessica thought. It wore well, and as a result, no one ever pried any further. The subject also gave it an added advantage. Contract law was not the stuff of scintillating dinner conversation.

They paid the bill about an hour later, struggled into their fur coats, and stepped out of the restaurant and into a blast of icy arctic air, winter's last hold on the city. Julie and Liz caught the first cab that came by and headed for the West Side, while Jessica decided to walk Meredith to her boyfriend's East Side apartment.

"Are you free tomorrow for some shopping?" asked Jessica, her words nearly lost in the numbing wind.

"Sure, Jess. What did you have in mind?" replied Meredith.

"Can you get us into Oscar de la Renta?"

"Are we changing our image or moving up to a better class of people?" It was a subject Jessica was not prepared to discuss, so she was thankful when she found a free cab on Seventy-ninth Street. "Okay, don't answer that," said Meredith to herself. "Just let me fantasize."

Jessica and Meredith walked slowly up Seventh Avenue. The blustery winds of the previous night had died away, but the bitter cold remained. At Forty-first Street Jessica readjusted the large garment bag she had draped over her right arm.

"Can I help with that?" asked Meredith.

"No, I'm fine," replied Jessica.

"You got some lovely things. I think the green silk is incredible."

"No, I'm not fine," Jessica said abruptly. "Meredith, I think I'm falling in love with a married man."

"Oh, Jess, not again," she said, recalling their first summer together in New York.

"Meredith, this isn't the same," Jessica declared. Her eyes were sincere. There were also tears streaming down her face.

"I'm sorry, Jess," said Meredith. "I'm sure this isn't

easy for you. Why don't we go somewhere, sit down, and talk this out."

They found a small coffee shop on Broadway and settled into a booth away from the counter. They were quickly joined by an overweight, middle-aged waitress in a pink polyester uniform who had sauntered out from behind the counter to take their order. Simply the sight of this woman with a folded handkerchief, the size of a road map, pinned above her left breast was enough to lift Jessica's spirits.

"Reminds you of Texas, doesn't she?" said Meredith as soon as the waitress had left.

Jessica nodded and smiled, appearing to recover somewhat in the less frenetic surroundings.

"Except for the gracious hello," Meredith added sarcastically. "Okay, who is he?"

"Meredith, you have to swear this conversation won't go any further," Jessica insisted. "If it does, it could screw up a lot more than something I'm not even sure exists, and please don't ask why."

"Trust me. Nothing you say will leave this room." Meredith raised her head and carefully examined the four elderly patrons at the opposite end of the restaurant. "In fact, it looks like no one who ever ate here ever left this room."

The best Jessica could manage was a feeble grin.

"Well, then, who's the mystery man?" asked Meredith.

"Mark Laidlaw."

"The one who owns the basketball team?" Meredith was one of those people who seemed to know or know about everyone in New York.

"Uh-huh," Jessica confessed reluctantly.

"Jesus, Jess. You really are moving with a better class of people. What's he like?"

Jessica drew a deep breath. "Honestly? Remember when you were sixteen, how you wished your father would look and act?"

"Sure, like anybody else."

"Why am I talking to you?"

"Because I'm your friend and I care about you," said Meredith apologetically. "Where did you meet him?"

"This is where it gets worse," Jessica answered. "I work for him."

"He's Delta Associates?"

"No, I'm Delta Associates. He's . . . Oh, it's not important," said Jessica, twisted in her own deception.

The waitress finally appeared with their coffee. She set two large mugs down in front of them, then tossed two stained packets of Sweet'N Low on the table. "Anything else, girls?" she asked indifferently. The woman wore her apathy on her sleeve like military service stripes.

"Just the check, please," answered Meredith. When they were alone again she leaned over and whispered to Jessica, "Why is it in New York, waitresses, bank tellers, and everyone who works in Bloomingdale's all seem to be the kind of people who wouldn't call for help if they saw you being raped in their own living room. . . . So, how does he feel about you?" she continued without missing a beat.

"I don't know. I'm not sure." Jessica began to stumble over her emotions. "There's just so much baggage there. His wife, his children . . . his affairs."

"He's told you all this?" Meredith asked incredulously.

"We've been seeing a lot of each other."

"How much?"

"No. We haven't slept together, if that's what you're asking," replied Jessica. "We're just not there yet."

"How do you know this is what you think it is?" Meredith asked as she stirred Sweet'N Low into her coffee.

"Meredith, I know what it isn't," answered Jessica gloomily. "And that's a normal business relationship . . . I can't define it. It's just I can't stop thinking about him, of wanting to be near him. I feel like he's a part of me, and that I'm incomplete without him."

"Keep in mind, Jess, loving a man like Mark Laidlaw is not going to be easy," Meredith cautioned. "Take it from your Jewish mother, life with him may be a lot more difficult than it was with your carefree cookie peddler."

"Barry was a sweet, decent guy, a little impetuous, a little crazy . . ."

Meredith scowled and her eyes narrowed.

"Fine. A lot crazy," Jessica conceded. "But that was different. I think we both knew it had no future."

"And this does?"

"Yes," Jessica answered emphatically. "And it's only because Mark is so open and caring. He has a strength, a sureness that you think will never fail him, that can overcome anything."

"God, Jess, you sound so convinced."

"I am. I just don't know if *I* have that strength," replied Jessica as she wrapped both hands around the coffee mug, trying to ward off a sudden chill. "Meredith, I know if I let this go any further, I'll get hurt, but I also know that if I don't, I'll be miserable. That's why I'm so confused."

"You know, Jess," said Meredith. "You never learn anything from being miserable, and it doesn't build character."

"I'm not interested in building character, Meredith. I want us to be happy."

"Are you happy when you're with him?" asked her friend.

"If I'm not holding myself back, yes," answered Jessica.

"Then stop holding back," Meredith scolded. "Jess, you're not testing the water in a bathtub. This is life. You've got to jump in over your head to find out if this is right. . . . Look around you," she went on with a wide gesture. "How many people you know even have a chance at happiness? Jess, you have that chance. Don't be afraid to take it."

Meredith's words struck home. Up to this point in her life Jessica hadn't been afraid to take on the world, tackling the challenges and wresting the opportunities, but with Mark she felt threatened. To gain what she wanted this time, she had to gamble more than a job or money or a way of life. She had to gamble her emotions. And for a very long time her emotions were the last thing she'd been prepared to risk.

Chapter 14

Easter came late that year, but Jessica was still caught with too much to do and too little time to do it in. As a result, she had to forgo one of her semiannual trips to Houston to visit her mother and sister. She spent the holiday with Julie Ann and her boyfriend, Ronnie Cogan, a promising New York actor who liked to brag that he was finally making more money acting than driving a cab.

It was the first time Jessica had vaguely felt like the "other woman." Mark had gone to Utah with his children for some reconciliation and spring skiing. He had discussed calling off the trip, but Jessica insisted that he go. He called her everyday from Alta to reassure her that he hadn't broken anything and to hear a sympathetic voice. But the phone calls didn't make the holiday any less lonely.

Jessica arrived at the office the following Monday before Stephanie and checked the messages on the answering machine. There was an urgent call from

Bobby Zerndorfer: "Jessica, we've got a problem. Call me when you get in. I'd like to come over and discuss it with you." His voice had a brittle tension that made Jessica uneasy. Bobby was the consummate professional. There was rarely a difficult situation he couldn't talk his way out of or an ideal one he couldn't talk his way into. He was adept at nuance, and the fact that he was out of character bothered Jessica.

An hour later Bobby Zerndorfer was ensconced in one of the gray leather Brno chairs in front of Jessica's desk. He struggled to look relaxed as he attempted to keep his sleeves from slipping down the polished chrome armrests.

"It's lot number fourteen, the small warehouse on West Street," he said, removing papers from a brown leather envelope balanced on his lap. "The title search took a little longer than expected. We had to go through three out-of-state holding companies before we found the owner."

"Who is?"

"John Arcaro."

"Come on, Bobby. I've never heard of the man," said Jessica, trying to control her impatience. "Who is he?"

In a unmistakable gesture, Bobby Zerndorfer took his left hand and bent his left ear forward; at the same time, he pushed his nose toward the left side of his face with his right index finger.

"Oh, shit, no," groaned Jessica.

"He ain't with the welcome wagon."

"Are we talking organized crime?"

"We're talking *major* organized crime," replied Zerndorfer. "John Arcaro is Philip Arcaro's nephew." He scanned Jessica's face for a sign of recognition. She shrugged. "And Philip Arcaro is the boss of the DeTesta crime family, one of the five equal-opportunity firms in the metropolitan area specializing in loansharking, pornography, labor racketeering, and general knee-breaking. It appears that Mr. Arcaro—the nephew, that is—makes his living as an X-rated movie producer and distributor of pornographic cassettes and magazines. The warehouse on West Street seems to be his main distribution center."

"Terrific," exclaimed Jessica. "Exactly what we needed—a smut peddler for the mob."

"Do you think your people knew?" asked Bobby.

"I'm not certain, but you can bet the rent check I'm going to find out."

"I don't rent," replied Zerndorfer, with a Cheshire-cat smile. "I own."

Jessica ignored Bobby's joke and plunged on, all business. "Share something else with me. How far have you gone with this?"

"I contacted Arnold Samuels," began Zerndorfer. "He's the lawyer for one of the holding companies, and I told him I had a client interested in purchasing the building and I wanted to know if it was for sale and at what price. Then came the normal round of phone calls. 'No, they're not interested in selling, but maybe a figure could move them.' I come up with one. 'It's too low.' The usual crap. We finally settled on a million two."

Jessica shifted uneasily in her chair.

"I know it's on the high side," Bobby continued, "but I thought it was worth it to get the deal done. It's one of the last parcels at the site. That was all well and good until this morning, when I got a call from Samuels. It seems his client, Mr. Thomas—aka John Arcaro—would like to meet with my client before he closes the deal."

"You think they've figured out what's going on?" asked Jessica, an edge of alarm in her voice.

"It's a distinct possibility."

Jessica began drumming on the table with a pencil. "Sounds like more than a possibility. How much more than what's on file is available to them?"

"Only what they could get from the other property

owners we've approached, and we've been very careful, so it couldn't be much."

"Good. Let's meet with 'Mr. Thomas,'" said Jessica with an enigmatic smile. "Set it up for this Friday, Bobby. Make it lunch at La Côte Basque."

"La Côte Basque? Are you serious?"

"Why not? The contrast appeals to me."

The party had been an unmitigated disaster. The gallery was a crude, makeshift affair in a loft next door to a firehouse in blue-collar Astoria, and the paintings consisted mostly of "found objects" glued to an array of garishly colored canvases. To add insult to injury, the artist, a former classmate of Jessica's at Vassar, also had the temerity to make a pass at Mark twenty minutes after they arrived.

In spite of having only flown back from Utah late that afternoon, Mark had been a surprisingly good sport through it all, which only served to make Jessica feel even more responsible for accepting the invitation in the first place. In addition, the nagging Arcaro question had thrown a cloud over the entire evening. She had to know if Mark had been aware of the connection between the mob and the West Street warehouse.

There was little traffic on the Fifty-ninth Street Bridge as Mark's limousine sped across it, taking them back to Manhattan. Jessica watched the red gondola of the sky tram rush past them on its journey across the East River to Roosevelt Island below.

"You've been awfully quiet. Was it the party or something I said?" Mark leaned in closer to Jessica.

"More of a sin of omission than commission," she replied coolly.

"Jessica, when you begin to sound like a lawyer, I know I'm in trouble. What is it?"

"Did you know one of the properties at the site was owned by Philip Arcaro's nephew?"

It was obvious the question caught Laidlaw by surprise. "Christ, Jess, no wonder you're annoyed. Honestly, I had no idea who was down there. How bad is it?"

It didn't take Jessica long to summarize her discussion with Bobby Zerndorfer and their plan of attack. Mark listened intently, interrupting only once for a clarification. "I don't think there's anything more you can do," he said when she had finished. "He'll most likely lay all his cards on the table at the meeting. These are not subtle guys we're talking about. Does he know you're a woman?"

"I'm not sure," she answered. "You think it will make a difference?"

"You better believe it will."

"How?"

"Damned if I know. I just know it will," he said. "The mob guys have not dealt well with women's liberation. They're still loaded down with a lot of machismo and old-world tradition. You might throw him off stride, disrupt his game plan. It's not easy for these guys to threaten a woman or, for that matter, even to negotiate with one. On the other hand—"

"He might find me too pushy and aggressive and come down on me like a ton of bricks," Jessica interrupted. "That makes me feel so much better," she added sarcastically.

"Relax, Jess," Mark said, smoothing the skirt of her dress with one hand.

"I'm trying, but this is my first gangster."

"Look, bottom line, if he tries to hold you up, let me know. I'm sure we can find a way to end run this guy," Mark said confidently.

"As simple as that?"

"As simple as that."

The car turned slowly onto East Seventieth Street and into the driveway of Jessica's apartment building. Jessica wasn't sure why, but she suddenly felt surprisingly at ease about the meeting with Arcaro. Perhaps, she thought, Mark's assurance was contagious.

"By the way," he added, "La Côte Basque? It was a nice touch."

It took Jessica an extra hour to dress Friday morning. Finding something right for the "sitdown," as she and Bobby half jokingly referred to it, proved to be more difficult than she had anticipated. Intent on hedging her bets, Jessica aimed for a look that would project both power and femininity, which wasn't easy. Out of whim or grand design, the items in her wardrobe suggested one quality or the other, but not both. Finally, after three outfits and any number of turns in front of the mirror, she settled on a navy-blue Chanel suit, some understated Chanel pearl and gold earrings, several layers of gold chains, and a simple strand of pearls.

Bobby picked Jessica up at her office around twelve-fifteen. It took them ten minutes to reach Fifty-fifth Street and twenty to thread through the snarl of midtown traffic that clogged the side streets from Third Avenue to the edge of Fifth. They waited fifteen minutes at a table near the large mural at the far end of the restaurant before they were joined by Arnold Samuels and John Arcaro.

Although contemporaries, Samuels and Arcaro stood in stark contrast to one another. Samuels, a thin bespectacled man in his early forties, was dressed in a well-tailored blue suit of a shade and fabric meant to temper the ferocity of his unruly red hair and magnify his importance. Arcaro, on the other hand, was all flash and style. He looked like some great silver peacock, as he swaggered about, his muscular chest puffed out, his sharp jaw set with an intimidating scowl. His massive body was fitted into a light gray silk and wool double-breasted suit that accentuated his V-shaped upper torso. His black hair was generously flecked with gray and had been shampooed and coiffed to a lustrous sheen. Buffed and polished, he was ready to do battle.

Arcaro's head moved restlessly on his thick, broad shoulders as he assessed the opportunities for defense or escape from this alien environment. His gaze fell on the mural of the small Basque fishing village above the red leather banquette and, for a moment, a glimmer of recognition or familiarity softened his brutal features. Shifting his eyes from the mural to the banquette, Arcaro noticed Jessica sitting next to Bobby Zerndorfer. He made no effort to hide the look of displeasure that swept across his face. He quickly leaned over and whispered something to Samuels.

Samuels nervously adjusted his glasses and cleared his throat. "Mr. Zerndorfer, we were under the impression we were going to meet—" he began as Bobby rose and extended his hand.

"Gentlemen, I'd like you to meet Jessica Wheeler, president of Artaud Enterprises," interrupted Bobby smoothly.

The rest of the introductions were completed with less drama, although Arcaro cautiously maintained his pseudonym. It was soon clear to Jessica that even with his gangster-gray suit and physical posturing, Arcaro was very much a man of the eighties. Her introduction into the equation had little or no effect on Arcaro or his plan of attack. One has to admire such single-mindedness, Jessica mused, no matter how sociopathic the motivation.

"If we can get right to it," Arcaro began, after the captain had taken their order. "Certain facts have come to the attention of my associates and myself that now make your proposed million-two figure unacceptable." His words were studied and purposefully chosen, but his accent betrayed his Brooklyn origins.

"And just what might those facts be, Mr. Arcaro?" asked Jessica pleasantly, first inspecting her glass of white wine and then Arcaro's face.

A smile teased the corners of his mouth. "So, you know who I am."

"I'd have to be a fool if I didn't. Wouldn't you agree?" replied Jessica. "Now, why do you find an offer of over a million dollars unacceptable?"

"Lady, you don't have to be a genius to figure out you're putting together a big deal down there," said Arcaro. "You and some company called Delta something or other have already bought up almost two blocks. Now, we've done some asking around and we figure our little warehouse is one of the last pieces in your site. It seems reasonable to think that fact makes it worth a premium above a million two."

"I'm not sure that's entirely true," answered Jessica judiciously. She glanced over at Bobby, who slowly shook his head. "But for the sake of argument," Jessica continued, "how much of a premium are you talking about?"

"Six million," replied Arcaro deliberately.

"Considering what we have spent so far and what we have available, Mr. Arcaro, I think that paying over seven million dollars for your warehouse is a little unrealistic," said Jessica. "Perhaps we could negotiate a compromise. Let's say a million seven."

Zerndorfer was struck by Jessica's determination and control.

"Now I think *you're* the one being unrealistic, Miss Wheeler," replied Arcaro. His voice was unyielding. "The seven million two is non-negotiable."

"Seven million two is a lot for fifteen thousand square feet of warehouse."

"And peace of mind?" added Arcaro. "Not really."

"Oh, I see," said Jessica. "You're offering me peace of mind."

"A very rare commodity, these days," Arcaro said, shaking his head almost sadly. "Even for seven million two hundred thousand dollars."

When the meal had ended, Jessica summoned the

check. After exchanging friendly words with the captain, she signed the charge slip then turned back to Arcaro. "I'll consider what we've discussed today and get back to Mr. Samuels. You should be hearing from us within a few days," said Jessica, getting up from the banquette and extending her hand. "I'm glad we had this opportunity to meet."

"So am I," replied Arcaro, shaking her hand. "And thanks for the lunch."

Samuels and Arcaro left Jessica and Bobby at the table and walked toward the door. Arcaro reached into his pocket and pulled out a pack of cigarettes, at the same time snatching a box of matches off a nearby table. "You know, I've got to hand it to her," he said, turning to Samuels. "The bitch's got balls."

Chapter 15

A tall, young, black man in a red jersey stood in a corner of the Arena floor, a basketball poised between his outstretched hands. He feigned a quick step to his left then fired the basketball in a wide looping arc toward the translucent backboard. The ball hung in the air, suspended for an instant in time and space, then dropped with a faint whoosh through the bright orange hoop and the soft cotton netting beneath it.

"Jesus Christ, Dominic," yelled Philip Arcaro, trying to make himself heard over the crowd around him, "where the hell is the defense?"

"I think they traded most of it away last year for that forward. What's his name," shouted Dominic Conti, hoping his comments filtered through the noise to his companion's hearing aid.

"You mean Hayes?"

"Yeah, that's the guy."

"That was some great deal. The son of a bitch hasn't played a game in the last two months."

"Whoa, Mr. Arcaro," said Dominic Conti, coming to the man's defense, "the guy's got a broken ankle."

"Correct. But he got it falling off a goddamn ladder, instead of under the backboards."

As the crowd stood and cheered, Philip Arcaro remained seated, lightly tapping the ash from the end of his aristocratic Macanudo-Rothschild cigar. Although a mafia don for more than thirty years, Arcaro was a man to whom polish and good taste had first been a minor preoccupation, and later in life, a major obsession. Eventually it went so far that he insisted his bodyguards dress in no color lighter than medium gray. Always seen wearing dark custom-tailored suits, Arcaro preferred to look like an investment banker instead of a crime-family chieftain. He had his thick pearl-white hair styled once a week by a fashionable barber in the Pierre Hotel. He dined in only the finest restaurants, lived in a lavish Central Park West apartment near Lincoln Center, and prided himself on his love of art and music. Yet for all the vanity and trappings of refinement, Philip Arcaro managed to live his life quite unobtrusively and still rule the DeTesta family with an iron hand.

"Can I get you anything, Mr. Arcaro?" said Dominic Conti as the second period ended. People had begun to file out of the Arena, heading for the concession stands, the bathrooms, and—the more disgruntled—for the exits. Houston was leading New York by twenty points.

"How about a side bet on Houston?" Arcaro joked to his associate.

Dominic Conti flashed a broad smile. He liked working for the old man. At the beginning it had been tedious. He had understood little about the world outside the family and spent most of his time sitting behind the wheel of a parked car, waiting. That had been ten years ago. Since that time the don had come to recognize the handsome young man's potential. He dressed him, schooled him in the social graces, offered him insights into the Machiavellian intrigues of the mob, and finally named him a trusted lieutenant.

As Conti rose from his seat to stretch his long legs, he noticed a young-looking redheaded man in a dark blue blazer on the court ten rows below him. The man was counting row numbers from his position on the floor. Conti watched warily as the young man suddenly sprinted up the aisle and stopped in front of him.

"Mr. Arcaro?" he inquired.

Arcaro turned toward the voice. At the same time a tension, barely perceptible, washed over Dominic Conti's body.

"Yes?" Arcaro's reply was cautious without being tentative.

"Mr. Laidlaw would like to invite you and your companion to join him for a drink during the half," said the young man.

Arcaro was quick to understand and appreciate the tastefully worded summons. "It would be our pleasure," he answered, nodding at Dominic Conti.

Philip Arcaro had first met Mark Laidlaw over a plate of risotto with white truffles at Nanni's on East Forty-sixth Street late one rainy afternoon twelve years ago. Laidlaw was having some problems at a plant construction site and a friend of a friend of a friend recommended a discussion with Arcaro. Each man was surprised by the other. Each had come to the meeting with preconceptions and had left with them stripped away. Rather than admiration, they forged a mutual respect for each other and, more importantly, a mutually beneficial compromise to end the labor unrest at Laidlaw's plant. Since that lunch they had run into each other on several occasions, usually at concerts or gallery openings, and had exchanged pleasantries, but neither had sought out the other, until now.

"Philip, it's so good to see you again," said Mark as

Arcaro entered his office. "I'm glad you could come up."

"How could I refuse an old friend and such wonderful seats," replied Arcaro, walking over to shake Laidlaw's hand. As he crossed the room, Arcaro noted an ornately framed watercolor set on an easel in a corner of the room. "You paid a hefty price for that Boudin, didn't you?" said Arcaro.

"More than I really wanted to spend," replied Laidlaw. "How did you know?"

"Who do you think was bidding against you?"

"I thought a very attractive brunette."

"My daughter," said Arcaro, smiling proudly.

"Well, she cost me a pretty penny."

"And you cost me the Boudin."

Laidlaw and Arcaro huddled for a short time by the black leather chairs near the window. As Laidlaw spoke, the old man could be seen nodding in silent agreement.

"Dominic," he said to his associate, who was standing by the door, "could you please wait for me outside."

"That won't be necessary, Tim," Laidlaw said to the man in the blue blazer awaiting his instructions in the doorway, "why don't you take Mr. Conti into the conference room and get him a drink. I'm sure he'd be more comfortable there."

Arcaro walked back over to the easel and studied the delicate watercolor. "Really fine work. Now, what's your problem, Mark?" Arcaro asked. The two men were alone, but Arcaro's attention was still focused on the Boudin.

"Your nephew."

"Which one?" Arcaro asked, turning to face Laidlaw.

"John." Laidlaw could see the disappointment settle painfully on the older man's shoulders at the mention of his nephew's name.

" 'The Prince of Porn' they call him in the papers,"

Arcaro replied angrily. "I think he's my curse for fathering daughters. Tell me, what did that *cetrule* do now?"

"Easy, Philip, it's nothing that can't be undone," Mark assured him. "I just think John didn't fully grasp the enormity of the undertaking."

"And this undertaking?"

"Certain people are assembling a site at Houston and West streets for a major neighborhood improvement project."

"Major neighborhood improvement project? Anything with white paint and new windows is a major improvement project in that neighborhood." Arcaro could sense Laidlaw was reluctant to reveal much more, and was discreet enough not to pursue it. "How does John fit in?" Arcaro continued.

"He's holding the last parcel."

"What's his plot worth?"

"Fair market value? Nine hundred thousand," replied Laidlaw.

"And what did these 'certain people' offer?"

"The final offer was a million seven."

"What did he ask for?"

"Seven million two."

"Christ, I don't know how the kid can sit down with balls that big."

"Look, Philip, I really can't say much more, but timing here is very important," said Laidlaw. "I think you should also know that if this deal doesn't go through, it's going to cost you a lot more on the construction side than six million."

"This thing's that big?"

"It's that big," replied Laidlaw.

"I'll talk to John."

"Thank you, Philip. That's all I really wanted," said Laidlaw. "Now, how about that drink?"

Arcaro looked down at the gold Patek Philippe watch half hidden under his white cotton cuff. "Maybe another time, Mark. I'd really like to get back downstairs and catch the end of the game."

"I'm flattered that you think the Knights could come back from being twenty points down against Houston," said Laidlaw as he walked Arcaro to the door.

"Be serious, my friend." Arcaro grinned. "I'm just hoping your boys can beat the fifteen-point spread."

Chapter 16

Sunk in the bowels of the Arena, the Knights training room had all the cachet of a pair of well-worn sweat socks, not to mention the aroma. Despite mirrored walls and bright red carpeting, the room couldn't overcome the claustrophobic cheerlessness that resulted from being buried two and a half stories below the nearest window. Jessica found Mark there three days after his meeting with Philip Arcaro. He was alone, working his legs back and forth on a Nautilus machine, the perspiration soaking through his gray New York Knights T-shirt.

"I'm really impressed," Jessica shouted, hoping to be heard over the clanging pulleys and weights.

"I'm glad someone is," said Mark, as he swiveled around to face her.

She stood framed in the doorway, a study in black, white and sexy: an ivory silk blouse was tucked carefully into her tight black miniskirt, and a boldly striped linen jacket was tossed nonchalantly over her shoulder. But it was the expression of exhilaration on her face that made her truly desirable.

"Why don't you end this charade and get dressed, so I can take you out to lunch?" she said.

"Is this a celebration?" asked Mark, wiping his face with a towel.

"I'd like to think of it as more of an emancipation," she answered. "Now get dressed."

"I'll be ready in twenty minutes."

"Make it ten. I'm double-parked."

"My God, you're strict."

On Eighth Avenue Jessica led Mark to a black Porsche Targa, parked by the curb and guarded by a beefy New York City police officer.

"Thank you so much, officer," said Jessica. "And you have to tell me what it'll be. You mustn't let the fact that Mr. Laidlaw here owns the Knights influence your choice. The Mets or the Knights."

"Make it the Mets," replied the officer.

"Mets tickets it is," Jessica declared with a wink at Mark. She got into the car, then beckoned Mark to join her. "You see? The people have spoken. Come on, get in." Jessica waved to the officer as he walked back toward a waiting patrol car.

"I can't believe you just bribed a cop," said Mark, sliding into the seat next to her.

"Don't be ridiculous. George and I are old friends," replied Jessica, hiking up her miniskirt so she could be more comfortable driving.

"Old friends?"

"Yes, old friends," Jessica answered defensively. "George and his partner Morris investigated my very first burglary in New York. And besides," she added, "this is his lunch hour." Jessica fearlessly whipped the shiny black sports car into the heavy Eighth Avenue traffic. The sudden acceleration threw Mark back against the tan leather seat.

"I've really got to start checking your expense account more closely," said Mark, reaching for his seat belt. "Where *did* you get this car?"

"Relax, boss. I borrowed it from a friend," she replied.

"Male or female friend?" he asked, scooping an athletic supporter and a ragged baseball glove off the backseat.

"A female friend, if you must know," she answered. "And she happens to be dating the first baseman for the Mets." Jessica took the mitt and the supporter from Mark's hand and tossed them over her shoulder. She gunned the Porsche, making a sweeping left turn across two lanes of traffic onto Thirty-fourth Street and leaving a cacophony of blaring horns in her wake.

Forty minutes later the black Targa was winding along the Hutchinson River Parkway, the suburban Westchester countryside racing by. With the top removed, Jessica's hair flew about her face, giving off intermittent flashes of honey and gold teased from the warm afternoon sun. Mark marveled at her strength and skill as she manuevered the speeding Porsche through the dips and turns of the old highway. They spoke very little. Conversation was unnecessary and impractical, since most of it was lost in the steady roar of the engine and the wind streaming overhead.

"So tell me," said Mark, as they slowed for an exit. "What are we celebrating and/or emancipating?"

"We are celebrating a morning phone call from Arnold Samuels," Jessica replied. "It seems Mr. Arcaro has reconsidered our offer and now thinks it was more than fair. What did you say to his uncle?"

"Nothing really. I simply asked him to try and make his nephew see the bigger picture."

"I'm sure," she said skeptically. "Well, whatever you said worked. The site is complete. Except for the paperwork on the warehouse, you're ready to make your next move."

"You mentioned an emancipation."

"Mine. I get to leave the purple-woolen majesty of the Twenty-eighth Street office for the fruited plaintiffs of Turner, Welles and Lambert."

Mark turned suddenly silent. He realized that what had first attracted him to Jessica—her irrepressible spirit and sense of independence—now threatened him.

After a quick swing through the town of Larchmont, the Porsche finally came to a stop across the street from a small, squat pagoda. Curious iron lanterns hung from the corners of its steep weather-beaten copper roof.

"What the hell is this?" asked Mark, his sober reflection shunted aside by incredulity.

"Lunch," Jessica replied, swinging open the car door. "Actually, this is Walter's, the home of the best and most inscrutable hot dogs in the entire metropolitan area."

"You've got to be kidding," exclaimed Laidlaw.

"You mean you don't believe a celebration of this magnitude warrants something special?"

"Of course I do, but—"

Before Mark could finish, Jessica yanked him from his seat and walked with him, arm in arm, across the street to the line of people in front of the stunted temple.

Ominous dark gray clouds churned over the skyline as the black Porsche roared over the Third Avenue Bridge into Manhattan. Jessica expertly downshifted into third gear and swung the car onto the FDR Drive, racing the impending storm.

"Maybe we should pull over and put up the top," suggested Mark, eyeing the threatening clouds.

"I take it you don't think I can get us back to the Arena before it rains," replied Jessica.

A bolt of lightning suddenly fired across the sky, followed by the distant rumble of thunder.

"You're darn tootin', Mario Andretti," Mark said facetiously. "And I'm not about to bet this suit that you can."

"You should have more faith," said Jessica, her attention fixed on the road. "And besides, I have a sixth sense about these things. Don't forget I'm from West Texas. I grew up with storms like this. Anyway, we don't want to lose time getting off the Drive." The engine screamed as Jessica downshifted a second time and spun the Porsche into the left lane. "Come on, live dangerously. Take a chance with me," she yelled, glancing over at Mark.

"I thought that's what I *was* doing," he replied.

His words cut across the moment, finally giving meaning to their weeks together. Her eyes lingered on his face, waiting for something more.

"Excuse me, miss, the road," said Mark, breaking the spell. "If I have the choice, I'd really prefer wet to dead."

The first drops of rain began to splatter against the windshield just as the car disappeared under Carl Schurz Park. Halfway into the tunnel a brilliant flash of lightning froze the traffic in an eerie strobelike luminescence; the accompanying clap of thunder shook the covered roadway down to the core of its underwater foundations.

The black sports car had scarcely traveled fifty feet from the tunnel when the southbound traffic came to a standstill and the sky opened up. The rain, buffeted by swirling winds, fell in twisted sheets, obscuring everything but the rows of menacing red taillights.

"Tell me some more about this sixth sense of yours," said Mark, a wide malevolent grin on his face and a stream of water dancing off the end of his nose.

"It's nothing really," replied Jessica sheepishly.

"You're not kidding," said Mark, as he started rummaging behind his seat. "Now where's the top?"

"Isn't it there?" she yelled. The rain had become almost deafening.

"No," he said in a mock growl. "It isn't here."

"Oh, my God!" Jessica screamed as she caught sight of herself in the rearview mirror. Her mascara was running down her cheeks, cutting dark channels through her makeup. Her new sixty-five-dollar haircut was matted to her head.

"What is it?" asked Mark, fearing the worst.

"Nothing," she answered, wiping away the makeup and casually running her fingers through her wet hair, trying to look aloof and detached. "Maybe the top's in the trunk."

"Don't you know?"

"Not exactly," she answered. "The top wasn't on the car when I picked it up."

"It wasn't?" he said, the words transforming the water cascading off his nose into a fine spray.

"No," replied Jessica. "But there is a sensible solution to all of this."

"Which is?"

"We're right near the Seventy-first Street exit. We'll get off the Drive and get the top out of the trunk."

"But we're not moving."

"We will be."

Jessica slowly eased the Porsche across two lanes of stalled traffic amid catcalls, terse epithets, and wild horn blowing. Five minutes later they were on East Seventy-first ripping apart the contents of the trunk.

"There's no top in here, Jess," said Mark calmly. Any ranting or raving at this point was obviously useless, the worst of the storm having passed on to Queens.

"Enough is enough," muttered Jessica. "Nothing is going to ruin this day. Mark," she ordered resolutely, "get in the car."

They slid hesitantly back into the wet leather seats. Jessica started up the Porsche. For a second the rear wheels spun hopelessly on the rain-slicked street. Then, with steam rising from the tire tracks, the car shot forward, barreling through the intersection at York Avenue.

The garage underneath Jessica's apartment building was at the end of a narrow, circuitous driveway. Empty, it surely was an awesome space, but it was made suffocatingly claustrophobic by the odd array of Volvos, Saabs, and BMW's squeezed, bumper to bumper, between the gray concrete pillars. Lording over this subterranean used-car lot was Manuelo, a beefy Puerto Rican with hands like ham hocks and little understanding of the English language.

Jessica and Mark looked like drowned rats as they stepped from the Porsche and walked toward the garage attendant's tiny office. As Jessica wrote her apartment number on a slip of paper, Manuelo couldn't resist sneaking sidelong glances at the waterlogged pair. Small puddles formed around their shoes and flowed, with an amoebalike symmetry along the painted floor. Jessica tossed Manuelo the keys to the Porsche then brazenly led Mark to an elevator at the far end of the garage.

"Terrific rug," said Mark as he stood in his bare feet at the entrance to Jessica's empty living room.

"I'm redecorating," Jessica shouted from the bedroom.

Mark stared across the large ivory and blue Oriental rug and out the terrace window at the clouds racing toward the horizon.

"They were supposed to have the furniture here last week," said Jessica as she emerged from the bedroom, drying her hair with a thick bath towel. "So I got rid of my old stuff. Then they called and told me it would be two weeks late. But you know how furniture people are, don't you?" she added, looking up at him. "Or maybe you don't." Wearing a long peach terry-cloth robe with a wide collar she had pushed up around her neck, Jessica looked warm and secure. "I left a towel and a robe for you in the bathroom, if you'd like to get out of those wet clothes," she said. "Maybe I'd better have your suit cleaned too. You might want to leave through the front door."

"Are all your guests treated this well?" said Mark, trying to work his fingers through the soaked knot of his tie.

"Just the ones that come to my door dripping wet," she answered.

"You get many of those?" he asked cagily.

"Funny you should mention it," she said. "I had four people show up that way only last week."

When he returned from the bathroom, Jessica was sitting cross-legged in front of the window, watching the storm. A bottle of cognac, two glasses, and a small plate of chocolates were arranged in front of her. Around her were several overstuffed pillows and a fancifully embroidered quilt.

"Penny for your thoughts," said Mark as he walked over and sat down beside her, discreetly tucking the ends of the brown terry-cloth kimono under his legs.

She watched as he adjusted the collar of the robe. "Right now I'm thinking you must be the 'all' the one size fits," Jessica replied.

"This didn't fit your other guests?" asked Mark. His voice had that curious inflection that men use to give a meaningless question tremendous import.

"Guest. Actually, it wasn't everything he really wanted in a robe," she answered obliquely. "Now, what about some dessert?" she said, changing the subject. "We've got chocolate truffles from Manon's and some very old cognac."

"Are you sure this is 'the' dessert to follow a Walter's hot dog?"

"Of course. There are rules here," she reminded him. "The hot dog was for the stomach. The cognac is to warm the heart, and the truffles to nourish the soul," she said, handing him a brandy snifter.

"Clever," he answered. As he took the glass he touched her hand. Then he held it. "You're cold," he said softly.

"No," she whispered. "Afraid."

"Of what, Jess?"

"Of you and me," she answered. "What it means to me. And what it would mean to you."

"What does it mean to you?" he asked in a tender voice.

"Happiness. Sharing. I hope it means the freedom to be what I want to be without losing you."

"And that scares you?"

"Only when I think what it would mean for you."

"Jess, don't try and protect me from my own happiness," Mark said, putting his arms around her and pulling her close. "I want to be with you. Hold you. Love you." He kissed her tenderly, cradling her head in his hands.

As their lips parted, Jessica stood up and took Mark's hands. "Not here," she whispered. "I want you in my bed."

A white satin coverlet flowed down off the queen-size bed and hung loosely against a pale peach dust ruffle. The brass bed was set at an angle in the room, projecting out from a corner in a forceful diagonal. Beneath it was a large white circular rug with the same peach color woven in a delicate geometric pattern on the border. Except for the bed, a brass nightstand, and a striking Empire bench upholstered in a printed cotton damask, the room was open and uncluttered. Its color and simplicity reflected its occupant's personality.

They stood silently by the bed, Mark gently caressing her cheek with the tips of his fingers. Jessica grasped his hand and lovingly kissed his palm. She studied his face, memorizing every angle, every line. She wanted to own this moment for eternity.

He dropped his hands to her waist and slowly unknotted the belt to her robe. It fell away in an unwinding serpentine, uncoiling at her feet. Then he moved to her shoulders and with an almost effortless motion slid the robe down over her arms to the floor. She stood before him nude, completely exposed. He could feel the heat rise from her body and engulf him. He felt consumed by her.

"My God," he said, taking in her exquisite form, "you're beautiful."

His words only confirmed what she had seen in his eyes. She helped him out of his robe, then took his hand and placed it on her breast. He could feel her tiny, velvety nipple stiffen against his touch, the passion flooding her body.

"Love me, Mark," she murmured, drawing him down on the bed. She threw her arms around him, holding him tight, as the icy coolness of the satin raced up and down her body. She could sense his anticipation, feeling him growing against her. When he kissed her again, she sighed as though she were giving up her life to him.

His lips moved to her neck, then to her breasts, finally settling on her razor-thin appendectomy scar. "I like it," he said, looking up at her. "It gives you character."

"Now you know I'm not perfect," she answered mournfully.

"But you have the most perfect imperfection."

She shuddered as he ran his breath along the raised pink incision line. Then he moved lower, opening her like a flower and exploring the feminine recesses of her body with his tongue. She held his head firmly against her groin and began to rotate her hips. She moaned languidly, the sounds escaping from deep within her throat. Mark continued his tender explorations and Jessica started to tremble.

"Please, Mark, now!" she cried. "I want to feel you inside me."

Mark raised himself up and kissed her. She could taste her sex on his lips. Mixed with his sweat and saliva, it tasted warm and sweet. She ran her hands through his damp gray hair, then reached down and guided him into her. She gasped as he entered her, the inner reaches of her body suddenly inflamed by his desire.

"You're so wet," he whispered.

She hugged him anxiously, embarrassed and at the same time proud of the level of her arousal.

With their passions unchecked, their lovemaking slowly built to a feverish crescendo, ending in a joyousness that neither one of them had experienced before. Afterward, he covered her with the white satin bedspread and held her in his arms, protecting her like some rare, fragile treasure.

Chapter 17

The regular season ended April 20 with the Knights thirty-two games out of first place and Mark Laidlaw's reputation barely intact. The local sportswriters, already whipped into a mad frenzy by a final ten-game losing streak, had a post-season field day savaging the Knights' players, coaches, and management.

As the storm of controversy swirled around the team, the last of the checks for the Houston and West streets site quietly cleared the account of Delta Associates. With the real estate secured, the second phase of Laidlaw's plan was set in motion. Stories, attributed to unnamed members of the Knights' management, began to appear, expressing Laidlaw's personal dissatisfaction with the "team's present situation" in New York.

Laidlaw's comments, first considered posturing, were quickly reinforced by carefully choreographed trips at the end of the month to Kansas City, Orlando, and Albuquerque. Then, three days after returning from his grand tour, Laidlaw, ready to confirm the rumors, called a press conference at the Arena.

It was three-thirty, and the narrow, windowless press room in the Arena was crammed with television cameras, photographers and reporters falling all over each other, vying for position. The gray folding chairs, empty coffee cups, and the smell of stale cigarette smoke in the room contributed to its pervasive atmosphere of decay and deterioration. Honed to *Front Page* perfection over the years by the press, the basic character of the room was now impervious to any amount of disinfectant or general sprucing up. It stood as a testimony to the average journalist's basic disregard for private property other than his own.

Mark Laidlaw made his entrance through a door next to a low riser at the front of the room. Adjusting his jacket and tie in a broad Kennedyesque gesture, he stepped onto the platform and into the harsh glare of the television lights. He was quickly flanked by his press aide, Marty Green, a balding, slightly pudgy, ex-reporter; Frank DeCicco, his tall, curly-haired general manager; and Abbie Rudolph, the cantankerous, cigar-chomping owner of the New York Blades. The four men conferred for a minute before Laidlaw approached a lectern bristling with microphones and removed a small note card from his inside pocket.

"Ladies and gentlemen," he began, "I have a few opening remarks to make and then I'll turn this thing over to you for questions." Laidlaw looked down at the blank note card in his hand, pausing purely for dramatic effect. "First," he continued, "about some of the recent speculation about moving the franchise. I have made no secret that I have been dissatisfied with conditions here in New York. I don't think it's necessary to elaborate on that. However, I will say now that we have been entertaining offers from several cities to move the Knights out of New York. In addition, we have received a serious offer from a German consortium to purchase the Arena for the eventual construction of an office tower at its present site.

"Naturally, all of these discussions are tentative and we understand that any decision that is made will have far-reaching effects, not only for the Knights and the Blades"—Laidlaw motioned toward Abbie Rudolph—"whose lease expires in a year and a half, but on all professional sports in New York. And for this reason we are not going to make any decisions hastily or without considering their impact on the New York fans. Now, ladies and gentlemen, your questions."

Angry, hostile, double-edged and barbed, the questions flew at Laidlaw in a seemingly unending barrage. For an hour he dodged, ducked, and parried, surviving the onslaught bloodied but unbowed.

Jessica pressed a button on the console and the television set disappeared behind a wooden panel. She got up from behind Mark's desk and walked over to the window. To the southwest the late-afternoon commuter flights were landing and taking off from Newark in a steady rhythm. Jessica watched the planes, their metallic skins bathed in sunlight, circle lazily over the airport then glide silently down to the long concrete runways.

"Well, what did you think?" asked Mark as he entered the office, still charged up from the press conference.

"You were clean, brave, and reverent," replied Jessica, turning back into the room. "And you were lucky they didn't eat you alive."

"Come on, Jess, seriously."

"Seriously? You handled them masterfully," she said curtly. "You showed understanding. You answered their questions. And, most importantly, you didn't tip your hand. By the way," she added, "bringing in Abbie

Rudolph was a good idea. It made it look like both of you were sticking it to the city instead of just you."

"Easy, Jess," said Mark, caught off guard by her sarcasm.

"I'm sorry, Mark," she replied. "The press conference went wonderfully. It's just that we really have to talk."

"No problem. Let's talk," he said, ushering Jessica over to the chairs by the window.

"Mark, it's over," Jessica announced solemnly.

"What is?" he asked cautiously.

"My work here, of course."

"Of course," he repeated, clearly relieved.

"Please, Mark, don't patronize me," she said, misinterpreting his reaction. "All the contracts are signed. The checks have all cleared, and all the escrow accounts are closed. There's nothing left for me to do."

"I need you here, Jess."

"No, Mark, you *want* me here," she corrected. "You must know how much I care for you, and I would stay if I was needed, but I'm not. Look, Mark, I'm a lawyer. I love the practice of law. It's as much a part of my life as you are. I need its challenges. And without it, I'll be miserable."

Jessica knew asking for change was a risk, but the endless boredom of the past two weeks, though punctuated by romantic evenings with Mark, left her empty and without a purpose. She was simply not content to live her life through a man, no matter how dynamic.

Mark took her hand, trying to exorcise her unhappiness. "How about this?" he said. "You go back to Turner, Welles, after I close the deal with the Germans."

"When will that be?" she asked, determined to stand her ground.

"Two weeks, three at the most."

"Agreed," she said emphatically. Then she slithered her arms around Mark's neck. "You can have me for three more weeks," she whispered in his ear, her voice forsaking determination for reckless abandon.

Jessica sat in the chair with her eyes shut tightly, reveling in the angst of an overdue haircut. Listening to the sound of the scissors flying around her, she wondered how she could ever trust someone who was not a blood relative with such an awesome responsibility. However, she reasoned, haircuts, like tax audits and pelvic examinations, were something you had to endure while hoping for the best.

Del Pritchard was the best. He had flair. He had style. And the most outrageous red spit curl in the middle of his forehead. It spilled out of a gelled coil of other red curls and ringlets and had embedded itself, like an inverted question mark, above his eyebrows. Del also had something rare in a twenty-five-year old—the ability to weave his magic and still put his clients at ease.

He floated around Jessica, snipping a millimeter here and there, then assessing his handiwork in the mirror. Thin strands of blond hair drifted in the air as he worked, some adhering to the sleeves of his black silk shirt, others disappearing into the pattern of the tiled floor.

Del made one last pass with the dryer, then fluffed her hair. "You can open your eyes now, Jessica," he said reassuringly. "It's over."

Jessica slowly opened her eyes as though awakening from a deep sleep. She studied herself in the mirror, casually turning her head from side to side. It was very important, in the rarefied atmosphere of chic New York hair salons, not to show any dissatisfaction. Even if your trusted stylist has turned you into Cher on Academy Award night. Dissatisfaction—or more likely, tears and screaming—was reserved for a scene with a hapless husband or lover, or a phone call to a sympathetic girlfriend.

Thank God, Jessica thought, as she spun herself

around in the chair, I'm still me. "It's terrific," she told Del approvingly.

"Maybe for the summer I'll make it a little shorter," Del mused aloud.

Jessica smiled. "You'll have to let me think about that," she said diplomatically. "It might not work in the office. I don't want to look too young."

As Del shrugged his shoulders, Jessica beat a tactful retreat to the changing room.

Ten minutes later she was out on East Fifty-sixth Street. She looked over her shoulder at her reflection in the salon window, shook her head, then took a deep breath, sucking in the moist spring air. Jessica began to head toward Lexington Avenue when she noticed Billy Richmond standing next to a shiny black Mercedes 560 sedan parked by the curb.

Billy, a tall, handsome black man in his late fifties, was Mark's driver. He was an enigma, a gracious and warm man with a past shrouded in mystery. There was some speculation that Billy was an ex-convict or a wanted criminal, but no one could say for sure. And no one could say how Mark and Billy met or why Mark had hired him ten years ago. Their secret was their compact, and neither man would violate it by revealing its terms.

"What brings you over here, Billy?" asked Jessica, walking over to the car.

"Mr. Laidlaw asked me to pick you up," Billy said. "He thought you might like a ride in the new car."

As Billy opened the rear door, the air around Jessica became suddenly thick with the heady scent of fine leather. "When did Mr. Laidlaw buy this thing?" asked Jessica, sliding into the butter-soft rear seat.

"This morning," replied Billy. "I just picked it up."

Waiting for Billy to cross around to the driver's side, Jessica began to laugh, overcome by the giddiness of such luxury and decadence. Billy gently edged the car into traffic, swinging wide to avoid a gaping pothole.

Jessica was looking for a mirror in the backseat when the phone, hidden between the two front seats, began to chirp. Billy picked up the receiver, listened for a moment, then handed the phone to Jessica.

"Well, how do you like it?" Mark asked with boyish enthusiasm.

"Now I know how my keys feel in the bottom of my Bottega Veneta bag," replied Jessica. "What is this all about?"

"I thought we'd celebrate," he answered.

"What?"

"May Day."

"You're two weeks late."

"I've been busy."

"You're crazy."

"That might well be, but I thought that since it's a beautiful, warm day, you'd like to go for a swim."

"You bought a new car just to take me swimming?"

"Don't be absurd. I need that car. And what makes you think you're going alone? I'm the one who borrowed Jonathan Lambert's house in Litchfield."

"Damn," replied Jessica. "Then I'll need a bathing suit."

"Listen, Jess," said Mark, "Billy's going to drop you off at your apartment, then pick me up at the Arena and take me home. It'll be about an hour, then I'll come by and get you."

"Great. I'll see you soon. By the way, do you say good-bye with these toys or is it over and out?" asked Jessica.

" 'Good-bye' works fine," he said, " 'I love you' works even better."

Mark dropped his keys on the small marble-topped Louis XIII washstand and began to leaf quickly through the mail. He fished a copy of *Business Week* from the stack of bills, junk mail and invitations, and headed across the foyer toward his bedroom in the west wing of the apartment. As he turned into the hallway, Mark suddenly found himself face to face with the young Irish housemaid. Apparently startled by "the master's" presence, the timid girl involuntarily gulped down a breath of air, which touched off a minor fit of gasping and coughing.

"Relax, Emily," said Mark, trying to calm her, "it's only me." To live with such fearfulness amazed him. He often wondered why poor Emily traded her Gaelic idyll for this urban horror she now called home.

"I'm sorry, sir. But you gave me such a start," she said apologetically. "I didn't know you'd be coming home early."

"That's because I didn't tell anyone," Mark replied. "Are you all right now?"

"Yes, sir. Thank you, sir," answered the young woman. "If there isn't anything else, sir, I'll be finishing my work." She tucked her hands into the pockets of her starched apron and began to edge her way down the hall.

"Oh, Emily," said Mark.

"Sir?" replied the girl, frozen in her tracks.

"Is Mrs. Laidlaw in?"

"Yes, sir. She's with Mr. Breed, sir."

"Breed?"

"Her trainer, sir."

"Right, her trainer," answered Mark dryly. "Thank you, Emily."

He continued down the hall, shaking his head. He just couldn't understand why New Yorkers, with all their endearing, albeit pathological, skepticism, were so quick to embrace this particular southern California scam. Paying someone to watch you sweat was, he reasoned, much like paying someone to watch you gargle or perform any other essentially private bodily function.

Entering his bedroom, Mark tossed the magazine on the bed and stepped into a small dressing area where he hurriedly changed his clothes. He had settled into this spartanly furnished suite two doors down and across the hall from his wife's room after leaving her bed two years ago. It was a way station between here and there and his last foothold in Ruth's world.

He grabbed a dark brown cowhide duffel bag from the bottom of one of the large walnut cabinets and set it on a small leather bench in the middle of the dressing room. He opened it, double-checked its contents, then zipped it up. On his way out of the bedroom, he scooped up a brown leather Loewe baseball jacket from a chair by the door. Throwing it over his arm, he stepped into the hall. It was now time to pay lip service to civility.

Ruth's exercise room was at the far end of the hall. Mark discreetly set his bag down to the right of the doorway, reviewed his list of excuses and apologies, then slowly opened the door. Thinking back on the incident, what Mark remembered most was how surreal it all seemed—the twisted images of his wife and Teddy Breed repeated in the mirrors lining the wall, the smell of wanton lust hanging in the air, the crosscurrent of emotion that swept over him.

Ruth sat on a bench in a corner of the room, naked, her head thrown back, her eyes shut tightly. With one hand she kept a secure grip on the edge of the narrow bench; with the other she held Teddy Breed's head firmly between her legs. Teddy licked at her furiously, eager to prove himself an able employee. Ruth's breathing quickened.

"Oh, yes," she hissed as her body began to stiffen.

Mark stood paralyzed in the doorway, astounded at how it felt to watch his wife ministered to by another man.

Although his back was turned toward Mark, Teddy was the first to sense his presence in the room. After years of these extracurricular training sessions, he had developed a sort of sixth sense, a kind of human radar.

But this time carelessness and overconfidence had gotten the better of him. He was naked, on his knees, his back to the door. So when the tiny hairs on the back of his neck bristled, he froze, his mind racing to find a way out.

"No. No. Don't stop, baby," Ruth groaned, moving her hand to the top of his head. "Just a little more."

"No, don't stop," Mark growled at Teddy, taking two steps forward. "Give the lady her money's worth."

Ruth tilted her head forward and opened her eyes. Her lids were droopy, her eyes glazed over with passion.

"You really needed this, didn't you?" said Mark, caught in a swirl of rage and pity. "I thought our mutual humiliations had some limits."

A small, vengeful smile crept across Ruth's face. "There are no limits, darling. Not anymore," she snarled.

Teddy, fearing a violent escalation and hoping for a less vulnerable position, started to get up off the floor. Mark crossed the room in an instant and jammed his foot into the small of Teddy's back, forcing him face-down onto the black floor mat.

"I don't want to see your face, mister," snapped Mark angrily. "Stay right where you are or I'll remember I'm the aggrieved husband and kick your teeth down your throat." Holding Teddy at bay, he looked down at his wife. He suddenly felt empty, drained of any feeling for her. "We should have gotten a divorce before you had to cheapen yourself," he said. She tried to respond, but he interrupted. "There's nothing for you to say. I think we both know what we're doing and what has to be done. I'll let you file," he added coldly. "And do it right away." He took one last look at his wife, searching futilely for some trace of the woman he once loved, then turned and left the room.

As Ruth grabbed for a towel, she began to sob

uncontrollably. She had made her point, but at what cost. She had traded her pride and dignity, not to mention her marriage, for three minutes of her husband's attention.

A tree-lined road led to another tree-lined road which led to Jonathan Lambert's weekend home. It was at the end of a long, shaded, gravel driveway, and stood quiet and regal in the midst of a carefully tended English country garden. The black Mercedes swung around and stopped in front of a small portico. Jessica slowly inspected the house, hoping to find some antidote for Mark's pain in the cheerful white facade. The trip up had played like a horrible, sad cliché; a 1960s French melodrama with oppressive, impenetrable silences, blurred landscapes flying by the windows, and the faint strains of a Bach fugue on the car stereo. She had tried to reach him, to cut through or sidestep his defenses, but it was useless. Angry and frustrated, he built new walls with each new approach.

Mark switched off the engine and took off his sunglasses. He took a deep breath, as though weighing all the options left him in the world, then ended his silence. "I've never asked you this before," he began hesitantly. "Actually, I've never asked *anyone* this before," he added after a moment's reflection. "What do you think about what we're doing?"

"You mean coming up here for the day?" she asked warily.

"Of course not," he said, dismissing her insecurity. "I mean the whole business with the Arena."

"Isn't it a little late for that?"

"I'd still like to know what you think."

"You looking for reassurance or absolution?" Jessica said softly.

"What can you grant me?" he said tentatively.

"Whatever you'll need, I guess," Jessica replied,

sensing the turmoil raging inside her lover. At that moment he seemed locked in an unmerciful tug-of-war with his feelings, trying mightily to confront them.

"You know I need you," he said, struggling to reveal his sense of failure.

"You have me, darling," she answered tenderly.

"And I love you very much."

"Mark, you're frightening me," she admitted. "Please, what's happened?"

"I'm getting a divorce."

After dinner they sat in front of the fire in Jonathan's den and talked, trading misgivings and revealing their private nightmares, trying to bridge a lifetime. Mark spoke about the disappointment he felt as his marriage fell apart, about the alienation of his children. These were his mistakes, the sins of his generation. He worried about the years between them, but she reassured him with the depth of her love. Her youthful optimism seemed to give her an inner strength and wisdom. So, as they reached out for each other, it was easier for Jessica to learn and Mark to remember. Finally, when they had made that bond, when each understood what the other felt and feared, they made love.

Jessica held Mark close as they watched the embers dying in the fireplace. She wanted more than anything else to protect him from the cold and the fallout from his life. She was aware of never caring this much about anyone in the world. She stroked Mark's head until he fell asleep, then gazed out into the early morning darkness, waiting for the dawn.

Chapter 18

The starboard wing of the airplane dipped as the Concorde made a wide sweeping turn on its final approach to Charles DeGaulle Airport. Through the small porthole across the narrow aisle, Jessica could see the lights of Paris shimmering in the distance. A rush of excitement overwhelmed her. It was all so impulsive, so romantic, so reckless. Then the wing rose again and the lights below slowly disappeared.

They had remained in Litchfield for the weekend, returning to New York Monday morning. On Tuesday Mark met with the mayor, and later with members of the city's Board of Estimate, fine-tuning an agreement for a new Arena. Concerns were expressed and assurances finally granted. It wasn't an easy victory for Mark, but it was a victory nonetheless. After the go-round with city hall, events seemed to take on a life of their own. The following day the Germans were contacted and plans were made to close the deal that Friday in Bonn.

Mark had spent most of Wednesday on the phone, but still managed to speak to Jessica and arrange for dinner that night at Le Cirque.

"To your return to Turner, Welles," Mark said, as he raised his champagne glass.

"Are you serious?" she replied, a little stunned by the news.

"We close the deal this Friday in Bonn," he said. "And if I may gloat, three weeks from the day you and I made our deal. So you see, I am a man of my word."

"So you are, sir. And I drink to your good health and good fortune," said Jessica playfully, reaching for her glass. She was elated at the prospect of returning to the firm.

"But there is one more little thing," Mark began hesitantly.

"Which is?" she asked, peering at him suspiciously over the edge of her champagne glass.

"I'd like you to come with me to Bonn," he said.

"What about closing up the office?"

"Let Stephanie do that."

"Really, Mark. You don't need me over there," Jessica insisted. "Winston and I have gone over all the paperwork. All that's needed is your signature. And besides, how do you think Winston will feel if you take both of us along? Not to mention what the Germans will think when you show up with a phalanx of attorneys."

"I'd feel more comfortable if you were with me," countered Mark defensively.

"Now I get it," she replied slyly. "You want a little fluff, a bedwarmer for those cool spring evenings along the Rhine." A knowing smile teased the corners of her mouth.

"If Germany's out, what about Paris?"

"Don't tempt me," Jessica answered, her resistance beginning to crumble.

"How about I meet you at the Ritz Friday evening

and we spend the weekend in Paris?" said Mark, sensing victory. "You could take the Concorde over and we could have a late supper together."

"Christ, what you won't do for a little free sex on the weekends."

"Free!" he exclaimed. "Have you any idea what round-trip airfare is on the Concorde?"

Jessica smiled again, this time coquettishly, then kicked Mark under the table, barely rippling the champagne in their glasses. He grimaced and reached for his shin.

"I really am sorry, darling," she said, rubbing his arm affectionately, "but that was the only way I could think of keeping you from putting your foot in your mouth. You see, I *do* love you."

The golden chandelier, threaded with strands of glass teardrops, glowed and sparkled in the warm morning light. Below it, on a squat cherrywood coffee table, sprays of blooming Casablanca lilies filled the master bedroom of the Duke of Windsor Suite with a intoxicating perfume. The pale green walls and darker green draperies absorbed the vernal sunshine flooding through the enormous French windows like giant leaves and forced the radiant energy into the gilded bas-reliefs above the doors.

Jessica slept peacefully in the curve of Mark's body, her head scarcely visible above a large, feathery, marshmallowlike duvet. For long minutes Mark watched her sleep, lulled by the deep, steady rhythm of her breathing, but soon he was gently caressing her neck, kissing her soft shoulders. She was like an exotic opiate he couldn't resist.

Awakened by his kisses, Jessica slowly rolled over and reached her arms around Mark, pulling him close. "I think you've convinced me," she whispered. "We should become lovers."

He kissed her, aching to capture the essence of her

being, and she responded hungrily. Mark's hands moved down along her legs, kneading the softness of her inner thighs. Suddenly, a piercing ring interrupted their lovemaking.

Mark slid across the bed and grabbed his watch from the night table. "Damn it," he said.

"What is it?"

"It's ten-thirty."

"So?"

"If it's ten-thirty, it must be breakfast."

"Tell them to get their own breakfast," replied Jessica huskily, wrapping her arms around Mark.

"No, Jess. It's our breakfast. I ordered it for ten-thirty."

"Who's hungry?"

"I am," said Mark, struggling into a robe.

"I thought I was enough for you," she replied sexily, her blond hair falling over her forehead.

"You're too much for me," he answered. "I'm an old man. I need energy."

"My ass."

"A subject worthy of Rubens's adoration," he said, dashing for the bedroom door.

"Bastard!" she yelled as she jumped naked from the bed, hurling a pillow in the direction of his retreat. Coming abreast of a full-length mirror on the inside of a closet door, Jessica stopped, looked herself up and down, then did a quick pirouette. "He's crazy," she said to the mirror after the short physical inventory. "It's perfect."

Minutes later they were back in bed, two white breakfast trays laden with fresh strawberries and crois-sants in front of them. On a small serving cart next to the bed, a bowl of thickened crème fraîche stood at the ready, along with jam pots filled with glistening pre-serves lined up in neat rows beside an ice bucket containing a bottle of Cristal.

Mark poured the champagne. A glorious, golden

foam rose up in the glasses then meekly subsided. She took a glass from him and set it on her tray.

"Jess, now that you're over here I think there's something you should know," said Mark.

"If you're going to tell me the Bonn deal fell through, I'm going to kill you," she replied, secretly hoping that was the worst possible revelation.

"It's more serious than that," he said, sounding ominous.

Jessica leaned back against a pillow, wondering why men needed a preamble to deliver bad news to women. In times of crisis, it was always something like, "Darling, I think we should talk," or, "How would you feel if . . . ?" They were never that way with each other. With men it was always the direct approach, like, "It's no deal, Burt," or "Sorry, Charlie, you're fired." So Jessica waited.

"Jess, I love you and want to marry you," he said slowly.

Mark's declaration caught her by surprise. The fantasy she had secretly hoped and wished for had, in an instant, become reality. It was almost too overwhelming to be believed—the perfect place, the perfect time, and the perfect man. She had never felt such happiness, such elation. Jubilant, Jessica fell into Mark's waiting arms.

"You know we've got a long way to go," he said softly.

"I don't care," she answered as she stared into his eyes. "As long as we do it together."

"Then you'll marry me?" he asked.

"And love you, and cherish you, and—"

He interrupted her with a long lingering kiss, knowing there was no longer any need for words between them.

Chapter 19

Ruth Laidlaw hated the holidays. She hated the snow and the cold weather. Thanksgiving and Christmas only made her feel more alone and unwanted. As for New Year's, there was little to be said at this stage in her life for marking time.

Mark had moved out of the apartment after he had returned from Europe in May, subletting a small duplex on Park Avenue. As far she knew, he was living alone, but Ruth knew there was another woman. There had always been other women. Only this time, things had gone too far, and now there was no turning back for either one of them. Somewhere along the way their marriage had become a hopeless, degrading affair that had robbed her of her self-respect and destroyed her dignity.

No one in the office seemed overly concerned by the wind gusting up Fifty-seventh Street or the fact that it rattled and shook every window on the sixteenth floor. All the lawyers went about their business with a quiet, professional air. Only Ruth flinched every time a new burst of winter roared outside.

Walter Hamel paused as his secretary handed a cup of coffee to Ruth Laidlaw, then, assured that all was in order, dismissed her with a polite nod. Adjusting the knot of his silken ancient madder tie, Hamel cleared his throat and, in hushed professorial tones, continued his appraisal of her husband's last settlement offer.

A wiry, thirty-five-year-old man with a pronounced overbite and a devious posture, Walter Hamel reminded Ruth of a well-dressed weasel or some similarly unscrupulous small mammal who had, in a long forgotten fairy tale, inveigled other small furry creatures out of hearth and home. It was a childhood impression that the attorney's expensive Italian suits and lightly tinted, oversized tortoiseshell glasses did nothing but reinforce.

Ruth had struggled with this image of Walter Hamel because he was one of the most highly respected divorce lawyers in New York. However, she had quickly come to the conclusion that a weasel was what she needed, since no one in their right mind would want Prince Charming to handle their divorce, especially with so much money at stake.

"Ruth, I really think you should consider this offer," said Hamel, watching helplessly as the ash on Ruth's cigarette grew longer and longer and finally, under its own weight, fell onto the deep royal-blue carpet. "Your husband's been more than generous."

Ruth shifted uneasily in her chair, crossing and uncrossing her legs and rewrapping herself in her lynx coat. "Generous. Is that what you think, Walter?" she said, beginning to mentally question Hamel's reputation. "Tell me, what's the price on years of neglect, humiliation, and betrayal?" Her words were edged with bitterness. "I'd like to know the mystical equation you lawyers use to convert dollars and cents into self-respect."

"Ruth, I know this is a trying time for you emotionally," Hamel said sympathetically.

"Do you?" snapped Ruth. "What do you know about being an abandoned woman?"

"Please, Ruth," said Hamel reassuringly, his voice taking on a soothing, paternal quality. "You've hired us to represent you in this action because we're experienced and knowledgeable. And because we have no emotional axe to grind. We're your advocates and represent your best interests. And right now, experience tells us that accepting this offer is in your best interests.

"If we reject this offer or delay our acceptance for any length of time, we run the risk of eroding the guilt factor and/or stiffening your husband's—or at least his lawyer's—resolve to retrieve concessions made earlier simply to speed the process along.

"Look, Ruth," he said, removing his glasses, "you'll have the income from a hundred fifty million dollars, and a magnificent apartment. Plain and simple, the agreement permits you to more than maintain your present lifestyle and provides for your future security. You couldn't ask for more."

"What about his undying hatred? What about his contempt?" Ruth said, each question rising a note in hysteria. "How do I get that?"

"I'm sorry, Ruth. I don't understand," replied Hamel.

"I thought I could make him show some emotion before this was all over, but it's obvious I can't. There are simply too many lawyers in the way," she said pointedly. "You see, Walter, I know that what you assume is guilt-induced generosity is simply a wealthy man's indifference. And all those years of indifference have left me empty and bitter."

"But you can put that all behind you now. Begin a new life," said the attorney confidently. "That's what this is all about."

"I *had* a life," she replied softly, staring into the folds of the fur coat, "and I don't want another one."

"Well then, Ruth, what do you want us to do about this offer?" he asked solicitously.

"Draw it up and I'll sign it," Ruth answered. "It's what I want, isn't it?"

"Trust me, Ruth. It's what you want," he replied. Hamel shuffled the papers on his desk. He always managed some minor housekeeping chore to cover these awkward silences. Women, Hamel had noted early on, passed through three stages during a divorce. He called them the three R's—realization, revenge and resignation. A clever attorney, Hamel was quick to exploit the first R and careful to temper the second to get the best settlement for his client; but as a man, he had a hard time understanding the resignation. His success offered these women a new start, but when it was over, it was as though he had shot them through the heart. Hamel could never see that his victory was their defeat.

As Ruth Laidlaw stepped out onto Fifty-seventh Street, a sheet of newspaper, caught in an invisible eddy, soared past her head and continued on its flight across town. Pulling the pair of sunglasses perched on her head down over her eyes, Ruth dug her hands deeper into the pockets of her lynx coat and headed up Madison Avenue against the icy chill. In her present mood a taxi was out of the question; this afternoon she was resigned to be the victim: of her husband's indifference, her lawyer's insensitivity, and nature's ferocity.

On Madison near Sixty-ninth Street Ruth stopped suddenly in front of the Pratesi linen shop. She felt herself inexplicably drawn to the display of luxurious pastel bedding in the window, the colors and textures so comforting and peaceful. She whisked herself into the small boutique without a moment's hesitation, exiting twenty minutes later with one ivory silk nightgown, two lilac cotton sheets, two matching pillowcases, and a bill for three thousand dollars.

"If your mother is as rocky as you say she is, maybe this whole thing is a bad idea," said the sandy-haired young man. "Maybe you should be home for Christmas."

"Don't be ridiculous. She won't mind," replied his girlfriend. "When I was home for Thanksgiving she seemed fine. I didn't even see her drink that much. Maybe getting away from my father was the best thing for her. I know it did me a world of good. Anyway, what about your father?"

"Shit. He wouldn't care if I never came home," answered the young man. He took a long drag on a joint, then passed it to the girl, who was sitting next to him on the couch. "At least let her know now instead of two days before Christmas. That way you won't have to beg for money."

The tip of the cigarette glowed bright red as the girl inhaled the acrid smoke. "Why not? This way my brother will look like a jerk for a change when he cancels out at the last minute," she said. She ground the last of the joint into the glass ashtray on the coffee table, then stretched languidly like an awakening cat. Her large gray sweatshirt rode up her taut abdomen, revealing a pair of white cotton bikini panties. The girl lowered herself into the corner of the sofa, throwing her bare legs over the lap of her handsome roommate.

"Patty, are we going to study or fuck?" he said as she began to rub her legs against his jeans.

She gave her head a quick shake, tossing her dusky brown hair around her face. She parted her lips seductively, her velvety tongue outlining the softness of her mouth. Patricia Laidlaw was a beautiful, sexy, and dangerous young woman. Intuitive and experienced, she knew how to manipulate men and bend them to her will. She was a nineteen-year-old enchantress who hunted men for sport. Fortunately, her predatory range did not extend beyond the University of Vermont campus, where she was quite satisfied torturing young men's souls and disrupting the occasional faculty marriage.

"*We're* not going to do anything," she growled. "*You're* going to get me off." She pressed her feet into her boyfriend's groin, her toes massaging his penis through his faded jeans.

The young man grinned and began unbuttoning his plaid flannel shirt.

"Uh-uh, lover," she reminded him, "your clothes stay on."

The young man looked at her forlornly. He could feel the pressure building inside him. He wanted her to touch him, to feel her fingers, her lips, her silky warmth, but first he had to play her game. He moved his hands to the inside of her thighs and began to stroke her gently, his nails lightly raking her soft white flesh.

Patricia slowly raised one leg over the young man's head, resting it on the back of the sofa. Then, throwing her arms over her head, she closed her eyes, anticipating Brian's touch.

It was nearly one o'clock in the morning, and a fire still crackled in the wide living room fireplace. Embers shot from the center of the flames, ricocheted off the finely woven fire screen, and died on the apron of the marble hearth. In a corner of the large room, by a window overlooking Central Park, a tall Douglas fir stood majestically in a red and green stand, awaiting the ornaments and lights that would transform it into a symbol of the season.

Ruth stared at the pine, running her fingers over the short green needles. She felt the stickiness on its branches and breathed in the fresh, clean scent that infused the living room. *This tree is still a living thing,* she thought. *The last living thing in this apartment.* She walked over to an antique escritoire where she had spent the evening addressing Christmas cards and retrieved a bottle of vodka.

Retreating from the oppressive stillness that had invaded the empty apartment, Ruth made her way down the west corridor to her bedroom. The room had been readied to welcome her. Emily had laid out her new Pratesi nightgown and turned down the bed before she had left for the evening. She had also remembered to make up the bed with the new lilac sheets.

Ruth went into the bathroom and took a long hot bath, soaking away a day's worth of filth and grime. She removed her makeup and replaced it with just a touch of color to her lips and a hint of cover cream under her eyes. She brushed out her hair, then walked back into the bedroom and slipped on the nightgown, the cool silk chilling her as it fell over her powdered and perfumed body.

Plucking a crystal water glass from a silver tray near the window, Ruth walked over to the inlaid maple nightstand by the bed. On it, next to the bottle of Stolichnaya she had carried in from the living room, was an amber vial and the final draft of her divorce agreement. She opened the vial and tapped a dozen little red capsules into the palm of her hand. Methodically she swallowed all twelve Seconals, washing them down with a glass of vodka. She refilled the glass then slid between the soft cotton sheets.

For fifteen minutes Ruth stared at the ceiling, smiling contently. But soon her eyelids became heavy and she began to feel a comforting weightlessness. She felt herself drifting away. Her breathing became shallow. Her heartbeat echoed faintly in her abandoned body. Ruth slowly released her grip on the now empty glass. It rolled off the lilac bed, the thin crystal embedding itself in the thick white carpet. As her chest rose and fell one last time, an imperceptible moan freed Ruth Laidlaw at long last from her earthly pain and anguish.

It should have rained the day Ruth was buried. Instead, cold, damp air blanketed coastal South Carolina. It was the kind of weather that drained the color from Beaufort, leaving it with a monochromatic loneliness.

Set on a gently sloping hill, the small cemetery overlooked the harbor. It was bordered with rows of sleeping magnolias that, in early spring, colorfully trumpeted the reawakening of life in the quiet southern town.

Mark walked back alone to the line of waiting limousines. Behind him, his two children followed at a distance that spoke less of respect than of simple disdain. As the driver swung open the door, Mark turned and looked at his children. Tall and blond, his son Douglas, a self-styled writer, had, at twenty-two, ambition enough for ten and compassion for no one. He had grown into his rugged good looks and would age with considerable grace, provided his malicious nature didn't twist and distort his classic features.

Patricia frightened Mark. She was the spitting image of her mother twenty-five years ago, with the same beauty and intelligence, but without the same passion or fire that had made Ruth truly captivating. Mark found Patricia lifeless and sometimes brutal, especially in her candor about her life and his. Suddenly, standing there amid the ghosts of the southern aristocracy, Mark grasped that it wasn't Ruth's suicide but these two unfeeling children that were to be the bitter legacy of his failed marriage. The realization left him angry because he knew, no matter how hard he tried, that there would be no second chances with Douglas and Patricia. But still he tried.

"Why don't you ride back to the airport with me?" Mark asked as the two approached him.

"Why?" said his daughter. "What's the point?"

"I thought we could talk," replied Mark, trying to span the gulf between them.

"She's dead. What is there to talk about?" Patricia answered coldly.

"You think I'm responsible for your mother's death, don't you?" said Mark defensively.

"Yes!" she hissed angrily. "It was you and your goddamn apathy. You took away any meaning she might have had in her life."

"And what about you and your brother?" countered Mark. "Were you two any comfort?"

"You never understood, did you, Daddy? You put all three of us in the same boat and then pushed us out to sea," she answered. "Mommy always had us, but she wanted and needed you."

"Is that what you think too?" Mark asked his son, who had judiciously detached himself from the proceedings by staring out over the tops of the limousines at an elaborately carved stone monument tucked away in the far corner of the cemetery.

"Me?" Douglas replied, after being forced back into the exchange. "Me, I'm past caring. About mother or your temporary guilt. Being in this family I've learned one thing. You either sink or swim. My concern is if you're still going to pay for my swimming lessons. Now, if you're through with this charade," he added, sliding into the backseat of the car, "I've got a flight to catch back to Los Angeles. I've got a meeting with an agent first thing tomorrow morning."

Douglas's car pulled away and the conversation was over. Mark walked with his daughter back to a second limousine. "The offer of the ride still stands," he said.

"I think I'll spend the night in Beaufort," Patricia replied. "Aunt Charlene asked me if I would stay."

"You and Brian still going to spend the Christmas break in St. Croix?"

"Uh-huh."

"I'll call you on Christmas. Maybe we can get together after the holiday?"

"I don't think that's such a good idea," she answered impassively.

As the limousine driver saw Mark and Patricia approaching, he started for the handle of the car door.

"Are you going to move back into the apartment?" she asked abruptly.

"I don't think so. Why? Do you want me to?"

"Does it really matter?"

He watched her walk down the line of cars and join the small circle of local mourners. She never turned around to wave. For that matter, she hadn't even said good-bye.

Mark sat slumped on the sofa, his back to the city. Emotionally drained, he found little solace in the dramatic setting behind him. He had caught the last flight out of Savannah and, after two hours on the ground in Charleston, finally arrived back at Jessica's apartment around a quarter to eleven, exhausted and disheartened.

"Ice?" asked Jessica, trying to remember the last time Mark drank scotch.

"Please."

She reached into a silver ice bucket with a pair of tongs and dropped three ice cubes into the pale amber liquor. "Was it that bad?" she asked sympathetically.

"Worse," he answered, taking the drink from her hand. "Standing there, in the middle of that cemetery, I learned my daughter thinks I caused Ruth's death and our failure as a family."

"And Douglas?"

"Douglas's approach is candor, not guilt," Mark replied, after a quick sip of scotch. "He was glad to find out I had feet of clay but was worried the revelation would undermine his sole source of support. After all, a struggling writer needs a patron. God, Jess, I never felt such contempt, such hatred."

"Mark, they'll get over this," she said, sitting down next to him and taking his hand.

"They might, but I don't know if I will."

"You will," she insisted. "You'll see. We'll change things."

Chapter 20

From his vantage point in the shadows above the Arena floor, Frank DeCicco carefully scrutinized the activity on the court. He was a handsome man with seductive Mediterranean features, dark probing eyes, and jet-black hair.

"There's not enough grunting down there," he said as Mark sat down next to him.

The two men watched in silence as the Knights' afternoon practice went on for another twenty-five minutes, with enough uninspired plays and lackluster drills to sicken even the most diehard fan. During that time scarcely a grunt, a sneaker squeak, or any other manifestation of effort or enthusiasm managed to reach the ears of the owner and his general manager.

"I'm sorry Mark, but Louie's got to go," DeCicco announced somberly. "I love the guy dearly, but there's nothing happening on that floor. Those guys are just going through the motions."

"Agreed," Mark replied, "but no announcement or

search for a replacement until the end of the season. I see no reason to embarrass the man at what is probably going to be the end of his career. And at this point, what's another six weeks?"

"With Louie still on board? The difference between a very long shot at a play-off spot and a definite first-round draft choice," answered DeCicco.

Mark had liked Frank DeCicco from the moment they first met. It was during the heyday of the early seventies, when "championship" and "all-pro" were synonymous with the Knights. At the time DeCicco was finishing his second season with the Knights and had just been named all-pro. He was bright, eager, and, from the start, ambitious. He possessed a dizzying mix of talent and personality, that rare thing that makes actors movie stars and athletes sports heroes. And more importantly, he knew how to use what he had.

It was almost preordained that Mark would bring Frank DeCicco back into the Knights' organization when he bought the team. Mark felt a certain kinship with the former power forward. Both men had the uncanny ability to win over an opponent and make him an ally without the usual macho posturing or "good ol' boy" arm twisting. This kinship made DeCicco the logical choice to succeed Randy Singer as vice-president and general manager after Singer, who had been with the club for fifteen years, had retired a year and a half ago.

"Assuming a first-round draft choice," said Mark, turning to DeCicco after the players and coaches had left the floor, "have you thought about what you're going to do with Milford after we pick Johnstone? We're not going to need three centers."

"Aren't you being a little premature?" answered DeCicco. "We haven't washed out the rest of the season yet. And what about the lottery?"

"I'm feeling optimistic."

"Be careful. Around here too much optimism is suspicious."

"I'll keep that in mind."

"You know Phoenix is interested in Milford," added DeCicco.

"Terrific. What kind of deal do you think we can make?"

"I'd like to go for that guard of theirs, Nickerson," said DeCicco, "but if it's a no go, I think we should consider settling for a first-round draft choice."

"That's fine with me," replied Mark. "You're in charge of the rebuilding. Which brings me to the reason for this meeting." He paused for a moment, his eyes fixed solidly on DeCicco. "Frank, I want a winning team," he said resolutely.

"So do I, Mark," answered DeCicco, troubled by Laidlaw's intensity.

"You know I've asked you to rebuild this team because I have confidence in you."

"I know that. And I appreciate your faith in me. You know I'm going to do everything I can to deliver a championship," said DeCicco, wondering where this was all leading.

"I'm sure you will, Frank," Mark said confidently. "I'm putting all my resources at your disposal. As I've told you before, you're going to have everything you need to bring in a winner." Laidlaw looked out over the empty arena, then back at DeCicco. "Except time," he added soberly. "The bottom line is the new Arena is going to be bigger and we're going to need a lot more season-ticket holders. So I want to see something out there next year besides good intentions. And in three years I want to be renegotiating your contract and fending off requests for play-off tickets, not looking for a new general manager."

"Understood, Mark," DeCicco answered impassively.

"Good. No more to be said. Now the rest is up to you," Laidlaw declared, rising from his seat. "By the way, how's the restaurant doing?"

"Great. We've been booked solid almost every night since we opened," he replied. "It's a real kick."

A year ago DeCicco had decided to indulge the second of his two grand passions, fine food. The first, beautiful women, had already cost him a two-and-a-half-year-old marriage and a pound of flesh. Finally, in late October, he and two partners opened Spoleto, an elegant Italian restaurant on East Sixty-second Street. Within a few weeks there were praises from *New York* magazine and chic, wealthy patrons lined up at the bar.

"It's really a beautiful place," Mark said. "Your people did a wonderful job." He glanced down at his watch. "I've got to run, Frank. I've got a meeting uptown in half an hour. I'll talk to you tomorrow."

As Mark's footsteps faded in the distance, Frank DeCicco's gaze wandered up to the championship pennants hanging limply from the rafters. Suddenly they had become harsh reminders of Mark's politely worded ultimatum.

"Well, what did Neddy—"

"It's Nedra," interrupted Liz.

"What?" asked Meredith, distracted by the interruption.

"Jessica's mother's name is Nedra," repeated Liz doggedly.

"Is it?" asked Meredith, nonplussed.

"Yes, it is," answered Jessica softly. "But Neddy's a nice name too," she added, indulging her friend's forgetfulness.

"I'm sorry, Jess. It's just Texas names are so . . . so," Meredith said, straining for the right word.

"Foreign?" interjected Julie, with a cunning smile.

"Exactly. Foreign," Meredith said, nodding in Julie's

direction. "The names are foreign to an easterner's ear."

"Foreign, my sweet Aunt Fanny," responded Liz. "Face it, Meredith, you have this odd mental block about the people in our lives."

"That's not true," Meredith protested. "I remember Mark's name."

"Mark's your brother's name," said Liz, throwing up her hands in disgust.

The friendly cuts and asides didn't seem to bother Jessica. Her happiness blotted them out. She felt impervious to any outside threat, as though what she and Mark had shielded her from everything ugly or menacing.

"So what did . . . mother," said Meredith warily, "and baby sister think of Mark?"

"Nedra and Kendall," replied Jessica, "thought he was simply wonderful. Frankly, I was lucky to get him out of Houston in one piece. I found out that where men are concerned, the Wheeler women show no loyalty. God, can my mother flirt."

"Does this mean the two of you are going public?" asked Liz tactfully.

"Not until the first weekend in July," answered Jessica.

"And, pray tell, what is so special about the first weekend in July?" inquired Liz.

"That, dear friends, is the weekend I am getting married."

"Oh, my God, you mean all that lust and passion wasn't just lust and passion?" Meredith exclaimed.

"Jess, I'm so happy for you!" Liz exclaimed.

"Me too," added Julie. "This is such a wonderful surprise."

"And I want you to hold the entire weekend open for us," Jessica continued. "We're planning something unforgettable."

They ordered champagne and toasted Jessica and Mark. The sisterly affection felt by the three women for the fourth was genuine and sincere, but there was no escaping the jealousy and panic that accompanied Jessica's announcement. The tensions were obvious. They were all over thirty and single. There were too few good men—forget great ones—and so little time. And while the possibilities and opportunities paraded by, their biological clocks kept ticking.

Liz and Meredith stood in front of the restaurant after the others had left, waiting for a taxi to take them across town. A gentle spring breeze fluttered the hem of Liz's black linen skirt and brushed a soft strand of hair over her eyes. She played nervously with the thin strand, then tucked it back into the delicate wave falling over her forehead.

"By the way, you'll never guess who called me to set up an interview and, I think, tried to ask me out to dinner at the same time?" said Liz.

"I have no idea," answered Meredith, looking up the street for a taxi.

"Who's the most ambitious man in New York?"

"My uncle Nathan."

"Don't be absurd."

"You never heard of Nathan's Dry Cleaners? There must be a hundred of them in the metropolitan area. The man has cornered the market in cleaning fluid. Taxi!" Meredith screamed as a cab sped by, ignoring her hail for a more promising fare. "Bastard. How do they know you're a lousy tipper?" she said, turning back to Liz.

"It was Bernie Abrams," said Liz.

"Who's Bernie Abrams?"

"The man who called me. It was Bernard Abrams, the Manhattan district attorney."

"Ah, that Bernie Abrams," Meredith replied knowingly. "The ambitious one. Right . . . Right. The man who runs for something every two years and loses. I'm impressed."

"No, you're not."

"You're right, I'm not. Seriously, Liz, are you going to go out with him?"

"I don't know."

"Journalistic ethics, or are you just tired of Jewish men?"

"Meredith, he hasn't even asked me yet," Liz answered coyly. "The phone call was more a case of his hints and my intuition."

"Don't worry, he will," Meredith replied. "Look, there's another cab coming. Take a few steps back into the doorway before they see you." She jumped out into the street and raised her hand.

"God, you are impossible," said Liz as she stepped back into the shadows in front of the restaurant.

The fourth day of a mid-June heat wave had just started to soften the New York City streets when television crews began stringing cable into and out of the Sheraton Centre Hotel. By eleven A.M. the air-conditioning was straining against the bright lights and a crush of people packed into the main ballroom in anticipation of the NBA players' draft. Seated at long tables, in front of banks of phones and computer terminals, were the team representatives. Surrounding them like a diamond horseshoe were the lights, cameras, and reporters. Above them all, crammed into a narrow balcony, were the fans and spectators who had come to cheer on the first-round choices and give the event some color for the evening news.

Frank DeCicco sat calmly in front of a computer screen, rechecking his strategy, as Evan Murtaugh, the NBA commissioner, emerged from a small group of people huddled on the bandstand and approached the podium. Murtaugh, a former U.S. senator from Geor-

gia, was still a southern aristocrat at seventy. He made
no effort to angle his six-foot-four-inch frame over the
microphones jammed haphazardly into the lectern. He
simply projected his deep resonant voice toward the
back of the room and within seconds had complete
command of the proceedings.

"Ladies and gentlemen," Murtaugh began, "I'd like
to welcome you to the National Basketball Association's
annual players' draft." Murtaugh looked quickly
around the room, running his fingers through his thick
white hair. "We've got a lot of business to conduct this
morning, so if everyone is ready, I'd like to begin." He
adjusted his heavy black-framed glasses as an aide
handed him a sheaf of papers. He thumbed through
the pages and removed the appropriate sheet. "The
first choice in round one goes to the New York
Knights," Murtaugh announced, "and the Knights
select, from Georgetown University, Ralph Johnstone."

Cheers and applause erupted from the balcony.
Frank DeCicco glanced briefly up into the sea of waving
pennants, then whispered something to Marty Green,
who had joined him moments earlier. It had all been
carefully orchestrated, like the "spontaneous" demon-
strations at political conventions; yet for all its press-
grabbing appeal, the hooting and flag waving truly
represented what many Knights' fans had hoped for,
the rebuilding of a New York dynasty.

Chapter 21

The morning sun turned the inky water an azure blue as the *Néréide* cut a course through the untroubled Tyrrhenian Sea on its way to some isolated Corsican beach. Below decks, in the master suite of the seventy-foot sailboat, amid the rumpled Porthault sheets and empty champagne bottles, Mark and Jessica made love. Bubbling with playful exuberance, they celebrated their freedom. After three days they had finally managed to elude their wedding guests by slipping aboard the *Néréide* and stealing out to sea.

Not that the wedding had been an unpleasant experience. Mark had spared no expense in fulfilling Jessica's fantasies and, from appearances, many of his own. Chartering a 727, he had flown Jessica's mother and sister plus fifty of their friends to Sardinia to help them celebrate. One dark cloud did hang over the festivities, however—the conspicuous absence of Doug and Patricia Laidlaw. Mark had phoned and written, but his efforts were fruitless. And this failure to reach his children and heal the rift between them troubled him deeply. Nevertheless, it was a cross he was determined to bear alone and keep from overshadowing Jessica's happiness.

The sheer beauty and glamour of the Costa Smeralda melted even Meredith's hardboiled New York cynicism. First developed in 1962 by a consortium headed by the Aga Khan, this once rugged stretch of shoreline on the northeastern coast of Sardinia had been transformed into a haven for the wealthy and a harbor for their playthings.

Mark had taken over the Hotel Pritrizza for five days. The Pritrizza, long considered the resort's most secluded and romantic hotel, was made up of private terra-cotta and stone villas, set amidst tiny gardens richly perfumed with hibiscus and bougainvillea and sheltering a large saltwater pool carved out of natural rock.

The evening after they had arrived, Mark and Jessica were married on a hill overlooking the bay of Liscia di Vacca, a vibrant pink and purple sunset painted behind them. Frank DeCicco stood up for Mark. Jonathan Lambert, looking quite paternal, gave the bride away.

The women's airy, diaphanous skirts billowed lightly in the soothing winds wafting over the bay. Nedra Wheeler, nearly overcome by the moment, fought back her tears as her daughter moved slowly up the makeshift aisle past her.

Young and more beautiful than ever, Jessica wore an off-the-shoulder dress of delicate Alençon lace over ivory silk chiffon and carried a nosegay of yellow and white wildflowers. Her blond hair, swept to one side, was held in place by a chaplet made up of the same wildflowers. She was radiant, a picture-book bride in a picture-perfect setting. As she stood next to the man she loved and pledged a lifetime of commitment, Jessica realized there could never be any limits to her happiness.

Hours later, alone in their isolated villa perched high above the sea, Mark watched Jessica as she began to undress. With her blond hair shimmering in a pool of moonlight, she looked more like an angel than a bride. The cool night, the dizzying scents flooding the room, the opaline light—Mark felt as if he were in a dream. He walked toward Jessica, joining her in the pale circle.

"Wait. Let me," he said softly, taking her hand from the back of the dress. As Mark unzipped the wedding gown, he tenderly traced a path down Jessica's bare back with his lips.

She shuddered and began to turn around.

"No, not yet," he whispered. As he kissed the base of her spine, the open dress tumbled around her ankles. "Now," he said.

Jessica turned. Her body was flushed, glowing. Trapped in the frosty beam streaming through the window, Mark thought she was the personification of fire in ice.

"Hold me, Mark," Jessica said.

He held her. And where he saw the passion pulsing through her body—at her neck, her wrists, her breasts —he kissed her. "God, Jess, I love you so much," he said.

Never before had Jessica felt so safe, so secure, so wanted. It was as though every fear, every childhood demon, every anxious moment, had suddenly been put to rest by Mark's words.

He picked her up in his arms and carried her to the bed. As he removed his robe, she studied the hard muscular lines of his body, the firm curves of his legs. Soon he was pressed against her, and then inside her. And soon wave after wave of unbounded joy washed over her. Clinging to the man she loved, Jessica wept, overwhelmed by desire and her own happiness.

It was barely three weeks after the wedding and it seemed to Jessica, as she rushed down East Seventy-fifth

Street, that there were more demands on her time now than there had been during the entire six weeks leading up to the wedding. She glanced down to the end of the block and saw a distinguished-looking man in his early sixties leave a taxi, walk several steps to the front of a red brick town house, and ring the bell.

"Damn," she muttered to herself and picked up her pace.

The man rang the door bell a second time and again waited patiently.

"Mr. Calloway," Jessica said as she approached the house. The man turned to face the disembodied voice. "I'm so sorry I'm late. I had some problems getting out of the office." Jessica took a key from her bag, opened the front door of the town house, and ushered the man inside.

"This is a lovely space," remarked Calloway as they stood in the wide foyer. His eyes roamed over the pale walls, along the white and black patterned floor, and up the grand marble staircase at the far end of the hall. A tall window towered over the twisting stairway and flooded the entryway with sunlight. "It's quite dramatic, isn't it?" he mused.

"We think so," replied Jessica cautiously, a bit awed by the man's reputation.

There was no question that Marshall Calloway, with his ample proportions and ruddy face, was an intimidating figure. He had cultivated that image for the last thirty years as "the" interior designer, confidant, and chronicler of the *Town & Country* set. Although reputedly opinionated, arrogant, and churlish, he remained on the cutting edge of his profession.

"Now let me show you the rest of the house," Jessica said, leading Calloway into the living room.

As they crossed the threshold of the room, Calloway reached into the inside pocket of his navy blazer and removed a small leather-bound notebook. A gold Cross pen soon followed, and his tour of the house was in full swing.

The town house had seemed to fall into their laps. Mark had moved back into the Fifth Avenue apartment after Ruth's death; however, he immediately put the co-op on the market once he and Jessica had set a wedding date. The circumstances of Ruth's death aside, neither one of them was anxious to begin their life together under his ex-wife's roof. Fortunately, a week after he listed the apartment, a producer friend, who lived three doors down from the Seventy-fifth Street building, phoned to tell him that it was up for sale.

It was the small, stately, half-moon porch with its four limestone columns at the entrance that first convinced Jessica that this was their house. The fireplaces, the indoor swimming pool, and the marble staircase were only the icing on the cake.

An hour and a half later they returned to the foyer. "Once we approve your drawings, Mr. Calloway, we should be out of your hair," said Jessica as Calloway scribbled away in his leather notebook. "However, we would like monthly progress reports and budget revisions," she added, having found her confidence. "Also, we will want direct approval on any item over five thousand dollars."

"I have no problem with that," replied Calloway.

"Oh, there is one other thing, Mr. Calloway."

"Yes?" he answered suspiciously, his furrowed brow knitting itself into a tiny crimson knot.

"If it's at all possible, we'd like to be in by Thanksgiving, Christmas at the latest."

With divine grace, like a priest granting absolution, Calloway nodded and smiled. "We'll shoot for Thanksgiving."

After she had shown him out, Jessica leaned against the front door, her eyes raised to the heavens, grateful that she had survived Marshall Calloway.

* * *

Although he had been living with Jessica since they returned from Sardinia, Mark still made occasional side trips to the Fifth Avenue apartment to replenish his supply of shirts or pick up the odd suit. But by the end of August the apartment was sold and he moved what was left of his dressing room into Jessica's apartment on Seventieth Street. As for the furnishings, he sent the children the items Ruth had bequeathed them, plus a few other things he felt had sentimental value, and the rest he put up for auction. He was determined to make a clean break with the past.

Jessica had forgotten the hardship of sharing a bathroom on a daily basis. Not that Mark wasn't the perfect roommate. He was clean, considerate, and tidy, always willing to lend a hand. It was just that there was so much of him. The fact that Mark prided himself on his appearance was no secret. And Jessica loved the way he looked, but his wardrobe took her breath away. There were Italian suits for daytime and summer, English suits for evenings and winter, plus assorted casual and weekend wear for every season and contingency. And shoes! There were thirty-two pair, at least, in various shades of brown and burgundy.

To keep a temporary inconvenience from becoming a permanent torment, Jessica immediately called Marshall Calloway to redesign the master-bedroom suite in the town house. Then she phoned a rental company for clothing racks, and within two days had transformed the living room, with the help of the building's handyman, into a gentleman's dressing room. Jessica took great pride in the remodeling. The living room was, after all, her first major sacrifice in the name of their marriage.

Mark propped himself up against the pillows, the satin coverlet sliding down his bare chest to his waist. He switched on the television with the remote control, then eased his head back against the soft down to watch the news. His right hand lingered on the empty place beside him, the crumpled bed linen still warm from their lovemaking.

"Well, how did it go this morning?" Jessica yelled from the bathroom as she readied herself for dinner.

"Come on out and see for yourself," he answered. "They're doing a story on it now."

Jessica stepped out into the bedroom. Wearing only a pale beige silk camisole, matching tap pants, and a white terry headband, she plunked herself down on the bed next to Mark.

He kissed her lightly on the shoulder. "Um, you smell wonderful."

"I'm not wearing anything," she said, trying to wriggle away.

"Who said anything about perfume? *You* smell wonderful," he said, shifting his attention to the nape of her neck.

"Come on. No distractions," she protested. "I want to see this."

On the screen a reporter, reduced to shirt-sleeves in the late August heat, was standing in front of a large sign, announcing the future site of the NEW YORK CITY ARENA.

"Today," the reporter began with unctuous enthusiasm, "the city received its most tangible commitment from owner Mark Laidlaw that the Knights basketball team will remain in New York. This morning, at this site at Houston and West streets, Mark Laidlaw and the mayor broke ground for what, in two and a half years, will become the new home of the Knights and the New York Blades hockey team."

Mark and the mayor, both in hard hats and team jackets, could now be seen with shovels, digging into a roped-off corner of the vast empty lot.

"How did you ever get him into that jacket?" Jessica exclaimed. "The man looks like an orange penguin."

"Believe me, you don't want to know."

Soon the Mayor appeared on the screen. "I'd like to express my appreciation to Mark and his management team," said the mayor, from under an orange hard hat, the perspiration running down the side of one cheek, "for passing up some very lucrative offers and keeping the Knights in New York. He has kept faith with the city and with its fans."

The mayor's image was quickly followed by a close-up of Mark. "And I'd like to thank the mayor and Borough President Seidel," he said, "for all their assistance in straightening out some difficult administrative curves that ultimately allowed us to keep the Knights in New York, where the team belongs."

Jessica got up and headed back to the bathroom.

"Well," asked Mark, "what did you think?"

"I don't know if it was the set or all that orange around him, but I thought the mayor looked a little green."

"Probably. Keeping sports franchises in the city has become a political hot potato, and I think he found our deal a little difficult to swallow," replied Mark. "Let's face it, the man's into Chinese food, not sports. If I'd been trying to relocate a dim sum parlor, he would have led an army to my defense."

"Just thank God he's a political animal," Jessica shouted from the bathroom, "and gave you what you wanted."

"Believe me, he got as good as he gave."

"By the way," she said, peeking around the bathroom door, her eyes sparkling with mischief, "you looked very sexy in that hard hat."

Chapter 22

At precisely 8:25 P.M. the black late-model Cadillac turned slowly onto East Sixty-second Street from Park and pulled up in front of Spoleto. A heavy rain danced on the hood of the car then rolled down the sculpted fenders, joining the rushing torrent in the gutter. Emerging from the driver's side of the car with an umbrella in his hand, Dominic Conti tugged at the collar of his raincoat to ward off the unusual late September cold. He walked around to the passenger side of the car and opened the door. Philip Arcaro, his face briefly illuminated by the headlights of a passing cab, rose from the front seat and joined Dominic Conti under the umbrella.

As the pair moved toward the doorway of the restaurant, they were approached by two men in raincoats huddled under a large black umbrella. They seemed to appear out of nowhere.

"Mr. Arcaro?" one of the men called out.

There was an instant of recognition as Arcaro turned

toward the familiar voice, which was immediately followed by an explosion and a brilliant flash. Almost simultaneously the second gunman raised a revolver to within inches of Dominic Conti's head and fired, killing him instantly. The first shot hit Philip Arcaro in the chest, ripping a hole the size of a quarter in his overcoat and throwing him against the rear door of the Cadillac. As he sat wide-eyed on the wet pavement, blood began to percolate from the open wound, spreading a vicious red stain across his expensive wool coat. Bending over the slumping figure, the first gunman jammed his pistol into Arcaro's mouth and methodically pulled the trigger. The second man maneuvered around Dominic Conti's body, firing a second round into the dead man's chest and a third into his groin.

As the rain washed the gun smoke from the air, the two men returned their weapons to their coat pockets, and walked back into the shadows.

Bernie Abrams peered through the venetian blind, straining for a view of Central Park through the heavily frosted windowpane.

"You can't see Gracie Mansion from here," said Liz Copley, her voice heavy with sleep and sex. "The Fifth Avenue elite get in the way, but I guess that's always been your problem."

Abrams turned away from the window, looked at her and smiled. "Very clever. Now go back to sleep," he whispered. "It's early."

"What time is it?" she asked.

He glanced over at the clock radio on the nightstand. "Almost four."

He cut an odd figure, standing in the darkness by the bedroom window, nude, a pair of light tortoiseshell glasses perched on top of his tousled gray hair. His body was hard and lean, his shoulders slightly rounded, the result of years of tennis and late nights at his desk. He was forty-eight years old and at best could pass for forty-seven, which didn't bother Abrams since he considered looking younger a political liability.

"It's snowing," he said.

"Just what we need—a white Thanksgiving," Liz muttered. She was lying on her side, the bed covers gathered around her naked waist, the fury of their lovemaking still evident on her neck and breasts.

Watching her, open and inviting, Abrams immediately felt a pleasing warmth flow through his body.

"I think you'd better come back to bed," purred Liz, tapping the mattress. "Your ambition is beginning to show."

At first his passion for her was unrestrained. He pounded into her with a fierceness and intensity that drove her wild. Then, suddenly, he withdrew, leaving her angry and unfulfilled. She clawed at him, begging for him, pleading for release.

"Finish yourself," he whispered, a malevolent grin creasing the corners of his mouth.

"No," she whined, shaking her head. "I want you."

"Do it!" he commanded.

"Bastard," she snarled as she began to work her fingers furiously between her legs. Tiny beads of sweat appeared in the thin lines on her forehead. Her hips rolled uncontrollably. And the room became heady with her scent. She glared at Abrams, her teeth clenched in a carnal frenzy.

Then, all at once, he pulled her hands away and plunged himself into her.

"Oh, my God," Liz screamed, feeling him throbbing inside of her. "Now! Come now!"

Her words rang in his ears. He pushed into her harder, more urgently. Then a tremor swept his body and he came, collapsing on top of her.

Bernie Abrams pursued everything in life with a savage intensity. He had been elected Manhattan district attorney seven years ago after a brutal campaign. He had beaten the aging incumbent in a bitter primary fight, then had to face his Republican challenger, a prominent state senator. This was no mean feat, considering the mayor—a very successful vote-getter and a member of Abrams's own party—had given the senator his tacit endorsement. As a result, his victory became a constant source of embarrassment and irritation to the mayor, who, every six months or so, found himself or one of his appointees the target of an Abrams grand-jury investigation.

Interestingly enough, it was Abrams's own energies that had short-circuited his political ambitions. The public perceived him as such an effective political gadfly that it refused to elect him to any other office.

During a lull between elections, Abrams and his first wife divorced, after eleven years of marriage and three mistresses. Oddly enough a moral man, he had found the guilt from his affairs intolerable. And since giving other women up was out of the question, Mrs. Abrams had to go. It wasn't a particularly messy or scandalous divorce. In fact, the timid, mousy woman was quite relieved to be rid of him.

Abrams had become intrigued with Liz Copley after he had watched her reports on the Taxi and Limousine Commission. He was impressed enough to begin an investigation of his own. And it was only a matter of time before he called her to suggest an interview, which was followed a week later by dinner at the Four Seasons.

Their relationship didn't blossom as much as it metastasized. At first fraught with intense passion, it was soon crawling with Freudian delights. It became a love affair based on brinkmanship. They played games with each other—sexual games, manipulative games, dangerous games—for power and control. It was a match made in Krafft-Ebing.

Liz's bedroom, on the second floor of her small but expensive duplex apartment, was streaked with orange ocher. The snowstorm had ended around seven and the morning sun had drifted across the park, splashing against the row of stately prewar buildings on Central Park West.

With her ear to Abrams's chest, Liz could hear his heart beat. How strange, she thought, that we can simply count down our own mortality. She raised her eyes and studied their reflection in the mirror across the room. A title came to her—"Naked Bodies in Quiet Repose." Her concentration was broken by the touch of his fingertips on her skin as Abrams began to lightly trace ever-widening circles on her right breast.

"I have a little gift for you," he said.

"Gold, jewels, or small pelts on a large coat?"

"Something more professional than personal," Abrams replied, enlarging his circles to include Liz's left breast.

"A job at the network?" she asked, shifting slightly to her right to accommodate his deft fingers.

"Could be a stepping-stone."

"Stop playing around, Abrams. What is it?"

"A story, but it's not for attribution."

"You've just become 'a source within the district attorney's office,'" said Liz, her interest piqued. "Now be specific."

"Because my office has the Arcaro murder," Abrams began, "we requested the FBI surveillance reports on Arcaro that were made before his federal indictment six months ago."

"So?"

"So last week the Justice Department sent the whole kit and caboodle over, and you'll never guess whose name popped up in the reports."

"Abrams, I'm not a jury," Liz protested. "You don't have to walk me through this. Just tell me who it was."

"Mark Laidlaw."

"What!" she exclaimed, sitting up and facing him.

"Naturally, I called Joe Masini at the U.S. Attorney's Office," Abrams continued, "and he was quick to assure me they found nothing there."

"And you think he's wrong. That there's something you can hang on him."

"*And* the mayor, if I'm lucky and they were stupid," he added. "I'm sure there was some sort of quid pro quo deal cut between the two of them over the Arena."

"Ah, now it's becoming clear," said Liz. "I break the story, make your wild allegations public, then you come riding to the rescue to save the poor ripped-off taxpayer. Isn't that your scenario?"

"More or less."

"What if I say thank you but no thank you?" She got out of bed and went searching for a robe.

"Look, Liz, the public has a right to know," answered Abrams willfully. "You're either going to be out front with this story or back in the pack fighting for the scraps. Because this story is going to get told with you or without you."

She found a gray silk robe lying on the floor at the foot of the bed and struggled into it. "You know what your problem is Abrams?" Liz taunted. "You're a great fuck, but a fucking louse." She pulled the robe tightly around her waist, then stormed into the bathroom and slammed the door. Leaning her head against the bathroom mirror, Liz realized that no matter how compromising the source, a story like this was something she could never turn down.

The next morning Liz called Jessica and asked if they could meet as soon as possible. From Liz's tone of voice, Jessica sensed it was something urgent, so she left the office early and rushed uptown to meet her friend.

The trainers were grouped around the reception desk on the mezzanine level, sorting out their next assignments, as Jessica entered the health club. Located in what had been the basement and subbasement of a former midtown Masonic lodge, the club was one of those acclaimed health spas in New York where devotees went for a "serious workout."

Side by side on computer-controlled exercise bicycles, Liz and Jessica pedaled fiercely up an unseen grade, rivers of perspiration soaking through their faded blue sweat pants, reminders of their vow to avoid Spandex chic.

"I'm sorry, Jess," Liz added breathlessly after she had detailed Abrams's accusations, "I can't kill this one. The best I've been able to do is buy you and Mark some time so you can organize a defense."

"I don't understand it, Liz," replied Jessica. "You report that John Arcaro is about to be indicted for the death of his uncle. And *Mark and I* need a defense?" The tension on the bicycle increased another increment, forcing Jessica to quicken her pace. "I told you Mark only asked Arcaro if he would intercede on our behalf in negotiations we were having with his nephew," Jessica added. "John Arcaro was trying to gouge us on some property at the new Arena site. Look, Liz, those people down there were paid better than fair market value for those buildings. And there was nothing illegal or unethical in the way the deal was done." Jessica lowered her voice as she felt the anger welling up inside her. "And you can tell Bernie Abrams if he's fishing for the mayor, he'd better do it in another pond."

The timers ended their ride and the conversation. With little left to say to each other, the two women, accompanied by their respective trainers, completed the rest of their individual workouts.

Forty-five minutes later they stood at opposite ends of a long mirror in the locker room, Liz drying her hair and Jessica reapplying her makeup. When she had finished, Jessica walked slowly down the row of sinks and confronted her friend.

"Before you go ahead with this," Jessica said, addressing Liz's reflection in the mirror, "there's one thing I'd like to know . . . Why are you with that man?"

"Why?" Liz replied, turning to face Jessica. "Because it's so intense. He makes me feel alive. When I'm with him I'm on fire. And it's been that way from the very beginning." Hopelessly, she searched Jessica's face for understanding. "Physically, it's incredible. It's raw, almost violent. We just don't want each other, we want to possess each other, totally, completely. It's like nothing I've ever felt before." When she had finished, her lips were trembling and her cheeks were flushed.

"But where is it going?"

"Why does it have to go anywhere?" said Liz. "Jess, in your whole life have you ever done anything truly dangerous? Where you've risked something really important? Something you felt you could never afford to lose?"

"No, I haven't," Jessica whispered, embarrassed by her timidity. "Maybe I've lived my life too cautiously."

"So have I, until now. I know this thing with Abrams is risky, but living on the edge has made me more aware of what's going on around me. I feel now I know who I am . . . Relax, Jess," she added, sensing her friend's concern. "He's what I need at this point in my life."

Hurrying up the stairs from the club, Jessica knew, though no opening salvo had been fired, that the battle lines had been drawn. As she opened the front door to the street, cold air swirled around her, washing away the helplessness she had felt moments earlier in the locker room.

She walked west on Forty-eighth Street toward Third Avenue, wondering how she was going to explain everything to Mark. She knew he would understand Abrams's role in all of it. It was Liz's complicity that was going to be difficult to justify. At the corner she tried to hail a cab but was forced onto the sidewalk by a speeding bicycle messenger. "Bastard," she muttered under her breath. Stepping back into the street, Jessica immediately realized that the focus of her hatred was not the young man who had almost run her down, but the famed public servant who was intent on smearing her husband and destroying her friend.

"I'm just not lucky Thursdays," Mark explained to Frank DeCicco and Jessica as they started down the hall from the sky box after watching Boston rout the Knights, 129–100.

"I think you're right," said Jessica, catching sight of Liz and her TV crew exiting the elevator at the far end of the corridor.

"How the hell did they get past security?" DeCicco asked angrily.

"I hope you're ready for this," Jessica said, taking Mark's arm.

"As ready as I'm going to be," he answered.

Seconds before the two groups collided, there was a silent exchange between Liz and Jessica—one woman asking for forgiveness, the other denying it—which evaporated in the harsh glare of the television lights.

"If I could have just a word, Mr. Laidlaw," said Liz, thrusting a microphone in Mark's face. "Would you care to comment on allegations that there are FBI surveillance reports that link you to Philip Arcaro?"

"I'm afraid, Ms. Copley, I had no idea I was the subject of any FBI investigation," Mark replied calmly.

"Then do you deny you've ever met Philip Arcaro?" Liz persisted.

"Ms. Copley, I appreciate your ability to ask the loaded question," Mark began, trying not to sound arrogant or self-serving, "but what you're asking me is comparable to asking the American ambassador to Germany, before the war, if he ever met Hitler. Although it may leave some doubts and suspicions in the minds of your viewers, I think it would be foolish to answer your question before determining the source of any allegations, which may have been leaked simply to smear me or others by association."

"Mr. Laidlaw, couldn't you—"

"Look, Ms. Copley," said Mark, interrupting the reporter, "I don't mean to appear evasive. As soon as I have more concrete information about any charges against me, I will gladly invite questions from the news media."

"Can you give us an idea when that will be, sir?" Liz continued stubbornly.

"I hope within the week," Mark replied. "Now, if you'll excuse us please, we'd like to get by."

As Mark guided Jessica through the small crowd that had gathered in the hallway, Liz zeroed in on Frank DeCicco. "Mr. DeCicco, you knew Philip Arcaro, didn't you?"

"I met the man several times," DeCicco answered coolly.

"Everyone knows he was gunned down in front of your restaurant," Liz reminded DeCicco, "but isn't it true he was a regular patron?"

"Yes, he was. So are two former Secretaries of State, a federal appeals court judge, the center fielder for the Mets, and your boyfriend," replied DeCicco smoothly. "What can I say? The food is good."

The trio finally managed to reach the sanctuary of an empty elevator and headed down to the garage.

"What do you think? Did we win that one?" asked DeCicco.

"Let's call it a draw," Mark suggested. "Remember —this was only the first go-round."

Jessica stood close to Mark, trying to come to grips with her feeling of abandonment. She had never imagined that the first casualty of marriage would be friendship.

Chapter 23

Early December saw an unusual number of "A" list parties, which invariably raised the yuletide spirits of florists, caterers, limousine drivers, and dry cleaners. It was fascinating, some wry critic had noted, the way wealth trickled down in New York.

Strains of Gershwin and Cole Porter wafted up into the uninhabited recesses of the new Phoenix Insurance Center as three hundred formally attired guests milled about on the atrium floor. Constructed like some ancient Egyptian totem with multicolored tiers of granite and marble, the building stood as a monument to corporate ego and architectural megalomania.

Mark stood in front of a large Pomodoro bronze, nursing a drink and admiring his wife, a few feet away, as she mesmerized Jonathan Lambert and the governor. And mesmerizing she was, glittering in a heavily-beaded and -sequined Bill Blass bolero jacket which she wore over a slender, strapless column of black silk crepe; the sparkle was accented by a pair of long diamond-drop earrings, a gift from her husband by way of Harry Winston.

"Your wife is a beautiful woman."

The comment jolted Mark from his trance. "Thank you," Mark began, turning to his right and coming face to face with Bernie Abrams. "I'm a very lucky man," he added deliberately.

"Really?" replied Abrams. "Well, you know what they say—lucky at love, unlucky at cards."

"I guess I must be the exception to the rule," said Mark. "I'm lucky at cards too."

"What a coincidence. So am I," answered Abrams. "You know, I always seem to be holding the winning hand."

"With me, I can just sense when the other guy's bluffing," Mark replied. He took a sip of his drink, then smiled.

"Perhaps you and I should play some poker one evening," said Abrams, struggling to return the smile.

"That sounds a little like entrapment, counselor. You're not suggesting anything illegal, are you?"

"Certainly not. I'm just talking about a friendly game of cards."

"Well, then, I'll look forward to it," replied Mark, staring into Abrams's eyes.

"So will I. Until our game, then," said Abrams. "Have a nice evening." He bowed slightly, then turned and walked away in the direction of the mayor and his entourage.

Over the governor's shoulder, Jessica could see Mark and Bernie Abrams talking. As soon as Abrams departed, Jessica politely excused herself and rejoined her husband.

"Christ," she whispered, "what did *he* want?"

Mark casually worked his arm around Jessica's waist. "Actually," he said, pulling her close, "he came over to tell me how beautiful my wife looked."

* * *

The following Monday Mark had lunch with Ira Krumholtz, a noted criminal attorney, in the dining room of Krumholtz's law office on Madison Avenue. Jonathan Lambert had recommended him to Mark after Jessica first received word of Abrams's intentions. A flamboyant personality crammed into a size forty-four portly, Krumholtz had an annoying penchant for Churchillian cigars, tall blond women, and legal precedents, though not necessarily in that order.

A very attractive young woman in black trousers and a white jacket buttoned to the neck cleared the dishes from the long mahogany table. Mark noticed a small black Bakelite name tag pinned above her right breast, but the girl moved so deftly around her two charges, Mark was unable to read it. Ira Krumholtz took little notice of the girl's efficiency. He was lost in culinary rapture, waxing poetic over his new chef's artistic use of saffron threads with crayfish. Disappearing from the room with the dirty dishes, the girl returned moments later with the coffee service and small rosewood humidor. She served the coffee, offered the men cigars, then, on Krumholtz's cue, left the dining room.

"I spoke to some people at the Justice Department," said Krumholtz, expertly piercing the end of an enormous cigar. "And they said they had nothing working against you. There was a surveillance report that put you and Arcaro together and a wiretap that confirmed what you and the old man had discussed. But frankly, what they've got doesn't interest them." Krumholtz carefully lit the cigar and exhaled with evident pleasure, the smoke rising in a languid spiral toward the ceiling.

"No, I think what we have here, if you'll excuse the pun," he continued, "is one of Mr. Abrams's famous trial balloons. He tries to tie you to one end of it and then jerks you around until you grab for someone to incriminate or you shoot down his balloon."

"So how do we handle him?" asked Mark.

"We call in the artillery and blow his fucking balloon out of the sky."

"I take it you're talking press conference."

"Right. Only we're going to have to work quickly," Krumholtz added. "You don't want to get bogged down in this guy's ambition."

"How soon?"

"I think we've got all our facts, and I'm free tomorrow. Have your people set it up for tomorrow afternoon," replied Krumholtz. "Oh, and if I were you, I'd invite the Copley woman personally. Maybe you could kill two careers with one stone."

"I don't think so," Mark said, considering for a moment his wife's friendship with the reporter. "No, on this one she gets a pass."

The swimming pool in the Laidlaw's Seventy-fifth Street town house was neatly tucked into a basement room two doors down from the wine cellar. The ceiling was honeycombed with recessed lights and the walls masked with pale yellow tiles. At the corners of the room lush areca palms in large terra-cotta tubs stood thriving in the moist, tropical atmosphere, thick with the smell of chlorine. The pool itself was painted a light aquamarine to approximate the color of shallow Caribbean inlets, and ran practically the entire length of the sixty-foot room.

Mark sat down on a chaise by the edge of the pool, loosened his tie and watched Jessica finish her evening swim. Naked, her long, smooth body, propelled by a steady kick, glided gracefully through the water, sending tiny swells breaking over the narrow gutter lining the pool. Five laps later, Jessica pulled herself from the pool and grabbed a towel from a nearby chair.

"Ah, the sweet blush of youth," said Mark, his voice booming off the tile walls.

"Jesus!" Jessica exclaimed as she spun around, drawing the towel in front of her.

"Relax. It's only your husband."

"You should have let me know you were here," she scolded, wrapping the towel around her head.

"Sorry, I didn't want to break your rhythm," he answered. "Come over here and I'll dry your back."

Jessica threw her robe over her shoulder and walked over to Mark's chaise. She moved with a catlike suppleness, betraying a fragmentary innocence, at once aware, then unaware, of the effect her nude body had on her husband.

"How come you're so late?" she said as she set her robe down on the edge of the chaise and sat down. "I thought you were going to watch the news here with me."

Mark took a towel off the back of a chair and, using broad circular strokes, began to work the heavy cotton terry over Jessica's back.

"I'm sorry I didn't call," Mark said. "The press conference ended late and Ira wanted to go over the television coverage with me. So we watched the Channel Two news live and the other two on tape. You couldn't tell it from the length of the stories, but the press conference ran an hour and a half. You'd have thought I shot Arcaro instead of just had a drink with him. By the way," he added parenthetically, "your friend tried to eat us alive. She didn't seem to want to accept the truth as an answer."

"What did Krumholtz think?" asked Jessica, ignoring the reference to Liz.

"From just the six o'clock pieces, he thought we pretty well neutralized Abrams's charges and pushed him on to the defensive," replied Mark. "If Abrams has anything more than innuendo, he's going to have to present it to a grand jury. This shit won't work a second time. Now what did *you* think of your husband's defense?"

"Me? I thought you kicked ass," Jessica replied resolutely.

"Is that a private assessment?" he asked, reaching around and gently cupping her right breast.

"Of course," she murmured, responding to his touch. "Nice lady lawyers don't talk like that in public."

"Jess, before this gets out of hand," Mark whispered, nuzzling her neck, "why don't you get dressed and I'll take you out for a big steak and a bottle of red wine."

Jessica slowly turned around and faced Mark. Her cheeks were flushed, her nipples erect. She shook her head and, without saying a word, began to methodically unbutton Mark's shirt.

"Right," said Mark breathlessly, "why don't I just keep my mouth shut?"

As she finished with the last button on the shirt, Jessica nodded knowingly and smiled.

They spent the two days before Christmas in Houston visiting Jessica's mother and sister, then flew back to New York in the hope that Mark's children would respond in some way to his invitations to spend Christmas with them. But there were no replies.

Mark did all he could to make their first Christmas in the new house a memorable one. He took great pains in finding the right gifts, in decorating the house, and in searching out the perfect tree, but there was no escaping the tremendous disappointment and frustration he felt at the rejection by his own children. Soon his gloominess became pervasive, and for the first time since they had moved in, the house began to take on an empty, hollow feeling.

Two days after Christmas Jessica dragged Mark to Bergdorf Goodman to help her return some gifts. She wanted more than anything to be with him, to penetrate his depression. It was a bracing winter day, the air clean and crisp. Along Fifth Avenue ever-vigilant Senegalese street peddlers hawked fake watches and imitation cashmere to the unsuspecting as crowds of shoppers and tourists surged in and out of the elegant shops. The woodsy scent of chestnuts roasting over blackened braziers blended with the aroma of bus fumes and expensive perfume, creating that singular essence that, if somehow bottled, could only be called "Christmas in New York."

Jessica, with a floor plan in her head and Mark securely in tow, flew through the store, alighting in three departments only long enough to make exchanges or receive credit. Skirting bottlenecks with out-of-the-way elevators, and buttonholing the most accommodating sales people, she managed to magically complete her errands and exit Bergdorf's in a mere thirty minutes. This was no mean feat, considering it was accomplished by someone under thirty, trailing a man, and with little experience at being "a rich lady."

"Come on, I'll buy you some chestnuts," said Jessica brightly as she pulled Mark from the revolving door. "Then you can take me someplace absolutely divine for a drink."

"You've got a deal," replied Mark, his veil of self-pity beginning to lift. Suddenly, in a group of people passing in front of them, Mark caught a glimpse of his daughter, her arm around a young man in a blue parka. "God, that was Patty," he said to Jessica, grabbing her arm.

"Are you sure?" asked Jessica.

"Not really," he replied anxiously.

They hurried after the couple, down Fifth Avenue toward Fifty-seventh Street, where a crowd was stopped at the traffic light. As the light changed, Mark called out. The young woman, in a ragged beaver coat, froze at the curb then turned slowly in his direction. It was his daughter. She whispered something to her boyfriend, as Mark and Jessica approached, forcing him to share her look of dread.

Mark and Patty exchanged a mechanical embrace, any emotion between them a faint memory. "It's good to see you," said Mark awkwardly as they moved in a group away from the corner. "Why didn't you call and let me know you were going to be in New York?"

"Actually, we're just in between trains," she replied, making no effort to mask the lie. "We got bored in Vermont and thought we'd go down to Washington for the weekend. But you know what to do for boredom, don't you, Daddy?" she added, drawing first blood.

Ignoring his daughter's gibe, Mark began to introduce Jessica. "I was really hoping for more relaxed surroundings for this first meeting," he told Jessica, trying to control his embarrassment, "but I guess this will have to do. Jess, this is my daughter, Patricia. Patty, this is Jessica."

"It's a pleasure to finally meet you, Patricia," Jessica said, extending her hand to the young woman. "Your father has told me so much about you." Jessica sensed a pervasive sadness under the young woman's thin veneer of hostility. She could see it in her face, in the way she stood and how she held fast to her companion's arm.

"I'm sure he has," answered Patricia, limply returning Jessica's handshake as she shot a searing glance at her father. "Look, I'd love to stay and chat with you both, but we have a train to catch," she added, tossing her head in the direction of her boyfriend.

"I understand," said Mark, disheartened by his daughter's resentment. "What about having dinner with us on the way back?" he asked. "Both of you," he continued, struggling for some common ground.

"I'm sorry, Daddy," Patty replied coldly. "I don't think I'm up to entertaining stepmothers, yet . . . Good-bye, Daddy."

As Patricia led her boyfriend off to join the flood of pedestrians crossing Fifty-seventh Street, he turned quickly and shouted something over his shoulder.

"What did he say?" Mark asked Jessica, unable to make out the young man's words.

"You're not going to believe it," she replied. "He said, 'It was a pleasure meeting you both.'"

"The boy may have poor taste in women, but at least he has good manners," Mark said facetiously.

Jessica looped her arm through Mark's and steered him up Fifth Avenue. "I'm sorry, darling. I know how much it hurts you," she said, trying to comfort him.

"She's made up her mind to despise me, and right now I see no way to change that," he replied.

Jessica pulled Mark closer and kissed him. "Why don't we have that drink now, at home, in front of a fire."

Chapter 24

"Why couldn't we have gone to my place?" said Liz nervously as she looked down at the crowd of onlookers lining the sidewalk. "I'll never get through that mess and back to the office on time."

"I thought you might like to watch the parade," Bernie Abrams replied, joining Liz by the bedroom window. "And besides, aren't you Irish on somebody's side of the family?"

"It's English," she answered with a scowl, "and it's on my father's side."

"Then Saint Patrick is not your man," Abrams said blithely. "He's not mine either, but at least the noise should liven things up." He raised Liz's long hair off the back of her neck and kissed the soft down that began at the top of her spine.

"Mmmm, that feels good," she murmured.

"Did you do what I asked before you came here?" he whispered in her ear.

"Yes," she answered huskily. As Abrams slowly spun

her around, Liz threw her head back, feeling the pressure of his lips move to her throat.

He reached his hands up to her head and pulled her to his mouth. His kiss was demanding, manipulative, asking not for love, but obedience. "Take off your clothes," he said, suddenly backing away from her.

She stared at him and smiled confidently. The game had begun, and the first move was hers. Liz ran her hand through her hair, then took a step back toward the curtains.

"No," he exclaimed, "leave them open."

She stepped away from the window, leaving only the skirt of her gray wool wrap dress bathed in the afternoon sunlight. "You want me, don't you, Abrams?" she said provocatively as her hands toyed with her wide black leather belt.

"Yes," he answered softly, his gaze fixed on her waist.

"You're going to have to speak up, Abrams," she teased. "I can't hear you."

"Yes, I want you," he confessed, his voice rising above the din that invaded the room from the street below.

"That's good. Because I have a treat for you. Now sit on the bed and watch me," she ordered.

Liz removed the belt and slid it languidly to the floor. Then, drawing her hands seductively down the front of the dress, she reached inside the waistband and unfastened the two hooks that held the swathe of gray jersey in place. Deftly, she peeled back the soft wool, pinning the loose material at her hips and revealing her nude body.

"Oh, yes," murmured Abrams ecstatically.

"I took my panty hose off in the cab," Liz said obediently. "Just like you asked."

"Come closer," he ordered breathlessly.

"Not yet," she replied, releasing the material from her hips. Her body momentarily hidden from view, Liz shrugged her shoulders, sending the dress cascading onto the floor. Feeling the warm sunlight on the back of her legs, Liz slowly turned around, bent over and picked up the gray dress. Frozen in the brilliant rectangle of light, she was a study in contrast, her unblemished alabaster skin and the contours of her supple body defined by cool shadows and her dark hair. Folding the dress and carefully setting it on the chair by the window, Liz got up and walked toward Abrams. "Now, I'm ready," she said.

Beneath the bedroom window a cheer went up on Eighty-sixth Street as the Police Department's Fife and Drum Corps filed by in their dress-blue uniforms, the booming bass drums resonating down the twin rows of buildings. Perched on their parents' shoulders, small children bobbed gleefully amidst a sea of green pennants and strained for a look at the next float rounding the corner from Fifth Avenue.

Liz and the bed moaned and creaked in a synchronous rhythm as she and Abrams wrestled with each other's libido. Grasping and clawing, heaving and sweating, they brazenly fought one another for an orgasm.

Feeling momentarily weightless, Liz opened her eyes and saw Abrams reaching across her and retrieving what appeared to be a long black silk scarf from the drawer of the night table.

"More games, Abrams?" she sighed.

"No, more pleasure, darling," he answered as he lightly drew the scarf along the damp valley between her breasts.

The silk was cool and soothing. She stretched, raising her arms, opening herself to his touch. She let out a low moan as Abrams trailed the scarf up the inside of her arm. At her forearm the featherlike caresses abruptly ended and she could feel the end of the scarf being wound around her wrist.

"What are you doing?" she asked anxiously, wondering if the games had gone too far.

"Trust me, darling," he said reassuringly. "This is going to feel wonderful." He finished tying the scarf around her wrist, then quickly slipped the loose end through an opening in the headboard and around her other wrist. He kissed the palms of her hands, then traced the path of the scarf down her arms with his lips. With his hands, he fondled and stroked her until her misgivings faded and her body took up an unmistakable rhythm.

Then he pulled a leather pouch from under the bed. He opened the bag and removed two large, pink, bullet-shaped objects, one much thicker and longer than the other. Abrams turned a small switch in the bottom of the larger dildo and it began to hum.

Liz, straining against her silken bonds, looked down horrified at the thing poised between her legs. "Please, Bernie," she begged. "Please, not that. You're going to hurt me."

"Baby, I won't hurt you," Abrams said as he began to gently rub the vibrating end of the device between her legs. "You're going to love this." His voice was even and measured.

"Please, no, Bernie," Liz whimpered. She scissor-kicked her legs in an attempt to knock his hand away, but quickly succumbed to exhaustion and Abrams's slow, steady pressure. Maybe he meant what he said, she prayed. Maybe he was only trying to please her. Maybe the games were over. Suddenly, the gentle, teasing vibrations stopped and Liz felt herself being ripped apart. She screamed, but her cries died out at the bedroom window, smothered by the tortured strains of "New York, New York" played by the Archbishop Stepinac High School band.

Liz picked up her dress from the chair and glared at Abrams lying in bed. "You son of a bitch," she cried, tears streaming down her face. "How could you do that to me?" she demanded hysterically. She hastily wrapped the gray jersey around herself, furiously cinching in her waist with the black belt. "I begged you not to. What is the matter with you?" She slumped down at the foot of the bed and dissolved into tears. "Goddamn it! What is the matter with us?"

Intimidated by Liz's emotional display, Abrams slid across the bed and tried to calm her.

"Don't touch me," she screamed as he began to put his arms around her.

"Liz, honey. I'm sorry," Abrams pleaded. "I never meant to hurt you."

"Bernie, I begged you," she said.

"I thought you really wanted me to do it. I thought it was all part of the game."

"It is a game, then? Isn't it?" she murmured. "But the pain is real. Tell me Bernie, is what we feel for each other . . . is that a lie too? A cheat, a trick!"

Abrams looked at her for a moment, unable to grasp what she was saying.

"Why won't you answer me?" she implored him. "Or can't you?"

"No, that's not a lie," he finally admitted. "What we have is real. I don't know how to analyze it, nor do I want to. I just know it fulfills a need deep down inside each of us. Liz, honey, I care about you very much," Abrams added, pulling her into his arms, "and I promise you this won't happen again."

Liz rested her cheek against Abrams's shoulder and thought about what he'd said. She felt terribly confused and frightened. Months ago she knew that they had both unleashed something in each other that neither one of them wanted to admit to. And yet now neither one of them could find the words to bring these feelings under control. They were trapped, trapped in a horrible downward spiral that threatened to destroy them both.

*   *   *

Jessica had been ecstatic about her elevation to partner at Turner, Welles, and Lambert. Naturally, the promotion had been the result of hard work and dedication to the firm, but the size and location of her new office did much to fuel the idle rumors to the contrary. Although hardly of palatial dimensions, her new corner office on the forty-third floor was twice the size of her previous cubicle and had a commanding view of the East River and New York harbor. Not to mention that it was a mere five doors down from Jonathan Lambert's baronial suite, placing her at the perimeter of the inner circle and the center of office gossip.

Raymond Healy sat patiently in the reception area as Jessica stepped off the elevator. She scarcely noticed the bearlike man reading the newspaper, but he had noticed her. As a New York City detective, it was his job to notice people, and he had been making mental notes of everyone going in or out of the office since he had arrived. Healy took a good look at Jessica while she waited to be buzzed in. From her expensive clothes, delicate features, and the brief description he had from an aide in Abrams's office, Healy knew at once that she was the one he'd been waiting for. Still, he remained seated behind his newspaper, not wanting to appear too assertive in such a subdued setting.

"Ms. Wheeler, there's a Mr. Raymond Healy here to see you from the Manhattan district attorney's office," her secretary said as Jessica passed by on her way to her office.

"Lois, give me five minutes," replied Jessica, caught off guard by the announcement, "and then bring him down to my office."

While her secretary meandered down to the reception area to escort the detective back to her office, Jessica quickly gathered up the files on her desk and moved them to the top of the burled walnut cabinet behind her chair. Why tempt fate? she reasoned.

At six-three and 250 pounds, Raymond Healy filled the doorway of Jessica's office. Physically, Jessica concluded, this man had no other choice than to be a cop. His slightly graying red hair, his protruding beer belly, and the rosy, wrinkled cheeks were almost too stereotypical to be true.

"Ms. Wheeler, my name is Raymond Healy," the detective said deliberately, removing his identification from his coat pocket and handing it to Jessica. "I'm a New York City detective assigned to the Manhattan district attorney's office."

The tedious introduction made Jessica restless. She found Abrams's attempts at official intimidation laughable. But Healy lumbered through it anyway, as though he were auditioning for some absurd television police drama.

"And?" She quickly returned his wallet, in an attempt to speed him along.

"And I have a subpoena for all your records dealing with Artaud Enterprises Incorporated and any of its subsidiaries," Healy added, slipping a folded sheet of light blue paper into Jessica's hand.

Jessica glanced through the subpoena, then tossed it on her desk. "Well, detective, I am sorry I kept you waiting for something like this," Jessica said politely. She led Healy to the threshold of her office. "I'll have my secretary show you out."

Alone in the office, Jessica stared at the subpoena lying on the desk. "That son of a bitch," she muttered, walking around to the telephone. She was angry and frustrated. She'd always seen the law from the inside, from a position of relative power. For the first time she understood how an innocent man felt when swept up in an unfamiliar legal system. Now she was the innocent, and the system, although not unfamiliar, was being twisted and perverted by one man's blind ambition.

She dialed Mark's private number at the Arena and waited. It took ten rings, but Mark finally answered.

"Did I get you at a bad time?" she asked.

"Actually, I was about to fire Quinn McDonald," Mark admitted.

"I guess this is a bad time," said Jessica apologetically. "I'm sorry. You know I really like Quinn."

"Jess, we all like Quinn. We all liked Louie," answered Mark. "But I need a winning head coach, not Miss Congeniality. Now, what's up?"

"It seems you didn't kill the snake. You merely stunned him."

"What are you talking about?"

"Bernard Abrams," she answered. "I was just served with a subpoena for all my Artaud files, answerable in ten days."

"Bastard . . . What's our next move?"

"I'll go into court and request a protective order against the subpoena. I think we can claim the files are privileged information. That should slow him up for a while."

"Is there anything we can do about what's over here?"

"I don't think so. But I'll call Ira Krumholtz and see if we can put together a united front that will get us back on the offensive."

"Fine," said Mark. "While you're doing that, I'm going to read Quinn the riot act."

"So you're not going to fire him?" she asked.

"Maybe."

"Maybe? What kind of answer is maybe?"

"If he wins tonight, maybe I'll postpone my decision. Is that fair enough?"

"Throw in dinner and you've got a deal."

"How about Le Cirque after the game?" he asked.

"Perfect. I'm going to be on the late side, anyway. I have a lot of work to do. Around ten, then?"

"Fine. I'll have Billy pick you up at work and take you home."

"Thank you, sir."

"Jess, have I told you lately how much I love you and how happy you've made me these last nine months?" Mark asked affectionately.

"Not since this morning," she teased. "But don't let that stop you. I'm young and insecure and I need constant stroking."

"I guess that means I'm going to have to pay for dinner."

Chapter 25

A big tawny cat lay dozing contentedly on a countertop in front of a narrow kitchen window as a tiny orange-striped kitten batted and chewed at its tail. Every so often the small needlelike claws and teeth would penetrate the larger cat's dense fur and she would swish her tail, sending the youngster tumbling back toward the sink.

From the bedroom window of the town house, Jessica watched the kitten's playful antics through sunken, hollow eyes. Her face was ashen, the color drained into the widening river of hopelessness that seemed to be carrying away her dreams. She sat on the small daybed by the window, her knees drawn up against her chest, the soft folds of Mark's cashmere robe gathered close to her body to ward off an icy chill.

Finally spent, the kitten fell asleep in the warm curve of its mother's belly, its oversized paws clasped firmly around the mother cat's thick tail. Existing for days on nothing more than sleeping pills and coffee, Jessica longed for that same secure, untroubled sleep.

The bedroom door opened slowly. Jessica's mother, a striking gray-haired woman in a black suit, entered and quietly approached Jessica. There was concern on the woman's face. It was written in the slender creases around her sympathetic brown eyes and strong mouth. Although she walked with the aid of a slim ebony cane, the woman carried herself ramrod straight. Her vanity and stubborn southern pride would permit no less.

"Jessica, honey," the woman whispered, gently placing her hand on her daughter's shoulder. "Kendall and I are ready to leave. Are you really sure you want us to go? I could stay on longer, you know."

Jessica held her mother's hand against her shoulder, then turned from the window. "Really, Mama," she said, "I can't lean on you forever. You've got a life of your own, and I've got to start rebuilding mine."

"You can give yourself time, honey."

"Time, Mama?" said Jessica. "You know it's been a month, and I haven't set foot outside this house. And I have responsibilities. People are depending on me."

"If you're sure," her mother replied.

"I'm sure," answered Jessica, secretly wishing she would stay forever to hold and protect her.

"I'll send Kendall in to say good-bye, then."

"Don't Mama. I'll be down in a minute and see you both off."

"All right, honey," said Nedra Wheeler, bending over to kiss her daughter on the cheek. "We'll wait for you downstairs."

After her mother left, Jessica got up from the daybed and went into the bathroom. She washed her face, scrubbing furiously at the spot where her mother kissed her. Her mother's perfume had contaminated Mark's fading scent. Trapped in the weave of the cashmere robe, it was her last contact with his physical presence.

Her face washed and dried, she pulled the robe close

to her. She rubbed the soft cashmere against her cheek, now inhaling just the faintest traces of her husband. Tears welled up in the corners of her eyes. She was losing him.

Jessica stared at herself in the bathroom mirror as her tears, caught first in the deep circles under her eyes, ran down her colorless cheeks. She tried to remember her life before Mark, before the happiness, before the joy. How had she survived? she wondered. How, in such a short time, had two people's lives become so intertwined that one couldn't exist without the other? For the past month her life had sailed along effortlessly, guided not by any inner will or force of character, but by the bitter, heart-wrenching rush of events.

After warning Mark about the subpoena, Jessica had telephoned Ira Krumholtz to work out a strategy for a common defense. They had agreed to meet the following week to review the scope of the subpoena and figure out a way to put an end to Bernie Abrams's witch hunt once and for all. From four-thirty to seven she had patiently labored over the wording of a lengthy, twice-revised contract, until she was bleary-eyed. Then she stuffed it with other files into her briefcase and trundled down to Wall Street, where Billy Richmond was waiting for her with the car.

Jessica sent Billy back to the Arena to wait for Mark while she got ready for their dinner at Le Cirque. She agonized for nearly an hour over her wardrobe that evening, as though she were dressing for a blind date. After his playfulness on the telephone, she was determined to drive Mark crazy with something short, black, and clingy yet still within the bounds of good taste.

Arriving at the restaurant around ten, Jessica had been warmly greeted by Sirio Maccioni, who led her to their table on the right side of the room. She was positively aglow with anticipation, but her mood changed abruptly when she noticed that the table was empty. In all the time she had known Mark, he had never kept her waiting in a restaurant, and his absence made her uneasy. Some might have considered this attentiveness old-fashioned, but Jessica adored it and found it reassuring that Mark was always there for her.

The phone call that ended everything came only minutes after she was seated. There had been an unsettling calm in Frank DeCicco's voice as he described Mark's condition. His tone, bordering on resignation, did nothing but sow the seeds of panic in Jessica's heart.

In the sky box moments after the game, as Frank and Mark discussed Quinn McDonald's future with the team, Mark suddenly complained of a terrible headache, then collapsed. Within minutes, DeCicco reported, they had Mark in an ambulance, rushing him to New York Hospital. All Frank could tell her now was that they had just moved him into intensive care.

Horrible thoughts began to churn in her head. She felt dreadfully alone and afraid, cut off from the rest of the world. She started to cry.

Sirio chivalrously commandeered a limousine from one of his guests, racing Jessica to New York Hospital. In the lobby she was met by Billy Richmond, who whisked her up to the fifth-floor intensive care unit. Frank DeCicco was waiting for her by the nurses' station. He was leaning against the wall, a trench coat thrown over his shoulder, his eyes riveted on some invisible spot on the floor. In the brightly lit corridor he seemed to Jessica to be standing in his own shadow, his head shielded from view by the poplin raincoat. Hearing footsteps, DeCicco looked up. His eyes were red, his jaw firmly set.

"How is he, Frank?" she asked quietly.

"Still unconscious," DeCicco replied. "They worked on him in the emergency room for an hour and then brought him up here about twenty minutes ago."

"I want to see him," she insisted.

"I'll take you in," he said.

DeCicco led her through a set of double doors and past the intensive care nurses' station. For some reason she thought the room would be larger, with more beds, more injured bodies. She stood with Frank DeCicco at the foot of Mark's bed and stared at her husband in disbelief. There were tubes running all around him like plastic snakes bent on devouring their prey. His chest rose and fell in a slow, steady rhythm, the air forced in by a blue-gray respirator next to the bed. Above his head a red light skipped from left to right across a screen, monitoring his heartbeat. This can't be Mark, she had thought. He looked so small, so helpless. It had to be a mistake, someone's idea of a cruel joke.

She sat down on a chair by the bed and, leaning over, touched his cheek. His skin felt smooth and warm.

"Mark, I love you so much," she whispered in his ear. "Please don't leave me."

A small teardrop had formed in the corner of his left eye. Jessica watched it swell then dart down the side of his face. It was life, she reasoned, a sign that he wasn't giving up.

She had been sitting by his bed for nearly an hour, half hypnotized by the relentless push-pull of the respirator, when the monitor over her head suddenly let out a high-pitched whine. She looked over at Mark wide-eyed, trying frantically to detect what had set off the ghoulish device.

Within seconds a nurse touched her on the shoulder. "I'm afraid you'll have to go now," the woman said firmly.

"But I want to stay," Jessica cried desperately. "I have to stay. He needs me."

"Please, Mrs. Laidlaw," the nurse replied. "You have to leave."

As Jessica backed away from the bed two nurses and two doctors appeared out of nowhere with a crash cart and began working on Mark. They moved with blinding speed, hands flying, each member of the team complementing the other. While this furious scene unfolded in front of her, a thin, redheaded nurse approached Jessica, took her hand and guided her out of the ICU and back into the hall where Frank DeCicco was still waiting.

Fifteen minutes later they were joined by Steven Askew, the attending neurosurgeon, and Marvin Granger, Mark's personal physician.

"He's gone, isn't he?" she asked, staring helplessly into the doctors' faces and hoping for some sign that would put a lie to her words.

Granger gently touched her arm. "I'm sorry, Jessica," he answered softly.

All at once the muscles around her stomach seemed to contract and she gasped for air. She felt as though she had been hit by an iron fist, and reached out to Frank DeCicco to keep from doubling over. Although tears were there, she couldn't scream or cry out; instead, a mournful wail echoed in her brain. Gradually a frigid mist began to surround Jessica as DeCicco and Billy Richmond led her into a nearby waiting room.

Jessica strained to listen as Dr. Askew quietly catalogued his efforts to save Mark's life. "Cerebral hemorrhage," "cranial pressure," "cardiac failure"—the snatches of medical jargon jabbed at her until the cold veil completely enveloped her and the voices were muted. She stared at the compassionate faces as the air around her seemed to freeze, trapping her and the memories of the man she loved in a large icy crystal.

The days that followed were a blur. Familiar faces appeared to advise and console, then disappeared. Mark's children returned to New York for the funeral, but would have nothing to do with Jessica. Spurning her invitation to stay at the Seventy-fifth Street house, the pair took condolence calls in a small suite at the Regency Hotel, trying unsuccessfully to isolate the young widow from Mark's old friends.

Arrangements for the funeral were handled by Jonathan Lambert, Mark's executor, in accordance with the provisions of his will. A private nondenominational service was held at a funeral home on Madison Avenue. Careful to avoid any possible confrontation, Lambert had discreetly seated Jessica and the children on opposite sides of the aisle. The unusual seating plan left many mourners with the uncomfortable option of having to choose between Mark's children and his wife.

Mark was buried later that day on a terraced hillside above a sea of granite tombstones in a northern Westchester County cemetery. The ranks of mourners who had made the trip north from Manhattan had thinned considerably. Most who stood at the graveside that afternoon had also stood with Mark and Jessica on that bluff overlooking the Tyrrhenian Sea nearly nine months ago. Even Liz Copley, out of a sense of guilt or devotion, stood with the others on that quiet knoll, silently making her peace with a memory.

During the three weeks following Mark's death, Jessica cloistered herself in her bedroom, first angry, then depressed. She railed against Mark for leaving her, for breaking his promise to love her forever. She needed someone or something to blame, to accept responsibility, and when Mark and God failed her, she turned inward.

Curiously, the only one who could reach Jessica was Frank DeCicco. He began to visit her regularly, talking about Mark and his plans for the team. She began to look forward to his visits, and soon came to view DeCicco and the Knights as an extension of Mark. And as the time approached for Jessica's mother and sister to return to Texas, it was apparent that Frank DeCicco had become an invaluable friend and trusted adviser.

Chapter 26

Jessica put down the phone. It had been only a week since her mother and Kendall had flown back to Houston, but it seemed like an eternity. She missed them dearly. She looked forward to the daily conversations with her mother. Now that she was alone, they gave her a sense of being part of something, of belonging to someone, of being loved. She had friends in New York, good friends, but like many New Yorkers, a part of Jessica was still from somewhere else. Her roots, her memories of love, security, and family, were still anchored in the dusty plains of West Texas. And the only thing that comforted her now was the past.

As she sat down at the makeup mirror at the far end of her dressing room, her housekeeper, a diminutive woman with an hourglass figure, knocked softly and entered the bedroom suite.

"Mrs. Laidlaw, Billy is out front with the car," she said in almost a whisper.

"I know I'm running late, Emma," replied Jessica.

"Why don't you tell Billy to pick up Mr. DeCicco first and then come back for me."

In forty-five minutes she was due in Jonathan Lambert's office to view a videotape Mark had made when he had revised his will four months ago. Jonathan had warned Jessica about the tape a week after the funeral. During the next several weeks he had avoided any mention of the tape out of consideration for her, but now that Mark's children were about to leave the city, Jonathan had no choice.

Jessica had invited Frank DeCicco along for moral support. Not knowing what was on the tape, and screening it in the presence of Douglas and Patricia Laidlaw, was an unnerving prospect.

At the appointed hour all the concerned parties were seated in Jonathan Lambert's office. As with Mark's funeral, the seating arrangement reflected an adversarial proceeding. Just to the right of Jonathan's ornately carved desk, facing a television built into a dark wooden bookcase, were two padded armchairs separated by a four-foot aisle from three similar chairs. Jessica sat anxiously with Frank DeCicco on one side of this demilitarized zone while Douglas and Patricia Laidlaw and their attorney, Michael Rosen—a thin, taciturn man—waited on the other.

Standing in front of the television set, Jonathan carefully explained that what they were about to see was simply a personal message from Mark and that any oral bequests or codicils contained in the tape had no legal validity. With that, he switched on the television and started the tape.

A jumble of black and white hash quickly gave way to a title card indicating the date of the recording, then Mark was on the screen. Jessica gasped at the image frozen in time. He looked so relaxed, she thought, dressed in a black polo sweater and gray flannel slacks, as though death were the furthest thing from his mind. He was sitting in one of the Barcelona chairs at the far end of his office, his arm slung over the back.

"Well, I'm sure this feels as strange to you as it does to me," he began, "but, Doug and Patricia, I wanted to make sure that things I may never have had a chance to tell you finally got said. I know I haven't always been there when you needed me, and many times I seemed distant and remote. But that didn't mean I didn't think or care about you. You and your mother were always in my thoughts. Yes, I cared for your mother. And I tried to help her, but she was too intent on destroying herself for me to make any difference. That I failed her and you is something I will always regret. I guess in the end the only thing I can do is repeat the same lament of every troubled parent, 'I did what I thought was best for you, and I loved you.'"

Much to everyone's surprise, the tape ended without any mention of Jessica. She sat stunned, devastated. She looked first to Frank DeCicco for some explanation, then to Jonathan Lambert, who, in an unaccustomed gesture, nervously adjusted his eyepatch as he walked over to his desk to continue the proceeding. She felt the same numbing cold she had felt in the hospital corridor begin to wash over her. The ruthless fate that had taken her husband was now clawing at her memories.

"It was Mark's wish that a formal reading of his will should follow this tape," said Lambert, reaching for the open file in front of him.

The resemblance between Douglas Laidlaw and his father was striking. At first glance it had held Jessica spellbound. Douglas's mouth, the shape of his face, the way he carried himself, were all grim reminders of what she had lost. However, it wasn't until Jonathan began to speak that she noticed something else about the young man, something that made him much less his father's son. It was in his eyes—a smug, self-serving malevolence that seemed fueled by some deep-seated contempt for the people around him.

After the tone of Mark's videotape, his will came as a shock. Although he had generously provided for his children in the form of two fifteen-million-dollar trust funds, he had left the bulk of his estate—cash, real estate holdings, and stock estimated at $360 million—plus the administration of assorted charitable trusts to Jessica.

"That sanctimonious hypocrite," growled Douglas Laidlaw, breaking the uneasy silence that had settled over the room. "He loved us and screwed us at the same time. That bastard." He shot a cruel look at Jessica. "There's no goddamn way you're going to get my money, lady," he said viciously. "I put up with too much shit from that bastard for too many years to hand you what's rightfully mine."

"Take it easy, Douglas," said Frank DeCicco, rising from his chair. "I don't think you want to say anything you'll be sorry for later."

"Stay out of this, DeCicco," snapped Douglas. "This has nothing to do with you, unless you've got designs on my father's money as well as his woman."

As DeCicco started for the young man, Jessica grabbed his arm. "Don't, Frank, please," she said softly.

Michael Rosen whispered something to Patricia, who immediately rose and took her brother's arm. "I think we'd better leave," she said, ushering her brother out of the office.

"I'll be talking to you soon, Jonathan," said Rosen after he and Jonathan Lambert exchanged well-seasoned shrugs. "And don't forget to send me a copy of the will." Lambert nodded and Rosen left the room.

"Jonathan, you drew it up. Tell me, why did Mark do this?" Jessica asked plaintively.

In answer, Lambert pulled a second video cassette from his desk drawer, walked over and slipped it into the tape machine. "He made this one for you," he said. Then he looked over at Frank DeCicco. "We'll wait for you outside."

Jessica sat alone for several minutes before she started the tape. Feeling angry and cheated, she needed time to compose herself. Mark had left her his fortune, but he had also left her without saying good-bye, without holding her, without loving her. She hated him for it and herself for believing it.

"Jess, the most difficult part of all this is trying to imagine being without you," Mark said as the tape began. "I have loved you more than I have loved anyone or anything in my entire life. You have brought me laughter, happiness, and contentment. I know your life will be different now, but please remember, Jess, nothing that happens from this moment on will ever diminish what we've had. I will always love you and always be with you. Good-bye, my darling."

"Good-bye, my love," Jessica whispered through a veil of tears. She suddenly felt relieved, as though things were finally complete. Mark had given her the greatest gift anyone could ever know, the chance to say one last good-bye.

Three nights later, during halftime, Frank DeCicco stood at center court in the Arena, reading a tribute to Mark. Like many of these eulogies, the glowing sentiments and fine words seemed to fall on deaf ears. The crowd was more interested in the close score and a second beer.

It was only when the teams returned from the locker rooms and DeCicco introduced Jessica that the crowd seemed to perk up. New York, a sports town, is ever sensitive to changes in a team's ruling elite, and, as in any dynastic succession, the fans like to take measure of the new owner.

Polite applause trailed Jessica as she stepped quickly to the microphone, her blond hair gleaming in the harsh Arena light. Dressed in a dark gray suit, Jessica looked more the heir to the house of Dior than to the New York Knights. But as she spoke, her spirit and emotion slowly began to win over the crowd. She spoke eloquently of the relationship between the team and the fans, and the responsibilities each had to the other. Yet it was her closing words that roused them all.

". . . and so we're going to dedicate ourselves to bringing an NBA championship back to New York," she said, her voice echoing through the hall, "for the glory of our players, for the pride of our loyal fans, and for the memory of my husband. . . . Thank you."

There was a thunderous ovation for the young widow as she walked back to the stands with Frank DeCicco at her side.

"I guess they believed you," said DeCicco.

"Why shouldn't they?" answered Jessica, practically shouting to make herself heard over the enthusiastic crowd. "I'm going to do it."

PART 3

Chapter 27

Spread across the beige sofa in Jessica's office, Ira Krumholtz looked more like a beached baby whale than a high-powered criminal attorney. Although quite at ease, he puffed furiously on a huge black cigar, keeping a small cloud of smoke in an odd geosynchronous orbit over his head; when Ira moved, so did the cloud, adding a surreal touch to an already comic tableau.

Back to work almost two months now, Jessica still found herself occasionally struggling to focus her attention and fighting periodic bouts of depression. But fortunately, the frequency of these episodes had diminished as time passed and she finally felt able to start rebuilding her life.

"I just finished a case in State Supreme Court when I got the good news, so I thought I'd come over here and tell you in person," said Ira, stopping to take a sip of coffee from the cup in front of him. "Mm, good coffee." He put down the cup and returned to his cigar.

"It seems Abrams has decided to drop the investigation into Mark's relationship with Philip Arcaro and the acquisition of the Arena site."

"I don't understand," replied Jessica. "Why the sudden change of heart?"

"Politics," Krumholtz answered matter-of-factly. "I know it's cruel to say this, but with Mark's death, the investigation has lost a lot of its political impact. And to take you on in your husband's name would look more like widow-bashing than anything else. And that would mean bad P.R."

"So it really all came down to image?" said Jessica angrily.

"Exactly . . . But Mark knew that. That's why he hired me. He knew this thing would never go to court, let alone to a grand jury, and that we'd end up trying this case in the papers." Krumholtz responded to the pained expression on her face by explaining further. "Look, Jessica, Abrams finally realized, after he got all the documentation, that the deal was a terrific one. Everyone benefited. Mark. The builders. The mayor. Even the people. And with no losers, there was no crusade and no glory, so exit the crusader."

"So it's over," she said in frustration.

"It's over."

"But what about Abrams?"

"What about him? . . . Just play it safe," he told her. "You'll be moving in loftier circles now, so keep one eye open for him. Remember, after you cut off a snake's tail, it doesn't take long for it to grow a new one back. On the other hand, the man is pragmatic. Who knows, some day he may come knocking on your door for a campaign contribution."

"That'll be the day."

"Stranger things have happened in New York politics," said Krumholtz, rising from the sofa. "Now I think I'll go pay my respects to your senior partner and perhaps talk him into buying me lunch."

"Thank you for stopping by, Ira," said Jessica.

"Oh, and by the way," replied Krumholtz, stopping at the door. "I was at the Arena the night you spoke, and if you'll excuse a bit of sexism, I think you're one classy broad and you're going to get through all of this just fine."

"Thank you, Ira," she said softly, touching his arm as he left the office.

Sitting down at her desk, Jessica looked over at Mark's picture. It was a photograph taken during a fall weekend in Litchfield three months after they were married. Mark was wearing the brown leather jacket he loved so much and was leaning against an oak tree next to Jonathan Lambert's guest house, a pile of golden-yellow leaves at his feet. As she studied the photograph, Jessica realized that in his face there was still enough comfort and love and understanding to help her through the loneliness and sorrow. "I know, darling, it's hard for me too," she whispered, "but I'm trying."

The Mercedes hit a row of steel plates sunk into the asphalt and jarred Jessica from her thoughts.

"I'm sorry, Mrs. Laidlaw," Billy Richmond apologized. "Looks like they're tearing up Third Avenue again."

Jessica glanced out the car window at the orange and white barricades squeezing the impenetrable uptown traffic into two lanes. She noticed the eager young men and women sweeping in and out of the cafés and restaurants dotting the broad avenue. Resplendent in cotton and linen, the celebrants of this early June evening tried to appear undaunted by the day's hot and sticky weather.

It's all still going on, Jessica thought, *as though nothing happened.* Her depression, her sense of isolation, were just islands in the stream around which life continued to ebb and flow. She knew these islands were slowly eroding away and soon the time would come when she would have to sink or swim. Yet she was determined to avoid such an arbitrary fate by rejoining humanity on her own terms.

After Ira Krumholtz's visit, Jessica phoned Meredith and asked if she might attend that evening's dinner at Sistina. Since the December confrontation between Mark and Liz at the Arena, Jessica had politely excused herself from the monthly dinners. Everyone understood, but no one ever pointed a finger at Liz.

"We've kept your seat empty," Meredith replied, elated at the prospect of Jessica's return. "Believe me when I tell you there wasn't anyone we could find to replace you."

"You mean there was no one who wanted to," Jessica added smartly. "Face it, Meredith, spending fifty dollars for dinner and getting your social life savaged by three sociopathic cynics isn't everybody's idea of a good time."

"Whoever promised you a good time?" asked Meredith. "And how can you be catty enough to compare a little honesty and healthy skepticism with savagery?"

"Personal experience."

"All right, I'll concede one time."

The two women laughed. Jessica no longer felt guilty about being vital and alive. It felt good to laugh, to express something more than sadness and pain. She suddenly remembered the warm company of her friends.

"God, I've missed you guys," said Jessica.

"All of us?" asked her friend cautiously.

"Yes, all of you." There was an uncomfortable pause as Jessica struggled with her next question. "Well, how is she?"

"Doing penance," replied Meredith. "Seriously, Jess, she's not doing very well. You know, after Mark died, she and Abrams broke up. The best I could make out is they had gotten into some really heavy dominance thing. She just hinted and we never asked. Then she became very depressed. She still hasn't been able to get over the guilt she's been carrying around because of Mark." Meredith waited for some response from Jessica, but when there was none, she continued. "She's wanted to see you."

"What for, absolution?" Jessica shot back. She immediately regretted the words. "I'm sorry, Meredith. That was uncalled for."

"Maybe you're right. Maybe she does want absolution . . . or just a chance to apologize."

"Then why didn't she call me or come by the house?"

"After seeing you at the funeral—"

"I didn't know she was there," interrupted Jessica.

"She was also with us at the cemetery."

"Why didn't you tell me?"

"She asked us not to," Meredith answered. "She didn't want to upset you or make things worse."

"And afterward? Not a word from her. Why?"

"Because she's afraid to face you. Because she thinks you blame her for Mark's death."

"I don't know. Maybe at the beginning I did, but when this all happened, I blamed everyone, even Mark," Jessica admitted. "Now I know that was a natural reaction, trying to make sense out of something so irrational."

"It would help Liz if she heard you say that. I think it would help both of you."

"I'm not sure if I'm ready for that."

"Then why did you want to come to dinner?" asked Meredith.

"God. I hate it when you're right," answered Jessica. "Have I become so transparent?"

"Let's just say I've become more intuitive."

"I can't believe the world has changed so much in three months that you actually bothered to spare my feelings."

"Congratulations, you've caught me on a bad day."

"Listen, Meredith," said Jessica, "please don't tell

Liz I'm coming. I don't want to create any unnecessary pressures or false expectations. I don't know how I'm going to deal with this yet."

"Okay. Just don't worry about it, Jess," replied Meredith confidently. "I'm sure you'll work it out."

"I hope so," said Jessica. "Well, then, I guess I'll see you at eight."

Billy Richmond stopped the car in front of Sistina and rushed around to open the door for Jessica. They had been trapped in traffic on Third Avenue for nearly ten minutes and the delay had made Jessica nervous. She had never intended to make a grand entrance. She had almost taken a cab to avoid being seen arriving in the Mercedes. Anything to feel less self-conscious about rejoining the group.

With her head down, Jessica nearly ran into Julie Vericki coming up the sidewalk. The tall blonde deftly sidestepped Jessica, then realizing who it was, threw her arms around her.

"Jess, it's so good to see you," said Julie as she hugged her friend. "Meredith said you'd be coming."

"You haven't spoken to Liz, have you?" Jessica asked anxiously.

"Not about you. Meredith told me about your little talk."

Jessica stepped back for a moment to give Julie a thorough inspection. Tan and lean, and radiant in a white linen dress, the doe-eyed model was as beautiful as ever.

"You look terrific," said Jessica. "No, don't tell me. You're working out twice a day now."

"No, it's something better and much more fun," said Julie, taking Jessica's arm and walking her into the restaurant.

"What is it?" Jessica demanded. "You can't keep a secret like this all to yourself."

"I'm pregnant," she whispered to Jessica.

"You're kidding," Jessica said incredulously.

"Really," answered Julie, a wide smile breaking over her face. "Two months. Go ahead, Jess, tell me I'm beaming."

"You are. God, Julie, I'm so happy for you," said Jessica, kissing her friend on the cheek. "But you've got to tell me, how is Ronnie taking all of this?"

"Oh, you mean the free spirit I've been living in sin with for the past two and a half years? The man who thinks plants are too much responsibility?" joked Julie. "Well, Mr. Iconoclast wants us to get married next month. We've already started looking for a bigger apartment."

"You're kidding!"

"No. And are you ready for this? He's got us looking on the upper East Side. Ain't family life grand?" added Julie gleefully.

"It certainly is," Jessica said. There was a touch of wistfulness in her voice as she thought for an instant about what might have been.

"God, Jess. I'm sorry," replied her friend. "I didn't mean to—"

"Of course you didn't. It's just me," explained Jessica. "Sometimes it's so hard to forget that I'm alone."

With sisterly affection, Julie put her arm around Jessica and walked her through the dining room.

Liz and Meredith had arrived early and were having an animated discussion as the two women approached their table. Meredith, her hands whipping around her head, was chastising Liz, as usual, for some real or imagined shortcoming of broadcast journalism. As a culpable member of the electronic press, Meredith felt Liz had a moral obligation to endure these periodic harangues. And Liz accepted it, much like a starving atheist would sit through grace before a free meal.

"Hey, look who I found!" said Julie exuberantly, interrupting Meredith in the middle of a lofty argument.

"Is this still a table for four?" asked Jessica.

Liz glanced anxiously at Meredith, then turned toward the familiar voice. She looked up at Jessica, her eyes filling with tears. "It always has been," Liz said in almost a whisper, trying to hold back her pain. But it was no use. The months of guilt and anguish were just too much for her and she broke down. "Oh, God, Jess, I'm so sorry," she sobbed. "Please forgive me."

Jessica bent down and wrapped her arms around her despondent friend. "Honey," she said softly, stroking Liz's head, "don't do this to yourself. It wasn't your fault."

Several days later, standing by her office window, Jessica watched as a small sailboat fought its way up the East River against the strong current. The limp sails flapped in the late afternoon breezes that whipped through the canyons of lower Manhattan and out onto the river. Her eyes followed the ketch along its journey, but her mind was on another boat, riding with gentler winds off the coast of Sardinia.

"Am I interrupting anything?" asked Jonathan Lambert as he stuck his head in the office.

"Not really. Just a memory," Jessica said, turning from the window.

"If this is a bad time, I'll come back later."

"No, Jonathan, it's fine. Please sit down."

Lambert slipped into one of the chrome and brown leather chairs in front of Jessica's desk. She never ceased to marvel at Jonathan's endurance. At seventy-seven, still a full-time partner and more recently a best-selling novelist, he seemed driven, not by the uncertainties of time, but by a belief in the inherent redemption of excellence.

"Is it any easier than it was a month ago?" he asked as she sat down across from him.

"Being back at work or dealing with the memories?"

"Both, I guess," replied Jonathan. "One has a lot to do with the other."

"Well, my work is getting more focused. And the memories," she added pensively, "they're getting slightly soft around the edges. Does that sound like progress?"

"It sounds like the natural order of things."

In the two years and some months since Jonathan loaned out the beautiful and ambitious associate to Mark Laidlaw, a warm, almost father-daughter relationship had developed between them. After Mark's death, Jonathan seemed to always be hovering somewhere just out of sight, ready to swoop down when he was needed. A man of simple truths, with an unbridled joie de vivre, Jonathan Lambert did much to fill the void left in Jessica's life by the death of her father fourteen years earlier.

"You think you're ready to talk about Mark's estate?" asked Jonathan as he pressed his fingertips together in a rather distracting exercise.

"Don't try to be coy, Jonathan. It doesn't become you," Jessica replied. "They've contested the will, haven't they?"

Jonathan nodded half-heartedly. "I just got the papers from Surrogate's Court."

"And what are they claiming?" asked Jessica.

"The only thing they can. That you exercised undue influence over Mark at the time he drew up the will."

"I didn't even know he changed his will."

"I know that."

"God, Jonathan, if this whole thing wasn't so venomous, it would almost be laughable."

"But it isn't. Laughable, I mean," he said, smoothing the ends of his moustache against his upper lip. "Look,

Jessica, we both know this is only a strike suit. They're just trying to tie up the estate and squeeze you financially. They know the house is in your name and that you'll need money to maintain it and to keep on Billy and the housekeeper."

Jonathan paused as he always did when he had to frame what he considered an indelicate or indiscreet question. It was part of an old-world charm that Jessica found quite endearing.

"If I might pry, at this moment, Jessica, exactly how liquid are you?" asked Jonathan.

"Personally? . . . I think there's around fifteen thousand in a household account that I've been drawing on, and about fifty thousand in assorted mutual funds. That's my profit from the sale of my co-op . . . Oh, yes," she recalled, "and about twelve thousand or so in an IRA. That's me, lock, stock, and gold card."

"Good. That should hold you while I petition the court for your household expenses."

"Jonathan, I want you to understand that I will refuse to post the house for the executor's bond," she said emphatically. It was the last stronghold of her memories, and she was determined to defend it at all costs.

"Don't you worry about anything," Jonathan reassured her. "I'll post the bond, and if we run into any trouble with the petition, I'll advance you anything you may need to keep the house."

"Thank you, Jonathan," she said, walking around the desk to embrace him, "I can't tell you how much that means to me."

"Well, now that that's all taken care of," he replied confidently, "we can find out what it will take to get your darling stepchildren to settle. Of course, if that's what you want."

Chapter 28

Frank DeCicco's beach house sat squarely at the edge of the dunes fifty yards from Dune Road. Constructed of a series of juxtaposed boxes sheathed in barn siding, the modest, unpretentious house curved around a wide sun deck, leaving it open to the sea. The morning sun had just begun to bake the deck and the fashionable Hamptons' shoreline, sending fresh ocean air wafting ashore.

Sitting on the edge of the bed, bleary-eyed, Frank DeCicco ran his hand through his hair while he peered around the bedroom then out the open glass door leading out to the deck. He reached for a pair of shorts that were hanging precariously off the side of the wooden headboard and pulled them on. Struggling to the doorway, he flipped on a large overhead fan to purge the room of the pungent aroma of sex and perspiration.

In the kitchen at the opposite end of the house, DeCicco glanced over the dirty dishes in the sink, then rummaged through the cupboards looking for a clean glass. He found one at the back of the dishwasher and poured himself some orange juice.

"You never did tell me what you were doing in Southampton," DeCicco yelled out through the open window.

"Looking for you." The sultry, incorporeal voice came from the distant reaches of the sun deck.

"Seriously. What were you really doing in town yesterday?" he asked.

"Like I said, looking for you. I wanted to talk to you. I thought we could get to know each other better," the woman's voice teased.

DeCicco refilled his glass with juice, then slid aside a glass door and stepped onto the deck. At the far end of the wooden platform, was a young woman, her nude body glistening with suntan oil, stretched out facedown on a towel-draped chaise lounge.

"I brought you some orange juice," said DeCicco, pressing the cold glass into the small of the woman's back.

"Bastard," the girl shouted, flipping on her side. Patricia Laidlaw stared up at DeCicco, a bawdy smile inching up the corners of her mouth. "Thanks for the juice," she said, reaching for the glass. She drank slowly, purposely spilling some of it down her chest.

DeCicco watched, transfixed, as thin rivulets of the icy, orange liquid trickled over the young woman's breasts and hardened her nipples.

Patricia flicked her tongue around the edge of the glass then sucked the remaining ice cube into her mouth. Setting the glass on the deck, she tugged at the waistband of DeCicco's shorts. "You look warm, Frank," she said, first gazing dreamily at DeCicco's groin, then up at his face. "And I've got just the thing to cool you off," she purred.

* * *

By Monday morning the skies over Long Island were darkening and DeCicco was growing restless. They had spent most of the weekend in bed, punctuated by brief interludes on the deck or in the dunes. And although their lovemaking had been raw and almost ruthless in its intensity, DeCicco had become tired of the young woman. At times, she seemed insatiable. Young and more than desirable, Patricia Laidlaw was any eighteen-year-old's fantasy, but for someone with considerably more notches on his belt, the initial flattery was soon replaced by boredom.

Large raindrops started to splatter against the windshield of the red Maserati as DeCicco leaned into the window and kissed Patricia Laidlaw good-bye.

"When can I see you again?" she asked breathlessly as their lips parted.

"Whenever you're back out here," replied DeCicco cavalierly.

"It can't be until Friday," she said. "I'm taking some courses at the New School during the week."

DeCicco paused for a moment, assessing his possible opportunities for the weekend. "Why not?" he answered, deciding to go with a sure thing. "Let's make it Friday." Suddenly he heard the insistent chirp of the phone in the beach house.

"And if I can get away sooner?" she asked.

"Call me first. I may have a meeting in the city this week and could be late getting back," he lied. The telephone continued to ring. "I've really got to get that," he said, edging back slowly toward the house. "I didn't turn on the damn answering machine."

"Then I'll see you Friday," she shouted as she revved the car's engine.

"Right, Friday," he said. He waved as Patricia put the car in gear and spun the small, fiery-red coupe out of the driveway. As DeCicco sprinted up the front steps to the house, he realized that in the two days they had

been together he had learned very little about Patricia
Laidlaw. But what was there to know? he wondered.
Wasn't she just another spoiled rich kid out for a
good time? Anyway, the sex had been good, he con-
cluded, and it was something to look forward to on
Friday.

Once inside he snatched the receiver off the phone
on the kitchen wall. "Hello," he said, struggling to
catch his breath.

"Frank, this is Jessica," said the voice at the other end
of the line. "How's the vacation going?"

"Relaxing, Jess, very relaxing," DeCicco replied as
he stared out the window and watched the Maserati
disappear down Dune Road.

"Then I'm sorry I have to ask this favor."

"Don't be ridiculous, Jess. We're friends. Ask away."

"Do you think you could come into the city on
Wednesday?"

"No problem. What's up?"

"Marty Green has scheduled me for an interview
with a sports reporter from the *Daily News,* and I'd like
you to be here with me."

"Who's the reporter?" DeCicco asked suspiciously,
knowing Marty Green's penchant for pairing players
and staff with ambitious reporters and hoping for the
"big splash" story.

"Daniel DiNome," answered Jessica.

"What time's the interview?"

"At two, in the conference room."

"I'll meet you there at noon, so we can talk first."

"Come on, Frank. Who is this guy?" Jessica asked
uneasily.

"The man who once compared the owner of the
Miami franchise to naval lint."

"Dear God . . . What has Marty gotten me into?"

"Don't worry, Jess. It'll be a cakewalk," answered
DeCicco calmly. "You should have absolutely no trouble with this guy. One, you're a lawyer. Two, you'll have

me there coaching you. And three . . . three? Maybe
you should think about firing Marty Green."

Danny DiNome sat in Mark's outer office reading a
dog-eared copy of Shaw's *Man and Superman* and
chewing on a toothpick. Although one of the highest-
paid sports reporters in New York, he looked as bat-
tered as his volume of Shaw. His suit, a tan lightweight
Brooks Brothers affair, looked slept in, the shiny lapels
and elbows underscoring years of wear. He had pale
white skin made even fairer by a massive head of dark
hair which slid down his forehead and dangled in front
of his wire-rim glasses each time he turned a page. A
frayed pink button-down shirt, a pair of scuffed leather
deck shoes, and the absence of socks, topped off this
well-aged collegian's image.

The missing socks aside, DiNome was a premier
reporter. Strongly opinionated, with a rapier wit and
limitless ingenuity, he was one of the new breed of
writers who were changing the face of sports journalism in New York.

Recently DiNome, in his inimitable style, had begun
to focus his attention on the arrogance and mismanage-
ment of team owners. The series had been lavishly
promoted by the paper. And DiNome's opening salvo
against the owner of one of New York's baseball teams,
published under the title "Raping the Public: A Team
Owner's Guide to Fun," resulted in more than an
increase in newsstand sales. DiNome was banned from
the Bronx stadium indefinitely.

In response to this affront to his first-amendment
rights, the plucky reporter had outfitted a twenty-foot
Winnebago with food, drink, and half a dozen stunning
female acquaintances, and parked it just outside the
players' entrance to the stadium. He called it "The
Daily News First Amendment Freedom Van and Taco
Parlor," and offered "an atmosphere of unrivaled
self-indulgence" for the post-game interviewee.

The widespread publicity over the stunt prompted a reconciliation, and so, barely two weeks after DiNome's hospitality suite rolled into the stadium parking lot, he was back in the press box bumming cigarettes.

Shortly after two, Jessica emerged from Mark's office and greeted Danny DiNome. She had been warned by Frank about the schoolboy demeanor and combative reputation, and so was quite at ease as she ushered him through Mark's office and into the conference room just off it.

Nothing had been changed in Mark's office since his death. Jessica had insisted on it. She had also made it clear that in the future all team business that involved her would be conducted in the conference room. It was as though the large office was still Mark's domain and, as his surrogate and not successor, she had no rights to it.

A row of windows masked by sheer draperies cast a diffuse light around the narrow room. Jessica and Danny DiNome took seats at the far end of the long, elliptical oak table and were immediately joined, as if on cue, by Frank DeCicco.

As the interview began, DiNome was plainly leery of Jessica's good intentions. Her short speech at the Arena several months earlier had only proved to him that she could effectively memorize lines. His true measure of her would come in the next hour or hour and a half. His questions, sometimes probing, in many cases abrasive, were met with candor tempered with a fierce concern for Mark's memory and her own personal privacy. At the outset Jessica had impressed on DiNome that she would discuss anything bearing on the team, but he constantly tried to press the limits of this one ground rule.

"With the challenge to your husband's will by your stepchildren," DiNome said, beginning his next question, "don't you foresee a lengthy period of instability for the Knights?"

"Frankly, Mr. DiNome, I don't," replied Jessica. "Within the next ten days we intend to petition the court to appoint an administrator for the team. Someone with an expert knowledge of the game, who has the respect and confidence of both sides."

DiNome noticed the look of surprise on Frank DeCicco's face. Clearly, he thought, this lady keeps her own confidences. "Would you care to mention any of those up for consideration?" he asked, turning his attention back to Jessica.

"I don't really think this is the appropriate forum for such a discussion," she replied. "After all, the naming of an administrator is a part of a judicial procedure. However, I could call you," added Jessica, leaving open the door to a future exclusive, "when we have the approval from the court. Would that be fair enough, Mr. DiNome?"

"If that's as good as I'm going to get."

"It is."

"Then I'll just have to wait for your call, Mrs. Laidlaw," said DiNome, graciously accepting defeat.

With a complete picture of Jessica Laidlaw still eluding him, but satisfied he had enough material for a respectable column, Danny DiNome packed up his tape recorder and note pad and ended the interview. Frank walked him out to the elevators while the two of them made macho small talk. When he returned to the conference room, DeCicco was shaking his head and smiling.

"You know, Jess," he said, plainly delighted with the outcome of the interview, "you don't look like an owner, but you sure as hell sounded and acted like one."

"You think so?" she asked.

"No question."

"Good. Jonathan and I hope positive comments in the sports press will strengthen our case."

"Speaking of which, DiNome tried to pump me for the name of the administrator on the way out," said DeCicco. "Why didn't you tell me about this business before?"

"To avoid having you lie to him," Jessica explained. "You see, Frank, your credibility is very important to me. Because I want you to run the team."

Surprised by the announcement, DeCicco was also quietly relieved that his future would remain in his own hands. Mark's ultimatum was now just an unpleasant memory. "I'm flattered, Jess," he replied modestly.

"Don't be, Frank. You and I both know you're the only logical choice. You were the person closest to Mark in the organization, and you'll provide valuable continuity for the players and the public. And besides," she added, "you're the only one I trust."

The room dimmed dramatically as an errant cloud momentarily blotted out the western sun.

"The only problem we have now is getting Douglas and Patricia to accept you as administrator," said Jessica pessimistically. "And after what happened in Jonathan's office, I think it's going to take some hard-nosed negotiating to win them over."

"I don't think so," Frank replied. "Douglas may have a short fuse, but I don't think he's stupid. He's got to know a winning team is worth more on the auction block than one dragging around last place. That much he has to have learned from his father."

"And Patricia?"

"I don't understand her at all," he answered, thinking back to the past weekend. "But somehow I feel certain she'll follow her brother's lead."

"I wish I could share your optimism."

"Why don't we work on that over dinner? We'll celebrate your victory over Danny DiNome and your emergence as an owner."

"Aren't we jumping the gun?" Jessica asked skeptically. "The man hasn't written a word yet."

"Trust me. He'll sing your praises." Just then a gust of wind nudged the wayward cloud along and the room flooded with sunlight. "You see," he teased, pointing out the window, "a sign from God."

"Never mind me," she replied. "Let's just hope the good Lord starts singing your praises into my stepchildren's ears."

"Don't worry, Jess. I'm sure he will."

"Harder, harder," Patricia growled as she dug her nails into Frank DeCicco's back. Thin red trails scored his flesh and tiny welts covered his neck where her lips had been. The bed rocked noisily, and the moonlight, disrupted by the fluttering curtains, darted around them. The whole room seemed convulsed by their frenzied lovemaking.

DeCicco pounded into the young woman, his large hands spread across her behind, holding her tightly against him.

"Oh, Jesus!" the girl cried as wave after wave of passion swept over her. "It's so *good!*" Arching her back, she raised herself off the bed and wrapped her arms around DeCicco. Within seconds he began to shake and make low-pitched, animal-like sounds, his body racked by a shattering orgasm.

Lying in the crook of DeCicco's arm, Patricia watched curiously as a drop of perspiration maneuvered through the thickly matted hair on his chest. Then, just as it was about to plummet onto the sheets, she reached up and blotted it with her fingertips.

"Before I left the city today I found out she's petitioned the court to have you run the team," said Patricia impassively. "So I take it you haven't told her about us."

"How do you feel about that?"

"What? . . . That she wants you to run the team or that you haven't told her you're fucking her stepdaughter?"

"Don't be ridiculous. You know what I mean."

"Frankly, I don't give a shit," Patricia replied as she reached for a cigarette on the night table. "You want the truth? The ugliness between my parents has left me so numb, I play with fire to find out if I'm still alive. And let's face it, playing with you is playing with fire, but that's my thing." She lit a cigarette and followed the smoke as it spiraled up toward the ceiling. "Douglas's thing is the challenge to Daddy's will. I'm just along for the ride. Nothing personal, Frank," she added, turning back to DeCicco, "but I don't care if you're named administrator or pope."

"And what about Douglas?" he asked. "What does he care about?"

"Douglas believes in self-interest," she answered dryly, "and that's why he's going to agree to let you run the team while we're contesting the will. He knows you're going to work your ass off for a winning season because that's the only way you're going to prove yourself to either side. . . . Now, if you wouldn't mind getting me some tissues, you're beginning to ooze out of me."

DeCicco crawled dutifully out of bed and walked into the bathroom, more convinced than ever that he could broker both sides of this mess and still come out the winner. All he really had to do, he reasoned, was smooth a few ruffled egos and avoid tripping over the thin line between ambition and success. He had done it as a player and was certain he could do it again. Before leaving the bathroom, he rinsed his mouth, then tore a wad of toilet paper off the roll and strolled back into the bedroom.

Chapter 29

Julie was married at the end of July. It was a balmy Saturday evening. A string of hot, sticky, ninety-degree days had been broken by violent thunderstorms the night before and had left everyone in a festive spirit. Over the western shore of the Hudson River the sky was draped with varying shades of red and orange. A large motor yacht cruised up the river toward the George Washington Bridge. On the aft deck, festooned with white roses dyed magenta by the sunset, in the presence of family and friends, Julie and Ron Cogan exchanged wedding vows.

After the ceremony Jessica, Meredith, and Liz politely elbowed their way past the buffet table and ensconced themselves in a corner of the luxurious main salon with a bottle of champagne.

"Do you believe that dress!" exclaimed Liz as she filled their glasses. "She must have cornered the market on lace and seed pearls."

"Well, I'm furious," snipped Meredith sarcastically.

"I think she had some nerve finding something that gorgeous without asking for my help."

"Relax, Meredith," Jessica replied, "it was her mother's."

"And did you see her mother?" asked Liz.

"Like I could miss someone fifty-eight and breathtakingly beautiful," Meredith said enviously. "When I'm that age I would just like to be referred to as presentable."

"With luck and advances in plastic surgery, darling, that shouldn't be a problem," replied Liz cattily.

"Thank you for that vote of confidence, Liz darling," said Meredith, raising her glass in a mock toast. "Oh, by the way, Jess, some nasty little messenger dropped a copy of Wednesday's *Daily News* on my desk and I just happened to read an article about you in the sports section."

"You just happened to read Wednesday's sports section?" said Jessica, exchanging doubting looks with Liz.

"Right."

"And?" asked Jessica.

"And frankly, I was impressed. I had no idea you knew anything about running a basketball team," said Meredith.

"Let's just say I'm learning very quickly."

"You must be, to get such a glowing review," chimed in Liz, "because the people I know who know sports say Danny DiNome usually shows no quarter when it comes to team owners."

"Remember, I don't own the team yet."

"Maybe she just wore some sexy Armani suit and simply charmed the hell out of him," said Meredith. "You know, from his picture in the paper he looks really kind of attractive."

"Forget it, Meredith," warned Jessica, "from the neck down Danny DiNome looks like the aftermath of an explosion at Brooks Brothers."

When the champagne bottle was exhausted, Jessica left her friends and went up to the bow of the boat for some fresh air. The sun had set, and the air, washed clean by yesterday's rain, felt cool and crisp against her skin. Jessica closed her eyes and listened to the music drifting up from the fantail. For an instant she was transported to the bow of another boat in what seemed another lifetime. Overhead the sky was a blanket of stars, each one more brilliant than the other. Suddenly, in this netherworld of memories, Jessica sensed the presence of someone standing close to her. She turned and opened her eyes and saw a tall figure in the shadows. For an instant the past and present merged, causing her to gasp as the figure stepped into the light in front of her.

"I'm terribly sorry if I've startled you," said the man, his clipped English accent drawing the curtain on her fantasy. "I guess we both had the same idea."

"Excuse me?" replied Jessica shakily.

"To get away from the crowd and get some air," he answered.

"Oh, yes."

"Actually, that's not true."

"It isn't?" said Jessica, curious about this unusual man. "I thought that's why I came up here."

"Well, what I mean is," he confessed nervously, "I followed you up here."

"Did you?"

"You see, I've been watching you all evening . . . That doesn't sound very good, does it?" he said, interrupting himself.

"Not very," Jessica replied sympathetically. "By the way, should I be afraid of you?"

"Oh, my goodness no." The fair-haired man pushed his oversized tortoiseshell glasses back against the bridge of his nose. Normally self-assured, he began to feel dreadfully foolish. But what he had said was the truth. He hadn't been able to take his eyes off Jessica from the moment he saw her step out of the Mercedes in that pale chiffon dress. Radiant in the evening light, she immediately became the focus of his attention.

"In fact," he continued, "I'm really quite harmless. Honestly, I couldn't help noticing you. Everyone here seems to know you, and since I don't know anyone besides the bride and groom and a few of Ron's actor friends, I thought it important that we meet," he said with an inviting smile. "I'm Alton Shea."

"The producer?"

"Yes," he replied, flattered that she recognized his name.

"Well then, Mr. Shea," said Jessica, buoyed by the brisk night air and the champagne, "considering your situation and that I'm reasonably certain you're not an axe murderer, I feel it's my duty as a friend of the masses to meet you. I'm Jessica Laidlaw," she concluded, extending her hand.

A half hour later they moved inside to the forward lounge to escape the stiff wind that had begun to sweep down the Hudson. A vibrantly patterned modular sofa snaked around the coral and white cabin at the front of the boat. Except for two of Ronnie Cogan's maiden aunts, who had grown tired of the noise in the main salon, the lounge was empty. Jessica and Alton Shea sat across from each other at a bend in the couch and continued their conversation.

Although thirty-eight, Alton Shea looked forty-five. But he had the energy and vitality of a twenty-year-old. An attractive man, he was tremendously self-confident. His charm, wit, and intelligence—qualities lost on an era devoted to style—revealed him to be totally without arrogance or pomposity.

". . . so, decked out in heavy tweeds, I was packed off to Cambridge," he told her as they exchanged life stories. "Even after three generations of Bernsteins had lived and prospered in England, my parents were still worried about our fitting in. At Cambridge they'd hoped I'd cultivate old school ties and become part of the ruling elite. I did, but I think I took it too far when I came home to announce that David Bernstein had decided to become Alton Shea."

"And where on earth did you get the name Alton Shea?"

"My father's tailor. A lovely man, really. Yes, well," he stammered, trying to regain his original train of thought. "I was staging a modern dress version of *Richard the Third* at my college at the time. A simply ruinous production, as I remember it. Anyway, I was quite taken with myself and thought that David Bernstein on the program sounded much too much like some crass American motion-picture mogul, so that's when I decided to become a bespoke producer."

"And what did the real Alton Shea have to say about all this?" asked Jessica.

"I'm not sure I follow you."

"I guess what I mean is, what did he think of his namesake's success?"

"Sadly, I never found out," Shea replied. "The true Mr. Shea died before his name ever appeared on a theatre marquee."

It was only after the yacht began to nudge the creaking pier that the two realized how much time they had spent together. Alton Shea had found Jessica utterly captivating. In his circles, a beautiful woman with her honesty and lack of pretense was a rare if not impossible find. And for the first time since Mark's death Jessica felt comfortable with a man, able to talk and joke without the horrible specter of guilt or shame. But that soon ended when an awkward silence, prompted by the departure of Ron's maiden aunts, was followed by an unintentionally awkward question.

"Jessica, I would very much like to see you again.

Would you have dinner with me tomorrow night?"
Shea asked cautiously, as though he knew he was
risking any chance of seeing her again.

His question unleashed a sudden rush of memories
and conflicting emotions, leaving Jessica incapable or
unwilling to repress them. "I'm sorry, Alton," Jessica
replied soberly. "It's just not possible."

"Perhaps another time, then," he answered, realizing their moment together had come to an end.

"Yes," she said softly, "maybe another time."

They shook hands politely at the gangway, then
Alton Shea walked down to the pier to a waiting taxi.

"Wasn't that . . ." whispered Meredith as she approached Jessica by the railing.

"David Bernstein?" Jessica replied as she watched
him get into the cab. "Yes, it was."

"I was going to say Alton Shea," Meredith added
impatiently. "Who is David Bernstein?"

"Just a very nice man," Jessica mused out loud. She
turned back to her friend as the cab drove off, anticipating an unending stream of questions. "Meredith,
don't say another word, and I'll give you a lift home.
Open your mouth, and I'll have Billy run you over."

Chapter 30

Walter Nealy parked the patrol car at the edge of a shadowy tree line twenty yards from the northbound side of the Garden State Parkway. Before switching off his headlights he made sure the radar gun over his shoulder had a clear view of the oncoming traffic. Then he rolled up his window and checked his watch.

It was almost one-thirty, which meant he had six more hours on this shift. Then it was a week off followed by a welcome return to days. For most of the summer he had languished on the graveyard shift, monitoring the early morning traffic heading back and forth from the auto plant in Mahwah, and on Mondays catching the weekend stragglers speeding back to New York City. But now that Labor Day had come and gone and the work on the Tappan Zee Bridge was completed, the stragglers had disappeared and the highway was deserted till six.

Nealy was listening to some idle chatter on the police radio when the white Corvette rocketed past him.

Instinctively, he spun the police cruiser out onto the highway, then quickly glanced down at the radar control box mounted on the dash. The red digital display read eighty but began making incremental leaps of five as soon as he switched on the rooftop flashers.

The northern New Jersey countryside flew by as the police car picked up speed. In the distance Nealy could see the Corvette's taillights flickering as the car sliced through a series of sharp S-curves. He radioed the chase into the substation dispatcher, who, in turn, relayed the message to a second car four miles farther north.

A quarter mile from the Ridgewood Toll Plaza, the cruiser and the Corvette, both traveling around a hundred miles an hour, were still at least twenty car lengths apart. Hoping to alert the clerks and possibly slow the driver, Nealy flipped on his siren. But to the trooper's surprise, the Corvette accelerated. Nealy gradually eased up on the gas pedal, anticipating a roadblock and a pile of twisted, burning metal on the other side of the rise.

Ahead of him at the toll plaza Nealy could see the white Corvette stopped in front of a line of police cars and maintenance vehicles, their blue and amber lights cutting through the darkness. He pulled up behind the white sports car, drew his service revolver, then, using the car door as cover, slid out of the cruiser. Craning his head over the door, Nealy peered into the rear window of the Corvette. The driver, a large black man in his mid-twenties, apparently unconcerned or un-aware of his situation, was beating furiously on the steering wheel, as though keeping time to some obscure tune running through his head.

Nealy felt his heart begin to pound inside his chest. He grabbed the radio microphone off the front seat. "You, inside the car," he said, his voice booming from the bullhorn atop the patrol car. "This is the police.

Step out of the car slowly and put your hands on the roof."

It was late in the afternoon when Frank DeCicco got the message to call Marty Green in New York. He had been trapped in Miami Beach since Saturday for a league meeting, and by Monday his patience was growing thin. On this last day of the conference he had found himself mired in a fruitless discussion over salary caps with some of the more shortsighted owners, so he was grateful for the excuse to make an early exit.

"Fuck his agent, Marty," DeCicco shouted as he paced back and forth in his suite, the telephone receiver glued to his ear. "The bastard'll just screw things up. The way I see it, the kid's our responsibility. After all, the dumb shit called us first . . . What time did Krumholtz get him out of the Jersey lockup?"

"Around noon," Marty Green answered from New York.

"And where is he now?"

"At home."

"Fine. Now here's what we've got to do to contain this thing," said DeCicco. "First, I want you to get him into a detox program. And I don't mean some place that's going to slap him on the wrist. I want a place with a good track record. And I want him in there fast . . . I don't care what it takes, Marty. I want that kid repentant, reformed, and ready to play by the first week in October."

"I'll get right on it, Frank."

"Look, Marty, I don't think I have to tell you your business," DeCicco warned his press aide, "but let's remember to be entirely open about this thing with the press. Impress upon them that we still have great faith in Johnstone. And that a young, unsophisticated kid like him is certainly entitled to one error in judgment."

"Don't worry, Frank. I'll handle it," Green assured him.

"You'd better, Marty. Or both our asses are in a sling. You know, I may be running the team now, but I've still got three would-be owners and their lawyers breathing down my neck."

"I understand, Frank."

"Good. Then I'll see you tomorrow morning . . . Oh, my love to Deborah and the kids." DeCicco put down the phone and stared out the window. Out at sea a tropical storm was moving up the coast, the sky a swirling, impenetrable mass of gray and black clouds. The ominous weather convinced him that now was the time to get back to New York. He needed to tie down a few loose ends to ride out the impending storm.

By seven o'clock that evening DeCicco had returned to New York. By eight he was having drinks with Jessica in the small formal garden at the rear of the town house.

"I appreciate your coming over, Frank," said Jessica. "I know you just got in from Florida."

"No problem, Jess," DeCicco answered affably. "It's all part of the service. Anyway, I thought you should get your information on this business firsthand."

"Okay. Tell me what happens to Johnstone now. Are you going to lose him for the season?"

"Not for a first offense," replied DeCicco. "The kid's going to have to plead guilty to the speeding and driving-while-impaired charges, then agree to voluntarily enter a recognized substance-abuse program. That should satisfy the court and the league. As for us," he continued, "we simply have to hope this experience sinks in. Two more positive drug tests and Johnstone is going to have to work for a living." DeCicco finished his drink and set the glass on the white wrought-iron table. "The way I figure it, the kid got off lucky. He didn't kill himself or anyone else. We're going to get him into a good detox program. *And* I wasn't in town to beat his ever-loving brains in."

Jessica grinned. She liked Frank DeCicco's streetwise banter. It reminded her of the wisecracking New York toughs who inhabited the movies her father used to watch over and over again on television while she was growing up. Oddly enough, Frank's blue-collar dialect was as contrived as many of those old movies. Mark had once explained to Jessica that DeCicco, a middle-class kid from Long Island, perfected the accent so he could get into pickup games on Manhattan playgrounds after sneaking into the city from Oyster Bay. But that didn't seem to matter to Jessica. The flattened vowels and missing G's were familiar to her and made her feel an integral part of something that the rest of the country publicly condemned and secretly envied—life in New York.

Frank DeCicco stood up and clapped his hands together. "Okay," he said, "the basketball lecture is over. Now we go eat."

"Come on, Frank. You don't have to do this," replied Jessica. "You must be exhausted."

"Who's tired?" he answered. "Besides, I'll take us to a place where the owner will wait on us hand and foot."

"Great. Then, you're on."

They ate at Spoleto—DeCicco's restaurant—which had been closed for a month for renovation and was set to reopen the following night. DeCicco sat Jessica on a tall stool in a corner of the empty kitchen as he began the preparations for their dinner. Onions, garlic, and tomatoes quickly fell victim to DeCicco's masterful and hitherto secret knife-wielding ability. A few handfuls of flour and an egg were soon transformed into delicate strands of angel hair pasta while wild mushrooms and heavy cream were spun into a sauce. Jessica watched in awe as various sliced, slivered, and pounded ingredients flew from the worktable to the stove and, finally, to the dinner plate.

"Frank, where on earth did you learn to cook like

this?" asked Jessica as she stabbed at the last bit of veal on her plate.

"College," DeCicco replied. He reached across the wooden countertop for the bottle of prosecco he had left balanced against the edge of the ice bucket and refilled their glasses. "I wanted to impress a girl who wasn't impressed by basketball players."

"And?"

"So I read a few cookbooks and watched a few episodes of Julia Child and cooked us dinner," answered DeCicco casually.

"No, I meant how was your date?" Jessica said, her curiosity piqued by his offhand attitude.

"It's funny how those things stick in your mind," he replied. "All I remember was that she really didn't measure up to the effort."

"Well, so much for romance," Jessica said scornfully, then downed her glass of wine.

"Lighten up, Jess . . . at least something good came out of it."

"Yes, and what was that?"

"I learned how to cook and she got a decent meal."

"Since I just enjoyed the fruits of that disappointing evening," she replied apologetically, "I should be the last one to complain."

Jessica helped Frank clear away the dishes and clean up the kitchen. Then he drove her home. It was eleven-thirty by the time DeCicco's gray BMW pulled up in front of the Seventy-fifth Street town house.

"Dinner was lovely, Frank," Jessica said. "It was a real surprise. Thank you." She leaned toward DeCicco to kiss him on the cheek, but he suddenly turned his head and intercepted her kiss. He pressed his lips against hers with an urgency and restlessness that frightened her. "Please, Frank, don't," she gasped, pulling away from him.

"Why, Jess?" replied DeCicco, baffled by her reaction. "I thought there was something special between us."

"There is, Frank . . . a special friendship," she added compassionately.

"Friendships can change, Jess . . . can become even more meaningful."

"And *still* stay friendships," Jessica reminded him. "Please try to understand, Frank, it's just too soon for me to think about anyone else. My life is too complicated right now, and that's why I want to keep what we have. I know this may sound selfish, but I need you as a friend."

DeCicco's mind began to race. He realized he had made a terrible miscalculation that could cost him Jessica's confidence forever. "You know, it's going to be hard to change the way I feel about you," he confessed.

"I realize that, Frank, but it's important for both of us that . . ." Jessica paused, searching for some conciliatory phrase.

"This doesn't go any further?" interrupted DeCicco, retreating under the cover of his wounded pride.

"Yes. That this doesn't go any further," she repeated softly. She reached over and touched his hand. "I think I'd better go in."

An oppressive silence hung over the two as DeCicco walked Jessica to the front door. He felt an overpowering need to break through it and reestablish some of what he had lost moments earlier. "Well, then we'll just have to be friends," he said judiciously.

"Thank you, Frank," Jessica answered. "That means a lot to me."

Back in the car DeCicco glanced up at the red-brick facade as the lights went on in the upper floors of the town house. It had been a long day and he was tired. He had forgotten his own rules, and it had almost cost him everything. Angrily, he slammed his hand against the steering wheel. Patience, he thought. Have a little goddamn patience and eventually even she will come around.

From the hall Jessica could see the light by her bed and the nightgown laid out over the turned-down coverlet. Since Mark's death Emma had watched over her like a mother hen, trying, these long months, to restore order and security to the young widow's life and to keep the house running smoothly. She had succeeded. The house had become Jessica's sanctuary, the one place she could ward off the terrors of the outside world and feel safe from harm. But tonight the walls had been breached. DeCicco, intentionally or not, had churned up a witches' brew of emotions. Betrayal, guilt, sorrow—feelings she thought she had put behind her—were now threatening to overwhelm her.

Jessica walked slowly into the bedroom and sat down on the edge of the bed. For comfort or reassurance she reached for one of the two large pillows by her side and drew it to her chest. The perfumed scent of the small white tea roses in the crystal vase on the nightstand recalled another time, and her mind began to drift. Somewhere deep within the depths of her memory a little girl was crying, alone and afraid. Soon that fear and loneliness were no longer a memory and Jessica began to sob uncontrollably. "Oh, Mark," she cried out, "I miss you so much."

Chapter 31

In the morning Jessica had begun constructing simple rationales for DeCicco's behavior and her reaction to it. Looking back on it four days later, the incident seemed merely a minor misunderstanding. She had entrusted DeCicco with Mark's dream, and was determined not to do or say anything that would jeopardize it. The Johnstone business had been carefully managed, and the Knights' organization was readying itself for October's training camp, all of which left Jessica with little doubt about DeCicco's importance.

She was in her office at Turner, Welles, reviewing the team's financial statement, when her secretary buzzed her on the intercom.

"Ms. Wheeler, there's a Mr. Alton Shea on line one."

"Thank you, Lois," Jessica replied. At first pleased and then uneasy, she hesitated before pushing the green light on the phone. "Alton, how are you?" she said, after two deep breaths. As she waited for his answer she could hear her voice echoing down the line. Oh, the many dividends of deregulation, she thought.

"Just fine, Jessica. And you?"

"Getting by," she shouted, trying to make herself heard over the intolerable echo. "Alton, can I call you back?" she asked. "We seem to have a bad connection."

"I'm really not sure," Shea answered. "Could you hold a minute?"

In the background Jessica could hear a woman responding in clipped, measured tones to Alton Shea's questions.

"No, I'm sorry, Jessica," he said, coming back on the line. "I'm afraid that isn't possible."

"Alton, where are you?"

"In fact, I'm not quite sure about that either," he replied with mannered British distraction. "Just one moment." Again he began to confer with his mysterious female companion. "Jessica, are you still there?"

"Yes, Alton," she answered, amused by his controlled lunacy.

"Three hundred miles southwest of Greenland."

"Heading toward or away from New York?" asked Jessica, as though the madness were contagious.

"Toward New York, certainly," he said, sounding almost indignant. "That's why I'm calling. We're scheduled to land around five-thirty and I was wondering if tonight could be that 'another time.'"

"Another time?"

"The 'another time' we spoke about at the Cogans' wedding," he reminded her.

"Oh, you mean dinner."

"Or any other meal of your choosing within the next twelve to eighteen hours."

Perhaps it was because of the bright, sunny weather, or because she felt serendipitous, or simply because she remembered he had green eyes. Whatever it was, Jessica decided to accept Alton Shea's invitation.

"Marvelous," he said, barely able to contain his elation. "I'll pick you up around eight. Now if you—"

"Don't you want the address?" she interrupted.

"Already have it."

"You do?"

"Yes. Got it from Ron and Julie yesterday."

"That was very resourceful of you, and also very optimistic."

"I can't help it. It's genetic . . . Now, can I ask a favor of you?"

"That depends on the favor," Jessica answered with feigned suspicion.

"Could you make the reservations for dinner?" he asked sheepishly. "I don't want to take up any more time on the phone," he added in a whisper, "some of the Americans on this queue are getting quite surly."

"You know, Mr. Shea, you are a very strange man."

Le Bernadin's blue-gray walls, polished moldings, subdued lighting, and tables set discreet distances from one another, provided the perfect setting for the chef's seafood specialties. A small army of well-appointed captains, waiters, and busboys assisted in their presentation.

Jessica and Alton Shea sat beneath a large nineteenth-century oil of a Breton fishmonger and his wares. With a small silver spoon Jessica avidly scooped up tiny, glistening beads of caviar as Alton Shea marveled at her dexterity.

"I really am sorry," said Jessica, trying to sound sympathetic. "But you're from a country surrounded by water. How could I know you'd be allergic to seafood?"

"It's not all seafood, actually. Just shellfish. The rest is just a general aversion to slippery things," he said, munching on a crust of bread. "Didn't I mention my eastern European roots? . . . Frankly, I'm not sure the whole thing isn't some divine retribution for changing my name or, at worst, for popping down the odd banger at breakfast."

Jessica felt relaxed around Alton Shea. His sense of humor and spontaneity threw her delightfully off balance. He was life viewed from a new perspective, with childlike wonderment and boundless enthusiasm.

Between the coffee and the crème brûlée their conversation turned to their past relationships. Alton had been married for six years to a celebrated English actress who, after a messy divorce, had gone to live in Hollywood with "a short but very intense American movie star of Italian extraction." As Shea went on to describe them, the two were now "frolicking in the sunshine and making 'important' made-for-television movies."

"You sound bitter," said Jessica.

"I tend to think of it more as clinical disappointment," he replied dispassionately. "There was a lot of ego invested in our marriage, and when it ended, I had hoped she would have traded up, not down."

"Down meaning . . ."

"California, television, and small, swarthy men."

"Is that how you felt when she left you? Glib?" Jessica asked.

"Touché." He winced. Her question had hit a nerve.

"I'm sorry, Alton. I didn't mean to pry."

"It's my fault, really. I keep forgetting the American penchant for candor." Looking across the table at Jessica, he suddenly felt compelled to shed his British reserve and answer her question honestly. It was as though his reply would cement some bond between them.

"Actually, I felt numb at first," he said, quietly recalling the moment. "Then angry. Angry with her for leaving me, and angry with myself for not seeing it coming and doing nothing to stop her. Now I know that she was fighting for her emotional survival, and living with me was making that impossible. When you think about it, she probably did the right thing." He raised his coffee cup to his lips to cover his pained expression. "How did you feel when Mark died?" he asked her as he set the cup down.

"The same way," Jessica answered, surprised she was no longer uneasy about discussing these feelings with a man. "First numb, then abandoned and angry. But I've had nowhere to channel that anger. Mark's gone and though I've tried, I can't take it out on his memory."

"What about his children? They've given you every reason to unleash your wrath in their direction."

"At the beginning, yes. But the lawsuit is their reaction to what they saw as Mark's neglect and failure as a father," explained Jessica. "It's their anger, not mine. I'm trying to redirect what I felt, turn it into something more constructive."

"And have you worked that out yet?"

"I think so, but I haven't talked with anyone about it."

"And you don't have to discuss it with me, if you don't want to," he reassured her.

"But I'd like to," she said. "You may be the one person I know who will understand what I want to do. Alton, I want to run the Knights, turn the team around and fulfill my husband's dream."

"I'm not very familiar with professional sports in the States, but that sounds like quite an undertaking."

"Alton, I know I can do this," Jessica said confidently.

"Then, my dear, I suggest that you do it."

His words, unwavering and unequivocal in their support, were the words she wanted and needed to hear. Jessica reached across the table and took Alton Shea's hand. He had roused a spirit deep within her, reconfirming her belief in herself and her willingness to risk her emotions again.

Chapter 32

The preseason schedule brought the Knights to Los Angeles the last Friday in October. It was part of a three-city road tour that had already left two rookies sidelined and one veteran questioning his ability to make it through another season. Frank DeCicco had joined the team in Los Angeles, ostensibly to bolster his veteran's flagging resolve. In truth, he had come the three thousand miles in response to a polite summons.

Late that night DeCicco's rented car slowly wound up one of the narrow roads that threaded through the Hollywood Hills, a dimly lit neighborhood of speakeasy facades that masked mortal sins and madness. After a twenty minute search, DeCicco finally found the right address. He parked the car in front of a small, gray clapboard house whose front door, but for the intercession of an insignificant concrete step, would have opened directly onto the roadway.

As DeCicco got out of the car he could see Douglas

Laidlaw in blue jeans and a white pinstriped shirt framed in the doorway.

"I'm glad you could make it, Frank. I hope it wasn't too difficult to find," Douglas said, gesturing toward the inside of the house. "Come on in and I'll fix you a drink."

From the street the size of the house was deceptive. Wedged between the road and a hillside, it appeared more like the afterthought of a greedy builder than a home. Yet once inside, the layout of the rooms made it seem almost spacious; each room flowed into the other, creating the illusion. Douglas led DeCicco into the living room, where the creamy white floor, sparse Bauhaus furnishings, and glowing fireplace gave off an air of crisp elegance.

"Please sit down, Frank," Douglas said courteously. "Now, what can I get you to drink?"

"A small scotch will be fine. No ice," he answered. As Douglas left the room and went into the kitchen, DeCicco did a quick survey of his surroundings. The modesty and simplicity amazed him. He had expected youthful extravagance—a large house, a swimming pool, the usual trappings of mindless wealth—but instead found maturity and taste. This discovery only served to complicate his previous assessment of Douglas.

"Tell me, Frank," Douglas shouted from the kitchen, "how did you do tonight?"

"We lost, 123–110. Our defense collapsed in the third period," DeCicco yelled back.

Moments later Douglas reappeared with two drinks and joined DeCicco by the fire.

"First thing I want to do is to apologize for the scene in Jonathan Lambert's office," Douglas said, with just the proper blend of humility and contrition. "There was no excuse for the way I lashed out at you."

"Believe me, Douglas, it's forgotten," replied DeCicco magnanimously. He sampled the scotch,

whirling the smoky, oaken liquid over his tongue.
"Good scotch. Okay, Douglas, what's on your mind?
You didn't ask me up here just for a drink and an
apology."

"I wanted to personally pledge you my support as
general manager," answered Douglas.

"At eleven-thirty at night?" DeCicco responded,
taking another sip of scotch. "Anyway, I understood I
had that support when you agreed to have me named as
administrator."

"Yes, that's true, Frank, but that position is only
going to be a temporary one," Douglas reminded him.
"I've been thinking about something a little more long
term."

"How long?"

Douglas got up, put his glass on the mantle, and
began to jab at the coals with a brass poker. "I was
thinking of a five-year guarantee as president from the
time my sister and I take over as owners," he explained,
his attention still directed to the fire, "with a provision
for renegotiation if you bring in a division championship anytime during the five years."

"You know, Douglas, whether you like it or not, you
really are your father's son."

His face flushed from the fire or DeCicco's remark,
Douglas looked back at his guest, grinning antagonisti-
cally. Then he stood up and dropped the poker noisily
into its stand.

"Don't misunderstand me," added DeCicco tactfully.
"I like what you're saying . . ."

"But."

"But I feel you've overlooked an additional, and
probably more effective, incentive."

"Like what?" asked Douglas coyly, knowing all along
where this was leading.

"Like a percentage of the team."

"Frank, that's taking a giant leap on faith," Douglas

replied. "We could talk about possible ownership options, but why cloud the present with the future?"

"Let's just say it would be nice to know there will *be* a future."

"Trust me, Frank. There will always be a future for you with our Knights."

"And what do you want me to do in return for your support and my future?" asked DeCicco warily.

"Just watch out for our interests."

"What are we talking about now, Douglas? Spying?"

"Please, Frank, let's not be melodramatic," Douglas replied. "Simply keep us informed about what's going on in New York. Stay close to Ms. Wheeler and find out how she intends to fight us. That's all."

"But not too close, lover."

Wearing white shorts and a sleeveless gray sweatshirt, the armholes cut down to her waist, Patricia Laidlaw leaned coquettishly against one of the high-backed chairs in the adjacent dining area, eyeing Frank DeCicco with amusement.

"Douglas, I can't get the Jacuzzi to work," she complained. "There're too many dials and switches."

"There's only three settings and a temperature dial," answered her brother, annoyed by the interruption. "I can't believe you can't figure it out."

"Believe it. I can't," Patricia replied brusquely. "So could you please turn the thing on? I need to unwind . . . You don't want me taking pills again, do you?"

Setting his glass on a small chrome end table, Douglas got up and started out of the room. "I'll just be a minute," he said, turning back to DeCicco. "If I don't do it, she'll probably short-circuit the whole damn thing."

After her brother had moved out of earshot, Patricia walked slowly toward the fireplace, her bare feet making soft slapping sounds on the vinyl tiles.

"You really like to bust your brother's balls, don't

you?" said DeCicco as Patricia sat down cross-legged on the couch across from him.

"I do what I can . . . You know I've missed you," she whispered huskily.

"I told you once training camp began, weekends would be impossible."

"And weekdays, were they impossible too?"

"Weekdays I was stuck down in Princeton," he answered, using his favorite well-worn alibi.

"You're awfully transparent, Frank," Patricia replied indulgently, "but I'll help you make amends. What about tomorrow? We could make up for the lost weekends."

"I'm sorry, Pat. There's a game tomorrow in Portland and I'm flying up with the team," he told her. "Why don't I call you when I get back to New York?"

"You do that, Frank. Only I hope it's before dear, sweet Jessica and I have a long talk," Patricia snapped, her patience with his macho posturing worn thin.

"Do you think that's going to make a difference?"

"It might . . . to some people."

Just then Douglas returned from his struggle with the hot tub, the front of his shirt spotted with water. "It's on," he announced, pushing his sleeves down from his elbows. "Now go unwind."

"Thank you, brother dearest," Patricia answered sarcastically. On her way out she threw a glance at DeCicco. "Good night, Frank. I hope we see each other again soon."

"I'll look forward to it," said DeCicco, manufacturing a weak smile for Douglas's consumption.

Patricia's exit was followed by a brief, uneasy silence. DeCicco stared into the bottom of his empty glass while Douglas retrieved his drink from the end table.

"I think you should know I don't care who she fucks," Douglas said, breaking the silence, "as long as she doesn't fuck up my life. . . . She can be dangerous, you know."

Coming so late, Douglas's warning was worthless. DeCicco was already mired in something that wasn't about to disappear with a quick shower or the ever-popular "I'll call you."

"Look, Douglas, I've really got to get going," replied DeCicco. "It's late and I've got a plane to catch in a couple of hours."

"Well, at least we had our little talk," said Douglas. "I just wanted to be sure we understood each other."

"I think we do," DeCicco replied as the two walked to the front door.

"Oh, I forgot to mention, Frank, there is one thing that I'd like you to do for us."

"And that is?" DeCicco asked.

"Try and win some basketball games. It would make us all very happy."

DeCicco slammed the car door and started the engine. He had underestimated Douglas Laidlaw and had allowed himself to be manipulated. Whether it was their years around their father or their years of analysis, Mark's children certainly knew how to play Freudian hardball. Unfortunately for DeCicco, only time would tell how much of their behavior was calculated and how much of it was chance.

Chapter 33

Two days later Jessica stood in the doorway of Jonathan Lambert's office watching him proofread the galleys for his new book. Pages with red notes scrawled in the margins lay scattered on the floor around him, and others in a dwindling pile in front of him seemed headed for a similar fate. He tore through the manuscript with such gusto that she had second thoughts about interrupting this flurry of activity, but knocked on the doorframe anyway.

"Rachel told me you were free for a few minutes. I was wondering if we could discuss the lawsuit."

With his one hawklike eye, Jonathan looked up at Jessica over the stack of papers. "No problem. Come in and sit down. You'll keep me from reaching my wit's end with this gibberish," he said, leafing through the galley sheets. "After reading this—this tripe ten or eleven times, I keep coming to the oddly reassuring conclusion that artifice and contrivance, although tremendously commercial, always makes for truly lamentable fiction."

"Jonathan, you said that about the last book you wrote, and *it* was nominated for an American Book Award," Jessica reminded him.

"That only obscures the truth."

"Jonathan, you're a literary snob."

"Enough," declared Lambert, grabbing the remaining unread pages and dropping them on the sideboard behind his chair. "Let's talk about your case."

"I want to settle," Jessica announced as though the words had come to her as a divine revelation.

"I think that's best," said Jonathan. "I always felt that Mark had treated the children a bit unfairly in the will, but he was determined to punish them for the way they had treated you."

"I know," she answered softly, remembering Mark's disappointment and frustration.

"In that case, have you given any thought to how you want to approach this?" Jonathan asked, removing Jessica's file from a desk drawer. "Are there any assets that you feel strongly about, that are non-negotiable?"

"Just one."

"The town house, I imagine. I think we can safeguard that; it's your primary residence."

"No. The Knights."

"Christ, Jessica. You can't be serious. What on earth do you want with a basketball team? A *losing* basketball team."

"It was Mark's dream, and now I want to make it mine."

"Believe me, Jessica, the Knights are not a dream," Jonathan insisted. "They're more like a very expensive nightmare."

"Mark never saw it that way," Jessica replied defensively.

"Of course not. The Knights were Mark's mid-life

fling," he argued. "He treated that team like men my age treat their thirty-year-old mistresses. He overpaid for it, doted on it, and never felt the fool when it broke his heart."

"And, if I can complete your metaphor, it also gave him immense pride and a purpose."

"Is that what this is all about?" Jonathan asked doggedly. "You feel you need a purpose to your life?"

"Maybe."

"What about your career? What about your family? You're a young woman. What about enjoying your life?" Jonathan could see he was making little headway, and switched to a different tack. "All right, all right, my concern for your best interests and your 'maybe' aside, what do you know about running a basketball team?"

"I know I can learn and that I can hire the people to teach me," replied Jessica with unwavering determination. "I guess what I want in all this, Jonathan, is not so much your understanding as your support."

"You know you have that," the old man said affectionately.

Suddenly, Jessica felt confident about winning the team. "Yes, I guess I do," she replied.

"Then it's decided. I'll call Michael Rosen tomorrow and see what we can do to get you the Knights."

"Thank you, Jonathan," said Jessica, getting up from her chair. As she started for the door she turned, feeling compelled to ask one last and injudicious question. "Jonathan, there is one more thing."

"Yes?" he said, peering around the side of the desk as he collected the papers strewn about at his feet.

"About those men your age with the thirty-year-old mistresses . . ."

"Ms. Wheeler," Lambert bellowed indignantly, "I believe our business is concluded. Now get out."

Alton Shea threw a party at Sardi's two weeks before Thanksgiving to celebrate the opening of his latest

London import. It was Jessica's first real public appearance as his companion, discounting, of course, their quiet dinners and weekend strolls through Central Park. And she was anxious to make a good impression.

Being catapulted into the electric atmosphere of a Broadway opening was a new experience for her. With Mark, the situations or events had always been controlled, and although his name was well-known, they could still travel around the city with relative anonymity. As a result, Jessica was more than a bit unsettled by the lights and commotion outside Sardi's as she emerged from the limousine on Alton Shea's arm.

On the second floor of the restaurant a handful of television crews and paparazzi maneuvered around the tables, fishing for interviews, offbeat photographs, and new faces among the glitterati. Jessica, trapped at a corner table and uncommonly alluring in a black off-the-shoulder Calvin Klein dress, quickly became fair game for the columnists and entertainment reporters. She managed to deflect most of the questions—about her stepchildren and their lawsuit—gracefully; the others, about her relationship with Alton Shea, she simply ignored.

Seated at the table with Jessica and Alton were the stars of the play, Russell Janklow and Celia Hunt, and their respective spouses; David Viner, the director, a disarming, twenty-five-year-old Englishman, who, for some inexplicable reason, wore a tie designed to look like an Alaskan salmon; and the writer, Edith Hurlburt, a corpulent, middle-aged lesbian with an enormous ego, an intense dislike of David Viner, and a growing fondness for Jessica.

Shortly after eleven the celebrants gravitated toward the three small televisions set up by the bar. Secretly expecting to be savaged by the New York critics, Shea's spirits were buoyed by the unanimous praise for the production from the local television reviewers, and moments later he was rocketed toward elation by a rave notice from the *New York Times*.

Amid the laughter and euphoria Jessica finally understood the sense of achievement and gratification that Mark had been striving for with the Knights. It was here in this room. She could see it was more than winning a case or completing a deal. It was making that connection with the public, having them recognize what you had done and, at the same time, being grateful that you had done it.

The professional celebrities, in their never-ending quest for exposure and self-promotion, left the party around midnight to move on to other affairs or private clubs. Those involved with the play—the actors, assured of at least a three-month run, and the producers, assured of breaking even—reveled in their success and stayed on until one. That is, all but Edith Hurlburt, who, after being politely spurned by Jessica, left the festivities and waddled off into the cold November night in search of companionship.

When they got back to the town house around two in the morning, Jessica insisted that Alton come in for a nightcap. They were both tired, but still infected with the exhilaration of his earlier triumph. In the living room Jessica filled two crystal snifters with cognac, then began a description of the party as seen through a novice's eyes. Her vivid and sometimes stinging characterizations sent Alton into paroxysms of laughter. Soon they were both laughing, Shea almost uncontrollably.

"Irving Berlin was right," said Jessica, gasping for air. " 'There are no people like show people.' "

"Like no people you know?" Shea chimed in.

"Ri-ight," Jessica drawled, the brandy melting away her inhibitions and her Vassar accent. "Honestly, I haven't seen such back-stabbing, heard more snide insinuations and gutter innuendos, since my high school cheerleader tryouts in Midland."

"Don't look to me to agree or disagree," he said in self-defense. "I just threw the party. I didn't script it."

"Speaking of which, have you any idea what that writer of yours said to me in the ladies' room?"

"Edith? . . . Well, I hope something literary."

"You might say that, if your reading matter consisted of the graffiti on bathroom walls."

"Ah, yes, the proving grounds for contemporary British playwrights."

"I swear, that woman gives lesbians a bad name," Jessica muttered, falling victim to fatigue and the hour. She had been pacing off her monologue in front of Shea and had finally run out of steam.

"I think you'd better sit down," he said, offering her the place beside him on the sofa.

"My God, this has been a long day," she replied wearily as she eased herself against him, her head coming to rest on his shoulder. "You know, David," she said softly. She had begun using his given name their second evening together, having found Alton just too pompous. She liked the name David. It was strong and sweet and, at the same time, gentle, much like the man who had foresworn it nearly twenty years ago. "I realized tonight that I've started to see the frivolous and whimsical side of life again, and I loved it."

"Tonight I really don't think you had any choice," he replied, stroking her head. "It was either that or go mad. I probably should have warned you about dear Edith. She does, on occasion, tend to be a bit too aggressive."

"Really, David, you know what I mean," Jessica said impatiently. "These past weeks with you have turned my life around. You've given me back something I thought I had lost forever when Mark died—the chance to be close to someone, to care about them."

"Do you know you have the most perfect nose in the world?" he whispered as he traced the tip of his finger lightly down the bridge of her nose. "My people would have suffered an extra generation of persecution for a nose like that."

"Christ, David, why can't you be serious?"

"It's difficult to be serious around you."

"Why?"

"Because you're so vulnerable and so beautiful," he confessed. "And because I've fallen hopelessly in love with you." He moved his hand to the side of her face and gently touched her cheek. "But I'm afraid you may not be ready to love me."

"Oh, my dearest David," Jessica exclaimed tearfully, wrapping her arms around him, "I do love you . . ."

Shea could feel his happiness being sucked into the silence of her unfinished sentence.

"But maybe not the way we might both want," she added plaintively, "at least, not now and not here. There are too many memories. You don't know how hard it is to put your life back in order."

He held her close. "I can wait for you to finish," he said softly, then tenderly kissed her on the forehead as he would a child. "I can wait for us."

In the comfort of his embrace Jessica closed her eyes and, for an instant, felt herself in the arms of a memory. But that moment quickly passed, routed by the feel of her cheek against Alton Shea's soft wool jacket and the touch of his lips on her forehead.

Chapter 34

The attendance projections for the coming holiday season were spread out over Frank DeCicco's desk. The neat columns and demographic breakdowns revealed little that he didn't already know: he had a third-place team with one certifiable star and two disabled veterans and most of the Arena's attendance consisted of season-ticket holders.

From under the jumbled computer printout the latest concessionaires' reports glared out at him. DeCicco felt as though he were about to drown in a sea of bad news and red ink. He had spent most of the morning wading through a lot of medical jargon from an orthopedic surgeon about why his two veterans should be considering another profession. The last thing he needed that Thursday afternoon was a call from Douglas Laidlaw.

"Douglas, how's the weather in California?" DeCicco asked guardedly, aware an apology was really in order.

"I thought you and I had an agreement," Douglas

snapped angrily. "In return for certain considerations, you were going to keep me informed."

"Look, Douglas, lately it's been very difficult for me to see Jessica. Between her schedule and mine, days are impossible, and nights . . . well," DeCicco began hesitantly. "She's been seeing this English guy," he added, opting for truth over pride. "I think he's a producer—"

"And you've been frozen out." Taking his cue from DeCicco's silence, Douglas continued, "Frank, I'm just a little pissed that I didn't get this bit of news from you first. After all, it's going to mean a lot to both of us."

"What news?" DeCicco asked uneasily.

"It seems that little speech she gave at the Arena wasn't just bullshit. The lady actually wants the Knights."

"What!"

"Believe me, I'm just as surprised as you are," Douglas told him. "I thought all that talk was just to pump up the sale price. It wasn't until ten minutes ago that I found out from Michael Rosen that we were both way off the mark. For the past two weeks he and Jonathan Lambert have been trying to work out a settlement. Today Rosen tells me that Lambert, in a meeting this morning, made it clear that the Arena and the Knights would not be part of any deal. . . . Can you believe it? She wants to keep the goddamn team!" Douglas's voice raced up some unwritten scale. "Now, the way I see it, since the woman feels so strongly about it, who am I to stand in her way?"

"Provided, of course, the price is right," interjected DeCicco cynically.

"Easy, Frank."

"Douglas, I thought you wanted the Knights."

"I did, Frank," Douglas answered. "It's just that things moved faster than I anticipated. Look, when you suddenly find yourself in a seller's market, you have to be a fool not to take advantage of it. Trust me, Frank, there's not a big demand for bottomless pits these days, especially at premium prices."

"And our agreement?"

"I meant to keep to it," Douglas replied in an unctuous, patronizing tone. "But you'll have to admit that if I'm not the owner, it's a moot point. Isn't it? . . . I wouldn't worry, though, if I were you. Just finish out the season over five hundred and keep my sister happy and you'll be fine . . . Listen, Frank, I've gotta run. I'm late for a meeting. We'll talk soon."

DeCicco hung up the phone before the string of clichés had ended. As much as he fought it, he couldn't help picturing a smug, self-assured Douglas Laidlaw in his stylish Hollywood living room, gloating. His humiliation complete, DeCicco picked up a glass paperweight and hurled it across the room. It crashed against a framed photograph of the 1972 championship Knights.

A week after the party at Sardi's there was an open casting call at the Majestic Theatre for a musical that Alton Shea was bringing over from London. A pyrotechnics extravaganza, it required eleven principals and twenty-six chorus people with the ability to dance in hot, fireproof underwear for two and a half hours and hold their breath for at least two minutes. It didn't take long to winnow away the squeamish, the cowardly, and the untalented. By four that afternoon the original 250 actors, actresses, and assorted Gypsies had become a more manageable fifty.

A member of the production staff ushered Jessica to a seat at the rear of the darkened theater then disappeared. About fifteen rows in front of her she could see Alton, David Viner—this time sans fish tie—and two men and a woman she did not recognize, huddled in muted conversation over a stack of pictures. Appearing out of nowhere, the young woman who had seated Jessica joined the group, whispered a few words to

Alton, then made a discreet exit. Shea turned, waved, and whispered in a clipped sotto voce that he would be no more than fifteen minutes.

Jessica acknowledged his message with a wave and a smile, then tried to settle into the narrow seat, but it wasn't long before she began, more out of exuberance than impatience, to fidget—first tapping a finger on her handbag, then swinging a crossed leg in ever-widening arcs.

The meeting ended and Alton walked up the aisle toward Jessica. As he reached her seat she sprang at him as though catapulted by some faulty inner spring, throwing her arms around his neck and kissing him.

"David, David, David," she repeated breathlessly. "Everything is so wonderful." She kissed him again.

"For a moment," he whispered, when they finally separated, "I was going to apologize for having you meet me here, but it's clear we should have met here sooner." This time he kissed her.

"Good night, Alton," David Viner said matter-of-factly as he passed the couple in the aisle. "Oh, and nice to see you again, Jessica."

Without sneaking a breath or in any way disrupting themselves, Jessica and Alton both waved after Viner as he strolled out of the theatre.

"My goodness," gasped Shea as they parted again, "we are in a good mood."

"Ecstatic."

"Are you going to tell me why? Or are we going to stay here locked in each other's arms until the show opens?. . . Not that I would mind. Well, except for the rats at night."

"Rats?. . . What rats?"

"The ones that migrate from the subways. The stagehands tell me they're the size of ponies, or is it cats? I've never been quite sure," he teased.

"Wonderful. Now, are you through here?" Jessica

asked, propelling him up the aisle and out into the lobby without waiting for a reply.

"Just where are you taking me, young woman?" Shea protested facetiously.

"To see a sunset."

As they stepped out onto the street and into the beginning of a cool autumn evening, Jessica looked up at the faint blushes of pink beginning to wash across the western sky. "Hurry, David. We don't want to miss it," she said, pushing him in the direction of Billy Richmond and the waiting Mercedes. She unceremoniously shoved Shea into the backseat, then waited patiently for Billy to close the door and get behind the wheel.

The black sedan darted away from the curb and into the surprisingly light eastbound traffic on Forty-fourth Street. At the same moment, Jessica produced a chilled bottle of champagne and two glasses.

"I take it you haven't lost the family farm," Shea remarked ironically.

"Never had one to lose," Jessica replied as she eased the cork from the champagne bottle with a gentle hiss. She poured the icy, golden liquid into tall fluted glasses, catching a pillow of the escaping foam between her lips.

The simple sensuality of this act held Alton Shea spellbound, his eyes riveted on her soft, inviting lips.

Jessica handed him a glass, then, misinterpreting the blank stare on his face, leaned over and whispered in his ear. "David, dahling," she began with an overdrawn English accent, "it's time you stuck your cool English reserve where the moon don't shine. This is supposed to be a celebration."

"Of course it is. And so it shall be," he said, shifting his gaze from her mouth to the sparkle in her eyes. "I know a toast is in order on such an auspicious occasion, but the words simply fail me."

"How about, 'To the new owner of the New York Knights,'" Jessica suggested modestly, "'love and kisses.'"

"Jessica, that's wonderful! When did all this happen?"

"Jonathan told me just before I came over. The final papers will be signed next week."

"Well, then, to the new owner," he said, raising his glass. "Congratulations, darling. I know how much you've wanted this."

They emptied their glasses, then found themselves in each other's arms. As they kissed, Jessica felt whole again, experiencing once more the wants and desires that she had denied herself these many months. Tears ran down her cheeks. She was deliriously happy in this loving man's embrace but saddened that Mark's memory was now really just that, a memory—a glorious, bittersweet pas de deux forever frozen in the past.

The car slowed down, went through a gate, and stopped on a wide asphalt apron jutting out over the East River. Twenty yards from the Mercedes a red and white Bell helicopter sat in the middle of a large white circle, the tips of its rotor blades drooping gently toward the tarmac. "David," Jessica whispered tenderly, "we're here."

"Darling," he replied, readjusting his glasses, "where is here?"

"The Thirty-fourth Street Heliport," she answered as she quickly checked her makeup in a mirror set into the rear of the front seat.

"Do we need a helicopter for something?"

"Of course we do. Can you think of a better way to see a sunset?"

"From my apartment."

"This doesn't bother you, does it, David?" Jessica asked as Billy Richmond opened the car door. "I thought it would be terribly romantic."

Before he could answer, the blades on the helicopter began a slow, laborious rotation.

"Certainly not," he shouted, trying to make himself heard over the deafening, high-pitched whine of the engine. "It sounds positively charming." Alton Shea was sure he would burn in Hell for the magnitude of such a lie. The words had nearly stuck in his throat. But, he reasoned, his immortal soul was a small price to pay for the love of such an extraordinary woman.

On his way out of the car he shuddered one last time at the thought of his impending demise, then made a desperate grab for the bottle of champagne.

"Okay, then, it's helicopters and seafood?" Jessica asked good-naturedly.

"Make that small aircraft and shellfish," he corrected her.

"Honestly, David, how could I have known?" she asked compassionately.

"I could have told you," he half groaned from under the small white towel over his face. He struggled to keep the damp cloth in place as he slowly and painfully raised his head from the car seat. "You know, Jessica," he began stoically, "when you think back to this moment in the years to come—and you will—I want you to remember what I did for love." To cap his performance, he crumpled, like a house of cards, back into the plush seat.

"My God, now I know it's serious," Jessica said, turning toward Billy Richmond. "He's talking in song titles."

It was a sure sign of their growing love for each other that Jessica and Alton could joke about what had happened. For Shea, the helicopter ride had been a simple dare, but for Jessica it had been the replay of a nightmare.

Shea had made a valiant effort to deal with his phobia, but as the helicopter reached two thousand feet and started for New Jersey, he realized he had lost his battle. His mouth became dry. His throat seemed tight and narrow. Cold sweat soaked his trousers where he had rested his palms. He fought on until the outskirts of Hoboken, when Jessica noticed he was hyperventilating and ordered the pilot back to Manhattan.

His symptoms began to abate the moment they touched down at the heliport, and had completely disappeared by the time Jessica had bundled him into the Mercedes.

"What should we try next?" said Shea, slipping the cloth from his face and dropping it on the floor.

"Why don't I take you home?" Jessica replied, confounded by his tenacity.

"Perfect. But let's pick up some Chinese food first."

"Are you serious?"

"Certainly. Jews love to celebrate with Chinese food. It's traditional. I think it's even written in the Talmud . . . We are still celebrating, aren't we?"

"If you're up to it," answered Jessica, "I guess we are."

Shea checked his watch, then placed a detailed order with an obscure Chinatown restaurant over the car phone. Twenty minutes later the owner and two large shopping bags were waiting for him in a narrow doorway on a cramped and darkened Pell Street. Shea stepped from the car, exchanged a short bow and a handshake with the owner, then paid for the food. In an instant he was back in the car and they were on their way.

As Billy Richmond steered the Mercedes out of Chinatown and up past the gaily-decorated storefronts of Little Italy, the inside of the car began to fill with the pungent smells of oyster sauce and garlic and the sweet perfume of ginger, orange peel, and rice wine.

"How on earth did you find that place?" asked Jessica, no longer able to control her curiosity.

"My mother's cousin's son."

"You're kidding."

"No. He works in the mayor's office. That's where the mayor goes for takeout."

The food was still hot when the Mercedes pulled up

in front of Alton Shea's apartment on Riverside Drive. Jessica had been up to the two-bedroom pied-à-terre only once before, when they had gone to retrieve a script he had wanted her to read. Decorated in classic English motifs, the apartment spoke reams about acceptance and assimilation. To Jessica, the rooms, with their solid-colored walls and sturdy walnut and cherry furniture, did give off a feeling of comfort and elegance, but more of a men's club than a home.

Shea started a fire then retreated into the kitchen to set out the food. It wasn't long before he returned with a large tray piled high with steaming dishes of dumplings, spareribs, tiny shrimp, and glistening noodles. Jessica helped him clear the top of a large square coffee table in front of the fire to make way for their dinner. Then Shea disappeared into the kitchen, returning seconds later with an ice bucket, a bottle of champagne, and two glasses.

"Just think of it as fizzy rice wine," he said as he sat the ice bucket on the coffee table. "By the way, there's more warming in the kitchen. Considering the occasion, I thought we should have a real banquet."

They sat in front of the fire on large pillows and dined with silver chopsticks on fine English china. There was warmth and contentment in the room, as well as love and the stirrings of passion.

Toward the end of the meal a delivery boy appeared at the door with a dozen red roses wrapped in thick cellophane and tied with a large red velvet ribbon. Jessica plucked a small white envelope from beneath the ribbon and opened it. Carefully printed with an almost childlike precision on a stiff white card were the words, *To the Knights' new champion, All my love—DAVID.*

"I was searching for something a little more Shakespearean, but that's all the clerk at the other end of the phone could reasonably manage," Shea said with a wry, apologetic smile.

"It's lovely, David, really. And so are the flowers. Thank you." Jessica slid around the coffee table, raised her hand to Shea's cheek and kissed him. It was a gentle, loving kiss that seemed to fan the desire growing inside her.

"I'll clear the table and find you a vase," said Shea, breaking away. He sensed what was happening between them, yet he wanted her to be sure that it was what she wanted. He busied himself stacking the dishes and loading them onto the tray.

"Please, David. Let me," Jessica insisted. "After all, you made the dinner."

"Actually, I only uncrated it," he replied. "Why don't you finish your champagne, enjoy your flowers, and I'll be out in a minute with dessert."

"Dessert?"

"Such as it is."

While dishes clattered in the kitchen, Jessica picked a rose from the bouquet on the table and walked to the set of French windows that divided the living room from a small terrace. Below her she could see the soft glow from the lamps lining the pathways that twisted and turned through Riverside Park. Beyond, the Hudson River, black and foreboding, picked up reflections from the New Jersey shoreline and swept them out to sea, where they merged with the night.

Jessica held the rose against her cheek. She found the soft velvet petals and the sweet fragrance soothing, but she knew she wanted more. She wanted Alton's arms around her; she wanted to be a part of someone's life again; she wanted to love.

Soon Jessica heard Shea's footsteps in the living room. Without a word, as though guided by her thoughts, he switched off the lights and joined her at the window. Standing behind her, he slowly ran his hands along her shoulders and down her back, finally resting them on her hips.

Jessica turned. In the firelight she could see the concern and confusion written on his face.

"David, what is it?" she whispered anxiously.

"I want you so much," he answered.

"Oh, David, I want you too," Jessica confessed, trying to reassure him. The certainty in her words and the look in her eyes told him that there was no longer anything standing between them.

Shea took Jessica in his arms and kissed her. Her blond hair felt like silk in his hands. And as she responded to his kiss, nothing seemed to exist for either of them beyond this moment.

Jessica quickly gave herself up to her desires. It was as though she were riding the crest of a wave of passion. She felt free, open, and anxious to express her love for this gentle, understanding man.

"God, I love you," said Shea as their lips parted.

Jessica threw her arms around his neck and kissed him again. As she pulled away a wide smile worked its way across her face. "Oh, David," she said tenderly, "I'm *so* happy."

The room was lit with moonlight now; the fire, having gone unattended, was reduced to a soft glow. Shea led Jessica back toward the fireplace. He slipped two more logs on the blackened kindling then stoked the smoldering embers until the fire sprang back to life. As the flames crept through the new wood and light once again spilled out into the room, Jessica and Alton Shea knelt before the fireplace.

Looking into her eyes, Shea could see his reflection amid a backdrop of flames. He held her hand and gently kissed her fingertips, then touched the side of her cheek. It wasn't a plea or a question, but in response Jessica moved her hands to the bottom of her white cashmere turtleneck and began to raise it.

"No," said Shea, "let me."

He undressed her with great care, tracing the

smooth curves of her body with his lips and hands. He massaged and kneaded the long, lean muscles of her back and legs and lingered lovingly at her neck and breasts. Bathed in its steady heat, Jessica's body was burnished a lusty red and orange by the fire. As Shea painstakingly slipped off her black silk panties, Jessica, with a low moan, opened herself to him. His touch was explosive, and she writhed and twisted to be closer to it until it consumed her.

Jessica sat up slowly and grinned wickedly at Shea. "Now, darling," she said hoarsely, "it's my turn."

Her fingers worked furiously at the small pearl buttons on his blue-and-white-checked shirt. She removed the rest of his clothing with equal speed and determination, leaving him in his white cotton briefs. Now her frenzy died away and she kissed and stroked him languidly, starting with his mouth, moving on to his neck and throat, then down to his small pink nipples. She pressed her naked body against him and ground her breasts into the coarse sandy hair on his chest. His breathing deepened, and she could feel his fingers push into her flesh as she kissed and licked his abdomen and the inside of his thighs.

She could feel him growing against her through the soft cotton underwear. She reached her fingers into the waistband and slowly slid the shorts to the floor. She first teased him, running her hot breath over his groin, then covered him with tiny kisses, finally taking him into her mouth.

She sucked and fondled him until he pulled her up and kissed her with a hunger that made her weak. Then he laid her back against one of the pillows and let her guide him into her. As the fire consumed the logs, the passion of their lovemaking quickly engulfed them. They became lost in each other and with each other until they, too, were consumed.

Chapter 35

Jessica spent the Thanksgiving weekend in Houston trying to escape a holiday depression while Alton remained in New York to finish casting his new show. Jessica filled her hours lunching with old friends, shopping with her mother and sister, and getting reacquainted with a less frenetic pace of life.

The only unpleasant moment of the four-day trip came during Thanksgiving dinner at Kendall's apartment. Kendall's husband, Larry, an ambitious young reporter with the Associated Press, began quizzing Jessica about the Arcaro affair and the size of Mark's estate. Jessica politely sidestepped his questions at the dinner table while Kendall glared, mortified by her husband's tactless behavior. But the incident did little to mar Jessica's weekend—she was used to such grilling by now—and she returned to New York the following Monday renewed and ready to take her place as the owner of the New York Knights.

The final settlement papers, giving her control of the

team, had been signed the previous Wednesday. To Jessica it seemed that for all the heartache, aggravation, and vast sums, there should have been some sort of grand ceremony, something akin to the signing of a peace treaty. In fact, it was all over in minutes, with five copies signed and a hug and kiss from Jonathan Lambert.

Afterward Jessica returned to her office and dictated her resignation from the firm. She had discussed it all earlier with Jonathan, who had, of course, insisted she stay on. But Jessica was adamant. She knew she had neither the temperament nor desire to be a part-time attorney. And she knew she'd fought for the team too long and too hard to give it less than a hundred percent.

Monday evening Jonathan had given Jessica a small farewell party at Le Cygne. A steady stream of accolades and toasts rained down on her from both associates and partners across the long table. For most of the assembled it was a festive occasion. The firm wasn't losing a partner, it was gaining a client—and a very wealthy one at that, not to mention a newly freed corner office. But for Jessica and Jonathan it was an evening tinged with sadness. They had been bound up together in so many ways—as teacher and student, parent and child, and finally as friend and confidant— that they both had momentary doubts about the wisdom of the decision.

The next morning, with little fanfare, Jessica packed up her files, her photographs, and a few mementos and moved uptown to Mark's office in the Arena. Dorothy, Mark's secretary, was waiting for her in the reception area on the twenty-third floor. At Jessica's urging, she had remained after Mark's death, providing liaison for the lawyers sifting through the estate. And now Jessica hoped Dorothy could give her some valuable insight into the workings of the organization and Mark's approach to it. She could always learn the game, she reasoned, but the system was another story.

"Are you ready to go in now?" asked Dorothy, mindful of Jessica's reluctance to use Mark's office.

Jessica looked at her and smiled. "There's no point waiting out here, is there, Dorothy?" she said. "We've got a lot of work to do."

Jessica had been in the office often since Mark's death, on her way to the conference room or looking for papers in the desk; yet this time she wasn't haunted by the specter of the man, but took strength from it. As Dorothy stood aside, Jessica walked around the room, surveying the office and its contents as though she were seeing it for the very first time. Through a crack in the curtains a beam of sunlight invaded the room, cutting a bright diagonal across the top of the wide oak desk. Without disturbing the beam, Jessica stepped behind the desk and settled into the thickly padded, high-backed chair. As she slowly leaned back into the soft brown leather, Jessica and Dorothy exchanged knowing looks. After much soul-searching and fear, the torch had been finally passed. Jessica saw the approval in Dorothy's eyes.

"Is there anything you'd like me to do, Ms. Laidlaw?" asked Dorothy.

"Yes, Dorothy," replied Jessica, "Tell, Mr. DeCicco I've arrived and that I'd like to see him. Then I'd like to see the latest report you have from the Arena construction site."

Jessica spent the better part of the day in meetings with her various department heads. Although already familiar with most of them, she felt it necessary to reestablish herself as owner and impress upon them that her office door would be open to all.

Around five-thirty, after seven meetings and ten reports, she got a phone call from Alton Shea, canceling their dinner plans.

"I'm terribly sorry, darling," he said apologetically, "but I have to have dinner with Darcy Frame and her agent. We desperately want her for our lead, only she doesn't seem to want us."

"Then she's a fool," replied Jessica.

"Actually, she's more like a money-grubbing little bitch." Shea laughed. "But she's perfect for the part. I'm hoping Allan and I can convince them at dinner that art is more important than money."

"And if that fails?"

"We'll kidnap her children."

"That's persuasive."

"They say it worked for Joe Papp . . . Look, darling, there is one more thing," he added cautiously. "I have to fly to London over the weekend and meet with the writer. Allan thinks some of the punch lines are still too English. I disagree, but then again, Allan thinks *I'm* too English."

"I'll miss you," Jessica said affectionately.

"Yes, and I'll miss you," he replied, "and that's why I want you to come with me."

"Da-vid," she answered, with a tone of parental disapproval.

"Don't be like that. You sound like my mother's cousin from Great Neck."

"The one who works in the mayor's office?"

"That's her son . . . Really, Jessica you must come," Shea pleaded. "Consider it a part of the worldwide celebration of your victory over the evil stepchildren. Yes, I can see it now on the back of a satin jacket: 'The Jessica Laidlaw Victory Tour.'"

"I thought you people were supposed to be repressed, not crazy."

"The Jews or the English?"

"Jesus, David . . . What time does this so-called tour kick off?"

"Nine P.M. Friday, from British Airways," he answered promptly. "You can pick me up around six."

"David, you're not just doing this to get a free ride to the airport, are you?"

"Can you think of a better way? . . . Now, what about dinner tomorrow night?"

Friday morning Jessica donned a hard hat and toured the Arena construction site on West Street with Mal Drucker, the primary contractor, and Frank DeCicco. As they skirted small mounds of concrete and stacks of cinder blocks, Drucker, a heavyset man in his forties with bushy eyebrows and a crooked smile, explained that the shell of the building was nearly complete and that subcontractors were set to begin work shortly on the interior.

"Mal, are you still aiming for a September opening?" asked Jessica as they entered the arena through a gaping hole on the Houston Street side of the building. Inside, in the eerie light, forklifts ferrying palettes of marble tiles and glass bricks scooted by them and disappeared into the musty recesses of the cavernous space.

"It looks like it'll be more like late October, early November," answered Drucker.

"Is that with the projected three-percent overrun?" she asked pointedly. "Or are you expanding that projection?"

Drucker peered at Jessica obliquely through the thick lenses of his wire-rim glasses. "Well, I see you've read our report," he said as his lips curved into his crooked smile.

"Yes, I have," said Jessica. "Now what about that projection?"

"I assure you, Jessica," replied Drucker, "it won't be more than an extra two percent."

"If we have to, we'll live with the two percent, but remember, Mal," she stated with a wry smile of her own, "anything over that comes out of your pocket."

Suddenly, from a far corner of the building, came a

shout followed by a loud crash. The three spun around in the direction of the noise. In the distance they could make out a long piece of steel and the remains of four shattered crates spread across the gray cement floor.

"There goes one of your men's rooms," said Drucker, shaking his head.

"Terrific," muttered DeCicco.

"Try and look on the bright side, Frank," Jessica added sarcastically. "Maybe that's going on Mal's tab."

Forty-five minutes later, after a meeting with the architect, Jessica and Frank DeCicco headed back to the Arena. Forced to detour around a water-main break, it was almost noon by the time they reached Thirty-fourth Street. Jessica, determined to get in some last-minute shopping for the London trip and still make a one o'clock luncheon appointment, dropped DeCicco at the Arena and continued on to Bergdorf Goodman.

The store, decked out in Christmas finery and crowded with holiday shoppers, reminded Jessica of trips to Grammer Murphy in Midland when she was a child. The rich scents and crystal bottles of the elegant perfume counters made her think back to another Christmas, when her tiny fingers rummaged through box after box of lavender sachets, in search of her mother's favorite shade of pink lace.

With cold, damp days in mind, Jessica rushed to the third floor and snapped up two wool suits, then flew back down the escalator to pick up two wide belts on the first floor. While a saleswoman wrote up her charge, Jessica glanced at her watch. It was nearly one. The makeup, she decided, would just have to wait. Even though the Plaza was across the street, she didn't want to be late for this particular lunch.

As she left the store, Billy Richmond took her shopping bags and placed them into the trunk of the Mercedes.

"You know her, Billy," said Jessica nervously. "After

all that's gone on, why do you think she wants to see me?"

"Ma'am, after all my years with Mr. Laidlaw, I have never been able to understand those children, so I guess I'd be the last one to ask," replied Billy diplomatically.

"But there's nobody else to ask, is there Billy?" Jessica said dispassionately.

"No, ma'am, I guess there isn't."

"Thanks anyway, Billy," Jessica replied softly.

After Jessica turned and started across Fifty-eighth Street, Billy came after her. "Mrs. Laidlaw," he began, "I do remember one thing."

"Yes, Billy?"

"That child could get very nasty if she didn't get her own way."

Jessica hurried up the broad steps in front of the Plaza Hotel, wondering why Patricia Laidlaw had been so cryptic over the phone and why she had insisted on this meeting. With Billy Richmond's warning and half a dozen possible scenarios playing out in her head, Jessica crossed the lobby to the Palm Court.

She spotted Patricia, partially obscured by a palm frond, nursing a large glass of white wine at a table at the far end of the room. Wearing a black turtleneck, large tinted glasses, and with her auburn hair pulled back in a French twist, Patricia gave Jessica the feeling she was about to sit down with an assassin.

"I'm sorry I'm late," said Jessica as she approached the table. "Bergdorf's was jammed and it took forever to get a salesperson."

"Did you buy anything?" Patricia asked, looking down at Jessica's empty hands.

"Just a few things," replied Jessica. "I left them with Billy."

"Ah, yes, Billy," the younger woman said, as though remembering some past misdeed or indiscretion that had been set right by the tall black man, "the faithful family retainer."

A short perky waitress arrived to take their order, precluding any response from Jessica.

"Why were you so vague on the phone?" Jessica asked after the waitress had left.

"So I'd pique your curiosity and you'd agree to meet me face to face," replied Patricia through a smug, supercilious grin.

"Well, I'm here. But I still don't understand why," admitted Jessica. "Since the settlement has been signed, I didn't think there was anything more for us to discuss."

"You really don't understand me, do you, Jessica?"

"Did you ever give me the chance?"

"No, I didn't, but you weren't that important to us, at least as long as my father was alive," Patricia replied coldly. "But when he died and left you all that money, you suddenly became very important—to Douglas, at least. But money has always been Douglas's thing."

"And you?" asked Jessica.

"Oh, don't get me wrong," Patricia answered. "If Douglas could get his pound of flesh, I was more than willing to cut off my share. It's just that I felt cheated when my father died. There was no one to hate anymore . . . and believe me, I *hated* him."

"But why?" asked Jessica, taken aback by the searing contempt in the girl's voice.

"For what he did to my mother," she shot back. "He married a warm, loving woman and left her a pitiful, self-destructive drunk. That's why." Patricia lowered her glasses and peered at Jessica over the black rims. "Oh, don't look so hurt and offended. Nobody says you have to defend his memory . . . Tell me honestly, Jessica. Haven't you ever wondered, 'If he hadn't died, would he have made me another Ruth Laidlaw?'"

"Never," Jessica declared emphatically, trying to control her rage.

"Of course you wouldn't," replied Patricia. She

drained her wineglass and set it back down on the table. "You still see God's grace in men, or is it vice versa?"

"Look, Patricia, before I get up and leave I'd like to know if there's some point to all this. Or are you just in the mood to spill a little bile today?"

"How about the education of Jessica Wheeler-Laidlaw?"

"And what is that supposed to mean?" Jessica asked uneasily.

"It means I thought you should know that your friend and trusted administrator, Frank DeCicco, has been screwing Daddy's daughter and trying to screw Daddy's wife," Patricia said, transforming her voice into a tortured whisper as the waitress returned to the table.

Jessica watched impatiently while the effervescent young woman set down their order and then departed in flurry of good cheer. "Damn it, Patricia. Just what are you talking about?" Jessica said angrily.

"Fucking . . . At least between me and Frank," Patricia replied obscenely. "You know, he's very good. I could have gotten really attached to him . . . if he wasn't such a jerk. He actually thought he could screw you . . . out of the team, that is, with Douglas's backing." As she spoke, Patricia picked absentmindedly at the small mound of chicken salad on the dish in front of her. "And everything was set, until you offered Douglas a deal. Then he had no choice but to cut dear Frank loose. Douglas wasn't about to slice up the pie three ways."

"Patricia, why are you telling me this?"

"Because I like things neat and tidy," she answered. "And because it gives me great pleasure to strip away a little of that insufferable Texas naiveté of yours and, at the same time, cut the balls off my father's alter ego."

"You know, Patricia, you're a very disturbed young woman," said Jessica, rising from her chair, her stomach in knots and her face flushed.

"Honestly, Jessica, I don't know why you're getting so upset . . . You should be thanking me."

"What for? Spreading this filth?"

"No . . . for my bedtime prayers," Patricia shot back at her. "After all, they did make you a very wealthy woman."

It was all that Jessica could do to keep from tearing the young woman apart in full view of everyone in the Plaza lobby. Instead, as she swept her coat off the back of her chair, she reached over and deftly slid the plate of chicken salad into Patricia Laidlaw's lap. "Now, you little bitch," Jessica declared, "we both feel better."

A stream of obscenities followed Jessica out of the Palm Court, into the lobby proper, and through a sea of turning heads; however, she held her composure and marched triumphantly across the broad red carpet toward the front door.

Chapter 36

"David, do you think it will be all right if we walk back to the house?" Jessica asked as she adjusted the collar on her raincoat. A stiff breeze, carrying the ominous smell of rain, had sprung up, churning the last leaves of autumn and flinging them into the middle of Cadogan Square.

"I don't see why not. It probably won't rain again for another ten minutes," Alton Shea answered flippantly. He put his arm around Jessica to shield her from the wind.

They crossed Sloan Street, leaving Knightsbridge and the elegant white town house behind them for the reserved, narrow, tree-lined squares and crescents of Belgravia. Although it was early Sunday evening, the London streetlights had already been on for two hours, their brilliance bouncing off the rain-slicked roadways.

"Dinner was wonderful, David. And your parents are lovely people," said Jessica, "but they dote on you terribly."

"Please, Jessica, try not to confuse doting with sales-manship," he replied, somewhat amused by her obser-vation.

"David, I recognize doting parents when I see them," Jessica answered confidently. "Anyway, what could those two perfectly charming people be selling?"

"Me . . . And themselves as in-laws."

"Honestly, David. You're impossible."

"I'm serious, Jessica," he began defensively. "Those people were perfectly . . . charming?"

Jessica nodded, anxious to hear the rest of this rationalization.

"Yes, charming, and sensible and intelligent," he continued. "Well, those very same people become shameless hucksters in the face of their eldest—and only unmarried—child's bachelorhood. Ever since the divorce, whenever I visit with a lady friend, there is always a tremendous effort to show the advantages of being a member of the family."

"Oh?" she responded with mild consternation. "And how many 'lady friends' have they tried to impress?"

"Fifteen or twenty."

"What!"

"I'm sorry. Did you want the numbers for the last six months or the whole year?"

"You bastard," she said, laughing as she tried to elbow him in the ribs.

Deflecting the blow, Shea grabbed her arm, held it behind his back and kissed her.

"You know, they liked you a lot," he said as they continued walking.

"Now, how do you know that, David? They just met me."

"It's simple cognitive balancing," he answered. "They love me. I adore you. Ergo, they must be mad about you."

At Sloan Square a light rain began to fall, forcing the couple under Alton Shea's large black umbrella.

"Tell me, David," Jessica said, suddenly wondering aloud, "are your parents the reason you wanted me to come with you to London?"

"I guess they're one of the reasons," he answered. "But what makes you ask that?"

"I don't know. I've just begun feeling that this trip has become more to you than an impromptu getaway."

"If you mean meeting everybody," Shea replied, "I don't think you can fault me for wanting to show you off. And besides, I thought you might like to see who and what makes up my life."

"But why is that so important now?" Jessica insisted.

He stopped in the middle of the nearly deserted sidewalk and looked at her intently, then cast his eyes past her, up the Kings Road toward the gardens along Eaton Square. "Because," he began slowly, his gaze still directed to some spot far in the distance, "two weeks ago I concluded a deal with Paramount's theatrical division. They're going to underwrite my company in return for a percentage plus options on the film rights."

"David, that's wonderful."

"But it's going to mean spending most of my time in London," he added. In the seemingly interminable silence that followed, he looked back at Jessica to assess the impact of his words.

The rain became heavier now, bouncing off the street and their umbrella with brisk pops. Jessica started to say something but then turned away, her words lost in the downpour. All at once the incident at the Plaza, the hours in the air, the rushing from place to place, began to weigh her down. She felt tired, the last of her energy drained by his revelation.

"Jessica, I know we should have discussed this sooner," he said, trying to explain, "but you were so busy with the team, and I thought once you came to London and understood what my life was like here, it might be easier to ask you to share it."

As she turned back, he could see tears tracing glassy lines down her cheeks.

"David, you just can't ask me that," she cried as she tried desperately to fight off the growing feelings of anger, sadness, and frustration. "Please, not now."

"But Jessica, you must know how much I care for you."

"Yes, David, I do, but I also know this is the wrong time. I won't back away from something before I start it, especially something I've fought so hard for," said Jessica, reaching out for understanding. "And if you care for me, you won't force me to make that choice."

"But I love you, Jessica, and want to be with you."

"I love you too, David, but right now there can only be our love, not our life," she explained. "You and I have both set courses for ourselves, and yet, with all our planning, neither one of us has really considered what the other has wanted or needed . . . have we, David?"

The truth was too painful for him to admit. He simply couldn't bring himself to answer Jessica's question. Instead, he tugged self-consciously at his wool scarf. "It's getting cold," he said somberly. "I think we'd better get a cab."

The rain ended around one-thirty in the morning and was replaced by a dense rolling fog. From behind the heavy curtains of Alton Shea's bedroom, Jessica watched as a deep blue Rolls-Royce Corniche deposited an elegantly dressed couple in front of one of the columned entryways on Chester Square. The bone-chilling dampness quickly forced the pair into the imposing town house and the liveried driver back into the Rolls and off into the murky night.

"Can't you sleep?" Shea asked in a half whisper as he scanned the room, searching for Jessica in the darkness.

"No," she answered weakly. "I've just got too much on my mind." In that shadowy bedroom, Jessica felt as though she were again being forced to defend Mark's memory. Alton Shea's proposal and Frank DeCicco's deceit both seemed like assaults on a sacred part of her being. A part of her she was determined to protect.

Grabbing his silk dressing gown off the end of the bed, he walked over to the window and draped the robe over Jessica's bare shoulders. For a moment they stood together in the window, staring down at the row of diffuse circles of light that seemed to contain the square in the fog.

Jessica took his hand and held it against her cheek. "I have to go back to New York today," she said softly.

"I thought you wanted to stay a little longer, so we could talk this through. Maybe work out something."

"That's just it," she replied dejectedly. "If I stay, we might just work out 'something,' and it would be wrong. I don't want us to be accommodations in each other's lives, David. I care about you too much for that."

"I feel like I'm scaring you away," he said as he held her in his arms.

"You could never do that," Jessica murmured as she drew him to her lips, but she knew he had. Out of his love for her, he had threatened her whole world and forced her to choose between his life and a memory.

Chapter 37

Early Tuesday Jessica, fighting off jet lag and uncertainty over her decision in London, found herself back behind Mark's oak desk at the Arena, reading the morning papers. The headlines carried news of an arms accord, the release of another hostage in the Middle East, and the end of a police slowdown in Newark, but what caught and held Jessica's attention were the vivid accounts of the Knights' 120–99 defeat at the hands of Chicago. It wasn't so much the ignominy of a twenty-one point loss that troubled her, but the reaction of the fans, and even the coaching staff, to the ineptitude on the court. Banners defaming the players and the coaches had been unfurled in the stands. And by the beginning of the fourth quarter, the remaining fans had donned paper-bag hoods as an expression of disgust.

Even Quinn McDonald, a coach of near saintly disposition, had been overheard by one reporter berating his players on the bench and ultimately had to be removed to a hospital after suffering chest pains during the third period. McDonald's assistant, Don Remy, a former player and college coach, took over and managed to rally the team for the last five minutes of the third quarter. But even that couldn't save the stumbling team.

Precisely at ten Frank DeCicco entered the office with his usual morning exuberance and started around the desk for his customary greeting.

"Sit down, Frank," Jessica said firmly.

Her tone and the ensuing silence were ominous. DeCicco backed away from the desk. Noticing the newspapers spread out across the desk and the look of bitter enmity on Jessica's face, he sat down quickly and readied himself for the onslaught.

"How's Quinn doing?" Jessica asked.

"He's going to be fine," DeCicco answered carefully. "They said he was lucky. It was only a warning."

"I feel partly responsible for what happened," said Jessica, folding up the papers on the desk. "I should have let Mark fire him when he wanted to. Now the timing stinks, but it has to be done."

"Don't worry Jess, I'll take care of it," DeCicco replied solicitously.

"I don't think so, Frank," she said sternly.

"I don't understand."

"There's nothing to understand, Frank," Jessica continued coldly. "Because you're going too."

"Look, Jess, if it's about the game last night," DeCicco began contritely, "we've been—"

"It's not about last night, Frank," she interrupted. "I've simply decided to terminate your services with the team effective Friday and, of course, buy out the remaining year on your contract."

"With no explanations? . . . Just like that?"

"Just like that," she repeated slowly.

"Look, Jess, let's be fair about this," DeCicco argued, leaning forward in his chair. "After all we've been through, don't you think I'm entitled to some reason?"

"You know, Frank, that all-American attitude of yours is beginning to wear thin," Jessica snapped angrily. She leaned back in the chair and dug her heels into the rug, trying to keep her composure. "Look, I really don't care what went on between you and Patricia," she continued. "That's your own sordid little business. But when you conspire behind my back and betray my trust, I don't think that entitles you to a damn thing."

"Jess, I don't know what you're talking about," DeCicco replied with all the shock and innocence he could muster.

"Come on, Frank, drop the theatrics. It's over," Jessica said, shaking her head.

DeCicco dropped his eyes, took a deep breath, then looked back up at Jessica, a defeated man. "Now what?" he asked her calmly, apparently resigned to his fate.

"I've already told you," Jessica answered.

"I mean, how are you going to handle this publicly?"

"Is that important to you?"

"What is it? You want to drag my name through the mud? Will that make you happy?" DeCicco said, his resignation turning to anger. "Then go ahead. But just remember that your husband's children mixed up the mud."

"Don't worry, Frank, I'm not one of your outraged lovers," Jessica replied acidly, "although my first reaction after being humiliated by that rabid little girl was to have you fixed, like some unmanageable bull. Instead, I decided—for the good of the team—that we'd just issue a press release on Friday announcing your immediate resignation and citing irreconcilable differences with the new owner. If you want to take that any further," she added casually, "it's completely up to you."

DeCicco got up and stood in front of the desk. "You know, Jess, you're cutting off your nose to spite your face," he said with unbridled vanity. "I've been working on some major trades that could have just turned the team around."

"Then I guess we're both going to have to live with what we've done, aren't we?" answered Jessica as she swept the newspapers off her desk and into the wastebasket. "Good-bye, Frank."

DeCicco didn't leave the office with quite the measure of humiliation Jessica had expected. Facing down opposing teams and irate lovers had left the tall Italian with a resilience and strength of character that she had failed to consider. But then why shouldn't he be cocky? she thought. She had let him leave the Knights with his reputation intact, not to mention a year's severance pay.

Marty Green shoved a cassette of last night's game into the VCR across from his desk and began to fast forward the tape to the beginning of the third period. Girding himself for the replay, Green took a cup of coffee and a bagel off his desk and sat down on the small couch next to the television. With the tape at normal speed, boos and catcalls quickly filled his office as the Knights returned to the floor from the locker room.

Just then the door to his office opened and Jessica entered unannounced. She looked quickly from Marty to the television then back to Marty. "I think you'd better forget last night, Marty," Jessica announced dramatically. "You've got a lot of work ahead of you . . . because I plan to temporarily replace Quinn McDonald with his assistant while we find a new coach. And I've just fired Frank DeCicco."

It didn't take Marty Green long to recover from Jessica's bombshell, and soon he and Jessica were mapping out a strategy to deal with press reaction.

Quinn McDonald would be asked to resign, giving poor health as a reason. All of his medical bills would be covered by the team, as well as the remainder of his contract. Jessica also insisted that some place eventually be found for him within the Knights' organization. As for DeCicco's termination, Jessica offered Marty Green nothing more than "irreconcilable differences," which he accepted dutifully with a polite, understanding smile.

By noon, after a flurry of phone calls and consultations, drafts of the press releases were completed and locked away for Friday's distribution to the media, pending Jessica's final approval after her meeting with Quinn McDonald on Wednesday. Interestingly enough, it was only after Jessica had invited Marty back to the conference room for lunch that the full impact of what she had done hit her.

"Are you aware, Marty," Jessica began as a white-jacketed steward rolled in a cart, "that within the first ten days of taking control of the Knights I've managed to set the entire organization adrift?"

"Well, changes had to be made, and you had to start somewhere," Green offered by way of encouragement, "so why not at the top?"

"Because now I have to start looking for a new head coach and general manager," replied Jessica, dismissing the steward after he put down the plates. "Have you any ideas, Marty?"

"Several," he admitted. "But each one depends on your level of desperation."

"Fine, who do you have in mind for panic-stricken?"

"Panic-stricken, huh . . . For coach, it would have to be Willie Doges."

"Willie Doges!"

"You did say panic-stricken."

"Marty, I've already said I've set the Knights adrift, I don't want to sink them too," Jessica exclaimed. "From what I've read, the man's a lunatic."

"Don't you think you're being overly judgmental?" replied Green. "So he's a little personally undisciplined, a bully, and possibly even a misogynist . . . nobody's perfect."

"Exactly. He's a lunatic."

With his fork, Marty Green lifted up an unusually shaped lettuce leaf from his salad plate and peered at it suspiciously. "Maybe that's what you need," he said warily.

"Who knows, Marty," Jessica replied thoughtfully, "maybe you're right."

Tired and beaten, Quinn McDonald agreed to accept Jessica's proposal and formally tendered his resignation Wednesday evening. But it wasn't until late Friday afternoon, after the team had left for a four-game road trip in the west and the last edition of the *Post* had been put to bed, that the media were notified of McDonald's and DeCicco's departures.

After plowing through clippings and personnel files of coaches, players, and former players accumulated for her by Marty Green's assistant Tim Lindeman, Jessica sat down with Green to select candidates for head coach. Although using the team's director of public relations as a sounding board could have been considered more than a little unorthodox, Jessica appreciated Green's objectivity as a former reporter and his dedication to the Knights. He was also clever, resourceful, and diligent. She had first noticed that diligence during the Arcaro affair and then watched as he and DeCicco expertly contained the Johnstone drug incident. She was wary at first, realizing she'd been a bad judge of DeCicco's character, but long hours working with Marty convinced her he wouldn't let her or the Knights down.

They spent Friday morning pruning their list down to those who would even consider the job, then eliminated all but two names—Ben Beamish, a former head coach at Philadelphia, and the infamous Willie Doges. Personally telephoning each man, Jessica arranged for face-to-face interviews with Beamish on Saturday and Doges on Sunday.

Tall, with reddish-brown hair he kept swept back from his boyishly handsome face, Ben Beamish seemed the perfect coach for the cover of *Sports Illustrated*. He also had the credentials for the job. He had been an all-American at Notre Dame, an all-pro forward with Detroit, and then assistant and finally head coach at Philadelphia, where he had led the team to three division titles. Citing burnout, he had left the team three years ago and joined one of the networks as a color commentator on their basketball broadcasts, which afforded him time for trout fishing and trolling the waters for another coaching job.

Arriving with a list of recommendations under his arm, Beamish impressed Jessica as a bright, energetic, and analytical man, who, given time and money, could turn the Knights around. How much time Beamish would need and how much money Jessica would ultimately have to spend, were two questions that Beamish deftly avoided answering in their hour and a half meeting.

"You know," Jessica said to Marty Green after Beamish had left, "it makes you wonder—if an infinite number of monkeys with an infinite number of typewriters can eventually type out all of Shakespeare, what could a coach like that do with five years and all my money?"

"The mind boggles," Green replied.

"Christ, Marty, have we really got that much rebuilding to do?"

"Let's see what Doges says tomorrow."

"Right. Tomorrow I meet the lunatic."

* * *

Small clouds of noxious gray smoke hung like patches of California smog over the reception area in Jessica's outer office as Willie Doges puffed away on a short, stumpy cigar. A wiry bantam in his early fifties, he sat with his reading glasses perched at the end of his nose while he scanned a copy of the *Daily Racing Form*.

Willie Doges, whom a sports writer had once likened to "Billy Martin, but with a better right cross," had been through five teams and two wives by the time Jessica invited him to New York. While long considered a genius at turning ailing franchises into contenders, Doges consistently eclipsed his achievements with public feuds with his players, tirades against his owners and the occasional drunken brawl with a fan. Fortunately for the owners, this uncanny ability to self-destruct at the peak of success—the so-called "Doges Syndrome"—only impacted on Doges himself. The teams usually sailed on to glory, or at least to a playoff berth. Many skeptics, however, saw the final transformation of these teams as simply the players' grateful response to having a madman removed from their lives.

Jessica and Marty Green were standing by her desk as Doges entered the office. Jessica had expected someone bigger, taller. Then she remembered that Willie Doges had never been an athlete. In fact, he was really the last of the true coaches. He hadn't ever played the game, except in high school, but had studied it, learned its strategies and intricacies, and then, like a great classical pedagogue, impressed his knowledge on his players.

"We're glad you could come up to New York on such short notice, Mr. Doges. Won't you sit down," said Jessica, gesturing to the black leather chair in front of the desk.

As Doges sat down, he immediately spewed forth another foul-smelling, gray cloud.

"I really wish you wouldn't smoke," Jessica requested politely.

"Are you Mrs. Laidlaw?" Doges replied gruffly, his voice a raspy, abrasive growl.

"Would that make a difference?" Jessica asked curtly, sensing this test of will.

"Uh-huh."

"Well then, Mr. Doges," Jessica replied forcefully, "I'm Jessica Laidlaw." As she spoke she slowly pushed a large glass ashtray across her desk toward Willie Doges.

Doges removed the dampened end of the cigar from his mouth and obligingly stubbed it out in the ashtray. "Now, lady," said Doges as he sat back in the chair with a satisfied smile, "let's talk about this goddamn mess you've got on your hands."

Forthright, and at times downright rude, Doges laid out his assessment of the Knights in a scant fifteen minutes. He thought that except for one or two players, the team had what was needed to win a championship. But what the Knights didn't have, he told Jessica bluntly, was the ability to move and think like one man, to be a team. And that required discipline.

Coming from a man whose personal life was a shambles, Doges's espousal of discipline as a cure-all for the Knights surprised Jessica. Yet she quickly realized that to Doges basketball was everything, and life was something you did in your spare time. During their half hour together, he made no promises or guarantees and made clear that any contract he signed would only be for the remainder of the season, with any renewal contingent on a five-hundred-or-better season.

As the interview ended and they shook hands, Jessica felt the determination in the man. What he had proposed were not idle theories or game plans. There were no tricks, no mesmerizing plays, no grand revelations. It was just basketball according to Willie Doges, plain and simple.

Halfway to the door Doges stopped, removed a cigar from his jacket pocket, and, with great care and delight, lit it. Then, after tossing an irreverent wink at Jessica, he sauntered out of the office, leaving a noxious trail behind him.

"Now what?" Jessica asked, turning back to Marty Green. "Do we go with Attila the Coach or Captain America with his five-year plan?"

Chapter 38

The following Monday morning was officially the first day of winter. The air was icy cold and crystal clear. It was the kind of day that New Yorkers, huddled in warm, fashionable, winter attire and scurrying around frenetically before Christmas, believe the rest of the country envies.

Jessica was up early, her mind focused and alert. She took a quick swim in the basement pool, then went through the morning papers over breakfast. By a quarter after seven she was double-checking her Christmas gift list while she waited for Billy Richmond to bring the car around to take her to the Arena.

Stopped at a light in Central Park, Jessica rolled down the car window and filled her lungs with the crisp morning air which was still free of bus fumes and car exhaust. Just then a group of bicyclists, in a blur of bright colors, flew across the path of the Mercedes, heading up the park drive. A bit jealous of the freedom, Jessica rolled the window back up and settled into her seat, determined to pick a new coach before her nine o'clock meeting with Marty Green.

As the black car emerged from the park and crossed Central Park South, Jessica suddenly tapped Billy Richmond on the shoulder. "Billy, stop at the Carnegie Deli, would you?" she asked anxiously.

The traffic on Seventh Avenue was light; the rush hour crush wasn't due for another thirty minutes. Billy eased the car against the curb in front of the famed delicatessen, but before he could get out, Jessica bolted from the backseat. "Billy, I won't be more than five minutes," she shouted over her shoulder as she pulled open the heavy glass door to the restaurant. And exactly five minutes later, she emerged, beaming.

Bouncing into the backseat of the Mercedes, Jessica, now brimming with confidence, instructed Billy to continue on to the Arena. As the car began to move, she opened her briefcase, looking for a slip of paper. Finding it, she reached for the phone in front of her and began to dial.

"It's nothing, Billy. I just went in for some blueberry cheesecake," Jessica explained to the bewildered chauffeur as she finished dialing. "It's a kind of therapy. It helps me with difficult decisions after logic and reason have failed."

Jessica waited impatiently as the phone at the other end of the line rang and rang. Finally, after the tenth ring, a surly, gravelly voice came on the line.

"Mr. Doges?" Jessica asked.

"Yeah," Doges grunted, sounding as though he were struggling with a hangover as well as coming out of a deep sleep.

"This is Jessica Laidlaw. I'm terribly sorry about the hour, but I—"

"Who?" Doges interrupted.

"Jessica Laidlaw," she repeated. "We spoke yesterday morning at the Arena."

"What time is it anyway?"

"Nearly eight."

"Oh, Christ," Doges exclaimed, suddenly recalling the Sunday meeting.

Jessica could hear Doges rifling through his room, searching for something. She assumed the search had been successful when the rustling stopped and she heard the distinctive snap of a wooden match against the friction strip of a match box, followed by a horrible, wrenching cough. Jessica could picture the little man gasping for air as his face vanished into a poisonous gray haze. For a moment she was tempted to reconsider her decision.

"Mr. Doges," she began, once his fit of coughing had ended, "we've made our decision and we'd like you to become our new head coach."

"You mean *you've* made the decision, Mrs. Laidlaw," answered Doges. "You own the team, don't ya?"

"Yes, I do."

"Well, I've got to hand it to you, lady. You've got guts," Doges said between drags on his cigar. "Not many would take the chance you're taking."

"Maybe it's in my blood," Jessica replied. "My father was a Texas wildcatter. And he taught me big risks sometimes get you big payoffs. . . . Now, as far as a contract is concerned, I'm completely agreeable to the terms we discussed yesterday, with only one other stipulation."

"Which is?" Doges asked suspiciously.

"I get to fire you on the spot if you smoke one of those disgusting cigars anywhere near me," Jessica answered firmly.

There was a long silence at the other end of the line.

"Well, Mr. Doges?" asked Jessica. "I think that's an awfully small price to pay to get another crack at a championship, don't you? After all, there aren't that many owners in the NBA who'll talk to you on the phone, let alone sit with you in the same room."

"You may have a point," he said. "Maybe I should try and cut back."

"I think that would be a fine idea," replied Jessica. "Now, Mr. Doges, I was wondering if you could get up here Wednesday so we could get your contract signed and the press conference out of the way. Then maybe you and I can get down to work."

"No problem," growled Doges. "I'll be there tomorrow afternoon."

As she hung up the phone, the black sedan turned off Seventh Avenue and began its slow descent to the garage beneath the Arena. Jessica stuffed Willie Doges's telephone number back into her briefcase. She knew this was only the beginning of her education and that graduation would come only when a championship pennant was dangling from the rafters over the Arena floor.

For the next several weeks, with Willie Doges reshaping the Knights, Jessica learned about being a team owner. Under the tutelage of Marty Green and Tim Lindeman, she immersed herself in the game—screening hours of tapes, watching innumerable practice sessions from a shadowy seat in the mezzanine, and poring over hundreds of reports, contracts, and statistics. She also spent time dodging Alton Shea.

Since she had left him in London, he had been back to New York three times to oversee work on his new musical. They were short stays, but each time he made an effort to call Jessica, and each time Jessica made up some transparent excuse to avoid meeting him. Bogged down in the numbers, projections, and regulations—the nuts and bolts of any pro sport—she felt she just couldn't risk being swept away by his charm, his good looks, or worse, by some enticing transatlantic invitation.

Finally, toward the end of January, after a week of

persistent phone calls, guilt, and a tongue-lashing from Meredith, Jessica agreed to meet Alton Shea for lunch. With her nights tied up by an important five-game home stand, and his days occupied with rehearsals, lunch seemed like a reasonable compromise. They picked a new restaurant near the Flatiron Building, in more or less neutral territory.

The lunch was a fiasco. After four weeks apart, Alton and Jessica had each returned to the center of their separate worlds, with their brief romance a fragile link between them. He arrived twenty minutes late, and as a result Jessica had to leave before the end of the meal to make a three-thirty appointment on Houston Street.

Neither one of them could bring themselves to talk about what had happened in London. There were too many other things to worry about now, like budgets, season tickets, and theatre-party sales. For a brief moment Jessica and Alton Shea had been lovers, but the moment had been fleeting. Now they were nothing more than friends.

Jessica's crash course in team management continued well into February with the addition of weekly briefings by Willie Doges. They were usually late-night sessions that began an hour or so after a game and went on into early morning. Surprisingly, Doges delighted in them and guided his new employer through the arcane world of pro basketball with great patience and understanding, impressing upon her the rhythms of the game. When he discussed his plays and strategies, he sounded almost poetic, and as the hours stretched into morning, he seemed to become more perceptive, more penetrating, and more alive.

The first real test of Jessica's weeks of study came on Valentine's Day in the form of an article in the *Daily News*. The story, written by Danny DiNome and quoting an unnamed source within the Knights' organization, implied a lack of leadership by the new owner. Cited in the article as examples of this rudderless helm were Jessica's late-night tutorials, her failure to replace Frank DeCicco, the growing influence of Marty Green —recently elevated to vice-president—and Willie Doges.

When Jessica got to her office that morning, Marty Green was already inside waiting for her. He was standing by the window watching the snow fall, his face flushed a bright red, a copy of the *News* rolled up in his hand.

"I take it you've read it," said Jessica, dropping her attaché case on the desk.

Green turned away from the window, shaking his head angrily.

"I have to admit, the man writes with style," added Jessica. "I loved it when he described me as 'wrapped in the arms of the holy trinity of inexperience, indecision, and isolation.' He probably should have included inertia, but I can see where that would have loused up his metaphor . . . Tell me, Marty, you're a writer. What do you think about the story?" she asked, her voice tinged with sarcasm.

"I think the point is, what do you want to do about it?" replied Green, ignoring the question.

"Right. What *do* I want to do?" Jessica muttered to herself. "Damn it. What I want to do is start running this organization," she said forcefully. "Look, Marty, if you cut through all DiNome's snide comments, he isn't really off the mark. There is a big difference between ownership and leadership. I fought hard for this team, and the reality is, I've got to run it. I'm just sorry whoever went to DiNome didn't come to me first."

"Would you have listened?" asked Green cautiously.

"I'd like to think so."

"Jessica, I don't want to seem like an apologist for our rotten apple, but how are these people to know?"

"I'm going to tell them, that's how," she answered. "A week from tomorrow the team gets back from their midwest road trip. Nine o'clock the next morning I want everyone—and I mean everyone who draws a Knights' paycheck—in the Arena. We're all going to get reacquainted."

"Well, that's a start," replied Green. "But I hope you're planning on more than a pep rally."

"You can count on it."

"Is there anything you want me to do about this?" he asked, holding up DiNome's article.

"I want to know who spoke to DiNome."

"Is that really important now? The damage has already been done," Green said defensively.

"You know who it is, don't you, Marty?"

Green shifted nervously in his chair but looked straight at Jessica. He knew what her next question would be and he also knew he could not deny her his loyalty.

Jessica sensed the man's dilemma and offered an avenue of escape. "How about this, Marty? I promise whoever it is won't be fired," she declared. "But that's the extent of my magnanimity."

"It was . . . my assistant . . . Tim Lindeman," Green said meekly. "I just don't know what got into the kid."

"Jesus, Marty, I'm sorry," replied Jessica, genuinely shocked by the revelation.

"So am I," he said. "I guess he thought he'd be doing some good if he shook things up."

"I hope it was only that, because if it isn't, you've got a big problem on your hands."

"Jessica, if I find out it's more than that," added Green, "I'll fire him myself."

Five days later, on a late-morning shuttle and Jonathan Lambert's recommendation, Jessica flew to Washington for lunch at a fashionable Italian restaurant in suburban Virginia. The local aversion to snow kept away many of the regular lunchtime patrons and left

Jessica and her guest, Jerry Barnstable, with a quiet corner of the restaurant to themselves.

"I've looked over the tapes and the reports you've sent me, and I think that if Willie can whip them into shape, they can take you into the play-offs," Barnstable said with authority.

The tall, lanky man had a commanding presence, which he seemed capable of turning on and off at will. Around forty-five, with fine brown hair, a large square jaw, and deep-set eyes, Barnstable looked less like the lawyer he was than the basketball player he had been.

"You're avoiding the issue," Jessica said as she chased a small envelope of pasta around the plate with her fork.

"Which is?"

"Do you think you can work with Willie?" she asked impatiently.

Barnstable's gaze drifted slowly around the empty restaurant, then settled back on Jessica. "Don't you think you're putting the horse before the cart?" he asked, reining in his exasperation. "We haven't even discussed my working for you."

"You know, Jonathan told me a lot about you," she confessed, "but he never mentioned you were coy."

"Look Jessica, I've been around Washington for ten years now," responded Barnstable, "and one of the first things I learned was when you sit down to play cards, you'd better know what you're playing, who you're playing with, and what you're playing for, because there are no friendly games here. . . . So what is it you want, me or my advice?"

After nearly eight weeks of studying the Knights from the inside out, Jessica was desperate for an objective evaluation from the outside in. At breakfast at the Regency the day after DiNome's column appeared, she had discussed her problem with Jonathan Lambert and he had offered his six-foot-four-inch friend from the Harvard Club. Jonathan's ringing endorsement and two rather lengthy phone calls with Barnstable convinced Jessica that he was a man worth recruiting.

A former Ivy League all-star and guard with the Knights, Jerry Barnstable had had an illustrious career as a player. He had been named all-pro six times between 1964 and 1973, the last four times during the Knights' go-go years of 1970–1973, when the team won three consecutive NBA championships.

Retiring from the game at the end of the 1973 season with hall of fame statistics, Barnstable became a full-time lawyer at the firm he had been working for during the off season, and bided his time. His patience paid off in 1974, when, with strong Democratic backing and a weak Republican opponent, he won a seat in Congress from his home district in western Connecticut. But it wasn't that long before the tidal wave of conservatism that swept the country in 1980 dashed his political aspirations and he was forced to take refuge in a liberal Washington law firm, venturing out only occasionally to test the political waters.

"Jerry, I want both you and your advice," Jessica said resolutely. "I want you as vice-president and general manager of the Knights."

Barnstable had known this was coming after the first phone call. He had been following the team in the New York papers and had become curious about the Machiavellian machinations in the front office, even going so far as to discuss the team's situation with Jonathan Lambert on his last visit to New York.

"I know you've been thinking about getting back into basketball," Jessica went on, "and—"

"You really shouldn't believe everything Jonathan says," Barnstable interrupted.

"And I also know you're an old-time flower-power liberal stranded in a conservative town."

"That may change."

"If you move."

"Or if the country does," Barnstable replied wistfully.

"Well, let's say this will give you something a little different to do while you wait," Jessica said. "Who knows, maybe you're even finding law a little boring."

"What did you practice, Jessica, contract law?" asked Barnstable.

"Real estate, mostly. Why do you ask?"

"And I'll bet none of your deals ever fell apart," he said, recognizing a shrewd negotiator.

"Not many," she answered with a modest smile.

"Everyone left the table fat and happy?"

"You could say that."

"Then I'll talk over your proposition with my wife this evening and give you my answer tomorrow morning."

"Thank you, Jerry. I really can't ask for anything more from you. . . . Now, if you're going to leave fat and happy," she said, gesturing to the captain, "how about some dessert?"

The team returned to New York late Wednesday in fourth place after winning three of their five road games. The players were in high spirits as their plane touched down at La Guardia, and Willie Doges had to remind them several times of the meeting the following morning.

The doors to the Arena were opened by building security shortly after eight-thirty. Around five to nine the hundred or so employees of the Knights' organization silently entered the brightly lit hall and filled the first ten rows of center court seats. At exactly nine o'clock, Jessica walked onto center court accompanied by Willie Doges, Marty Green, and Jerry Barnstable. A table, three chairs, and a narrow podium had been set up in front of the team bench. Jessica approached the podium while the three men took the seats to her right.

"Good morning, everyone," she began. "I know

you're all busy so I'll try and be brief. First, I'd like to congratulate the players and the coaching staff on a very successful road trip. Incidentally, the last ten seconds against Detroit were especially sweet." Interrupted momentarily by applause and shouts of affirmation, Jessica continued, "I'd also like to thank the players for being here this morning. I know how late you all got in last night."

Out of the corner of her eye, Jessica spotted a tall black man in a brightly patterned sweater and black leather pants, trying to slip unnoticed through a set of doors to her right. "Clearly, some later than others . . . Mr. Tilden," Jessica called out to the new arrival, "your skulking is as bad as your outside shooting."

Good-natured laughter and hoots from the players followed, and Jessica couldn't help but smile. "Isaac," she said, "come on over here and sit down."

The young man strode quickly across the floor to take his place with the other players seated in the first two rows.

"By the way, Isaac . . ." said Jessica.

Tilden stopped in his tracks and turned, flipping his large, blue-tinted sunglasses up on his forehead and looking warily at Jessica.

"I like what you did against Chicago on Saturday," she added appreciatively.

A broad, self-conscious grin broke over the young player's face.

"Now sit down so I can finish," she ordered with mock indignation.

The rest of Jessica's speech took no more than ten minutes. She refuted many of the points raised in DiNome's column, but was careful to avoid any direct reference to it. Her intent was simply to convince the players and staff that there was an intelligent, capable, and determined owner watching from the sky box.

". . . there's no question the extra money would be gratifying," she told them, "but keep in mind that ten

years from now what you'll remember is not the
money, but the pride in knowing you were the best." To
emphasize her point and heighten the drama of her
announcement, she glanced over at Jerry Barnstable.
"And no one knows that better," she continued, "than
our new vice-president and general manager, Jerry
Barnstable."

Polite applause followed Jerry Barnstable as he rose
and joined Jessica at the podium. For most of the staff
and certainly the players, Jerry Barnstable was one of
those sports figures who showed up at old-timers'
games and reunions and was remembered when talk
turned to the team's "glory years." As a general
manager, he was an unknown commodity. As he spoke,
Jessica scanned the faces in the stands and realized it
was going to take some time for the full effect of her
decision to percolate up from the rank and file.

After the meeting Jessica and the three men remained behind as the staff filed out of the Arena.

"Marty," said Jessica, "would you do me a favor and
catch Tim before he leaves?"

"Jessica, are you sure you want to do this now?"
Green asked cautiously.

"This is as good a time as any," she answered.

Jessica was listening intently to Willie Doges's vivid
description of last night's win over Detroit when Marty
Green returned with Tim Lindeman in tow. Noticing
the pale, redheaded young man with the patrician
bearing, Jessica excused herself from the others then
shepherded Lindeman across to the visitors' side of the
court.

"I wanted to see you, Tim," Jessica began, "because I
wanted to know what you thought about my little
speech."

"I'm not sure what you mean, Mrs. Laidlaw," the
young man replied uneasily.

"I mean, did you approve of it? Was I forceful
enough? Did it satisfy you?" Jessica asked icily.

"What?" asked Lindeman, caught off balance by the flurry of questions.

"Look Tim," Jessica said firmly. "Let me make myself clear. I expect three things from the people who work for me—performance, loyalty, and honesty. You've already shortchanged me on two of those things, but because of a promise I made to Marty, I'm going to let it pass. But keep in mind, Marty may need you, but I don't. Do you understand?"

"Yes," Lindeman answered hesitantly.

"Good. Now get back to your office and try to justify Marty's faith in you," said Jessica.

Tim Lindeman walked quickly across the floor, deliberately averting his eyes as he passed Marty Green and Jerry Barnstable.

"Well?" said Marty Green as she rejoined them.

"Well what, Marty?" replied Jessica. "You wanted him. You've got him. I just hope we get something more out of him than his undying gratitude."

"Someone I should keep my eye on?" asked Jerry.

Jessica immediately shot a glance over at Marty Green, waiting for a response.

"No," Green said sullenly, "I'll handle him."

Jessica wanted to take her frustration out on Marty Green. Instead, she just shook her head, then led the two men out of the Arena.

Chapter 39

It was a little after noon in Houston when Nedra Wheeler, using an ivory-handled walking stick and wearing a sumptuous black mink coat, emerged from her steel-gray high-rise apartment at the corner of San Felipe and Post Oak Road to begin her daily promenade to the nearby shops and malls.

As she passed through the lobby, an elderly couple entering the building stopped to greet her. They briefly traded building gossip and decried the unusually cold February weather before Nedra Wheeler, not wanting to be late for her luncheon appointment with her younger daughter, cut short the conversation and hurried out the front door.

A cold, clammy wind snapped at her cheeks and jabbed at her withered knee as she walked the half mile from her apartment to the Galleria, the granddaddy of Houston's shopping malls. Halfway there Nedra stopped, set her cane against a nearby wall, and fastened the top button of her coat. Noticing a speck of gray ash on the sleeve, she gently swept her fingers through the rich black fur. The coat, a Christmas gift from Jessica, had become her prized possession. She loved the way it set off her boyishly short gray hair and delicate skin. At fifty-five, Nedra, unmarried and with two beautiful daughters mirroring the years, still coveted the attention of handsome men and the jealous whispers of married women.

Grabbing her cane, she hurried on her way. She was never late to the Wednesday lunch. It had been a tradition with her and her mother in Midland for over thirty years, and when her mother died and she moved to Houston five years ago, Kendall insisted that the tradition be maintained. They met once a week at a restaurant within walking distance of the San Felipe apartment to play out, in hushed tones, the antagonism, jealousy, and guilt at the root of every mother-daughter relationship, amid the quiet tinkle of silverware and the polite conversation of fashionable Houston society.

Nedra Wheeler took two more steps down Post Oak Road and suddenly everything—her seventeen-year marriage, her daughters, the new fur coat—everything in her life became irrelevant. Because at that instant a twenty-year-old girl in a white Datsun sports car, trying to avoid a pickup truck stopped in the middle of the road, hit the accelerator, thinking it was the brake. Her car leapt the curb and, before anyone could shout a warning, pinned Nedra Wheeler between the front bumper and the low brick wall.

Kendall Pointer hastily hooked the front of her brassiere, pulled on her silk blouse, then wriggled her black leather miniskirt over her narrow hips. In the distance she could hear the wail of sirens as they converged on the Post Oak Shopping Center, five blocks and twenty-eight floors away. After slipping into her shoes, she grabbed her jacket from a sleek black-lacquered Italian armoire, then checked herself in the long mirror inside the door. Fully dressed, she still looked like she had just made love. Her blond hair, cut short on the sides, tumbled carelessly over her face, and her lush red lips were swollen from her lover's bruising kisses.

She paused by the open bathroom door on her way out of the bedroom. "Wyatt, I've gotta run," she shouted, "or I'm going to be late for lunch, and that drives my mama absolutely crazy."

"Okay," a man yelled over the noise of the shower, "but will I see you tomorrow night?"

"I don't know," Kendall answered. "Larry said he had to go up to Fort Worth tomorrow to cover the opening of some museum or gallery. I'm not sure which. Why don't I call you tomorrow morning, when I know when he's going to get back?"

"Call me here, then," said the man. "I've got a breakfast meeting here at nine."

"Here?" Kendall asked suspiciously.

"Yes, here. Four Cowboy cheerleaders are flying down from Dallas to do me in the hot tub," replied the voice behind the shower door.

"You bastard," said Kendall. Slipping into the bathroom, she silently opened the shower door and turned off the hot water.

"Jesus Christ, Kendall!" screamed the man. "That's not fucking funny!"

"Neither was the crack about the cheerleaders."

"Fine, the president of First Commercial likes Marina's huevos rancheros. Does that make you feel better?" he asked.

"Only if it's the truth," she answered.

"Dammit, Kendall, you're impossible. Go ahead and ask Marina on your way out."

"Sure, I should ask your goddamn housekeeper who you're entertaining," said Kendall. "That woman would probably shoot her own mother to keep from being deported."

"What do you mean, deported? She was born in San

Antonio. . . . You amaze me," said the tall, chestnut brown haired man as he stepped from the shower and reached for a towel. "You're the one cheating on your husband, and you're worried about me being unfaithful."

"Fuck you, Wyatt," Kendall snapped as she looked down at her watch. "Oh, shit, I'm going to be late again." She turned and headed for the bedroom door.

"Don't forget to call me," he shouted after her. "I should be here until eleven."

"Have I ever forgotten?" she yelled back.

Downstairs, in the foyer of the penthouse apartment, Kendall stepped into the private elevator and pressed the button for the garage. As she descended to the basement, she wondered why she didn't just stop this charade and divorce Larry. Perhaps it was because he needed her. No one else did—not her mother, not her older sister, and especially not Wyatt Reynolds. He didn't want or need anyone.

While searching for a pair of gloves, Jessica found the large brown paper bag a hospital nurse had given Kendall after her mother had been taken in for surgery. It was jammed into the back of her mother's hall closet between a pair of well-worn suede boots and a carton of old clothes undoubtedly destined for some charity thrift shop. The top of the bag had been stapled shut and her mother's name and a number had been hastily scribbled across the outside in big black letters. As though discovering a precious artifact, Jessica loosened the staples with a fingernail then opened the bag, taking great care not to rip the paper.

Inside on top of the clothes, was a smaller bag containing her mother's black gloves, shoes, handbag, and jewelry. As Jessica removed the little bag and set it on the floor, she could see what remained of the black mink coat. The coat, its front caked with blood, had been cut apart in the emergency room by the trauma team and was now lying in shreds at the bottom of the bag.

Jessica gently stroked the matted fur. She remembered what joy the coat had brought her mother. At Michael Forrest in New York her mother had spent hours modifying the original design, and in the process had charmed the handsome salesman. Jessica remembered the nights her mother dressed to go to the country club with her father, when she looked so beautiful and smelled of peach blossoms and rain, and the nights after her father died, when her mother's strength was the only thing that seemed to hold them all together.

As she stood in the hallway, her childhood memories seemed to ebb and flow, breaking apart then fusing with her memories of Mark and her own unspoken fear of death. Jessica began to sob, her tears falling on the dark fur, giving the dried blood an unnatural sheen.

After the funeral in Midland, Jessica had returned to Houston with Kendall to help sort out their mother's affairs. As the youngest and the one closest to their mother, Kendall had been devastated by her death. Since she was a little girl, Kendall had fought valiantly to please her mother—trying to be prettier, brighter, more polite—but she never quite succeeded. There was always something—a smudged knee, a C on a test—that seemed to undermine her best efforts. But now there were no more chances to please, and Kendall realized she was going to have to live with her failure.

Wiping the tears from her cheeks, Jessica stuffed the stained and ripped clothing back into the bag and carried it to the service hall behind the kitchen. Then she walked slowly through the apartment, stopping at the faded pictures of her mother and father on the piano to reflect on the "what if's" of life. Soon the chimes from a small brass Tiffany clock on the mantle roused Jessica from her daydream. Picking her coat off the sofa, she threw it over her shoulders, and, without looking back, left the apartment.

Halfway down the hall Jessica could hear the telephone begin to ring in the empty apartment. Ahead of her a patch of light cut across the dimly lit hall as the elevator door opened. She stood silent and still for a moment, then made a dash for the waiting elevator.

Kendall and Larry rented a modest two-bedroom town house in a half-finished complex on Burgoyne Road about ten minutes from her mother's apartment. Although the occupied buildings were clean and well-maintained and the lawns around them well-manicured, the abandoned construction gave the compound an air of impermanence, as though the completed buildings were simply awaiting the fate of the denuded ones.

Jessica was about to press the doorbell when the door flew open and her brother-in-law rushed by her with a camera bag over his shoulder.

"Larry?" said Jessica, dodging the bearlike man.

"Oh, sorry, Jess," he replied. "I've got to run. The office just called. They want me to fill in for someone at a NASA press conference. Kendall's upstairs. I'll see you later."

Jessica's sister was waiting nervously for her in the circular foyer at the top of the landing. She was wearing one of Larry's old football jerseys, a pair of ragged jeans, and no makeup. Her hair was combed away from her face and her eyes were puffy and red.

"Where have you been?" Kendall demanded, clearly upset by her sister's tardiness. "I called the apartment three times."

"Looking for black gloves," Jessica replied as she hung up her coat in the hall closet. "I couldn't find Mama's," she lied, "so I stopped off at the Galleria."

"Why didn't you call me?" asked Kendall.

"Because I'm only five minutes late," said Jessica.

"You still should have called," Kendall insisted.

"Kendall, you've got to stop this," Jessica pleaded. "Everytime someone is late doesn't mean something terrible has happened to them."

"I know that Jess," Kendall replied softly. "Remember, I'm the one who's always late. Mama always used to tell me how rude I was and said how it reflected badly on her. Because in Midland it was a sign of poor upbringing."

Jessica smiled at her sister. Their mother's indisputable sense of right and wrong and her ability to instantly assess blame for any transgression had always sent Kendall running to her room in frustration. She often claimed that arguing with her mother was like arguing with Scarlet O'Hara.

"Anyway, waiting for her in that restaurant, I figured she was trying to teach me a lesson," Kendall went on, "so the longer I waited, the angrier I got. And then came that phone call . . . Oh, Jess, I can't forgive myself for being so furious, and I can't seem to forgive Mama for being so self-righteous."

"Kendall, you're being too hard on yourself," said Jessica, putting her arm around her younger sister. "And you can't blame Mama for being who she was."

"But Jess, she was on me all the time."

"Kendall, you were her baby," said Jessica. "She wanted you to be perfect."

"She didn't seem to mind what *you* did," Kendall argued.

"That's because I was Daddy's little girl," Jessica replied. "And when Daddy died, I guess too much of John D. had rubbed off on me for Mama to contend with. Oh, Mama loved me and I dearly loved her," Jessica said, her voice choked with emotion, "but what she felt for you, Kendall, was something special."

"Then she did love me?" Kendall asked as tears ran down her cheeks.

"Sweetheart," said Jessica tenderly, "more than you could ever imagine."

Jessica held her sister and stroked her head as she wept. Now that they were both alone, she felt closer to the young woman in her arms than she had at any other time in their lives. They were each other's only link to a wild, impetuous, West Texas oilman, his beautiful, genteel, lady, and to a carefree childhood on an endless plain.

An hour later they were sitting around Kendall's dining room table, their mother's papers spread out in front of them.

"And this was everything she left in your safety deposit box?" asked Jessica, jotting down figures on a yellow pad.

"This is it," Kendall answered.

"You know, Kendall," said Jessica, "it's just a rough estimate, but I'd say Mama left an estate worth somewhere in the neighborhood of four and a half or five million dollars."

"What! . . . That's impossible," Kendall replied incredulously. "I thought she just had enough to buy the apartment and live comfortably."

"Frankly, so did I," said Jessica. "Actually, she only had an income of around forty thousand dollars a year from some bank accounts and mutual funds. The bulk of the estate seems to be tied up with oil leases from Daddy's estate and a five-percent interest in an oil partnership."

"And that's worth four or five million?" asked Kendall.

"More or less. Depending on the price of oil," answered Jessica.

"I wonder why she didn't do anything with them?"

"Knowing Mama, she probably felt just fine with what she had coming in and didn't want any more,"

said Jessica, trying to second-guess her mother's mo-
tives. "And besides, when the price of oil plummeted, it
dried up the market for these assets. I'm sure during
the past several years the partnership had no interest in
buying back Mama's shares at any price."

"And now?" asked Kendall.

"Well, the market is rebounding," replied Jessica.
"And money is beginning to flow back into the oil
business."

"So what do we do?"

"We try to find a buyer. Someone who's willing to
take chances and has a lot of money," added Jessica
bluntly.

"Funny, I may know just the man," Kendall said with
a self-satisfied grin on her face.

"Oh, really?" Jessica said curiously. "Anyone I
know?"

"No. Just somebody I recently sold a penthouse
condo to in West Oaks."

"I hope it was a big one."

"The top three floors."

"Him we should talk to," said Jessica.

"I can set it up, Jess, but I'd rather you spoke with
him alone," replied Kendall. "I know how to sell real
estate. I know nothing about partnerships and oil
leases."

"Fine. I'll do it, but only on one condition."

"What?" said Kendall, as though they were teenagers
again and Jessica had asked to borrow her favorite skirt.
"What's the condition?"

"That you and Larry keep the entire estate."

"Jess, are you crazy?"

"No, Kendall. I mean it," said Jessica. "I'd just like a
few personal things of Mama's, that's all. And we can
go through those things together."

"I don't think it's right, Jess," replied Kendall.
"Mama left that money for the two of us."

"Well, I do," Jessica insisted. "Look, Kendall, it's no secret Mark left me a very wealthy woman. So it would please me, and I know it would have pleased Mama, if you and Larry accept the money. . . . Honestly, Kendall, knowing Mama, she probably made us equal beneficiaries just so my feelings wouldn't be hurt."

Kendall looked around the sparsely decorated apartment, then shook her head grudgingly. "Okay, Jess, I'll do it," said Kendall. Then she got up from her chair, walked around the table and hugged and kissed Jessica. "Thank you, big sister," she whispered. "Thank you for being here."

Houston Capital Holdings was located on the twentieth floor of one of the city's ubiquitous glass and steel office towers. Constructed in the early seventies, the blue-tinted building had become notable for its early postmodernist architecture and because it was one of the few in downtown Houston not to change hands during the cataclysmic collapse of the real estate market in the early eighties.

Seated in the beige and chrome reception area with a panoramic view of Houston behind her, Jessica casually flipped through the latest issue of *Sports Illustrated*, ignoring the short article on Frank DeCicco's appointment as general manager of the Philadelphia franchise. She had learned about DeCicco's negotiations with Philadelphia ten days earlier, when Chet Newberry, the owner, called her about the restrictions in her buyout agreement with DeCicco. Disgusted but not threatened by DeCicco, Jessica agreed to waive the restrictions in return for a pro rata payback on his contract.

"Mrs. Laidlaw?"

Jessica looked up from her magazine at the wavy-haired man in his early thirties standing in front of her. His face was incredibly handsome by any standard, but there was something about it that struck her as odd or eerie. It appeared that his perfect features had been perfectly assembled, without the slightest hint of the asymmetry that haunts every human face. It was as though he had been the product of a determined sculptor's chisel and mallet rather than the haphazard pairing of genes and chromosomes. Yet there was life and energy in his face. His eyes, a vivid green, sparkled and danced like sunlight on a remote tropical sea; the thin creases in his cheeks twisted into wide commas with the faintest glimmer of a smile.

"I'm Wyatt Reynolds," he said, politely extending his hand. "I was terribly sorry to hear about your mother's death."

"Thank you," Jessica replied softly. Rising from her chair, Jessica found it difficult to conceal her surprise. From her sister's balance-sheet description of the man, she had expected someone much older and somewhat more bookish, not this slightly raffish Marlboro man in gray flannel.

"I know," remarked Reynolds, sensing Jessica's immediate confusion, "it's amazing how much shorter I sound over the phone."

"I have to admit, Mr. Reynolds," Jessica replied, reaching for his hand, "you're not quite what I had expected."

"Don't worry," Reynolds said apologetically, "it happens a lot. I just wish people would learn to describe me less in terms of my assets, then I could avoid these awkward first meetings . . .

"And please, call me Wyatt." He couldn't help noticing the quizzical expression on Jessica's face. "It was my mother," he began to explain. "She had this thing for Hugh O'Brian, the actor who played Wyatt Earp. Anyway, she already had a brother named Hugh, which meant she wasn't left with much choice when I came along. I guess it could have been worse. She could have named me after his horse."

They both laughed.

"Let's go to my office," he continued, "and I'll tell you how a man my age came to own this firm, and you can tell me about your mother's oil partnership, and we'll both have learned what we wanted to know."

Reynolds's office, at the end of a narrow hallway, was a study in contrasts. Computers, telephones, a sophisticated audio/video system, and other assorted high-tech gadgets vied for space in the large room with row upon row of old books. Most of the volumes were gilded, with heavy leather bindings, and all rested securely on lightly stained oak shelves. At one end of the office, on a riser a step or two up from the floor and surrounded by a polished brass railing, was a large oak table. The identical shade as the bookcases, it was littered with stacks of oversized, accordion-pleated computer printouts, some of them spilling onto the floor.

Jessica glanced around the room. "Are you a collector?" she asked, fixing on the books.

"Just clutter and first editions," Reynolds replied as he ushered her to a circular sofa adjacent to a bank of tinted floor-to-ceiling windows. "Are you interested in books?"

"Only as a reader," answered Jessica.

"Well, that puts you ahead of most," said Reynolds, reaching for a folder on the coffee table in front of the sofa. "I've done a little research on your mother's partnership based on what little your sister told me," he said, getting right to the point, "and I think it's a fine investment. Frankly, I don't understand why you want to sell."

"Let's say the oil business is a little too cyclical," Jessica replied judiciously, "and I'd like to restructure these assets so that they generate more income."

"Excuse my presumptuousness, Mrs. Laidlaw—"

"Please, make it Jessica," she interrupted.

"Well, then, Jessica," he began, "based on what I've

read about *your* extensive holdings, I would strongly recommend against this type of restructuring."

"So would I, if I were presumptuous enough to believe what I read about my 'extensive holdings' and I wasn't talking about my sister's inheritance," Jessica answered, her tone mildly reproving.

"Forgive me," Reynolds replied, breaking into his best "aw, shucks, ma'am" smile. "I usually don't put my foot in my mouth so soon."

Jessica knew that syrupy grin, and she also knew that Wyatt Reynolds hadn't put his foot in his mouth since he was six months old. As a child she had seen her father flash that same milk-and-honey smile when she traveled with him around West Texas. Grinning from ear to ear, he snapped up oil leases between Midland and Odessa on his way to making and losing his second million. It was his way of thanking someone for showing their hand too soon. Jessica could easily imagine the number of corporate chairmen and Wall Street bankers who had succumbed to Reynolds's "good ol' boy" charm and had been beguiled by that well-oiled grin.

"You're forgiven, if we can get back to my mother's assets," said Jessica, waiting cagily for the other shoe to drop.

"Fair enough," he said. Then, taking a new tack, he began a lengthy and perceptive evaluation of the partnership.

"So you're interested?" Jessica asked as he wound down.

"Maybe."

"And what does maybe mean?"

"Let's say I'm interested, but in slightly more than your mother's five percent," answered Reynolds.

"How much more?" she asked, growing weary of this oblique conversation.

"All of it," he replied.

"All of it?" she mused aloud.

"Right," said Reynolds, reaffirming his position without any further explanation. "Now, why don't you go ahead and probate your mother's will," he added, as though he was used to making decisions for everyone in his life. "I'll make some phone calls. And then let's see if you and I can do a little 'bidness.'" The word seemed to roll out of his mouth with polished perfection, enhancing his myth as a Texas wheeler-dealer.

As Jessica stood and shook Wyatt Reynolds's hand, she was momentarily aroused by the energy in the fast-talking Texan's touch. She found something just a little sexy about so much self-assurance distilled from so much conceit.

"By the way, it's a Mercedes, isn't it?" Reynolds asked out of the blue as they were walking toward the reception area.

"Pardon me?" asked Jessica, trying to digest the non sequitur.

"Your car. You own a Mercedes, don't you?"

"Why, yes. But how—"

"It's the way you dress," Reynolds replied smoothly, "expensive but understated. Look, if you ever decide to trade up—"

"Don't tell me," Jessica groaned. "You sell Rolls-Royces too."

"It's the largest dealership in Texas," he said proudly.

"Why do I have the feeling I should have known that?" said Jessica, shaking her head.

"No reason. It's only a hobby."

"Is all this a hobby too?" asked Jessica as she gestured around the reception area.

"No. This was a challenge," he answered.

"Was? . . . Don't you have any challenges left?"

"A few."

"Such as?"

"No. I don't think I should," he said with unaccustomed modesty.

"Come on," Jessica insisted. "You just tried to sell me a car. I think that gives me some rights."

"Well, then, how about Texas women with New York manners," he answered.

"You know, Wyatt," said Jessica, finally returning his good-ol'-boy smile, "I've always admired men who go after impossible challenges."

Chapter 40

Emotionally drained, Jessica returned to New York a week later. Her first few days back were spent in bed nursing a bad cold and trying to crawl out of the unbearable depression that had come crashing down around her the moment she had stepped off the plane. In Houston, being with Kendall and sorting out her mother's affairs, she had had, even amid the sorrow, a sense of purpose, something to insulate her from the grim reality of her loneliness. Back in New York that all changed.

While she was away, the Knights, under Willie Doges and Jerry Barnstable, had begun playing consistent five-hundred ball and had moved into third place in the Atlantic Division. Jerry's periodic calls to Houston to update the team's progress and get her okay on trades and budgets had, for a time, made her feel useful and needed. However, she quickly realized she was just rubber-stamping Jerry's decisions. Not that they weren't the right ones. Jerry had been the ideal choice for general manager. There was no denying that the job fitted him to a tee and that his presence gave the entire organization a well-needed shot in the arm. To everyone, that is, except Jessica, who, for the moment, seemed to find herself out of two jobs—team owner and daughter.

In four days she was over the cold, but the depression took a little longer. She fought as hard as she could against it, dragging herself into the office every day and occupying her time with paperwork and the occasional staff meeting. However, she found she couldn't concentrate on the simplest things.

Toward the middle of the month Meredith finally managed to spirit Jessica away from the office to rejoin the gang of four for lunch. In deference to Julie's recent motherhood, they decided to meet at Julie's Yorkville apartment to ogle the baby, swap gossip, and comfort Jessica.

They had all agreed to limit lunch to an hour and a half so everyone could get back to work, but by three they were just having coffee. Everyone was solicitous of Jessica, anxious to wrest her from her depression and raise her spirits. Meredith and Liz, with the best intentions, offered their shoulders and company, while Julie simply offered her daughter, Megan.

After Meredith and Liz left, Jessica held the baby in her arms in a chair by the sunny nursery window and rocked her to sleep. She studied the baby's perfectly formed little fingers, curled up into tiny fists in front of her face, and painstakingly monitored the steady rhythms of her breathing. The warmth from the small body seemed to infuse her entire being, and for a moment, she felt her loneliness melting away.

Julie quietly entered the baby's room and stood next to Jessica. "It's magical, isn't it?" she whispered as she looked down at her daughter.

Jessica nodded. They both understood the meaning

of the magic. In the abstract it could probably be explained away by some simple hormonal change or some quantum leap in evolution a billion years ago, but to the two women it was much more. It was the purest form of love, a bond often tested but never broken, even by death.

"You know, Jess," said Julie, gently stroking the top of her daughter's head, "when Ronnie looks at Megan he sees continuity, the promise of the future . . . I guess I see that too, but I also see my mother, my grandmother, and I know it's that past that steadies us for the future and makes us what we are. I think it takes a birth or a death to make us understand that."

"Maybe it does," said Jessica. Then she leaned over and kissed the sleeping baby on the forehead.

By the beginning of April Jessica's veil of depression had lifted and she began to take satisfaction in the team's progress. Although ten and half games behind division-leading Boston, there was still the distinct possibility that the Knights could finish the season in second place.

With the promise of a winning season finally within her grasp, a buoyantly optimistic Jessica emerged from the elevator on the twenty-sixth floor on a breezy Monday morning. There was an exuberance in her step as she crossed the reception area and stopped abruptly at her secretary's desk to admire a striking floral arrangement.

"My goodness, Dorothy. They certainly are beautiful," said Jessica, picking her messages off the edge of the desk. "What's the occasion?"

"There's no occasion, Mrs. Laidlaw. At least, not that I know of," replied the secretary hesitantly. "They just said it was part of the order."

"I'm afraid I don't understand, Dorothy," said Jessica. "What order? And who is 'they'?"

"The designer and the delivery men."

"What designer?"

"I think you'd better have a look at your office," replied Dorothy, "and please understand, Mrs. Laidlaw, there was nothing I could do to stop them. They were already finished by the time I got here."

Fearing the worst, Jessica slowly opened the door to her office and was immediately overwhelmed by an explosion of fragrance and color. The whole office had been turned into a large floral tableau.

"Oh, my," Jessica murmured as she walked around the room, marveling at the careful integration of plants and flowers.

"They said they got here at six-thirty, but no one seems to know how they got in," said Dorothy, following closely behind Jessica.

"Just lovely," Jessica said, completely dazzled by the transformation. "Who could imagine . . ." Her voice trailed off as she ran her fingertips over a spray of rubrum lilies.

"Oh," exclaimed the secretary absentmindedly, "there's a card." Almost as an afterthought, Dorothy slowly removed a small white envelope from behind a white porcelain vase and handed it to Jessica.

Jessica opened the envelope and removed the card. The message read:

> Although Oscar Wilde was a morally bankrupt sodomite, most Texans would tend to agree with him that "nothing succeeds like excess." Will you have dinner with me this evening?
>
> Wyatt Reynolds

"Jesus," said Jerry Barnstable as he stood in the doorway of the office. "What's going on? This place looks like a float in the Tournament of Roses Parade."

"Well, if you must know," replied Jessica smugly, "it's a dinner invitation."

"From whom? A Texas florist?" said Barnstable.

"Well, you've got the right state, but the wrong profession," Jessica answered coyly.

Moored in the shadow of the Brooklyn Bridge, the barge bearing the River Café sat motionless in its slip amid the shifting currents of the East River. Jessica and Wyatt Reynolds sat at a table by a wall of windows that looked out on the inky river and the lights of lower Manhattan beyond. The scene, refracted and diffused by a misty rain, evoked the delicate and determined brush strokes of a Monet landscape while their conversation skittered from the mundane to the sublime.

"You said over the phone this was to be a celebration," said Jessica, watching out of the corner of her eye as the waiter, with great care, poured champagne into her glass. "Exactly what is it we're celebrating?"

"Our partnership," replied Reynolds.

"And what partnership is that?" Jessica asked warily.

"Well, if you've already renounced your claim to your mother's estate," answered Reynolds, "I'd have to say, more accurately, my partnership with your sister."

"You mean you've acquired the rest of the outstanding shares?" she asked.

Reynolds nodded and smiled.

"I am impressed," said Jessica.

"I knew you would be," he replied confidently. "That's why I pushed so hard to close the deal with the others. I wanted to see you again and I didn't want to wait."

"I'm flattered," she said, "but I find it a little difficult to believe you rushed a multimillion-dollar deal just so you could have dinner with me. You could've called."

"No, I don't think so," he answered thoughtfully. "That's too subtle."

Three hours later Wyatt Reynolds's limousine turned onto East Seventy-fifth Street and double-parked in front of Jessica's town house. The rain had stopped and the street was wet and shiny and criss-crossed with shadows from the barren trees in the ghostly, blue-white streetlights.

"Would you like to come in for a drink?" asked Jessica, somewhat surprised at her own impulsiveness.

"I'd really love to, Jessica, but I've got to be in Houston tomorrow morning for an eleven o'clock appointment," Reynolds said reluctantly.

"Eleven? Isn't that cutting it a little close? The earliest flight out of here is seven."

"Not really. I've had my pilot schedule us out of Butler as soon as it opens," replied Reynolds. "That's why I have to take a rain check on the drink."

"You never mentioned you had a plane."

"You never asked."

"A large one?"

"Big enough . . . Now, where are you going with this?"

"Nowhere," replied Jessica. "I was just being nosy."

"Well, in that case," Reynolds began, "it's a Gulfstream Four with twin Rolls-Royce turbofan engines, the latest computerized avionics, a complete galley, and a double bed in the aft cabin that sleeps two rather comfortably."

"That sounds very cozy."

"It is. Now, if I may be permitted a question?" he said.

"Sir?"

"When are you coming back to Houston?"

"Is that a personal or a professional question?" Jessica asked brazenly.

"Both," replied Reynolds with a hopeful look on his face.

"Well, the team does have one last away game with Houston two weeks from today," said Jessica. "And I'm sure it would be good for morale if they knew the owner was there cheering them on."

"Wonderful," he replied. "If you like, I'll send the

plane for you on Friday. We can settle with your sister's shares and maybe spend some time together. How does that sound?"

"I think I might like that," she answered.

"Then I'll make some plans for us," said Reynolds. He tapped on the window to alert the driver, then turned back to Jessica. "I had a wonderful evening, Jessica," he said. "Thank you."

"So did I."

Utterly captivated by Jessica all evening long and no longer able to control himself, Reynolds leaned forward to kiss her. As he did, an untamed shock of chestnut brown hair dropped over his forehead. Reaching up, Jessica gently brushed the errant strands back into place.

"Don't you think you may be rushing things?" she whispered.

"Do you like to be rushed?" he asked as he threaded his arms around her.

"Sometimes," she countered slyly.

Reynolds drew her close and kissed her. Her lips yielded to his and she felt him take her breath away. Then she kissed him back, rebounding off his passion, her arms wrapped around his broad shoulders.

Chapter 41

The early morning stillness was shattered by an explosion. At first it had sounded like a car backfiring, but something deep in Dennis Melchiorre's memory told him otherwise. Although the war had ended over forty years ago, he still couldn't forget that loud, sharp, cracking noise and the death and pain that accompanied it. He eased himself out of bed, careful not to disturb his wife, and walked slowly to the window. It took a minute or two for his eyes to adjust to the darkness as he peered out across his driveway, beyond his neatly trimmed hedge, at the wide expanse of lawn in front of his neighbor's house. After only a glimpse out the window, he rushed to a nearby nightstand and picked up the telephone.

"Operator, would you get me the police, please," he said, his voice firm, controlled.

"Dennis, what is it?" asked his wife, awakened by the rustling around her.

Suddenly they heard a woman shriek followed by

another explosion and the sound of breaking glass.

"My God, Dennis, what is going on out there?" she asked again, frightened by the strange noises and the look on her husband's face.

Ignoring his wife's pleas, Melchiorre finished his conversation with the police. "Just stay in bed, Harriet," he said as he returned to the window, this time cautiously peeking out from around the edge of the curtain.

Across the way, in the middle of the gently sloping lawn next door, Melchiorre could see a young black woman in her early twenties screaming obscenities and firing random pistol shots into the windows of the large, two-story brick house in front of her. The woman, slim and attractive, was naked to the waist, the remnants of an expensive ivory silk negligee draped around her hips. Blood was streaming from the young woman's nose and from a cut above her right eye.

Finally, with the gun empty and her rage sapped by exhaustion and cold, the woman dragged herself to the doorstep of the house and collapsed on the cold brick, sobbing uncontrollably. It wasn't long before a tall black man appeared at one of the shattered windows. Cautiously he scanned the front lawn, then disappeared from view. Seconds later the front door opened and the man, wearing only white satin shorts, emerged. He looked up and down the street, then scooped up the young woman and carried her back into the house.

An uneasy silence settled over the neighborhood— not unlike the deceptive calm in the eye of a hurricane —soon to vanish in a maelstrom of police sirens and flashing lights.

The blinking red light on the desk phone went unnoticed as Jessica entered her hotel suite late that Saturday afternoon, tired and a little tipsy. She had spent most of the morning with Kendall at Wyatt

Reynolds's office, finishing up the paperwork associated with the sale of her mother's oil shares. A long lunch at Tony's with Kendall and Wyatt Reynolds had followed and now she was eager to relax before meeting Wyatt again for dinner.

After kicking off her shoes, Jessica walked into the bedroom and dropped onto the bed. She tried to close her eyes, but the wine at lunch seemed to make the bed pitch and roll. Wide-eyed, she stared up at the stippled acoustical ceiling, then her gaze began to drift slowly around the room until it fixed on the pulsating red light on the nightstand. She debated calling down for the messages, then deciding there was little chance of sleep with the bed twisting and turning, she reached for the phone.

"A Mr. Barnstable from New York called you twice," reported the operator with a gentle drawl, "once at eleven-thirty and again at three. He'd like you to call him immediately at his office."

The words "at his office" made Jessica uncomfortable. Jerry always made a point of spending Saturday with his family, and in the two and a half months he had been with the team, she had never known him to let anything intrude on his weekends. Jessica flipped through her Filofax for the number of Jerry's private line, then dialed New York. The phone rang once before he answered.

"It's me, Jerry. I'm sorry I didn't get back to you sooner. I just got my messages."

"Did you finish all your business?" he asked, his question practically begging for a positive response.

"More or less," answered Jessica, now nearly certain that this conversation would end her plans for the weekend. "All right, Jerry, who or what is our problem? I know you didn't come in today to show your son where his father works."

"It's Ralph Johnstone," said Barnstable.

"Damn it, not again," Jessica replied. "Is it drugs?"

"And assault."

"Oh, Christ, and I thought we had gotten him cleaned up," said Jessica. "Who did he beat up?"

"His wife. Early this morning. Slammed her around pretty good. Broke her nose."

"Is he in jail?" she asked.

"No. She wouldn't press charges," replied Barnstable. "Anyway, it was the neighbors who called the police because of the gunshots."

"Gunshots?" exclaimed Jessica. "That's it, Jerry. Let's skip the sleazy highlights. I want to hear the whole story."

"Okay. Late last night Johnstone and his wife decide to get a jump on the weekend with a little coke," he began. "Instead of love and kisses, the scene turns ugly. At first words, and then left and right crosses."

"The wife too?" asked Jessica.

"She may have gotten in the first punch, because from what Marty tells me, Johnstone had quite a shiner," Barnstable replied.

"Marty saw him?"

"Right," answered Barnstable. "His agent called Marty to warn us. Then Marty went up to Larchmont to try and see about damage control."

"I'm sorry I interrupted," said Jessica. "What happened after the fight?"

"Well, after Johnstone slams his wife around, he decides he wants her out of his house, so he throws her, half naked, onto the front lawn."

"Jesus."

"That was just the beginning," Barnstable continued. "Now Mrs. Johnstone, her blood also boiling, goes into the garage and takes her licensed—and I want to emphasize, licensed—automatic from the glove compartment of her car. She returns to the front lawn and proceeds to shoot out all the windows in the front of the house. I think that's when the neighbors called the police."

"Prudent thinking."

"Fortunately," he went on, "she ran out of bullets and steam and collapsed on the front steps before she killed anybody. Then Johnstone, maybe realizing he'd been a bit hasty, carts her back into the house. End of story."

There was a pause as Jerry Barnstable caught his breath and Jessica considered a plan of action.

Jessica was first to break the silence. "I want to meet tomorrow. Let's say noon at the Arena. With Jonathan Lambert, Willie, and Marty. I'll try and get out of here as soon as I can. Also I want Johnstone, his agent, and his lawyer in my office at four. They shouldn't give us a problem, but if they do, tell them it's a command. . . . You know, Jerry," she added, her tone a bit more reflective, "just when you thought it was safe to start reading the sports section again, this has to happen."

"Think of it as a test of character," offered Barnstable.

"You think of it as a test of character," Jessica replied snidely. "I'll take it for what it is—a conspiracy to louse up my weekend. I'll see you tomorrow, Jerry."

After hanging up the phone, Jessica's eye fell on the royal-blue dress hanging in the open closet, the soft gathers around the bodice and waist creating vales of darker blue down the skirt. She had been looking forward to this evening. Wyatt Reynolds intrigued her. She liked his down-home blend of brashness and charm, not to mention the way he kissed. It was titillating, almost indecent. He seemed to have the power to release the passion she had controlled and resisted these many months, which both frightened and fascinated her.

Shaking her head, she removed a card from her address book and picked up the phone. "Hello, Wyatt," she said. "I'm afraid we're going to have to cancel our plans for tonight."

* * *

It was a cloudless night and from 25,000 feet, East Texas appeared in the moonlight like a piece of velvet stretched to the horizon, interrupted by black sequined rivers and tiny starbursts of light. As the sleek Gulfstream jet sped toward New York, Jessica and Wyatt Reynolds sat on a small horseshoe-shaped love seat, drinking champagne.

"Wyatt, dinner was wonderful, but was the helicopter ride from the restaurant parking lot to the airport really necessary?" asked Jessica, trying to fend off the irresistible look in his eyes.

"Crazy as it seems, yes," he answered. "We had to leave Houston by ten so we could get to La Guardia before it closes. New York may never sleep, but it does sort of catnap between midnight and six A.M. . . . You know, you have the most beautiful eyes," he said, running his finger lightly over her eyebrows and down the ridge of her nose. "They're haunting. They seem to draw you to . . ." He kissed her tenderly. "Your lips," he whispered as they parted.

Jessica raised her hand to Wyatt's face and repeated the path of his fingers, ending at his mouth, where her fingertips delicately traced the outline of his lips. She returned his kiss, but this time it was deep, the passion unchecked.

Responding to her challenge, he took her in his arms and held her tight. His lips moved to the pulse point on her long, graceful neck. Jessica inhaled his heady cologne and could feel herself being swept away by his caresses, the altitude and alcohol having rendered both of them impervious to restraint.

"Wouldn't we be more comfortable in the bedroom?" he asked, rising from the sofa and offering his hand.

Without a word she took his hand and walked down the dimly lit aisle to the rear cabin. Jessica knew at that moment that she wanted Wyatt Reynolds for all the wrong reasons, but it didn't seem to matter. This was reckless abandon, pure and simple. As the cabin door closed behind them, they fell into each other's arms, their longing intense, their passion boundless. Neither needing nor desiring tenderness, their lovemaking was urgent, insistent and demanding, overwhelming any notion of intimacy and romance.

Sunday's noon meeting produced several options, but none that could salvage Ralph Johnstone for the play-offs that were to begin in a few weeks. Jonathan left Jessica's office shortly after three while the others waited for the second act of the morality play to begin.

At precisely four o'clock Johnstone's agent, Allen Waxman, and his attorney, Sidney Perlstein, arrived at the office with Johnstone in tow. Although dressed in crisply-pressed gray slacks and a bright yellow cashmere sweater, Johnstone looked tired and haggard. The events of the past several days had obviously taken their toll. The three men were quickly shown into the inner office, where introductions were exchanged and every-one was seated.

With Jessica ensconced behind her desk and flanked by Willie Doges, Marty Green, and Jerry Barnstable, the proceedings took on the look of an imperial court. Their intent was to deliver a message from on high and to make sure the message was heeded.

"Gentlemen," Jessica began, "if it's all right with everyone, I'd like my secretary to sit in on this meeting and take notes. I'll have copies sent to each of you."

Waxman and Perlstein looked over at each other and nodded in agreement. In their mid-forties, the thin, balding Waxman and the athletic-looking Perlstein were partners in Interpro, a firm that represented professional athletes and managed their careers. Ag-gressively recruiting some of the finest college players and netting them impressive contracts, they had built Interpro into a multimillion-dollar operation. Yet with all their polish and six-figure fees, the pair had a reputation for caring about the welfare of their players. Compassion wasn't that difficult a crop to cultivate, they reasoned, and the harvest was always satisfying, both emotionally and financially.

"I want you to understand something, Ralph," Jessica said firmly to Johnstone. "We're not here to pass judgment. We're not in the blame department. We're here to try and help you with your problem and keep you playing for the Knights. . . . Now, if no one objects, I'd like you to tell me what happened Saturday morning."

Johnstone glanced at Sidney Perlstein for guidance. The silver-haired lawyer nodded once and the young man haltingly began his winter's tale.

From Johnstone's scrupulous recollection of events, it was apparent that his side had spent the earlier part of Sunday preparing his case. Johnstone's story was so chock full of remorse and mea culpas that mere exoneration seemed like an insult. Nevertheless, his frank admission that he needed help seemed to win the sympathies of all. All except Willie Doges, who chewed menacingly on the end of his unlit cigar while Johnstone spoke.

An accomplished negotiator, Jessica had no problem making clear to the Johnstone side the realities of his situation vis-à-vis the Knights. "Ralph, naturally, we are concerned about you," she said, "but you also must remember I have a responsibility to the team, just as you do. And I have to balance those responsibilities." Jessica got up and walked around the desk to stand in front of the three men.

"You know, you not only took yourself out for the rest of the season," she continued, "you've hurt our chances for the play-offs. And it's no secret we're going to have a big problem without you in the lineup. So I feel you owe us something. More importantly, Ralph, you owe yourself something. Now here's what we want," Jessica said, glancing over at Waxman and

Perlstein, then back at Johnstone. "We want you in a solid rehabilitation program, something you'll feel comfortable with, but it has to be approved by the team. We also reserve the right, once you're back with the team, to test you periodically for substance abuse. With the understanding that if you fail any of those tests, you're out, plain and simple. That's the deal . . . Ralph, you've got a lot of hard decisions to make," Jessica added. "And we're trying to help you, but we can only do so much; the rest is up to you. Take your time. Talk things over with Allen and Sidney and let us know what you decide."

The meeting ended as perfunctorily as it had begun. Marty Green ushered the three men out while Jessica, Willie, and Jerry remained behind for a brief postmortem.

"Well?" said Jerry, turning toward Willie Doges, who had planted himself in one of the chairs in front of Jessica's desk.

"Well, what?" he grunted, still chewing on his cigar.

"What did you think?" asked Barnstable.

"I thought she must have been something in a courtroom," replied Doges.

"Thank you, Mr. Doges," said Jessica, leaning back in her chair, "but I don't think that's what Jerry was talking about."

"I know what he's talking about," answered Doges. "I just think I'm the wrong guy to ask."

"Why?" asked Jessica.

"Because I've learned it doesn't take much character to develop a consistent hook shot," replied Doges, inspecting the sodden end of his cigar.

"And so?"

"And so I think you should be looking for a new center for next season," he said. Reaching into his jacket pocket he pulled out a book of matches, studied them longingly, then looked up at Jessica. "It all boils down to character and will," Doges added.

"And you have them, Mr. Doges?" asked Jessica, eyeing the matches in his hand with suspicion.

"No, Mrs. Laidlaw, I don't," replied the coach. "What I've got is an ironclad contract with a willful woman."

"Do you think I'm a willful woman?" Jessica asked as she stared up at the canopy of Wyatt Reynolds's four-poster bed.

Following the meetings, she had met Wyatt for dinner at an Italian restaurant on First Avenue, then moved on, for coffee and brandy, to the apartment he kept in the Carlyle Hotel.

"I think you know what you want, and you fight hard to get it," replied Reynolds, dabbing with the edge of the sheet at the tiny beads of perspiration that had settled between her breasts.

"Is that willful?" she asked.

"Well, it does make you quite a competitor," he said. Leaning over, he planted a light kiss on her neck.

"How do you know what I am?" she whispered as she responded to his lips.

"We just made love, didn't we?" he said proudly, as though their lovemaking had bestowed him with some rare insight.

"And you think I treat sex like some sort of competition?" said Jessica, covering herself with the sheet in a display of pique.

"Don't you?" replied Reynolds. "Isn't that what excites you? Winning. Controlling. Fighting to stay on top." A sly grin raised the corners of his mouth.

"Do you have a problem with women at the top?"

"At the top or *on* top?"

"Both," Jessica answered smugly.

"No, they're still the same challenge."

"Oh, that's right," she said. "You're the one who sees everything and everyone in the world as a personal challenge . . . But what, pray tell, happens to your egotistical little theory if, for example, *I* don't see *you* as a challenge?"

"What do you mean?" replied Reynolds, finding himself suddenly on the defensive.

"I mean what if I'm here because I just like the sex," answered Jessica.

"So you see me only as a sex object?"

"Not *only* as a sex object," Jessica teased. "You have a wonderful plane."

"Sex and my airplane . . . Is there anything else about me you admire?" Reynolds asked in mock dejection.

"Well," said Jessica, sliding her hand under the sheet and reaching between his legs. "You are easy."

"God, you are willful," moaned Wyatt Reynolds as he wrapped his arms around Jessica and pulled her on top of him. "You must be murder on a tennis court."

Chapter 42

A scalding witches' brew of hydrocarbons and humidity descended on Houston during the first week in May and drove Wyatt Reynolds from the city to his weekend home by the lake. "The Ranch," as Reynolds liked to refer to it, consisted of a sprawling fieldstone building set in the middle of an oasis of lush greenery, bracketed by the obligatory tennis court, swimming pool, and ten-car garage. Although modest by Texas standards, a mile of shoreline and seventy-five acres separated "The Ranch" from its nearest neighbors, ensuring Reynolds's privacy and those of his weekend guests, who were usually eager to preserve low profiles.

Wyatt Reynolds sat at the computer terminal in his study, redefining his strategy for the next day's futures market and preparing himself for a scene. He had just passed Kendall through the main gate, and from the tone of her voice, he could tell she was spoiling for a fight.

"I should have realized what you had in mind when we all went to lunch. The furtive glances and charming conversation," yelled Kendall as she stormed into the study. "You had to pick my sister, didn't you . . . You know, you're a real bastard."

"It's good to see you too, Kendall," Reynolds replied coolly. He got up from the computer and walked over to her, leading her to the brown leather sofa by the fireplace. "Come on," he said paternally. "Let's talk this out."

Kendall shook off his arm and sat down. "How could you?" she asked plaintively, her rage melting away at the sight of him.

"You think I planned it?" he said.

"Didn't you?" she snapped back tearfully.

"Honestly, Kendall, it just happened."

"Like it just happened with us?"

"No, this was different," replied Reynolds, sitting down next to her. He paused for a moment, considering how to phrase his next question. There was no easy way, so he just let the words spill out of him. "Look, Kendall, you haven't said anything to Jessica about us, have you?"

"God. I don't believe you," she exclaimed. "Of course not. She called me this morning to tell me about the two of you. And to thank me for introducing you . . . Tell me, Wyatt, how did this get so twisted and perverted?"

"You're talking like these things have rules. Kendall, affairs only break rules. After all, you're the one with the husband," he reminded her.

"Larry needs me," she said.

"Then go back to him."

"But I need you," Kendall replied.

"But I want Jessica," said Reynolds. He got up from the couch and walked over to the window. Heavy gray clouds were chugging across the sky, masking the lake with a black veil. "Look, Kendall, it's over."

"I could tell her," she threatened half-heartedly.

"I don't think you will," he said softly. "You know it wouldn't get me back and would only hurt the people closest to you."

"Then what do we do?"

"We stay friends," he answered.

There were tears and more threats and angry words, but Reynolds was able to wear the young woman down with patronizing rationales and self-serving excuses. He had tired of Kendall, but feared her vulnerability. It made her weak, but worst of all, unpredictable. He knew that at any moment she could wreck his future with Jessica, so he played her like a finely-tuned instrument, smoothly, without any waffling or hesitation. In the end she accepted what he said because he left her a tiny glimmer of hope, which was really the cruelest cut of all.

He walked her out to her car, then hurried back to the house just as the sky opened up. A deafening clap of thunder shook the house. As it rolled on north over the lake, Reynolds could hear the phone ringing in the study. He raced back into the room and grabbed for the receiver. His mood changed as he heard the familiar voice on the other end of the line.

"It's good to hear your voice too, Jess," he said affectionately. "I was just thinking about you."

Jessica zipped up the small makeup bag and hastily tossed it into the suitcase on the bed. Since she and Wyatt Reynolds had started seeing each other, she had made at least four trips back and forth to Houston plus four others to Detroit and Chicago, where the team had play-off games. When he could, Reynolds joined her, turning the weekends into a whirlwind of passion and excitement.

She reached for a flat brocaded jewelry bag just as the phone on the night table began its horrible electronic warbling. Throwing up her hands in disgust, she glared at the phone. It seemed as though the gods were determined to keep her from getting out of the house on time. Maybe they thought the game against Chicago and a weekend with Wyatt Reynolds was just too much of a sensory overload. There had to be some explanation for the bottlenecks and delays she had experienced all day.

"Where have you been?" Meredith demanded as Jessica picked up the line.

"Meredith, I'm sorry, I can't talk to you now," Jessica said abruptly. "I've got a plane to catch at seven and I haven't even finished packing."

"You hate us, right?"

"God, Meredith, where did you get the black belt in guilt?" replied Jessica.

"I was kidnapped from my Gypsy parents by a band of roving Jews," her friend shot back. "You shit, this is the second dinner you've canceled. Liz and Julie think you've become a basketball junkie. Me, I'm a romantic. I think it's a warm body."

"Well, if you must know, it's both," answered Jessica.

"My God," exclaimed Meredith, "you're having an affair with one of your players. Is he white?"

"Meredith, please. Is this really necessary? I've got to hang up," Jessica pleaded.

"Then I'll make it quick," said Meredith. "I need two million dollars to open a restaurant."

"Fine," Jessica replied without missing a beat. "I'll meet you Wednesday for lunch. Now, *good-bye*, Meredith."

They met at the Union Square Café on Sixteenth Street, a lunchtime retreat for the advertising and publishing crowd in the neighborhood. Meredith had chosen the restaurant because she thought the relaxed and unpretentious atmosphere was the most conducive to asking a close friend for two million dollars. Not that she wasn't used to asking people for things. She'd asked a lot of men for jewelry, stock tips, the odd weekend trip to Paris, but the important thing, at least to Meredith, was that none of those individuals had been friends.

Amid the muted tales of botched campaigns and ungrateful authors swirling around the lower dining room, Jessica told Meredith all about Wyatt Reynolds.

". . . so we commute every other weekend to be with each other," she explained.

"And?"

"It's, well, oddly romantic, and very sexy," replied Jessica.

"What does that mean?" Meredith asked impatiently.

"I don't know. I guess it means that because we're together for such short periods of time, everything is very exaggerated, very intense. I mean, look at this," said Jessica as she pulled up her sleeve and revealed an exquisite diamond tennis bracelet.

Against the white tablecloth, the perfect stones transformed the sunlight streaming in from the window above them into a kaleidoscope of colors that broke apart and reassembled with each slight twist of her wrist.

"Jesus," Meredith said breathlessly.

"That came with breakfast, Saturday morning, after the Knights lost the game," Jessica replied. "He thought it would cheer me up."

"Cheer you up?" answered Meredith. "Those stones could cheer up Cleveland."

"The problem with all this," Jessica said somberly, "is that sometimes I think he does things just for effect, just because of who or what we are, not what we mean to each other."

"Jess, why don't you talk to him about it?" asked Meredith.

"Probably because I look forward to those two days

so much," she replied, "I really don't want to hear the answer."

"God, Jess, why is it always the same thing with us?" asked Meredith. "We always seem to want 'the more' that they're unprepared or unwilling to give."

"Maybe it's because they put such a high price on commitment and feel that we're asking for too much," Jessica answered quietly.

Their conversation ebbed as the waitress brought their entrées and set them on the table.

"Now, what about this restaurant of yours?" Jessica asked.

"Well, it wasn't exactly my restaurant to begin with," replied Meredith, fidgeting with a fork, "but it could be now."

"Why do I have a feeling there's a long story here?" Jessica said suspiciously.

"Yes, but it's full of wonderful plot twists."

"Do I have to listen to this? Couldn't I just give you the money?"

Meredith paused for a moment to consider the proposition, then shook her head. "No, it wouldn't be right," she concluded.

"Okay, Meredith," answered Jessica, resigned to the inevitable. "Tell the story."

"Eight weeks ago I'm doing some work for a ladies' sportswear outfit," she began. "Over lunch one day the owner, between lewd suggestions, mentions that he and two other 'garmentos' are thinking about opening a restaurant. It's sort of this decade's thing for New York's bored lawyers, gynecologists, and lingerie barons . . . You know," she added wistfully, "I've always wondered what happened to the seventies' Arabian horse farm/country squire fantasy. Actually, the thought of all those polo clothes rotting away in some farmhouse makes my heart sing . . .

"Oh well," she went on. "Naturally, I advise him

against it, citing my family's background in the restaurant business. But the guy, anxious to prove me wrong, drags me over to an empty location at Twenty-fifth and Park. I think a bank used to be there. Anyway, while we're standing there, he's tapping my brain. 'What would I do with the space?' 'How big a bar?' 'What kind of food?' Finally, after about five minutes of this, a bell goes off in his head. It's come to him that I should be the one to run their restaurant. Now he starts to sell me like I'm a buyer from Macy's. Strange as it may seem, all the time I'm standing there shaking my head, I'm thinking what an ideal spot this is. Ten minutes from Seventh Avenue, just north of the new publishing and advertising district. Already I can see lines at the bar for lunch. Then, suddenly, ladies' sportswear turns to me and says the magic words, 'twenty-five percent partner,' and the next thing I know we're shaking hands."

"Wonderful, Meredith," Jessica interrupted wearily, "so why are we having this lunch?"

"I'm just getting to that," replied her friend as she gestured to the waitress for another glass of wine. "Jess, do you want another glass of wine?"

"Meredith, the rest of the story," Jessica implored.

"Right," she said, picking up the thread of her narrative. "Two weeks ago, four weeks before the contractor is supposed to begin gutting the site, the IRS slaps a lien on the assets of garmentos two and three, brothers in ladies underwear, for failing to report any income for the last seven years."

"Nice."

"Wait. It gets better," advised Meredith. "Without the support of the other two, dreamer number one begins to get cold feet. He's ready to call everything off and take the loss. Now I'm not about to start pumping confidence back into the guy, but I do have this vision of a glowing review of this restaurant in *Women's Wear Daily* with my name prominently featured in the first paragraph. So, the quick thinking, resourceful person I am, I immediately came up with a viable alternative to the three garmentos and me." Meredith paused long enough to stuff a forkful of risotto into her mouth and wait for her story to sink in.

"Is this where I'm supposed to ask what that alternative is?" Jessica asked obligingly.

"It's simple," Meredith answered. "We buy out the other three, offering to cover their costs plus a small profit, and run the restaurant ourselves."

"What we?"

"You and I," said Meredith. "Well, actually, it'll be your money. But we'll be partners. Seventy-five, twenty-five."

"Who gets the seventy-five?" Jessica asked warily.

"I'll run the place," Meredith replied, ignoring Jessica's question. "All you'll have to do is call for your table."

"A two-million-dollar table. That seems more than fair," Jessica said sarcastically. "You wouldn't happen to have any figures on this enterprise, would you? A budget, some projections?"

"I've got them right here," Meredith answered with a sly smile. Reaching into a large gray portfolio propped against her chair, she removed a thin black binder and passed it to Jessica. "If you're interested, I also have the architect's sketches of the interior."

Jessica flipped through the binder, stopping every few pages to study a particular item. "That's a lot of money for a chef," Jessica noted. "Is there someone you have in mind for the job?"

"I've narrowed it down to two. Both from California," answered Meredith. "One is the sous-chef at Chez Panisse in Berkeley, the other is one of Wolfgang Puck's wunderkind from L.A."

"And what about the front of the house?" asked Jessica.

"I hope to open in early December. That way I could use some of Honey's people from the Southampton place," she said, referring to her father by his family nickname.

"How is Honey?"

"Still talking about divorcing my mother."

"And how long has that been going on?" asked Jessica.

"Since my brother Joey was born."

"But he's nearly—"

"Twenty-seven, right," interrupted Meredith.

Jessica smiled, then continued thumbing through the business plan.

"I think you can trust those figures," Meredith said, flattered by the close scrutiny Jessica was giving the proposal. "I worked them over a second time with Honey last night . . . Look at it this way, we'll either make some money or you'll have a dandy loss against next year's winning season."

"Meredith, did you ever think seriously about weather forecasting as a career?" replied Jessica as she looked up from the numbers in front of her. "Can I hold onto this for a while?" she asked, closing the binder.

"Please," Meredith said anxiously.

"Good. Now let me see those sketches."

The architect's drawings envisioned a large dining room softened with light oak paneling, rice-paper screens, and saucer-shaped deco lighting fixtures. White pitched baffles hung at oblique angles from the high ceiling above the bar and swept back into the room just short of a secluded balcony. Included among the sketches were renderings of the restaurant by day and at night. The daytime drawings showed an open, airy room, a convivial space for lunches and meetings. At night, sculpted by light and vague shadows, the restaurant appeared warm and intimate.

At first the idea of a restaurant had sounded whimsical to Jessica, but the longer she looked at the sketches, the less the idea seemed like whimsy and the more it seemed like a workable, if risky, undertaking. And why not? she thought. She already owned a basketball team. A restaurant would merely be a natural extension of her image. And besides, she was tired of eating home alone during the week.

Chapter 43

That evening the Knights were knocked out of the second round of the play-offs by Chicago, 115–112. All the elements for a win had been on the Arena floor, but with Ralph Johnstone not playing, the Knights missed his rebounding and his consistent hook shot, which was enough to cost the team the game and the series.

In her office the following morning Jessica and Jerry Barnstable gathered to consider their options for next year. As Jerry entered the office, he found Jessica standing by the window, watching the city rush to work. When she didn't immediately acknowledge his presence, he took a seat in front of her desk and waited. Without saying a word, she turned away from the window and took her place behind the desk.

"I'm not going to say I told you so," said Jerry, breaking the silence.

"You just did," said Jessica, "but that isn't the point. I asked and you told me. I guess I wanted to believe we could get by without Johnstone. I've learned my lesson. So now what do we do for next season?"

"As I see it we've got three possibilities," he began. "We trade Nichols for a draft choice to back up Johnstone. We can go into the free-agent market, or we can sit tight with what we've got and hope he can hold himself together. If he can't, we'll just have to do some mid-season horse trading." Jerry paused while he debated presenting another option. "There is a fourth possibility," he said finally.

"Which is?" asked Jessica.

"We could trade him."

"No," she replied adamantly.

"That sounds more like compassion than good business sense talking," he said.

"Maybe," Jessica said. "But Jerry, you and I both know that coke or no coke, Johnstone's the hottest thing we've got on that court. He draws the crowd."

"But that could change if he costs us another play-off," he warned her. "That's why we've got to come to some decision on this. If we go to the draft, it could cost us a guard we really need. If we go the free-agent route, it'll cost us money, and maybe a player. All this to back up a twenty-four-year-old kid, who, depending on some East Side drug clinic, may or may not be the franchise. I guess what you have to ask yourself is, how important is Johnstone?"

"Good question," answered Jessica.

Just then the intercom buzzed. Jessica quickly jotted down some notes on a legal pad in front of her then picked up the phone. "Yes, Dorothy?" she said.

"Ms. Laidlaw, Wyatt Reynolds is on the line."

"Tell him I'm in a meeting and I'll call him right back," said Jessica.

"I told him, but he said it was urgent," she answered apologetically.

"That's all right, Dorothy," Jessica said, "I'll take it." She looked over at Jerry Barnstable. "I'm sorry, Jerry."

Barnstable started to rise from his chair, but Jessica stopped him.

"Please, Jerry. Stay where you are. This won't take a minute," she told him, then punched the red light on the telephone. "Hello, Wyatt. Now what's so urgent?"

"Lunch," replied the Texan.

"Lunch is urgent?" Jessica said, mildly annoyed by the intrusion. "Where are you anyway?"

"Wall Street . . . It was urgent because I wanted to catch you before you made other plans."

"Why didn't you tell me you were coming to New York?" she asked, her tone somewhat softened by his announcement.

"It was a last-minute thing," he said. "Now what about lunch?"

Jessica was momentarily distracted by an unaccustomed tension in Reynolds's voice. His usually smooth drawl sounded thin, almost brittle, as though he were out of breath or in a great hurry. In fact, he sounded anxious. "I'll be free around one-thirty," she replied. "How about the Gotham in the Village? It's about halfway."

"Terrific. I'll see you at one-thirty."

As she hung up the phone an uneasiness swept over her. Although more insight than premonition, the feeling hounded her for the rest of the morning. The call had somehow betrayed an insecurity that, while not a damning indictment of Reynolds's character, did reveal a chink in his armor. This first sign of frailty frightened Jessica. To shift their affair from the rare-fied world of lavish hotel suites and private jets to such mundane considerations as trust, respect, and under-standing, would require them to strip away the superfi-ciality from their relationship. Then she'd be forced to consider Wyatt as she had Mark and David.

Two rows of unadorned pillars, vestiges of the build-ing's earlier industrial legacy, divided the spacious dining room of the Gotham Bar and Grill and forced the eye up to the billowing fabric hanging from the ceiling. Tantalizing smells wafted through the expansive restaurant and a soft spring breeze floated in through the large windows at the back of the room.

Jessica waved away the maître d' as she spotted Wyatt at a table toward the rear of the restaurant, a half-empty martini glass in his hand and his gaze fixed firmly on the behind of a tall redhead heading for the ladies' room.

"Sorry to interrupt your fantasy," said Jessica, stepping in front of him and blocking his view.

"Think again, lady. You are my fantasy," he said huskily. Getting up from his chair, Reynolds edged around the table, took Jessica in his arms and kissed her passionately.

"This is an unexpected surprise," she said, slightly embarrassed by his ardor. "Is everything all right?"

"Of course," he replied. "Why do you ask?" The edge in his voice was gone, worn smooth by the right amounts of vodka and vermouth.

"I don't know," said Jessica. "For a minute on the phone you sounded like a New Yorker." In an unspoken sign of support she reached across the table and touched his hand. "Now tell me, what are you doing in the city?"

"I had a meeting this morning with some potential investors," he replied as he beckoned to the waiter. "I'm trying to raise the final twenty million for a new venture-capital company we're starting up."

"Is that the royal we?" she asked with a smile.

"Perhaps," he answered, besting her smile with one of his own.

"Private placement?"

"Naturally."

"What's your intended capitalization?" she inquired nonchalantly.

"Two hundred million . . . My goodness, you have an inquisitive streak," he said.

"You can draw up quite a nice little shopping list with that much," replied Jessica as she took a menu from the waiter. "So how did it go this morning?"

He paused until the waiter left the table. "To be frank, not that well," he conceded. "I think I shot myself in the foot. I guess I'm losing patience with decision by committee. Growing up in Texas, maybe I'm more at home with the man . . . sorry," he said, raising his hands apologetically, "or woman, who stands or falls on their own."

"I like it, Wyatt," said Jessica. "It has a real folksy, backwoods touch. I don't believe it, but I like it . . . Now, where are you going with this?"

"You know, I still haven't gotten used to your New York manners."

"We're even. I haven't gotten used to making love in an airplane," she shot back.

"Okay, I'd like you to invest with us," he admitted reluctantly.

"Us?"

"Me . . . Why are you making this so difficult?"

"I'm not," answered Jessica. "I just think you're a little hung up about asking a woman for money. Too much Texas machismo."

"That didn't seem to bother you before," Reynolds teased.

"And it doesn't bother me now, but it seems to be giving you a problem," she replied.

"I seem to be losing ground here," he confessed. "Would it be all right if we start again?"

"No problem . . . Are you ready?"

Reynolds downed the rest of his martini, leaving the olive rolling around in the bottom of the glass. "Ready," he answered, before taking a deep breath.

"Great, I love high drama," Jessica said facetiously. "What sector are you going to concentrate on?"

"We're not going to be looking at sectors so much as start-ups with growth potential," he replied.

"And what kind of return are you anticipating?"

"Anywhere from twenty-five to forty percent after the second year."

"That's rather optimistic, isn't it?" she asked, dubious.

"I can't help that. I just happen to be very good at what I do," he said as another wide, unimpeachable Texas grin broke across his face.

It was nearly three-thirty by the time they finished lunch. Almost all the tables in the dining room had been reset for dinner and their waiter had vanished, leaving a kind word and the check after he removed their dessert plates. The maître d' processed Reynolds's credit card while the pair got up to leave.

"You know, I really should check my horoscope," said Jessica.

"Why?" asked Reynolds.

"You're the second friend this week who's tried to talk me into investing with them," she replied. "It must mean something."

"It probably means you're a wealthy woman with a lot of opportunities," Reynolds said diplomatically.

Jessica had given Billy Richmond the day off, so they hailed a cab on West Twelfth Street and headed uptown. During the trip Jessica, in passing, asked Reynolds for a copy of the prospectus. At first he seemed offended, as though the request were an unpardonable breach of faith. Then he tried to mask his irritation with a weak, self-deprecating joke, after the startled look on Jessica's face told him he had overreacted. But it was too late. The seeds of doubt had been sown. And there was nothing more insidious or dangerous than doubt. There was no way to recall it, ignore it, or even contain it, without falling prey to it. Jessica had wanted to believe in Wyatt Reynolds, just as she had wanted to believe in every other man she had been with. Howev-

er, a relationship required more than excitement or
fascination to sustain such belief, and sadly, that was all
that had really developed between them.

Jessica dropped Reynolds at the Thirty-fourth Street
Heliport, then took the cab to Central Park to think. It
was warm and most of the leaves on the trees had
turned from the light green of early April to the deep
emerald of late spring. From the brown stone balus-
trade above the Bethesda Fountain, Jessica watched the
rowboats glide gently under the Bow Bridge and
huddle in the small shaded coves of the lake. Somewhere in the distance the driving beat from a street rap
scratched and pounded from a "boom box."

As she turned and looked down the esplanade behind her, Jessica wondered if she wasn't being overly
sensitive. Maybe she had just seen too much and been in
New York too long. What am I doing? she thought. I've
slept with this man, without question, for over a month,
and now that he wants something less than my being,
he's suddenly suspect. Still, she couldn't shake the
feeling that something wasn't quite right.

Crossing over to Tavern on the Green, Jessica caught
a cab back to the Arena. She was determined to put her
mind at ease and knew a few well-placed calls would do
it. Fortunately, Wyatt was going to be tied up with
business for the weekend, so she would be able to spend
the time in New York trying to get some answers and
sorting out her feelings.

The following Tuesday morning over breakfast with
Jonathan Lambert, her questions only brought more
questions. They ate in the garden behind the town
house, amid the sweet perfume of blooming roses and
apple blossoms. There was an air of Victorian elegance
about the breakfast meeting. They sat at a small white
wrought-iron table and ate fresh strawberries and
croissants and drank rich, dark coffee that they made
blond with hot milk.

Jonathan was impeccably dressed in a blue blazer and tan pleated slacks. He sported a magnificent burgundy and gold Sulka bow tie and a wide-brimmed panama hat with a black grosgrain band. Jessica looked far less aristocratic in her peach silk blazer and silk and cashmere gathered skirt, but the effect was dazzling. The sun seemed to follow her with each move she made around the garden, her hair shining like corn silk in the brilliant light.

She was glad to see Jonathan. He had become her personal confidant in matters of business and they spoke often. He was her voice of reason and understanding, and she hoped his presence would soften the impact of any bad news.

"Now, I agree with you that the prospectus is very vague," Jonathan said frankly, "but it does conform to SEC regulations. As a blind pool for private placement, it's as specific as it has to be. Look, Jessica, with these things you're buying the track record of the management."

"Which brings us to what your people found out in Texas," Jessica replied.

"You have to understand that you didn't really give us enough time for an adequate investigation," Jonathan said, as a way of prefacing his remarks.

"I know, Jonathan, and I'm sorry," she answered, "but there were things I just had to know."

"Well, what they found was a paper trail ten miles long," he began. "Apparently your friend has kept a lot of attorneys very busy. Oh, don't get me wrong. There are substantial assets, but nothing, of course, in his name. They're held by subsidiaries of four, maybe five—my people aren't exactly sure—offshore holding companies. They did find one curious thing, though. In the last two or three weeks there have been a flurry of sales and transfers of assets."

"To where?" asked Jessica.

"They're still working on that," replied Jonathan.

"Remember, you put limits on the investigation. So right now they have no way of knowing if he's using that money to capitalize the new corporation."

"So what is your opinion, Jonathan?"

"As far as my people went," Lambert continued, "they found nothing illegal. Questionable? Maybe. Unethical? Who's to say? All I know is that there's too much mystery down there. Spend your money on a new center."

"Not you too, Jonathan," she chided affectionately. "Why is it everyone wants to second-guess the owner?"

A sudden gust of wind blew up, scattering the apple blossoms across the finger of grass that jutted out into the garden.

"There is something else they found in Texas," Jonathan added ominously as he clutched the brim of his hat, "but it's of a rather personal nature."

The wind unsettled Jessica. As a child, red skies, billowing clouds, the hair on the back of a cat, were all signs to be reckoned with, and even with years of eastern education, she still found it difficult to slough off these omens.

"What did they find out?" she asked.

Lambert stared into the bottom of his coffee cup as though searching for an acceptable answer in the grounds. Finally he looked up, focusing his eye on Jessica. "It seems that up until a month or two ago," he said, "your friend was involved with your sister."

"Involved," Jessica repeated softly. The euphemism stuck in her throat, but other words quickly took its place—deceit, betrayal, humiliation. She blamed herself for falling victim to her own trust. But that guilt quickly turned to anger as she thought how she and her younger sister had been used. Her face flushed a deep red and tears began to collect in her eyes. She was enraged, but also bent on challenging Wyatt Reynolds's duplicity.

*   *   *

Jessica spent the rest of the week in meetings with Jerry Barnstable, plotting strategy for the June draft and going over Meredith's figures for the restaurant with her accountant. She also avoided two calls from Wyatt Reynolds, but accepted a third and his invitation for dinner Saturday night. By Friday Jessica had made three important decisions—to draft a center in June to back up Johnstone, to invest in Meredith's restaurant, and to ruin Wyatt Reynolds's dinner plans.

"Get a lawyer and start your demolition," she told Meredith that evening at dinner. "You and I are going to become partners."

Meredith muffled a scream that didn't prevent heads from turning in Le Cirque. "My God, I never believed you would do it," Meredith said excitedly.

"Why not?" replied Jessica. "The figures seem right. The location is right. And my partner is someone I trust and who won't rob me blind."

"If the deal is so good, why do I already feel guilty?" said Meredith.

"Probably because you're going to stick me for dinner," answered Jessica.

"Oh, right," Meredith admitted. "Well, maybe only seventy-five percent of it," she added with a wry smile.

The following evening Jessica waited for Wyatt Reynolds in the library. The room, the only one in the house spared the hand of Marshall Calloway, was painted a deep blue and lined with walnut bookcases. Although it appeared old and worn, there was a strength and resolve in the room as timeless as the volumes it sheltered.

Around eight Wyatt Reynolds arrived and was shown into the library. Jessica rose as he entered, but remained behind the massive desk which took up most of the floor space in the small room. The library had a slightly musty smell, reminiscent of old rugs and dusty, dog-eared books. There was also something decidedly

Gothic about the room, something that Jessica had always enjoyed and that now seemed to make him uneasy.

"Aren't we going out?" he asked, noticing that Jessica hadn't changed for dinner.

"I don't think so, Wyatt," replied Jessica.

"Are you feeling all right?" he asked.

"I'm fine," she answered coolly. "I just thought we should talk."

"About what, Jess?" he said, taking the chair in front of the desk.

"Private business."

"You mean the offering?"

"In part," replied Jessica. "You see, Wyatt, I won't be coming in with you on this."

"Can I know why?" he asked calmly.

"It's just too risky for me."

"Risky?" he said, his voice rising noticeably. "Aren't you the woman who gambled three hundred million dollars for a basketball team? Come on, Jess. This isn't about risk. Let's be honest with each other."

"Fine, Wyatt," Jessica began. "For openers, this is a blind pool that's going to be run like some huge discretionary account—"

"And you don't trust the management. Is that it?" he interrupted indignantly.

"Not anymore."

"And why is that?" he replied, trying not to appear belligerent.

"Because you lied to me."

"Lied to you?" he said. "Jess, I've never lied to you."

"Okay, you want to play games with semantics," Jessica shot back, "let's say hid things from me, avoided the truth. Is that close enough?"

"Look, Jess, I don't know what you're talking about or who you've been talking to, but you're wrong," he insisted.

"You know, Wyatt, I would have figured you'd be

way past denial by now," Jessica said sharply. "And at least into some wonderfully convoluted cover story."

"I never thought I'd have to defend myself in front of you, Jess," he replied, getting up from his chair, "so I'm not going to. I think I'll just say good night before we say things we both might regret. I'm just sorry you can't tell me what's really bothering you."

Jessica had heard stories about men like Wyatt Reynolds, men who couldn't or wouldn't accept responsibility for their actions, men who thought themselves blameless or simply misunderstood by some unbalanced woman. Jessica had heard these stories but had dismissed them as the dissembling of spiteful, insecure ex-wives or lovers. However, now that reality had reared its ugly head, she was of another mind.

"And don't worry about the money," he added offhandedly. "I've got other investors who may be interested."

"Stay away from Kendall, Wyatt," Jessica warned him. She could feel the blood pounding in her temple. "If you go near her again, I'll show you what risks I'm willing to take."

He hesitated, reevaluating his position and the timing of his exit. "How long have you known?" he asked.

"Long enough."

"You know, it wasn't what you think," he said.

"Tell me, Wyatt, how come it's never what we think?" she replied.

He didn't answer; instead, he looked at Jessica with an empty stare. "I'm sorry, Jess," he said at last.

"So am I," she answered. "I think you've already said good night."

After Wyatt left, Jessica felt drained and at the same time euphoric, as though she had completed some tremendous physical ordeal. And she had. She had managed to rid herself of an insensitive, manipulative man without any of the attendant guilt or recriminations.

Chapter 44

The June NBA draft came and went with more high drama than Wyatt Reynolds. On the first round the Knights acquired the guard they so desperately needed. Then Jerry Barnstable waited patiently for a crack at Jessica's insurance player. His chance came at the end of the second round, after a series of blunders by Houston and New Jersey, when he was able to snare Stanley Amos, the center from Maryland.

Maryland had had a terrible season, plagued by injuries and dogged by a year-old gambling scandal. Yet even with the low team scores and lower morale, Amos had still racked up impressive statistics. Both Jerry and Willie Doges saw tremendous potential in their surprise draft choice and, once the veterans were re-signed, could look forward confidently to the new season.

Jessica took a house on Long Island for the summer, a modest two-bedroom clapboard cottage midway between Amagansett and Montauk. Set on a bluff just above the beach, it had a small apple orchard in the front yard and a swimming pool at the rear. A long rocky driveway led up to a sturdy wooden gate at the entrance to the main road, connecting Jessica to the rest of the world. Settling in with a stack of books, a VCR, and ten Fred Astaire musicals, Jessica was determined to enjoy the quiet and the isolation.

She was determined, as was Meredith, to make their restaurant a success. Meredith trudged out to the cottage every weekend to go over contracts and discuss china patterns and fabric swatches with Jessica.

Anxious to see Jonathan before he left for his summer home on Nantucket, Jessica returned to the city for a few days in mid-July. They had a delightful lunch at Lutèce. In a rare moment of self-indulgence, Jonathan regaled her with stories of his youthful adventures riding the rails during the Depression. Jessica listened rapturously, captivated by his vivid imagery. After lunch they stood in the leafy shadows on East Fiftieth Street. She hugged Jonathan, made him promise to enjoy his vacation, then helped him into his car. She couldn't help smiling as his limousine rounded Second Avenue, feeling as though she had just packed him off to summer camp.

Afterward, walking up to Third Avenue, Jessica realized that for the first time in a long time she felt in control, that she was no longer reacting to life, but acting on it. Whether it was the financial security, the progress she had made with the team, or just the natural exhilaration of a warm summer day, she felt she could take on the world. And maybe even Meredith.

That challenge came the next morning. Meredith called and insisted that Jessica meet her at "the restaurant" at four that afternoon. With Meredith sounding imperious, Jessica knew better than to argue, so she moved up an afternoon meeting with the board of

Mark's charitable trust to free herself by the appointed hour.

As Jessica rushed across Twenty-sixth Street she could see Meredith waiting restlessly in front of a boarded-up building ahead of her.

"Would you believe I had to take the subway to get here on time?" Jessica said as she approached her friend. "The president is in town and they've closed off half of midtown."

"I appreciate the effort, but you were still late," replied Meredith with a smirk.

"God, you're strict," said Jessica.

"Poor toilet training . . . Now put this on," she said, reaching into a large Bloomingdale's shopping bag and removing a pair of hard hats.

"What's this for?" Jessica asked warily.

"Safe sex."

Donning the hard hats, the two entered the building and made their way through the construction and debris, dodging broken two-by-fours, dangling wires, and piles of plaster. Amid the detritus, on a freshly swept slab of concrete, they came upon a small marble cocktail table, set with two fluted glasses and a bottle of champagne, which was lying casually against the inside rim of a silver bucket.

"What is this?" asked Jessica as Meredith led her over to the table.

"A sort of christening," replied her friend, struggling with the champagne cork.

Suddenly, there was a loud pop and the cork flew across the room, disappearing behind a stack of plasterboard. Meredith poured the champagne, then raised her glass.

"I want to call it Muscari," she said, surveying the empty space.

"What is that, Italian for rubble?" said Jessica, brushing plaster dust from her skirt.

"Come on, Jess. I'm serious," replied Meredith.

"I'm sorry, Meredith," Jessica answered, picking her

champagne glass off the table. "It's really a lovely name."

"It's French for grape hyacinth," she said reverently. "Actually, Jess, this is really more than a christening. With all the contracts signed and the construction beginning, I just wanted to thank you."

"But nothing's happened yet," Jessica said.

"Oh, that's not true," replied her friend. "Look around you, Jess. You're doing for me what you're doing for this whole city with the Knights." Meredith raised her glass again. "Thank you, Jess," she said softly, "for making dreams come true."

Jessica was moved by her friend's toast. It wasn't often that Meredith let down her guard. She had cultivated the image of the sharp-tongued, streetwise New Yorker for so long, it was difficult for her real feelings to break through.

There was a distinctive ring as the two touched glasses to seal the toast.

"Is this Baccarat?" asked Jessica, pulling her glass back to examine the label on the bottom.

"Why not?" replied Meredith. "This is a formal celebration. And besides, it's your money."

Jessica finished the summer on Long Island, moving back to New York after Labor Day. The dog days of August had carried over into September and the city was still hot and inhospitable, dampening the spirits of those who had managed to "summer" somewhere beyond the stagnant air and soft asphalt.

With the new Arena nearing completion, Jessica busied herself her first week back with plans for the dedication ceremony. She and Marty Green drew up a guest list that included politicians, sports figures, and prominent New Yorkers. Then she added the names of a hundred fifty season ticket holders and fifty construction workers who had been on the project, all of whom she had chosen at random.

Although the ceremony was scheduled for Septem-

ber 21, which would have been Mark's fifty-sixth
birthday, the team offices were occupied the week
before. Jessica was ensconced in a dramatic suite of
penthouse offices, with sweeping views of lower Manhattan and the harbor beyond. She had given Marshall
Calloway virtually free reign on the design, and he had
imprinted her personality on the barren space. The
outer offices were inviting without appearing too feminine. There were bold sweeps of soft colors, and solid
furnishings with rounded edges. The inner office was
refined in its appointments, creating, at least for the
infrequent visitor, a subtle air of intimidation.

The morning of the twenty-first was gray and over-
cast, but the clouds broke around noon and the dedication went off as scheduled under a bright blue sky.
Jessica, standing among the dignitaries in front of the
new Arena, was quietly amused by the speakers praising
Mark's foresight and tenacity, many of whom had
privately vilified him and coveted the very things they
were now celebrating. Yet, for Jessica, all of the fine
words paled the moment she revealed Mark's name
chiseled into the polished marble above their heads.

Chapter 45

It was nearly seven-thirty by the time the dark green Jaguar XK-120 roadster rolled up the winding gravel driveway. The driver, a dark-haired man in his early forties, flipped down the sun visor to block out the blinding rays of the setting sun, then carefully maneuvered the sleek machine around the five or six cars parked in front of the imposing Tudor mansion. Turning left, he drove on until he reached the large stone garage at the end of the narrow roadway.

The people in the house were waiting for him. They were mostly old friends, who tolerated or understood his solitary comings and goings. For those with standing invitations to these Friday-evening dinners, it was an occasion for good food and thought-provoking conversation. For the others, this visit to Peter Sanzio's estate would be a test—a test of will, of intellect, and, most certainly, of good manners.

Sanzio lifted a brown leather envelope off the passenger's seat of the Jag, then eased shut the massive garage doors and walked slowly up the gently sloping lawn to the rear of his house. Midway, a cool breeze engulfed him, billowing his beige linen shirt and stirring his memories. A current of air, the scent of early autumn, the color of an evening sky, still reawakened in him painful emotions.

Everyone who knew him took it as one of life's bitter ironies that this mythically attractive man so rewarded by his vision should be burdened with such unhappiness.

Years earlier, while working as a molecular biologist, Sanzio had developed and later patented several genetically engineered bacteria that were soon to make a major impact on the pharmaceutical industry. These discoveries, in turn, led to licensing agreements, stock options, and consultancies that made him a very wealthy man. But his good fortune had been tempered by the death of his fiancée from cancer four years ago. A beautiful and vibrant young woman, she had wasted away before his eyes, an experience that had left him feeling helpless and frustrated. Her death laid the foundation for a wall he began to build around a part of himself. It became a storehouse for his vulnerability, a repository for the last of his compassion.

He entered the house through a doorway hidden from view by two large taxus, just below a heavily leaded bay window, and quickly made his way to a rear stairway. On the ground-floor landing he could hear voices coming from the living room, but he continued his climb to the second floor. His bedroom was at the end of a dimly lit corridor. Once inside, Sanzio flipped the leather portfolio onto the bed, then walked into the adjacent bathroom. The room was an eye-popping affair, circular, with terra-cotta niches containing a sauna, a shower, toilet, and sink. In the center, raised up like some aquatic shrine, was an immense black marble tub, recalling the excesses of ancient Rome.

Stripping off his clothes, he opened a glass shower

door, turned on the water and stepped in. The fine needles of hot water stung his olive skin, forcing his mind back into contact with his body. The memories retreated to the confines of his subconscious and he began to focus his thoughts on his guests downstairs.

He returned to the bedroom and found his valet, a reedy, thirty-five-year-old Englishman, laying out his clothes for dinner.

"Any of them getting antsy, Wilkes?" Sanzio asked the man in the dark suit.

"Just the newcomers, sir," replied the valet. "One or two do keep checking their watches."

Sanzio stripped the towel from around his waist and picked up a pair of undershorts off the bed. "The traffic this evening around Hartford was murder," he said, more as a statement of fact than as an excuse for his tardiness.

"Will you be returning to Boston the usual time tomorrow, sir?" Wilkes inquired, his words efficiently clipped and rounded.

"Yes, Wilkes. Right after breakfast," Sanzio replied.

Since his fiancée's death there had been thousands of these exchanges between the two men. Routine and ritual kept Peter Sanzio going. His days were measured in activities and undertakings, carefully planned and prudently scheduled. Ultimately, it was this orderly existence that kept his loneliness at bay.

"Sir, Mrs. St. Pierre called again about the dinner for Mr. Lasker at the Metropolitan Museum," said Wilkes. "She implored me to implore you to attend."

"When is it?" asked Sanzio, adjusting his tie in the mirror over a marble-topped chest of drawers. His brown eyes narrowed and the tiny lines around them deepened as he threaded one end of the silk jacquard through the other.

"In two weeks. A Friday evening, I believe," replied the valet.

"Make a note of it in my agenda, and I'll call Mrs. St.

Pierre tomorrow on my way up to Boston," he answered. "It would be nice to see Jacob again."

The towering date palms were fitted with lights to soften their shadows and were surrounded with tropical plants, while the tables were strewn with hibiscus and bougainvillea. The Hall of the Temple of Dendur in the Metropolitan Museum had been magically transformed from a cold barren space into a lush desert oasis for the evening.

The two hundred dinner guests quietly marveled at the metamorphosis of the space as they sipped champagne and nibbled on black beads of caviar. They had come to honor Jacob Lasker, an investment banker and major contributor to the museum, who over the years had become a driving force behind the museum's expansion.

Waiters were just removing the appetizer plates as Jessica tried to slip unobtrusively into her seat next to Jonathan Lambert at a table by the reflecting pool.

"You're late," whispered Jonathan as she slid into the chair next to him.

"I know," Jessica whispered back. "That's why I'm skulking and you're whispering. It was Allen Waxman. He came by to assure me that Johnstone's totally recovered, completely reformed, and ready to play."

"And *that's* why you're late?" replied Lambert.

"He laid it on pretty thick," answered Jessica as an aside, all the while nodding and smiling at the familiar faces in front of her. "I think he was trying to feel me out about what we're going to do with Amos."

Jonathan introduced Jessica to the few strangers at the table, ending with the dark-haired man seated to her right.

"It's a pleasure to meet you, Mr. Sanzio," said Jessica, extending her hand. Looking up into his brown eyes, she was surprised to find an incongruous sadness that seemed to belie the strength in his face.

"I have to admit, I was looking forward to your joining us tonight," said Sanzio. "I've followed your work with the Knights and have admired all you've managed to do in such a short time."

"Well, thank you, but I've had a lot of help," Jessica replied modestly.

"It was too bad you lost Johnstone for the play-offs," he added. "He might have made the difference. So," he began gingerly, "are you going to start him this year or are you going with Stanley Amos?"

"Funny you should ask that. That's the same question Mr. Johnstone's agent was trying to get me to answer earlier this evening," replied Jessica.

"And did you answer him?"

"Excuse me, Mr. Sanzio, but are you a fan or a team owner?" she asked with feigned suspicion.

"I assure you, I'm just a fan," said Sanzio, breaking into a disarming smile that seemed to wipe the unhappiness from his eyes.

"In that case, I'll tell you what I told Mr. Waxman," replied Jessica. "Everything will depend on what we see in training camp."

"That sounds fair. And what did Mr. Waxman say to that?"

"Oh, no," said Jessica abruptly. "Now it's my turn to ask a forward question."

"Fair enough."

"Why haven't we met at one of these dinners before?" she asked bluntly.

"How do you know we haven't?"

"Because I would have remembered anyone—and I mean *anyone*—who talked to me about basketball, that's why," she replied. "And you haven't answered my question."

"Well," he began tentatively. "I don't come to these things because I'm usually too busy."

Jessica shook her head.

"I live out of town?"

"Possibly," she said.

"And because I collect art, not patrons," he said.

"If that's true, then why are you here?" asked Jessica.

"Because I'm a friend of that particular patron," replied Sanzio, pointing to Jacob Lasker at the next table.

As the wines changed color and the various dishes came and went, Jessica felt drawn to this enigmatic man. At once, he seemed open and easily accessible, then, moments later, he would throw up roadblocks and detours, channeling her questions down less threatening avenues. But still she persevered, and little by little began to discover the outlines of his defenses.

After dinner Billy Richmond drove them to a small club on the edge of the East Village where an old man played a smoky saxophone and boilermakers were once the order of the day. The chipped tile floor was strewn with peanut shells and cigarette butts and the air was heavy with the smell of stale beer, but the jazz was pure and the company pleasant. They finished the night there, lost in the music and each other.

Around a quarter to four their barrel-chested waiter walked by and unceremoniously dropped the check on the table. "Lords and ladies," he announced, "we're closing."

"My God, is it four o'clock already?" said Peter, looking down at his watch. He reached into his tuxedo jacket, pulled out a black lizard billfold and dropped some cash on the table.

The waiter swept the money off the table then drifted back behind the bar.

"Why don't you come back to the house for breakfast?" Jessica asked. "I can fix us some omelettes."

"Maybe some other time," Peter said. "I've got to be in Boston by ten-thirty."

"Boston?"

"I teach a seminar at Harvard once a week," he

replied. "In precisely six and a half hours I'm going to have to begin inspiring twelve future Nobel Prize laureates."

"Then how about dinner Saturday night?" she asked with uncharacteristic persistence. Perhaps it was the easy conversation, or simply the time they had shared, but for some reason she didn't want this man to disappear from her life.

"Let me call you this evening when I get back," Peter said quietly.

At that hour, his sudden reticence frightened her. Jessica began to wonder if she hadn't misread the entire evening, or, used to having her way, had rushed things. What if what she was feeling wasn't real and Peter Sanzio was simply another dangerously charming man with an overdeveloped ego?

The doubts crept across her face, muddying her crisp features and forcing Sanzio to reassess his reply. "Oh, the hell with the call," he said, prepared to expose his vulnerability for the sake of her uncertainty. "I'll pick you up at eight-thirty."

Dinner on Saturday led to an auction Tuesday evening at Sotheby's followed by lunch the next afternoon. As the week progressed, Peter seemed to be in Jessica's thoughts almost every moment. She wondered about him, worried about him, and at the same time, tried not to think about him, which left her feeling guilty and confused. God, how she hoped this was love. The word infatuation embarrassed her. It dredged up images of pimply teenagers with fleeting borderline obsessions, and of crinkled photographs taped to dresser mirrors.

Upsetting both his meticulous schedule and the weekend plans of his Friday guests, Peter canceled the weekly soirée and drove down to New York to have dinner that evening with Jessica, and lunch and dinner the next day. By midweek he had abandoned his

Connecticut house completely, taking up residence in his pied-à-terre on Beekman Place. Ostensibly, the move was to allow an easier commute to Rockefeller University; however, his lab work there only served to punctuate the afternoons and evenings he spent with Jessica.

Rumors abounded about the whirlwind romance between the lady team owner and the reclusive scientist. How they were spotted somewhere for lunch and seen "deep in conversation" at the Café Carlyle after dinner. Yet, as exciting as it appeared, there was little of the whirlwind in their burgeoning relationship. Rather it was a gradually enveloping process of sharing their thoughts and their experiences. And in this sharing they found understanding, an understanding so basic and so primeval that it defied definition or analysis. It made silences meaningful and words unnecessary. It was two as one.

The huge white tent soared above the statue of Pomona, the goddess of abundance, atop the Pulitzer Fountain in front of the Plaza Hotel. Beneath it 350 very posh New Yorkers came to munch on smoked salmon, dance, and raise money for another worthy cause. At least a hundred different perfumes and colognes filled the air, rising toward the lights on the tall tent poles and fusing into some ethereal fragrance in the searing heat. At the tables thin elegantly-coiffed ladies in black silk jersey and richly brocaded velvets exchanged air kisses while their consorts paraded about stiffly in evening clothes, longing for the comfort of an easy chair, slippers, and an old woolen robe.

Peter guided Jessica around the makeshift dance floor with a dreamlike ease while the band played "Someone to Watch Over Me." He held her close and felt her soft breath on his cheek. Through the folds of her black strapless silk dress he could feel her firm body. The sexual tension between them was electric.

Moving through the shadow of the fountain, Peter lowered his head and gently kissed her neck.

She looked up at him, her eyelids heavy, her lips wet with anticipation. "God, Peter," she whispered, "I want you so much."

He kissed her, then led her off the dance floor, past their table and out of the tent, onto Fifty-eighth Street. The night had turned cold and brittle. Traces of steam had begun to leak around the edges of the manhole covers in the middle of the street. He covered her bare shoulders with his dinner jacket, then hailed a cab.

They laughed as they rode up in the elevator to his apartment. The whole world seemed to be watching them fall in love, from the guests at the party to the taxi driver with the "defective" rearview mirror. And now the doorman had his chance, through the tiny security camera embedded in the ceiling of the cab.

Peter shut the apartment door behind him, then took Jessica in his arms. "I've been thinking it all week," he said, "and now I think you should hear it. I love you, Jessica."

As she reached her arms around his neck, Peter's dinner jacket tumbled from her shoulders. They kissed, each arousing the passion of the other.

"I love you too, Peter," she said breathlessly as she ran her fingers down the deep crease in his cheek. Then she stepped back, unzipped the black silk sheath and let it tumble to the floor.

He swept her up in his arms and carried her into the bedroom. Inside, the narrow blinds sliced the moonlight into thin strips before it could drop onto the blue bedspread. Peter laid Jessica down across the iridescent rays.

As their naked bodies touched, Jessica felt a warmth like the glow of a summer sunrise radiate through her body. Peter felt it too and responded to it, caressing her with a gentleness she had never known before. Consumed by her desire, Jessica's fingers flew over his body, kneading his strong shoulders and raking the backs of his muscular thighs.

Lying beneath him in the darkness, she smelled of jasmine and tasted like the sea. He felt as though he were making love to life itself, feeding on its sweet pleasures and tearful sorrows.

She moved to meet him as he entered her, her delicate hands guiding him. "Oh, Peter," she murmured as she pulled him against her. His chest pressed against her breasts and she felt him penetrating her very soul. Then, suddenly, the emotional link between them broke. Jessica moved furiously to reach him, to restore the balance, but he countered her efforts by pushing them both physically closer and closer to the limits of their passion.

As her body shook and she held him deep inside her, Jessica felt shut out and closed off from the feelings she needed the most. Peter had taken his emotions and, at the critical moment, retreated to that safe place in his mind where he could never be hurt.

"Oh, Peter," Jessica cried out, clutching at him desperately, tears flooding her eyes. "Where were you when I wanted you so much?"

"I'm sorry, Jess," he whispered, wiping back her tears and cradling her like a child. "I haven't been this close to anyone since Karen died, and when I felt all of those feelings coming back, it was as though I was going to go through all that pain again."

"Peter, I understand," she said. "But closing yourself off from people is not living. It's existing, marking time."

"I know," he replied softly.

"Then let me help you," she said, turning her head up toward his.

"How?" he asked.

"By loving you so much that the world looks new again," she answered.

Chapter 46

As the weeks went by, Peter's defenses fell to Jessica's warmth and understanding. He began to open up, to reveal himself, to involve himself in her life. They found themselves falling in love all over again.

Jessica had never been happier. In the last month and a half her good fortune had been staggering. The Knights had made it through the preseason injury free, Ralph Johnstone had scored thirty-eight points in the season opener, and Danny DiNome had picked the Knights to finish first in the Atlantic Division.

As for Meredith and the future home of her two-million-dollar table, the restaurant appeared scheduled to open on time and possibly under budget, a phenomenon so rare in the world of high-priced New York eateries that Jessica was prepared to count Muscari a success even before it opened.

And then there was Peter. They had become practically inseparable. Jessica even accompanied him to Boston early one cold, blustery November morning, to sit in on one of his seminars, which quickly degenerated into a skull session on picking point spreads when some of Peter's students recognized Jessica.

"I never realized there were such inveterate gamblers at Harvard," Jessica said as they walked together through the yard after the seminar.

"What better pastime for a Ph.D. candidate with a lot of computer time on his hands," replied Peter.

"But where do they get the money to bet?" asked Jessica.

"Grants. Student loans. Rich parents. The odd loan shark."

"Are you serious?" Jessica asked incredulously.

"Only about the rich parents," he said with a smile. "Well, maybe once in a while someone will pad an expense account."

They stepped through the gates onto Massachusetts Avenue and were caught in the swirl of pedestrian traffic.

"What time is the game this evening?" he asked.

"Eight."

"Well, then, you want to use room service here or in Washington for lunch?" Peter asked mischievously.

"Let's make it Washington," Jessica answered. "I wouldn't want to miss the game."

"You know, it's only twelve-thirty," said Peter, looking at his watch.

"So?"

"So, I thought you might want to change your mind."

"Not really," said Jessica with an impish grin. "I'd rather we took our time in Washington." Then she ran her tongue seductively around the edge of her lips. "Wouldn't you?"

"Taxi!" yelled Peter as he ran into the street after a brown and white cab.

*   *   *

Peter went to California for four days the following week, but called Jessica twice a day. He missed a call Thursday night but caught up with her Friday morning at the Arena, when he got back to New York.

"I'm sorry I didn't call last night," he said. "I had to rush to catch the red-eye home."

"Are you in New York?" she asked hopefully.

"No. Connecticut," he answered. "I left some papers up here I promised someone in California I'd review. By the way, I just took a look at last night's game. Your guys looked terrific."

"Actually, they weren't bad, were they?"

"Not bad!" Peter exclaimed. "That makes ten out of their last twelve. I can't believe you. Where's your team spirit, your sense of achievement?"

"It's in storage for the play-offs," she half joked, mindful of the grim realities of pro sports.

"You know, I never realized you took good news so poorly," he said, his voice scratchy from lack of sleep.

"That's because I'm Jewish on my partner's side."

"Listen, I just got some good news," Peter told her. "I'll share it with you if you don't think it'll louse up your day."

"Very funny."

"Brodsky called me from Paris," he began. "He's found a small Cézanne still life in Bruges that he thinks, with a little coaxing, may be for sale."

"Peter, that's wonderful," Jessica replied.

"He thinks it would be a good idea if I went over to look at it, talk to the owner," he said enthusiastically. "Émile said the old man's a bit of an eccentric. Sort of a fading aristocrat. I told him I'd be there Tuesday."

"Oh . . . How long do you think you'll be gone?" she asked, making no effort to mask her disappointment.

"Two weeks," Peter answered. "He has some other things for me to see in Paris, and I want to visit the lab in Geneva. But that's not the point," he added. "I want you to come with me."

"I really can't, Peter," she said. "I'd feel guilty leaving at the beginning of the season."

"Come on, Jess," he replied. "You know Jerry can cover for you. And besides, what's the worst that can happen while you're gone? You drop one to Boston?"

"Bite your tongue."

"Seriously, Jess. What do you say to two weeks of great food and even better sex?" Peter asked eagerly.

"With whom?"

"With the ghost of Christmas past . . . Come on, Jess. What'll it be?"

"Do we land in Paris or Brussels?"

"Paris."

Émile Brodsky slowed the silver Mercedes as he crossed over the narrow bridge spanning the canal. After making a sharp left turn, he followed the equally narrow cobblestone street that ran parallel to the canal to a small square dotted with barren trees and surrounded by a row of five-story, weathered stone buildings with steep tile roofs and elaborate stone arches above the windows. The homes and offices of the burghers of Bruges, they had stood silent watch over this square and the canal beyond since the middle ages, when the city, crisscrossed by the canals that linked it to the thriving ports of northern Europe, flourished as a commercial center. But now the "Venice of the North," ivy-covered and cut off from the sea, slumbered peacefully through the late autumn, a medieval museum shut up for the winter.

The Mercedes came to a stop in front of a charming inn across from the square, just as a blanket of clouds, skittering off the North Sea, obscured the sun. The beige stone buildings suddenly turned a dark gingerbread brown, giving the tiny crescent a fairy-tale air.

"It looks as though I must leave you now, if I'm going to avoid the storm," Brodsky said to Jessica and Peter.

His English, like a complex wine, was blended with the accents of other places and times.

"I want to thank you for all your help, Émile," said Peter, extending his hand over the front seat.

"Please, Peter. I did nothing," replied Brodsky. "I really believe you have Madam to thank." Touching the brim of his gray fedora, he smiled at Jessica, who was sitting next to him in the front seat.

With his pince-nez and old-world manners, Émile Brodsky belonged to another age—a time when men knew the meaning of love and pursued it with grace and elegance; when beautiful women, great music and art, were objects of desire, and money was only a means to an end. He was a diminutive man with fine, almost feminine, features, and the winsome eyes, gray goatee, and long face of an El Greco portrait. A respected art scholar and now dealer, he had helped, years earlier in Paris, shape Peter's artistic tastes, and later his private collection.

"Peter, I should have the painting to you in Connecticut in about two weeks," said Brodsky.

"Wonderful. Now have a safe trip back to Paris, Émile," Peter replied as he slammed the door of the car.

"Good-bye, Peter," said the elderly gentleman. *"Et au revoir, Madame Laidlaw,"* he added, turning to Jessica and kissing her hand. *"Vous êtes vraimént une femme extraordinaire."*

"Jusqu'à New York, au revoir, Émile," replied Jessica mysteriously.

Jessica and Peter watched as Brodsky's car disappeared over the arching canal bridge, then walked up the steps to the inn.

"Goodness, two conquests in one day," said Peter as he held the door open for Jessica.

"Are you jealous?" she asked.

"Perhaps."

"Really, Peter. Émile and I are just good friends," Jessica replied jokingly.

"And Monsieur de Charleroi?" he asked. "By the way, what did you say to him in the garden that made him change his mind about selling me the painting?"

"Nothing. We just talked."

"About what?"

"About a summer in Arles a long, long time ago and a beautiful young widow named Denise," said Jessica.

"By any chance did Denise have blond hair and blue eyes?" asked Peter.

"Yes," Jessica replied, recalling the joy and sadness in the old man's eyes, "she did."

At the front desk the clerk handed Jessica a telegram. Of an age that still regarded telegrams as portents of disaster, she hesitantly opened the official-looking envelope. "Damn! Not again," she muttered after reading the two line message.

"Trouble?" asked Peter.

"What else," she answered dejectedly. "I've got to get back to New York."

She handed him the telegram. The two lines, in bold letters, proclaimed both the frailty of the human condition and the fulfillment of Willie Doges's prophesy: JOHNSTONE MISSING. IF POSSIBLE, SUGGEST YOU RETURN TO N.Y.–JERRY.

Peter looked at her, put his arm around her waist and began to walk her across the lobby. "Come on, let's go upstairs," he said quietly. "I'll help you pack."

Chapter 47

Allen Waxman drummed his fingers nervously on the long walnut table while Jessica and Jerry Barnstable shuffled papers back and forth between them. Out the conference-room window Waxman could see the rough chop on the Hudson River and knew he would have about as much luck shoring up Ralph Johnstone's career as stemming the tide. None of them really wanted to be here. Meeting to discipline the star player on a winning team gave no one any satisfaction, but Johnstone had not given them any choice.

"I'm sorry, Allen," Jessica began after Waxman offered up a weak explanation. "I don't want to sound heartless, but whether it's exhaustion or his dying mother, he has a contractual obligation to notify the team. You know that as well as I do."

"Try and understand," Waxman said. "The readjustment has been difficult for him."

"Allen, you told us in October he was in great shape

and ready to play. Now he isn't?" Jerry Barnstable countered.

"Really, Allen," said Jessica, tired of his feeble arguments. "It's not like he was late for a practice. He disappeared for four days and missed two games. And you want us to overlook it? I'm sorry; that just ain't going to happen. Not this time."

Waxman shook his head and drew a deep breath. "All right," he offered, capitulating. The words were wrapped in layers of resignation. "But I don't think the urinalysis was necessary."

"I'm not going to get into a debate on that with you," Barnstable said coolly. "You know we have the right to administer a urinalysis whenever we believe conditions warrant one."

"Okay," Waxman began. "Let's assume, for the sake of argument, he tests clean. What are we talking about for the missed games, a fine or suspension?"

Before Waxman could get his answer there was a knock at the door. Jessica's secretary entered with a large gray envelope in her hands. She walked around the conference table and gave the envelope to Jessica. "This just arrived by messenger," she whispered discreetly.

"Thank you, Dorothy," Jessica replied as the woman made her way silently out of the room. After peeling off a wide strip of brown tape from the top, Jessica opened the envelope and removed a legal-size manila folder. Clipped to the front of the file, on a sheet of white paper, was a short summary of its contents. Jessica read the summary, then handed it to Jerry Barnstable, who, after a quick perusal, pushed the file across the table to Allen Waxman.

"I guess this answers your question, Allen. I really am sorry," Jessica said sympathetically.

"Positive," Waxman muttered as he finished the summary. "That poor stupid bastard. What the hell is he going to do now? Christ, why couldn't I reach him?"

"You can't blame yourself for this, Allen," said Jerry. "He's got a serious problem. Basketball was only complicating it."

"But you know these kids, Jerry," he replied. "Basketball is the only thing they know. We try to position them so they've got something to fall back on, a cushion, but we didn't have enough time with Johnstone."

"I know, but this business is out of our hands now," Barnstable explained. "Under the league rules, his expulsion is automatic."

"Well, not completely out of our hands," said Jessica. "I think we should take some responsibility here . . . Allen, we'll cover his medical costs until he's drug free, but the rest is up to him. That gives him two years to get himself together. Then let him reapply to the league."

Disheartened, Waxman got up, leaving the report in front of him on the table. "I'll tell Ralph about your offer," he said as he gathered up his coat and briefcase. "I want you to know, Jessica, that Sidney and I appreciate all you've done for him. The kid doesn't realize yet how much worse it could have been."

"Nice man," said Jessica after Waxman had left the conference room. She walked across the room to stand by the wall of windows overlooking the river.

"That's why he's successful," replied Barnstable.

"You think Stanley Amos is ready to take over for Johnstone?" asked Jessica, staring blankly out the window, her thoughts divided between Johnstone's replacement and Peter, on the other side of the Atlantic.

"He's looked promising in his last three starts," Jerry answered cautiously.

"But will promising get us to the play-offs?" she asked, turning away from the window. Her patience was worn thin by jet lag and Barnstable's hesitancy.

"Who can say?"

"I can," she replied forcefully. "Let's get someone to back up Amos."

"If you like, I'll put out some feelers today," Jerry said. "By the way," he added, trying to ease the tension between them, "how was Europe?"

"Until I got your wire, cold, damp . . . and wonderful," Jessica answered. She remembered her last night in Bruges, lying by the fire in Peter's arms. It finally seemed as though nothing could come between them —not distance, not obligations, not even the past.

Ten days later Jessica dragged Meredith to a Knights' game at the Arena. They sat in the sky box, where Meredith watched television while Jessica finished half a bottle of wine. Afterward they had dinner at Muscari.

The restaurant had opened on time and with tremendous fanfare. Word of mouth and notes in the fall preview issues of the major fashion and entertainment magazines had kept the phones ringing and the reservation book filled. Even after the kitchen closed, the bar was still three deep with leggy young women and men in expensive Italian suits. They sipped frosty pale-green drinks from oversized glasses and compared health clubs, film courses at the New School, and profit-sharing plans.

Fortunately, the patrons at the tables seemed more interested in the talents of the chef than in the bartender's ability to produce a rainbow of colors in a blender. For this Meredith was grateful. It meant the restaurant had a better than even chance of surviving trendiness and becoming a viable money-making operation.

"I've never been to a professional basketball game before," Meredith said as she refilled their wineglasses. "It sort of reminded me of a fraternity party at Maryland. You know, all that yelling, the smoke, and the smell of beer."

Their table was in a secluded corner of the balcony away from the noise of the bar, their privacy assured by the maître d', who, at that hour, seated any new arrivals in the main dining room downstairs.

Jessica had hardly touched her food and said very little during most of the evening. She seemed distant, preoccupied. Meredith knew better than to interfere, but she also knew that Jessica wanted to talk. Why else had she phoned this afternoon and insisted on the game and dinner? So Meredith made innocent small talk and waited.

"How about some dessert, Jess?" Meredith asked as the waiter approached to clear the table. "Something chocolate might help."

Jessica looked around at the empty tables then back at her friend. "Meredith, I don't know whether to be angry and hurt, or terribly worried," said Jessica. She sounded frightened and confused.

"Is this about Peter?"

Jessica nodded. "After I left him in Bruges, he called me every day for a week," she began, "sometimes even twice a day. Then, day before yesterday, the calls stopped."

"Did you try calling him?" asked Meredith.

"Yes, this morning."

"And?"

"The hotel in Geneva said he had stayed only one night and then checked out," replied Jessica. "That was two days ago."

"What about a forwarding address?"

"Just the house in Connecticut."

"Did you call there?" asked Meredith, trying for some rational explanation.

"Yes. I spoke to his valet," she answered. "He hadn't heard from him either, but he didn't sound very worried. It was as though he was used to this sort of thing."

"Jess," Meredith began hesitantly, "when you spoke to the hotel, did you ask if he was with anyone?"

Jessica was stung more by the voicing of her doubts

than the implication of her friend's question. It was something she didn't really want to believe. It was too cheap, too sordid. It would mean she had never understood Peter at all.

"I'm sorry, Jess, really," said Meredith, after watching the effect of her words on Jessica's face.

"That's all right," she answered. "I wanted to ask, but I just couldn't."

The waiter brought them coffee and a plate with a sampling of chocolate desserts.

"It's sort of like chicken soup when you're sick," Meredith explained. "It may not do you any good, but it can't hurt." They each picked up a fork and began to round off the corners of a slice of chocolate hazelnut torte.

"I can't help feeling responsible for this. I just pushed things too fast," Jessica said, resignation in her voice. "I knew Peter was keeping something from me, some closely guarded part of himself, but I thought we had worked all that out before we went to Europe. I guess we needed more time together . . . only I couldn't spare it. . . . Damn it, Meredith, I feel like I'm caught between Mark's dream and Peter's nightmare."

"Jess, this isn't your fault," Meredith assured her. "You didn't desert him. He deserted you. Look, maybe you should have asked for more, some assurances. I don't know. But then again, these are the eighties. Independent women like us aren't supposed to need assurances. I think we lost the right to ask for any sort of commitment once we won the right to refuse them."

The torte finally whittled away, they moved their forks to the edge of the plate and the small round puffs of white chocolate mousse.

"You know the funny thing about all this?" said Jessica as she rolled one of the sweet spheres through a pool of chocolate sauce. "Nothing has changed. After twenty years of sexual equality and all we've achieved, the best I can hope for out of this is that Peter is as miserable as I am . . . wherever he is."

"Nothing has changed?" Meredith exclaimed. "Maybe I should remind you, we've just had dinner in *your* restaurant after sitting in *your* arena and watching *your* basketball team do whatever it was supposed to do."

"You're making my point," replied Jessica. "I have all of that because I was married to Mark."

"God, you're a closet cynic."

"Did you ever think you were contagious?" Jessica shot back.

"Did you ever think that you've achieved something that Mark couldn't with what he left you?" asked Meredith, putting down her fork and staring intently at Jessica.

"And what's that?"

"You're winning," Meredith answered.

Jessica thought about Mark, about Alton Shea and Wyatt Reynolds, then about Peter. "Oh, I'm winning," Jessica announced, her voice choked with emotion. "Meredith if I'm winning, why don't I have anything to show for it!" Tears ran down Jessica's face and she began to sob. "Oh, God, Meredith," she cried, "I thought he loved me."

During the next two weeks Jessica was tortured by the growing number of unanswered questions. She tried phoning the house in Connecticut several times for any word of Peter, but always got the same polite reply from Wilkes: "I'm sorry, Mrs. Laidlaw. I've had no further word from Mr. Sanzio since he called Monday last to say he would be delayed in Europe. . . . Of course, I will pass on your message."

Jessica tried to bury her disappointment in preparations for the holidays. She invited Kendall and Larry to New York for an elaborately planned Thanksgiving weekend, then, as Christmas approached, plunged herself into a whirl of cocktail parties and dinners, trying to keep her depression at arm's length. A fourteen-game winning streak helped dispel some of her anxieties, but even that couldn't erase a haunting image of Peter Sanzio from her mind.

Chapter 48

It snowed four days during the first week of February. The second day was the worst, with nearly a foot blanketing the city. The temperature remained frozen in the teens, so that by the fourth snowfall the streets had become virtually impassable, buses and subways the only sure form of transportation.

While waiting for Marty Green in her outer office, Jessica watched as a parade of snowplows made their way up and down West Street, building mountainous ridges of snow along the shoulder of the roadway. It had taken her nearly an hour to get to work this morning, and as a result, she had asked Billy Richmond to stay at the Arena rather than risk another round trip.

"Just got some interesting news," Marty said striding into the room. "Chet Newberry has agreed to let Frank DeCicco out of his contract with Philadelphia."

"Sounds like he's been cooking again," replied Jessica.

"You might say that. He's going to be named president of Detroit this morning," Marty added as casually as he could. He wasn't exactly fearful of Jessica's reaction. But since the holidays, she seemed a little edgy. And he saw no need to test her good nature on this cold, gray morning.

"Well, it's nice to know America is still the land of opportunists," Jessica cracked. "Come on, let's go into the office."

Marty nodded, smiled at Dorothy, then followed Jessica inside. Whether it was the weather or the time of year or Jessica's attitude, something seemed to make Jessica's office gloomy. Even the fire in the black marble fireplace seemed more ominous than inviting.

"I know it isn't going to look good in the papers," Jessica began as she slipped behind her desk, "but I'm going to have to press the city for more parking down here."

"You're right, Jessica," Marty answered flatly. "It's not going to look good. Remember, Mark made his original pitch based on improving mass transit, sprucing up the neighborhood, and putting in the park across the street. If you make a move to take back that space, they're going to come at you with both barrels. Paving over a green space in this city is considered a crime against humanity."

"I agree," said Jessica. "But I wasn't thinking about using the park. I was thinking about the west side of the Arena."

"Over the river?"

"Why not? If we—" Her explanation was interrupted by the intercom. She picked up the white phone and, in one practiced motion, removed the earring clipped to her left ear. "Yes, Dorothy," she said.

"Ms. Laidlaw, Peter Sanzio is on line one," announced the secretary in her usual businesslike manner. "Should I tell him you're in a meeting?"

Jessica had agonized over and prayed for this phone

call for two and a half months. Now she dreaded it. Her stomach suddenly knotted up. All the repressed feelings she had about Peter began to bubble to the surface, swamping her consciousness. She tried freeing herself from the rising tide of emotion, but the anger and the hurt seemed to hold her fast.

"No, Dorothy," she said softly. "I'll take it."

Jessica stared down at the phone, then up at Marty Green. "Would you excuse me for a minute, Marty?" she said shakily, her confidence and resolve shattered by wave after wave of doubt and suspicion.

"I'll be back in my office," he replied, then got up from his chair and slipped out of the room.

As she looked back at the telephone, the small red light on the console seemed to glow brighter. She had played this moment over and over in her mind, but now the carefully crafted invectives and smug, self-serving retorts seemed to escape her. Jessica took a deep breath, then pushed the button next to the red light.

"Hello, Peter. How are you?" she began, trying desperately to feign indifference. "Or should I say, where are you?"

"I'm fine," he replied tentatively. "I'm in New York . . . How are you, Jess?"

He sounded tired. But it wasn't the fatigue one associated with exercise or physical exertion. He sounded beaten, as though he had been subjected to some inhuman horror and had barely survived.

Her heart went out to him, but she was determined to protect a part of herself that had been wounded so many times before.

"Oh, just fine," she answered, controlling the tremor in her voice. "When did you get back?"

"Last night," he said. There was a pause as Peter collected himself, summoning what was left of his strength. "Look, Jess, we have to talk," he said at last.

"We are talking, Peter."

"I have to see you. There are things I have to explain."

"Why? I would think not hearing from you for two and a half months was more than enough explanation," Jessica blurted.

"I'm sorry, Jess. I know what I must have put you through," said Peter.

"Do you?" she snapped, her control giving way to her pain.

"Yes," Peter said quickly, "because I felt angry, scared, and alone too." He drew a breath. "Please, Jess," he begged her. "After what's happened I know you don't owe me anything, but just give me a chance to explain."

She heard her own tangled and twisted emotions in Peter's voice; to deny him would be to deny herself. "All right," she relented. "Come to the house tonight around eight and we'll talk."

The cars parked along both sides of Seventy-fifth Street were entombed, like sleeping bears, in great snow drifts glazed with a thin veneer of ice. The street itself, plowed once after the first storm, was still choked with almost a foot of snow. Only the sidewalks had been recently cleared.

Tiny crystals of rock salt crunched underfoot as Peter made his way down Seventy-fifth Street. It had started to snow again, and large downy flakes began to stick to his coat and hat. He hurried down the block, glad to reach the shelter of the town house before the snowfall intensified.

Jessica met Peter at the door and was shocked at what she saw. His face was thin and drawn and his once tanned skin had a sickly sallow cast. There were flecks of gray stealing back from his temples, and his eyes seemed dull and lifeless.

As she led him into the living room, all Jessica's

pent-up animosity drained from her. She had been prepared to loose her rage against the Peter she had known, not against this broken man.

They sat side by side on the large sofa in front of the fire, insulated from everything but themselves and what they felt toward each other.

"Are you all right?" Jessica asked, fearful of his answer.

"Believe me," Peter replied, "I feel better than I look." An easy grin appeared on his face, wrinkling the corners of his mouth.

There was a loud pop in the fireplace as an ember shot out against the fire screen. They watched it drop onto the stonework, flare for a second or two, then burn out.

"They told me in Geneva I was going to die," Peter said softly.

His words seemed to rip away the walls around them and usher the storm inside. Jessica felt cold. She wrapped her arms around her waist and leaned toward the fire. She asked no questions. Instead she sat quietly, waiting for Peter to begin his story, studying his face and trying to comprehend how he had survived his worst nightmare.

"I began to feel funny the day after you left," he said. "You know, a little weak, a sore throat. I didn't think much of it. Thought it was from missing you," he added with a weak smile. "Well, by the time I got to Geneva I *was* sick. I must have looked like hell too, because when I got to the lab, Daimler immediately took me down to the staff doctor. He poked and prodded, took some blood, then told me to go back to the hotel and rest.

"The next morning I got a call from the doctor. He told me to meet him at a hospital about twenty minutes from the lab. I knew I was getting worse. I hadn't slept all night. Through the fever and cold sweats, I tried a little self-diagnosis. I guess that wasn't a very good idea. All I could come up with was a textbook case of lymphoma."

Peter tried to be as dispassionate as possible, but Jessica could see the fear in his eyes as he recalled that night in the hotel room. Moved, she reached over and touched his hand.

"And that's what the hospital tests showed," he went on, "because they put me on chemotherapy two days later. After about a week of the chemo, I felt even worse. The fever had gone higher. My throat felt like it was on fire, and my white cell count had gone through the roof. That's when, out of the fog and haze, I called Paul Méyer, a colleague at Harvard, and asked him to get me into the Pasteur Institute in Paris.

"He got back to me later that day and said they'd see me. Then I checked out of the hospital and dragged myself to Paris. At Pasteur they did a complete workup and found they had screwed up in Geneva. It wasn't lymphoma, but a virus associated with Epstein-Barr." He looked away for a second, shook his head, then turned back to Jessica. "Are you sure you want to hear all this?" he asked uneasily.

"Yes, Peter, I do," Jessica said.

"Basically what they did was isolate me for a week, run tests, watch and wait. Then they began administering drugs to stabilize my condition. After a while I got lost in time. I was up for a few weeks, then down again. Finally, the virus seemed to run its course."

As he spoke, Jessica began to understand the depths of Peter's isolation. Her concerns and anger began to soften—she wanted to believe in him, to love him. She was suddenly ashamed at the things she'd said to him on the phone that afternoon.

"You know, I thought about a lot of things lying in that bed," he said. "I thought about dying, about what my life's been like these last few years. But mostly I thought about how much I missed you."

"Then why didn't you let me know what had happened, where you were?" she asked, thinking of the time they had lost.

"Because I loved you and didn't want to hurt you," he replied. "And selfishly, I didn't want you to hurt me . . . Jess, as I watched Karen get weaker and weaker, I realized she gradually came to accept her own death. But what she couldn't accept was the hopelessness and frustration she saw on my face every day. I couldn't control it, and I couldn't hide it, and in the end I was sure she resented me for it. . . . I didn't want that to happen to us."

"That didn't have to happen to us, Peter," Jessica insisted. "But you couldn't have known because you wouldn't give me the chance to prove you wrong . . . Peter, I loved you, and yet you still managed to keep me at arm's length. God, I'm glad you're better, but I just don't know if you and I can work things out unless we do it together. We have to be able to share the good and the bad. I love you, but I don't know if I can keep fighting to reach you."

"You won't have to, Jess," he reassured her. "I've learned one thing from all this. Good or bad, my life is meaningless without you . . . You are a part of me." Peter took her hands as he got up from the sofa. "I want us to be together again," he said, "but I'm not going to rush things. I know you're going to need some time to sort through your feelings." He took her arm and led her out of the living room into the foyer.

"Are you staying in the city?" she asked.

"For the time being. Wilkes is coming down to baby-sit me until I'm a little stronger," replied Peter. "I didn't have the heart to object, knowing how much he loves New York."

Jessica smiled. She understood what this temporary dependence would do to his ego. She looked out through the narrow windows on either side of the door.

It had stopped snowing. Outside she could see Billy Richmond clearing the front step and sidewalk.

"Can I have Billy give you a ride home?" she asked.

"No, I can catch a cab on Park," he said, slipping on his hat and coat.

"Peter, I want—"

"Don't feel sorry for me, Jess. It's taken a lot for me to get this far," he said. "Just call me when you're ready and we'll talk some more."

Peter walked through the vestibule and opened the heavy wrought-iron door. Stepping out into the frosty air, he greeted Billy Richmond, who had just begun salting the front steps, then moved quickly up the block toward Park Avenue.

Jessica could think of nothing except Peter all weekend. Seeing him again, she realized how much she had missed him, and at that moment, how much she had wanted to hold and comfort him. She knew he loved her, but she wondered if he would ever trust her with his secrets and fears. Would he ever let down his guard and let her into his life?

She left the house only once that weekend, to take a walk through the park with Julie Ann and her daughter. The sky was an icy blue with wisps of cirrus clouds trailing along the edge of the horizon. A light wind swept the powdery snow, which sparkled like diamond dust in the brilliant sunlight, across the Great Lawn and into their faces.

Bundled up and strapped down to a small sled, Megan was barely able to express her delight as Julie and Jessica dragged her along behind them on the freshly cleared footpaths. With fearless enthusiasm the little girl urged her stalwart team on, squealing and clapping with each downhill run.

When they reached a playground, Julie freed her daughter from the sled, following closely on her heels as the child, packed into a yellow snowsuit, waddled toward a circle of children building a snowman.

"He's back," Jessica said quietly as she trailed behind them.

"Who's back?" Julie asked over her shoulder, while she tried to anticipate her daughter's next move.

"Peter," Jessica replied, as though she almost didn't believe it herself.

"You're kidding!"

"No. In fact, I saw him the other night," Jessica admitted. "He came over to the house and we talked."

"Christ, Jess, what did he say?" she asked as she pulled Megan off the top of a small snow bank.

"He told me he'd been seriously ill and—"

"And you believed him?" Julie interrupted.

"Julie, you should have seen him," Jessica replied defensively. "He was so thin and tired."

"I'm sorry, Jess," said Julie. "Then why didn't he get in touch with you?"

"To protect me. To protect himself. To keep his past from becoming his future," she answered vacantly. "I don't know if he really knows himself."

They walked Megan over to a row of seesaws. Jessica got on one end and Julie and her daughter on the other.

"What are you going to do?" asked Julie as she and Megan rose into the air.

"I don't know," replied Jessica. "He wants us to get back together, but he's leaving it up to me to decide."

"Do you want him back?"

"Yes," answered Jessica, "but I can't stay with him if he keeps closing himself off from me."

"Then tell him that," said Julie. She steadied the seesaw and lifted Megan off her lap. "What have you got to lose?" she added as they rose to their feet. At that instant Megan sprinted off toward the swings. "Oh, no," Julie muttered, then yelled, "Megan, wait for Mommy."

As Julie chased after her daughter, Jessica couldn't help smiling. Maybe it came from being around Megan, or maybe it was just her uncomplicated view of the world, but Julie's advice was sensible and straightforward. There was no guile or subterfuge, no one-upsmanship to get in the way of what Jessica really wanted.

They walked back to Julie's apartment, Jessica carrying the sled, Julie with the sleeping child in her arms. The temperature dropped as the afternoon shadows lengthened. What had earlier been slush and water had become black ice.

They put Megan to bed and shared some hot chocolate before Jessica left for home. She had to make a phone call. She walked slowly, going over in her mind exactly what she was going to say. By the time she reached the town house, she was almost running.

Rushing up the stairs and into her bedroom, she tossed her parka on the bed and stepped over to the phone on the nightstand. She picked up the receiver, then hesitated a moment, staring at the faint green buttons. Then, just as the first hint of doubt began to worm its way into her mind, she punched in Peter's number.

Chapter 49

Jessica's phone call had been like a tonic to Peter. Over brunch at his apartment the next day he seemed stronger, his eyes flashed with renewed spirit, and he spoke openly about his anxieties. More importantly, he spoke enthusiastically about their future. The words, images, and ideas flowed from him in an unending stream. He was like a man suddenly freed from solitary confinement, eager to share his every thought with the world.

Over the days that followed it became clear to Jessica that Peter had changed, and not just physically. He was no longer brooding and secretive. The cool, almost mystical aura that had surrounded him was gone. The threat of death had stripped away his defenses and softened him.

Under Jessica's watchful eye, Peter's health steadily improved. His ghostly hospital pallor disappeared, his appetite returned, and he slowly began to gain weight. They spent hours together, taking walks along the river, visiting galleries and museums or just sitting by the fire in Peter's apartment. They lived day to day and from moment to moment, cautiously building a future.

Being with Peter gave Jessica's life balance. The quiet and solitude came as a welcome relief after life at the Arena. Since the first of the year, the Knights had become a whirring juggernaut, chewing up their opponents and piling victory upon victory. They were now winning nearly four out of every five games and were favored to clinch the division title by the end of March. For Jessica, for the fans, for the whole organization, it was a dream come true, but it was not without its minor inconveniences.

The Knights' comeback became the focus of media attention during this unusually bleak winter in New York. Everyone in the organization was sought out for interviews. It was as though the reporters were searching for the germ of the team's success, trying to pinpoint the one person or secret strategy that turned the Knights around. Willie Doges's theory for all the scrutiny was, simply, that after years of losing seasons, deep down no one really believed this wasn't just some fluke or aberration. And for most of the season he stuck to that theory, ignoring the insatiable curiosity of New York's sports fans and the aggressiveness of the people in the press office.

Jessica's office had been deluged with ticket requests from people who claimed they had met, worked for, and in one case even been emotionally involved with her. The crush was staggering, but Dorothy sifted through it, separating the deserving candidates from the lunatics, leaving Jessica, of course, with the final selection.

By early March Peter was well enough to travel. They decided on a weekend trip to Boston, where the Knights would be playing in the Garden and Peter's grandmother would be celebrating her ninety-first birthday. Peter was exuberant about the idea of the drive up, while Jessica, concerned about meeting his relatives for the first time, took four hours to pack.

Anticipating disaster on the court and total rejection at the apartment in the North End, Jessica was on edge the whole weekend. And it wasn't until the trip back to New York that she finally let go of her insecurities.

Peter's green Jaguar headed west on the Massachusetts Turnpike, slicing gracefully through the driving rain. Inside, Jessica was scrunched down in the passenger seat, her worn leather flight jacket thrown over her body and her face hidden under Peter's brown fedora.

"I know you're not sleeping," said Peter. "You've got to be too excited. You beat Boston in Boston!"

"That didn't seem to impress your grandmother," Jessica replied sullenly, peeling the hat back from her eyes.

"Oh, is that what this is all about?" he asked. "Really, Jess. My grandmother is ninety-one years old and she's had five children and been through two world wars. I'd think she's pretty much seen it all. Don't you? Let's face it, unless you're a fan, a basketball game isn't going to make much of an impression. And besides," he added, "there aren't that many Italians to cheer for in the NBA."

"But I wanted her to like me," Jessica insisted.

"Believe me, Jess, you charmed the pants off her," Peter reassured her. "Anyway, you were a shoo-in to begin with. You see, I told her you were Italian on your mother's side."

"Right," Jessica shot back, "with blond hair and blue eyes."

"I told her your mother's family was from Milan," Peter replied with a careful smile. "Trust me, Jess, you won her over. I know. Didn't she give you your own Maria Danielli panettone?"

"Be serious, Peter," said Jessica.

"I am," he answered. "That bread is better than the

Good Housekeeping Seal of Approval. As a matter of fact, the last outsider I ever saw get one was my uncle Joe's wife, Margaret, and that was a year after they were married. I think it took so long because Aunt Margaret was Irish."

"All right! Enough!" Jessica shrieked. "I believe."

The rain began to let up outside of Hartford, and for an instant a ray of sunlight broke through the gray sky, lighting up the cluster of mirrored towers in the middle of the city. Jessica sat up and watched as the clouds quickly returned, plunging the brilliant scene into shadows.

"Tell me, Peter," she said. "Why does your grand-mother still live in the North End?"

"Because it's home," he answered. "I tried moving her out, but she refused to go." He glanced over at Jessica. "You know, she took us in—my mother and me—after my father died, and made a home for us. But for me, home has always been a state of mind, an idea, an emotion that anchors you. For her it's the North End. That apartment, those cold, narrow streets, they hold her memories. That's why I didn't fight her. With so little future left, I just couldn't rob her of her past."

Jessica leaned over and kissed Peter tenderly on the cheek. "You know, I love you," she whispered.

Peter reached his arm around her and held her close.

With her head on Peter's shoulder, Jessica felt warm, secure, and protected. They had survived the test of his illness and had grown from it. There were no longer any secrets or barriers between them. And although it remained unspoken, she knew they were now ready to move on with their lives together.

As predicted, the Knights secured the division title by the end of March and ended the season with a record of 62–20. With the same energy that carried them through the season, they blew through the early play-off rounds, losing only three games and winding up in the Eastern Conference championship against Detroit in mid-May.

On the other hand, Detroit, young and energetic, had seesawed through the early part of the season while trying to build that cohesiveness so important in any team sport. Finally, after the all-star game, the team came back with a vengeance, taking seventeen of their last twenty starts and dominating the league in April.

Ten days after it started, the series between the two teams, a battle royal of close scores and aggressive play, stood at three games apiece. Scheduled for Friday night at the Arena, the prospect of the seventh and deciding game had turned the city on its ear. It had all the hype and hoopla of the NBA Championship, the Super Bowl and the World Series rolled into one. Although there was still Los Angeles to face, most of the fans and sports writers saw Detroit as the real threat to their city's championship hopes. The series had become more than just a semi-final round of basketball, it had become the realization of a dream that had eluded New York for nearly fifteen years.

Before the game Jessica and Jerry Barnstable met briefly with their players in the locker room. They were encouraging and low key, joking with the younger ones and trying not to upstage Willie Doges and his staff or interfere with any of his instructions.

Afterward, out in the hall, they ran into Frank DeCicco. He had been holding court in the middle of a group of reporters in front of the Detroit locker room until he spotted Jessica. Abandoning his entourage, he waylaid the pair at the elevators.

"I want to congratulate you, Jess," DeCicco said unctuously. "Oh, and you too, Jerry," he added, as though he'd just noticed Barnstable standing next to her. "You've really turned them around."

"Thank you, Frank. That's very kind of you," replied Jessica, attempting to mask her insincerity with a polite smile. "Actually, I think most of the credit should go to Jerry and Willie. And to you, Frank."

"Me?" said DeCicco modestly.

"After all, Frank," answered Jessica, "you did teach me to take nothing for granted."

"I hope that means you're not still holding a grudge," DeCicco replied, clearly missing her inference.

"No. I like to think I've become too pragmatic for that," Jessica said.

"That's good to hear," replied DeCicco as a smug grin etched itself onto his face. "Who knows, someday we might even work together again."

"I said pragmatic, Frank, not stupid," she added, the polite smile gone from her face. Her eyes sliced through him, recognizing, at last, what a mindless threat he had been.

"Well, it was nice seeing you both again," DeCicco said hesitantly, his confidence momentarily shaken.

"Yes, well, enjoy the game, Frank," replied Jessica, stepping into the elevator with Jerry Barnstable.

"You too, Jess," DeCicco added quickly as the doors began to close in front of him.

People were still streaming into the Arena as Jessica slipped unnoticed into her seat next to Peter, two rows behind the Knights' bench. This was only the second time during the play-offs that she had traded the security of the sky box for the exhilaration of the Arena floor. She found it positively electrifying sitting in the stands. Every shot, every rebound, seemed to send a spark through the crowd, and they responded as one, celebrating the baskets and cheering on the defense. It gave them all a sense of participation, as though extra encouragement could drive the basketball a little farther or a player a little higher.

Jessica grabbed hold of Peter's hand and squeezed it tightly.

"Nervous?" he asked.

"Excited," she answered.

As the players took the court, a roar descended from the upper reaches of the Arena. A howling wave, it grew louder and louder with each succeeding section it engulfed, until it crashed over the floor, seeming to shake the very foundations of the building. The sixth player had arrived.

From the tip-off it was clear that the teams were evenly matched. The previous games were now meaningless: there were no histories, no records, no statistics to intimidate or consider. There were only ten men, forty-eight minutes, and the desire to win.

The pace of the game grew furious and intensely physical, almost gladiatorial, with each team going beyond what the coaches and the crowd thought humanly possible. There were outrageous leaps of faith and outside shots made with nearly godlike perfection. The noise in the Arena became deafening. The fans, realizing they were witnessing something historic, kept up a thunderous, pulsating rumble.

By the middle of the fourth quarter the lead had changed hands at least ten times. Two Detroit players had fouled out and one from the Knights. Stanley Amos, the Knights' star center, had been held to only seventeen points and was just one foul away from the bench. On the sideline Willie Doges paced back and forth in front of the Knights' bench, perspiration dripping down his face while he shouted instructions to his players.

Caught up in the frenzy that swept the Arena, Jessica and Peter, like the others around them, were on their feet, urging the Knights on. For Jessica, her hair covered with confetti, her voice hoarse and raspy, it was like waking up from a wonderful dream and finding out it wasn't a dream at all. Together, Marty, Jerry, Willie, and Jessica, had made it this far, farther than anyone had expected. And their efforts had paid off gloriously.

When he wasn't watching the action on the court, Peter had his eyes glued to Jessica. He found her completely and totally irresistible. Amid the clamor, she seemed absolutely radiant, aglow with anticipation and desire. She had become the anchor in his life, and he knew he wanted to be with her forever.

Peter looked up at the scoreboard as the clock began to tick off the final seconds. Detroit was leading 119–117. Suddenly, a collective sigh echoed through the Arena as one of the Knights' guards missed a rebound under the basket, turning the ball over to Detroit with only fifteen seconds and no New York timeouts left in the game.

The sigh immediately gave way to the reverberating chant of "De-fense, De-fense," which became more strident with each unbroken Detroit pass downcourt.

The air was charged with energy, powered by the sheer determination of the fans. Possessed by it, Peter abruptly turned toward Jessica. "Will you marry me?" he shouted impulsively, trying to make himself heard over the crowd.

Jessica glanced away from the court for the first time and stared incredulously at Peter. "What?" she replied, dumbfounded.

With only seven seconds on the clock, Peter repeated it slowly: "Will you marry me?"

"You're crazy!" Jessica screamed, her eyes filling with wonder and hope.

"Absolutely," said Peter. "Now answer the question."

Her answer died in an ear-splitting roar. Lee Weathers, the Knights' best outside shooter, had stolen the ball with three seconds left in the game. Dribbling furiously to midcourt, with one second separating the Knights from their destiny, he raised the ball just above his forehead and fired it at the basket. The ball seemed to hang in the air forever, traversing the wide arc between Weathers's hands and the rim of the basket.

Then, coaxed by gravity and the will of twenty-six thousand screaming fans, it dropped effortlessly through the soft netting and onto the polished floor just as the buzzer ended the game.

Peter swept Jessica up in his arms and kissed her as the Arena erupted in pandemonium. Streamers of toilet paper flew from the upper rows of the hall, banners were unfurled, and delirious fans surged onto the court. Jessica felt light as a cloud, floating on the jubilation that swirled around her. It was a sweet victory, and sweeter still that it came in New York and in the hall that bore Mark's name. The championship and the fulfillment of her promise was next.

She held onto Peter tightly, then whispered in his ear. "You knew we'd win, didn't you?"

He nodded and smiled.

"And you know I'll marry you, don't you?" she added, beaming.

Peter kissed her again. "Let's just say, in all this confusion, I hoped you wouldn't lose your senses," he said.

"Never," she replied breathlessly. Then she took his hand and fearlessly led him down to the floor, through the euphoric crowd, for the trip to the locker room.

They returned to Peter's apartment late that night and fell asleep in each other's arms. At dawn they awoke and made love, then, from bed, watched the sun rise in the eastern sky. The burnt-orange light streamed through the venetian blinds, illuminating the particles of dust suspended in the air. Jessica looked on as the tiny specks danced in the sun-warmed updrafts like a memory that tumbled along the churning currents of her mind.

"What are you thinking about, Jess?" Peter asked as he caressed the soft curves of her body.

"Riding the wind," she replied softly, remembering a cool, distant, summer night.

"I don't understand."

"When I was sixteen," she began, "we still lived in Midland and I was going out with Bobby Ray Masefield. Besides being the quarterback of the high school football team, Bobby Ray had the most beautiful red 1970 Mustang convertible you ever saw. Well, some nights, when the weather was cool and still, instead of taking me straight home, Bobby Ray would take that red Mustang out on the Interstate between Midland and Odessa. He'd get the car up to about fifty or sixty, then I'd sit up on top of the front seat, spread my arms and ride the wind. It made you wonder how it would feel if all the world was yours and all your dreams could come true."

"And?" asked Peter.

"It feels wonderful," she whispered, "simply wonderful."

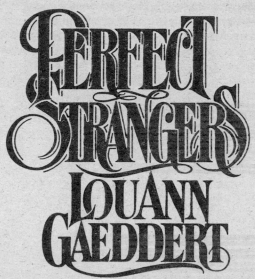

Rising high above the Hudson River, Riverside Drive—New York's most desirable address—is a boulevard of seasoned grace and classic beauty. But behind the serene facade of marbled mansions and palatial apartments, passions seethe and tensions mount, secrets are kept and hearts given away, as the lives of friends, neighbors and newfound lovers intertwine...

RIVERSIDE DRIVE

LAURA VAN WORMER

"A gem of a book. I can't shake her characters out of my mind. [Laura Van Wormer] is a born storyteller."
—Esther Shapiro, co-creator of *Dynasty*

RIVERSIDE DRIVE
Laura Van Wormer
_____ 91572-1 $5.95 U.S.   _____ 91574-8 $6.95 Can.

LANDMARK
BESTSELLERS
FROM ST. MARTIN'S PRESS

HOT FLASHES
Barbara Raskin
_____ 91051-7 $4.95 U.S. _____ 91052-5 $5.95 Can.

MAN OF THE HOUSE
"Tip" O'Neill with William Novak
_____ 91191-2 $4.95 U.S. _____ 91192-0 $5.95 Can.

FOR THE RECORD
Donald T. Regan
_____ 91518-7 $4.95 U.S. _____ 91519-5 $5.95 Can.

THE RED WHITE AND BLUE
John Gregory Dunne
_____ 90965-9 $4.95 U.S. _____ 90966-7 $5.95 Can.

LINDA GOODMAN'S STAR SIGNS
Linda Goodman
_____ 91263-3 $4.95 U.S. _____ 91264-1 $5.95 Can.

ROCKETS' RED GLARE
Greg Dinallo
_____ 91288-9 $4.50 U.S. _____ 91289-7 $5.50 Can.

THE FITZGERALDS AND THE KENNEDYS
Doris Kearns Goodwin
_____ 90933-0 $5.95 U.S. _____ 90934-9 $6.95 Can.

Publishers Book and Audio Mailing Service
P.O. Box 120159, Staten Island, NY 10312-0004

Please send me the book(s) I have checked above. I am enclosing
$ _____ (please add $1.25 for the first book, and $.25 for each
additional book to cover postage and handling. Send check or
money order only—no CODs.)

Name _____

Address _____

City _____ State/Zip _____

Please allow six weeks for delivery. Prices subject to change
without notice.
BEST 1/89